TAMESAN
THE LAST WIZARD SAGA
SONG 1

TONY SHILLITOE

First published in 1995 by Pan MacMillan Australia
as *The Last Wizard* ©

Short-listed finalist for the inaugural 1995 Aurealis Awards
for Best Fantasy Novel.

Republished in 2025 by Millswood Books
as *Tamesan: The Last Wizard Saga Song 1*

30th anniversary edition.

Cover art by Kirsi Salonen
Cover design by TS

Millswood Books

ISBN: 978-1-7641847-7-9

For Jaimee and Kim

One

Marc rubbed his thick stubble, his fingers tracing the long white scar running from his left eye to his collarbone. He was completing his day of sea-watch on White Eagle's Ledge promontory, and he was grateful that the late summer weather was warm. A lazy westerly breeze drifted from the ocean's empty reaches to break the day's rising heat, and he knew the dragonship's passage would be slow. He imagined the Dragon Head, Kevan, chafing at the lassitude and cursing the delay and the dragonwarriors would be tired and bored, but in the absence of a strong southerly no one could truly estimate the ship's time of return.

The villagers waited nearly ten weeks for the dragonship to come home. People who feasted on rumours of tragedy and misfortune were peddling tales of disaster – warriors torn asunder by a mighty dragon, rocks ripping the heart out of the dragonship in a surging storm – but Marc was too old to listen to morbid imaginings. He knew the weather's vagaries and why the ship was late. Before he received the near-fatal wound that left him scarred and unable to wield a battle-axe or pull an oar, he spent fifteen summers on the dragonship. More than anyone who remained in Harbin while the dragonwarriors searched for the fabled dragon treasures, he understood what might delay the ship.

Marc stretched his left arm in the warm afternoon light and stared across the deep grey water towards the village. A dark smudge against the light green forest, the village huts, the Warriors' Hall and the Long Hall clung like a bramble vine to the fertile strip nestled beneath the steep shoulders of Dragon Mountain. He was born in Harbin, thirty-five summers ago, first son of Arken and Jenna. His brother, Hendrik, became a dragonwarrior four summers after he did, but Hendrik was killed on his third journey. Dragonwarriors needed good fighting skills and luck, and Hendrik had only one of those things.

Marc sighed, shifted his stance against the granite rock, and squinted into the sun's glare on the grey ocean. Gulls dipped and rolled near Varst's Bluff on the bay's northern side, tiny dots flashing white when sunlight caught their feathers. Free creatures, scavengers perhaps, they came and went as they pleased, and he wondered if they ever considered the affairs of men, ever wondered why he and other men stood sentinel on the spray-moistened rocks while they wheeled and dipped above the ocean. 'Foolish thoughts,' he chided himself, but he had a lot of time for foolish thinking while he was on sea-watch. Strange ideas invaded his mind when he was alone, and he sometimes wondered if great Varst was playing tricks on him. He shook his head, as if that would clear his mind, and turned his gaze south.

That's when he saw the dragonship's red square sail rise into view. He blinked and checked again. It was the dragonship. He knew it well. Even as a man of thirty-five summers, he felt elation at the ship's appearance. By his estimation the dragonship would reach Harbin by nightfall, and in a few short hours the whole village would leap into celebration. How he loved to dance and sing the old dragon-hunting songs! There would be tales tonight, new tales to add to Harbin's rich history of dragon hunters.

He reached into a cleft between the granite rocks to retrieve the ivory horn handed down through generations of sea-watchers from Nakiades' era, and as he ran his calloused fingers across the fine carvings, pictures of powerful warriors locked in mortal combat with fearsome dragons, he felt a pang of regret for the old days, long gone before he was born. He yearned to be a hero, to have his likeness carved into the artefacts of his descendants, to be remembered by the future.

He shook his head and pushed the daydream aside. 'Too many foolish thoughts,' he reminded himself sourly. He sucked in air as he lifted the horn to his lips and blew hard and long, and the sound raced across the water to echo against the small islets and the great mountains. Summer was over. The Dragon Fang, the dragonwarriors of Harbin, were coming home.

Joy passed from mouth to mouth, shared by the women and children, as the sea-watcher's distant signal reached Harbin. Outside the Dragon Head's cottage, Eesa slapped a paddle against the interior of her heavy wooden butter churn, muttered an oath to Procra, the Mother Goddess and called, 'Chasse!'

The cottage wooden door swung open, hinges whining, and a willowy, broad-shouldered youth emerged, rubbing his eyes against the bright mid-afternoon sunlight. He flicked a loose forelock of red hair aside and stared at his mother's figure hunched over the churn, but when he heard the familiar bellow of the horn across the bay, and the excited cries swelling through Harbin, his pulse quickened. This time next year, sixteen summers old, he would be coming home aboard the dragonship as a dragonwarrior, as a man who faced a dragon's wrath and took a dragon's hoard to mark his coming of age.

'Are you listening to me?' Eesa demanded, waggling a butter-smeared finger before the boy's face to interrupt his reverie.

'Yes, Mother,' Chasse answered.

'Then do as I ask and find Tamesan. I need all the help I can get to prepare for the men's return. You make sure your sister comes back here.'

Chasse suppressed a smile at the sight of his mother, the wife of the Dragon's Head, the most powerful warrior in Harbin, standing with her sleeves rolled up, goat fat smeared to her elbows and across her forehead and cheeks, looking like a common village woman. His mother was considered a beauty, he knew that, but her beauty was hard to see when she dressed like a drab.

'Chasse!'

'I'm going,' he replied hurriedly, and he scampered away to find his sister.

Sitting cross-legged on the mountain ledge, Tam watched the solitary red sail, that hung above the bay's grey waters like a statement of intent, move painfully slowly in the eddying breezes. Beneath the red square, the hull was a darker suggestion on the watery mass, a shadow, and fractious gulls stooped and circled, acting as winged heralds to the ship's approach. The last sail she saw in Harbin Bay was moving rapidly seaward ten weeks earlier, carrying the village's dragonwarriors and a handful of would-be warrior youths into the untamed world of heaving ocean and dragon tales, seeking treasures, adventure and manhood, and Tam watched the ship leave with her usual mixed emotions of excitement and concern – and envy. Her father, Kevan, was perched on the curving prow, his mane of greying hair and full beard emphasising his status. As Dragon Head, it was his duty to lead the men on their annual pilgrimage to slay the fearful dragons, creatures that lurked in the wilderness and terrorised less fortunate villages along the coast.

Tam studied the sail's progress and assessed it would be late afternoon before the ship docked at the wooden jetty jutting from the stone embankment below the village. There would be rejoicing and reunions as families welcomed the safe return of their fathers and sons, husbands and brothers, but the night's celebrations would be neither lavish nor long because the dragonship's return was the forerunner to the Dragon Feast, the annual Harbin festival during which treasure gathered from the slain dragon's den would be shared among the villagers. On that night, a good deal of food and wine would be consumed, while the men told tales of their recent adventure, and sang older ballads about the past deeds of great dragonwarriors, like her father. They would share the traditional stories of their ancestors who first sailed into the bay, led by Nakiades, the legendary warrior who fought the silver dragon so that his people could settle in Harbin and start new lives. At the festival's close, the men would present the initiates who sailed away to battle the dragons for the first time. They would no longer be regarded as immature, eager boys, like her brother, Chasse. They would be true dragonwarriors, accorded the rights and trappings of the men who formed Harbin's Dragon Fang.

A pebble rattled above Tam and clattered down the rocky escarpment to her left. A second pebble ricocheted off a flat rock to her right. She shook out her finely braided red-gold hair, glared at a clump of bushes directly below, and said with mock anger, 'I know where you are, Chasse.' A third pebble arched out of the thick clump and clunked harmlessly against the granite rock face behind her. 'Chasse!' she warned. A red head popped into view from behind the largest bush, and a broad bright grin creased her brother's face. Disarmed by his comic appearance, Tam broke into a smile and asked, 'What do you want?'

'The ship's coming,' Chasse said.

'I know,' Tam replied. 'I can see it from here.'

'Mother is calling for you.'

'Let her call,' Tam answered abruptly.

'I'm coming up.'

Chasse disengaged from his cover and scrambled up the rocks to sit beside Tam in the early afternoon sunlight, and he gazed at the sun-speckled bay glittering like mica flecks in blue-grey granite. 'They return on a dark sea,' he murmured absently, recalling a village proverb.

Tam glanced up at the patchy ceiling of light grey clouds. The blinding sun hung in one brilliant patch of azure sky as if determined to warm the world, and she reflected on the village lore that they grew up with but never fully understood. A dark sea presaged a storm or conflict. The old village women spoke in riddles of red sunsets and grey seas, and ice on summer ponds, as if these events were portents of what was to come, but Tam saw little to prove the accuracy of their predictions. She recalled how so many of so-called confirmed predictions made by old crones like Sharmine, or the bent and wizened Marissa who claimed she could foretell the coming of bad things by reading fish entrails, were retrospectively assigned to earlier signs they claimed to have observed. The only time that Tam expressed her scepticism with her mother, Eesa bluntly warned her to be respectful of her elders and less critical of others until she was perfect herself before she handed Tam the mucking shovel to clean out the chicken roost. Tam never broached the subject again in her mother's hearing. 'Do you believe all that stuff?' she asked.

Chasse turned his bright blue eyes towards her, and Tam found herself feeling sorry for all the girls who would fall victim to her brother's handsome looks. 'Sometimes,' he answered cryptically.

'Meaning what?'

'Meaning I don't really know,' he replied, grinning. 'Sometimes things happen and it's easy to see there was a warning about it. Like when Defra fell into the stream at Watersdrop last year. The old women said Sharmine saw a red flower in the stream two days before and she called it an omen.'

'I don't believe it,' Tam snapped. 'The old women make it up to feel important. It's like they want to keep everyone aware of their presence.'

Chasse didn't pursue the argument. He was familiar with his sister questioning every value that their father and mother held sacred, and he enjoyed provoking her by taking their parents' side in discussions, but recently he found her criticisms of the village's customs and beliefs too passionate to be fun. She seemed to be brooding on a deep anger that was becoming more determined, obsessive. He was always close to her, being barely a year older, even despite her being a girl, but lately that closeness was changing. Someone he didn't recognise was emerging from within his normally effervescent sister, a stranger whose mood swung into serious contemplation on a whim or a thought, and he found that person frustrating.

Tam shifted her focus from the dragonship tacking in the mouth of the bay to the spread of slate-shingled roofs clustered along the strip of curved shore directly below her mountain perch. The incoming ship would berth at the finger of planking and poles forming the jetty. Moored fishing boats bobbed on the ocean swell and seagulls circled. Moving dots of colour on the jetty were the first people preparing for the dragonship's arrival. She knew her mother would be among them.

As wife of the Dragon Head, Eesa would ensure the jetty was clear of fishing nets and tackle and clutter that might hamper the disembarking warriors, and she would be accompanied by other wives, women she could cajole because they answered to her in the absence of their husbands, but she would already be cursing her daughter's tardiness. Eesa frequently berated Tam for lacking the necessary sense of duty expected of a girl-child of the Dragon Head, but Tam hoped that the occasion's importance would diminish her mother's anger by the time she descended the mountain to lend a reluctant hand.

Further up the steep bank, people moved between the wooden huts, going about their menial duties, apparently oblivious to the dragonship's return – especially the few remaining men – but Tam knew that most would be preparing for the dragonship's arrival. People were carrying bedding and furs to the Warriors' Hall, and gathering firewood, and taking food and mead to the Long Hall for the night's celebrations. Goat herders were mustering their free-ranging stock from the lower hillside and driving the patchwork animals towards the rough-hewn pens built to hold them until the ones to be killed for the feast were selected. The bustling village activity would intensify as the ship neared mooring.

'Coming down?' Chasse asked, tilting his head and cocking an eyebrow.

'Have I choice?'

'You're a girl,' he mocked. 'You have no choice.'

Tam laughed politely at his condescending observation, knowing he was teasing her, but the truth behind his statement rankled. She was a girl and, in the village, she had no choice but to do as she was told. That was law. 'I'll come down, brother Chasse,' she said, with feigned diffidence, 'but only because I choose to come down.'

'I'll tell Father that when he arrives,' Chasse threatened with a grin, and he began to slide down the rock. 'You know what will happen then.'

'You won't live that long!' Tam retorted, and she scrambled over the lip of the ledge to pursue him.

By the time the pair reached the base of the mountain, their faces were flushed, and they were breathless. Though he was a summer older, Chasse barely escaped his sister. Tam's agility impressed him, and she obviously knew the mountain and forest paths better than anyone, but that was because she spent a lot of time wandering the mountain, a habit that angered their mother. She was his sister, but he also loved her because she was so unlike the other village girls, and sometimes he wished that she was a boy, a brother, because she was willing to play the games he enjoyed. But he was leaving childhood, almost a man, and it was unseemly for him to be seen too often in her company, especially playing games. Tam would be a poor brother anyway, he decided. She was too different, not because she was a girl but because she had different ideas, different habits. Tamesan was unique. That word best described her.

Chasse heard the old woman, Sharmine, whisper the word to another when they were talking about Tamesan. They thought no one could overhear their conversation, but they didn't see Chasse bent over a fish barrel retrieving a leather-wrapped ball that he was throwing with Aska and Marron.

'Eesa will rue the day she bore that child,' Sharmine said solemnly. 'She doesn't want to be a woman. She sees this world too clearly, and I fear she doesn't like what she sees.'

The other woman – Chasse remembered she was called Laryssa; she died in the recent winter – shook her head and whispered a reply Chasse couldn't hear, but Sharmine's crusty old face wrinkled with mirth, and she said, 'I remember well enough what it was like. Oh, but I did infuriate my father then, and my mother swore she would throw me off Watersdrop to purge the village of me and my ways.' Her laughter subsided to a chuckle, and she made a sign with her open hand, the same sign she always made when she claimed to foresee an event. 'But this daughter of Eesa and Kevan is not like we were, Laryssa, not like us at all. We had a place here, and we knew it. It simply took us a little time to settle down, the way it does for some girls. This one is different. There is something in her presence, in her bearing, something that makes her unique. I fear she will bring great sorrow to her household. Some things I've seen are mere trifles, but this girl's future is as true as if Procra herself whispered it to me.'

Laryssa made a similar motion with her open hand, and started to reply, but Chasse moved away because his friends were calling.

The word 'unique' was new to Chasse then, so he asked Eesa what it meant. Eesa explained, but when she asked why he wanted to know he replied only that he heard it being used. The word merged with his vision of Tamesan thereafter, and he couldn't look at her or think of her without remembering Sharmine's prophecy. Tamesan was unique, but one day she would bring great sorrow to her family.

'Come on, Chasse!' Tam cried, and she sprinted across the open pasture where the village goats grazed, red hair streaming behind her like a banner. Hearing her challenge, Chasse took to his heels, drawing on his boyish pride not to be beaten to the village outskirts by a girl.

They reached the junction of paths inside the village, side by side, but stopped short when they spotted their mother, arms akimbo, blocking their way. Eesa met them with an angry glare, before fixing her attention on Tam, but her first words were for Chasse. 'Your father returns, boy. Get to the jetty with the other boys and do whatever tasks are required to ensure the dragonwarriors can disembark unhindered.'

Chasse mumbled a reply, briefly brushed Tam's hand, as if reassuring her he was only leaving because of his duty, and he ran past Eesa into the village.

Eesa's green eyes narrowed. 'Are you too proud to answer the sea-watcher's horn?'

'I came,' Tam replied, trying to judge her mother's mood and intent.

'I had to send your brother to fetch you, and your brother is nearly a man,' Eesa said, anger bristling. 'Men do not chase after foolish girls who think life is for nothing better than sitting on mountaintops to gaze at the sky. Your brother has far more important matters to attend. As do you. The men are coming home. Your father is coming home. And you will prepare for him, and for all the men of Harbin, like every other girl in this village. Do you understand me? No more foolishness. You are the Dragon Head's daughter. Behave accordingly!'

Tam nodded. She knew better than to publicly protest when her mother was angry. Her mother's will was also village law. Her only choice was to obey.

Two

Tam squared the sharp knife above the salmon before pushing down and severing its head. Scales and bone crunched under the blade. She scraped the fish head into the wooden bin at her feet, slit the fish's belly and dragged out its slippery entrails.

Eesa's intention was as unpleasant as her mood when she set Tam to cleaning fish for the feast. The task was menial, but Tam understood that the Dragon Head's daughter could not be seen to be above such work. Normally, Eesa would arrange for her daughter to be involved in less malodorous duties, like preparing vegetables, or cleaning the Warriors' Hall — duties reserved for young girls and the dragonwarriors' wives. Cleaning and gutting fish, smelly and dangerous, was traditionally reserved for widowed harridans, or fishermen's wives whose husbands did not travel south on the dragonship. Careless slips of razor-sharp knives cost the women more than the tips of their fingers over the years, so it was obvious to Tam that her mother was punishing her. *But for what?* she wondered. *Spending time alone? What is wrong with that?*

'Watch yourself, girl,' a cracked voice warned.

Tam looked up into the glinting eyes of Amarti, wife of old Berikan the fisherman. The woman pointed with the stub of a lost finger at Tam's knife, its sharp edge dangerously close to Tam's hand. With dark shiny pupils above her sun-cracked cheeks and snub nose, Amarti looked like a crab, an observation that secretly amused Tam because The Dragon Heart, Harbin's lore keeper, ironically chose the old language words 'A-Mar-Ti' for her name, and they approximately translated into 'tough little crab'. Amarti was a tough little crab.

Tam slid the gutted fish aside and pulled another from the pitted wooden bucket on the bench, and as she set to sliding her knife back and forth across the slippery scales she contemplated the names of her family to ease her boredom.

Her father was Kevan. His was a name for strength and perseverance, because in the old tongue he would be called 'Ka-Evar-Une': 'the man of rock'. She could not argue with the Dragon Heart's choice of name for her father. He was the veritable pillar of strength of Harbin, the keystone of the village's foundation.

Her mother's name came from 'Ere-Eesa', which meant 'daughter of fortune' in full translation. She knew, from family gossip over the years, that her mother was the only daughter and child of Maruki, a widow, meaning there were no men to carry the family name forward or to bring wealth. Perhaps fortune favoured Eesa through her marriage to Kevan.

Her brother was named by the Dragon Heart from 'En-Chai-Se', meaning 'he who triumphs'. Her cynical nature told her that the Dragon Heart named Chasse to impress the Dragon Head with a promise that his son would achieve greatness. Not that Tam doubted that Chasse would be a great warrior, but he was not of the same mould as their father. Chasse was softer, warm like a cosy autumn fire, whereas Kevan was cold like a rock. If Chasse ever rose to be a leader, he would lead by example, not by force or threat. He would listen to the needs of others. He was not at all like their father.

Tam considered her own name. The Dragon heart chose 'Te-Amen-San' from the old language. It literally meant 'the dawn's light', and when she learned her name's true meaning, as a child, she loved to hear its sound on her mother's lips. Her name drew her to the natural world, tying her to sunrises and their beauty. She sometimes rose before the first rays of daylight coloured the eastern skies over the backs of the mountains, slipped outside, and sat on the shingled roof of her parents' cottage to watch the sunrise set the world ablaze with golds and reds. 'Te-Amen-San

– dawn's light'. Mystified by her name, she whispered it softly to the morning sky and wondered why the Dragon Heart chose that special name for her. Even her red-gold hair matched her name. She began to believe that she was destined for something more than the mundane fate shared by the other women in Harbin: cleaning, cooking, mending and bearing children for men.

She checked her thoughts. Not every woman endured the common fate. The truly ugly, like old Asmae who lived in isolation at the northern reach of the village, never attracted a man in their lives, and were never blessed with children, but even Asmae carried a woman's burden in her working life. She cleaned her share of pots, mended her share of fishing nets, and cooked her share of meals in the Warriors' Hall. Now, her sight dimmed with age, her back bowed, and her hands gnarled and scarred from years of servile work, Asmae spent the long winters alone, and in the short summers the only visitors she received were young girls sent by Eesa to feed her. Tam felt pity whenever she thought of the old woman. She understood Eesa's reason for sending the young girls to tend Asmae. It was a blunt social lesson, a warning to the girls that the choices for young women were limited: accept the care of a strong man and his burden of marriage or live forever alone and dependent on the goodwill of strangers.

'You'll daydream away your fingers, girl,' Amarti rasped.

Tam brushed aside a wisp of hair dangling annoyingly across her cheek, and swept another fish head into her bucket, but as she bent to extract the next salmon from her basket she heard sniggering. She glanced up to see three girls sidling past, carrying freshly cut reeds in their woven baskets.

'Oh, excuse us,' the tallest girl remarked, with pouting indignity. 'We didn't mean to disturb the daughter of the Dragon Head from her important tasks.' The girl smiled sweetly, but her ice-blue eyes sparkled maliciously.

Tam forced a return smile, and scooped the fish from her bucket, letting it smack on the benchtop.

'I do hope you are being careful with that knife, Tamesan. It looks wickedly sharp,' the tall girl said, with false concern. She shook her long black plait and nudged a companion.

With a deft swing, Tam hacked off the fish head and smiled sardonically at her antagonist. 'Pray to Procra I don't slip and cut the tip off your wagging tongue, Katris,' she warned.

Katris' friends stifled their laughter, as Katris nonchalantly shrugged and replied, 'Oh well, can't stay to gossip idly with the fisherwomen. We have the Long Hall to prepare for the men. We'll leave you to your chores.' She turned and led her friends away from the pebbled beach and the fishermen's quarters.

'Good riddance,' Tam muttered, glad to be free of Katris' taunting face.

A few paces away, Katris turned and shouted, 'Please do bathe in scented oils before you come to the feasting tonight, Tamesan! I think the men will be sick of the smell of fish after so long at sea!' She wheeled, and the three girls continued up the foot-worn path to the village centre, laughing loudly.

'Pay no heed to them, girl,' Amarti croaked, waggling a limp fish at Tam. 'They've no call to be teasing you. Your mother would tan their rumps if she heard them.'

Tam watched the receding figures, thinking of all the answers she ought to have called after Katris. Katris had changed. Two summers ago, they were close friends, laughing together, playing games, sharing secrets, looking for any excuse to spend time in each other's company. Only Chasse was as close to her as Katris.

She remembered taking Katris to the higher slopes on Dragon Mountain and sharing her private aerie, where, from its heights, they could look over the entire bay and see all the islets out to Dragons' Mouth, until the deep ocean filled the horizon. It was the one place where Tam escaped her mother's constant demands for help and work. Village girls rarely ventured up the mountain, beyond the trees bordering the cattle pasture, but Tam led Katris higher to show her the world from a different perspective. She shared her love of the land and sea surrounding Harbin, revealing to Katris the forest's serenity and beauty, the strength of the mountains, the ocean's temperamental moods and the pastel sunsets, and the secret of the dawn's light. Katris sat and listened, staring in silent wonder, and Tam made her promise not to share the secret with anyone. As a pledge of trust, they shared the translations of their names in the old tongue. Katris came from 'Ke-Atry-Sis' meaning 'she of the moon beauty'. With pale skin, blue eyes and black hair, Katris was growing into a beauty of fifteen summers. As tall as Tam, and as sharp of mind, they were natural friends.

But the friendship waned when Katris' interests became less adventurous and more like those of other girls. She stopped asking to climb the mountain and began making excuses not to go whenever Tam invited her. While Tam sought opportunities to avoid women's work, Katris started going out of her way to learn cooking and weaving crafts, and how to care for children. The adolescent girls, Katris foremost, chattered incessantly about men and boys, comparing their respective merits, their physical attractiveness, their reputations as warriors. Tam feigned interest in their conversations to remain in the group and even took nervous delight in sneaking with Katris and the other girls to the hot springs at the Dragon's Cauldron, where the men bathed, to study them secretly, but she quickly tired of that fervent, furtive game. She tried to entice Katris away, but her friend laughed at her, calling her a little girl. Hurt, Tam tried to cling to the outer edge of the girls' group, but something had changed, and she could sense it because Katris frequently snubbed her, especially when Tam showed no interest in girls' talk.

Then the snide and poorly disguised insulting remarks began. The girls didn't approve of Tam spending time playing boyish games with her brother. They accused her of turning her brother – someone they all agreed was very handsome – into more of a girl than a boy. They chastised her for ducking her responsibilities and being slow to learn craft and cooking skills. Because her first period came later than Katris', they teased her for being slow to grow into a woman. Embarrassed, sick of the harassment, she spent less and less time with the girls, choosing to share her loss of social identity with the mountain's solitary beauty.

Alone on the mountain, staring across the expanse of the bay into the sweeping ocean, the taunts and ridicule of Katris and the other girls receded, and Tam lost herself by observing the gulls wheeling over the fishing shoals. Every now and then, gulls would settle on the water, dip their heads, and fly off with tiny sparkling weights hanging from their red beaks. She watched sparrows flit from bough to bough, chasing butterflies and insects, and she watched insects swarm around delicate mountain blooms, gathering pollen or nibbling at the fresh petals and leaves. The more she saw, the more she recognised that there was balance and purpose in everything, a harmony in the natural world that made the village girls' teasing games trivial. Tam could lie against the warm, flat granite on her favourite mountain perch in the morning sunlight and feel the pulse of the earth. High above Harbin, the whole world fell into perspective, and her tiny village diminished in significance.

When she tried to slip back into the group near the end of her thirteenth summer, two years ago, more bored with isolation than desiring their company, Katris deliberately told the others about Tam's mountain hideaway, and her secret hope that her name marked her for greater things than being the common wife of a Harbin dragonwarrior. The girls' ridicule trebled. They laughed in Tam's face and accused her of thinking that she was above everyone because she was the Dragon Head's daughter. Hurt by Katris' broken trust, Tam stormed away and vowed to have nothing more to do with their idle activities and their frivolous chatter about who was the best-looking man and who would pair with whom when the time came for choosing. She again sought the mountain's security, and the occasional company of her brother.

Sensing a presence that interrupted her thoughts, Tam spied a small shadow at her side and she turned her head to find her little brother, Jaysin, staring at the knife she held above a silver-pink fish. She waited for Jaysin to speak, but he remained silently staring. Tam felt immensely sorry for her auburn-haired brother. For a nine summers child, Jaysin was overly quiet and reserved, and he often sat at the edge of children's games. He was much like her – a thinker, unable to mix easily with his peers – but, unlike her, he seemed desperately unhappy. 'Well?' she asked, when it was obvious that Jaysin would not speak first.

'Mother wants you to feed Gramma,' Jaysin said in his reed-thin voice. He didn't lift his gaze from the knife.

'Do you want a turn?' Tam offered, and she lifted the knife carefully towards Jaysin's hand.

'No,' the boy blurted, and he ran towards the jetty.

'Now that there is a strange one,' Amarti remarked, cackling, as she lifted a gnarled hand to her forehead, feigning confusion.

Tam ignored the old woman's jibe as she watched Jaysin's retreat. Sometimes, she wanted to hug her little brother to keep him safe from the world's harms. Sometimes, like everyone else, she saw him as an odd little boy, and she felt guilty for thinking like that.

'I have to go,' she announced. She picked up a rag, wiped the scales and fish fluids from her hands, dipped her hands in a bucket of water used to rinse the scaling knives and shook them dry, before heading along the path to the village centre.

People were engrossed in organising for the dragonship's arrival. Girls bustled in and out of the Warriors' Hall. Some swept, others carried cloth and straw. Women carted woven baskets of fresh baked breads into the Long Hall, and armfuls of firewood, while an older man hobbled along the upper path bearing newly slaughtered chickens for the coming feast.

Most did not see Tam pass, but Banni smiled and waved. Three summers older than Tam, when Banni came of age the dragonwarrior Jared took her for his wife, as everyone expected. Though she was older, she was always friendly towards Tam, more so than Tam's peers. In fact, Banni never appeared unhappy or angry with anyone. She was a calm spirit at peace with everyone and everything.

Tam returned Banni's wave and continued towards the narrow wooden bridge spanning Watersdrop that led to her home, but as she approached the bridge she saw boys milling on the path, gathering into a circle. At the centre, two boys faced each other. One – tall, strongly-built, with a shock of dark hair – she immediately recognised: Marron, Trask's son. Trask was a fierce member of the Dragon Fang, a dragonwarrior considered by some as second in prowess only to Tam's father. Marron was Chasse's age, and next summer they would both be initiate warriors sailing on the dragonship. She was certain that the other boy with his back to her was Derin, the third son of old Galt, the herdsman, because he always let his long, dirty blond hair hang loose. Marron's head bobbed and Derin sidestepped. They held solid sticks in their hands, crudely fashioned swords. The boys were fighting again. Hardly a week passed lately without a brawl erupting because they were obsessed with proving who was the better fighter. The circle rotated across the path, cutting Tam's access to the bridge, so she was forced to watch the boys.

Marron and Derin had fought more times in the past four weeks than anyone could count, and although Marron won every encounter Derin did not accept defeat. Eesa stepped in to break up one brawl, not because she disapproved of the boys fighting – they were boys, and they had to sort out who was strongest and who would lead – but because the fights were becoming increasingly bloodier and determined. Her concern was that the village could ill-afford to lose a potential dragonwarrior because of a vicious boyish game. Derin emerged from the most recent fight with a long cut across the side of his neck, a broken nose, and a wound to his thigh. But Eesa's warning fell on deaf ears because, without the dragonwarriors to back her authority, the older boys were a law unto themselves.

Marron lunged and Derin stepped back, escaping Marron's first attack, but he was caught in a tangle of spectators, and Tam heard him grunt as Marron struck. A cheer rose from the circling boys, and they threw Derin back into the fray, clutching his stomach and gasping for air. Marron looked up, saw Tam was watching, and smiled, before he spun with excessive bravado and kicked, his right shin striking the hunched-over Derin under the chin. Derin collapsed backward amid a roar from the audience and lay still. Victorious, Marron turned to face Tam with both arms held high and executed an exaggerated bow before the boys jostled him and patted him enthusiastically on the back, congratulating him.

Tam was horrified. Derin was motionless, but no one stooped to help him. She pushed through the group, ignoring Marron, and knelt beside Derin. When she touched his bruised arm, he groaned, sucked in a lungful of air, and violently coughed.

'Leave him,' said a voice above her. 'He'll be fine.'

Tam looked up into Marron's dirty face and dark glittering eyes. Around him, a dozen boys of all ages stared down at her, curious as to her intent. Derin groaned again and spat a mouthful of blood on the ground. A broken tooth gleamed in the mess. 'You've hurt him!' she accused, attempting to make Marron sorry for Derin's plight.

Laughter burst from the boys. Marron grinned, and replied, 'Of course I hurt him. It was a fight. That's what you do in a fight.' More laughter greeted his sarcasm. Some boys complained that they wanted to leave until a distant angry voice scattered the group.

'So, you're all going to leave him here?' Tam asked in amazement.

'His father is coming,' Marron sneered. 'I'm sure a goatherd knows how to look after hurt animals.'

Derin winced, and the muscles bunched in his legs as if he was going to stand, but the fight was long gone from his body. He groaned and relaxed.

Tam glared at Marron, who was still standing over her. 'Stop taunting him,' she implored.

'I'll stop when he's had enough and knows his place,' Marron asserted. His determined expression was challenging anyone, even her, to doubt that he was the best fighter and natural leader of the boys, but she was also aware that his eyes were analysing her, as though he was anticipating an answer to a very different question, which made her suddenly feel uncomfortably vulnerable. Before Tam could make sense of her fear, the rhythm of running feet broke through her thoughts and Galt the goatherd lumbered towards them.

'Get away from my boy!' Galt snarled. He pushed past Marron to kneel beside Tam. 'In Varst's Name, what have you done, lad?' Galt asked. Marron sniggered. Galt's weathered face flared with rage and he rose to face Marron, growling, 'If you don't get out of my sight before I raise my arm, I'll break your smirking face with my fist.'

Marron instinctively retreated, but he didn't leave. Instead, he fixed Galt with an acid glare and sneered, as he said, 'I'll go, old man, but not because you frighten me. I don't like the stench of goat dung.'

Galt lifted his fist, but Marron skipped away, laughing, and jogged after the rest of the boys who were waiting for him. 'When your father comes ashore you will hear more of this!' Galt shouted. 'Mark my words, you cocky little rooster! You will hear more!' He watched, until Marron joined the waiting pack of youths, before he turned to his son. Tam helped Derin to sit up, but he wobbled groggily and constantly moaned. 'Here, girl,' Galt said, firmly pushing her aside. 'Leave my son to me. He does not need a woman's touch. Run along and do whatever it is your mother asked you to do.'

Tam wanted to object, but she saw the anger, hurt and sorrow competing in the man's lined face as he bent to cradle Derin in his arms, so she rose and moved back, and watched while Galt walked unsteadily, carrying his beaten son to his hut at the edge of the village beneath Dragon Mountain. Unable to do any more, Tam crossed the wooden bridge to her home, scattering a flock of chickens as she passed through them.

From her doorstep, Tam could see across Harbin Bay. The water remained grey, but the red sail was a large square now, the long low hull visible above the waterline, and the more adventurous fishermen were rowing towards the gap to meet the dragonship. Her father would be home soon, reasserting his authority as Dragon Head, and her mother would revert to being the Dragon Head's wife. Tam wondered how her mother felt each time her husband left her in charge of the village, only to return to take back the responsibility and the status.

Every woman in the village must experience something akin to that, she thought. When the men were away, the women made the decisions and controlled their own lives. When the men returned, the women fell back into place, letting the men decide, letting the men rule. Last summer, when she dared to ask Eesa why their lives were like that, she received a scolding for her curiosity, and a lecture on how it was that men were born to lead and women to follow. Later, Tam overheard her mother talking about her question with the other women and laughing.

'That child asks too many questions,' Eesa said. 'If her father heard her, he would go mad.'

'We would all like to ask too many questions,' said another woman. 'Thank Procra for summer and dragon journeys.' The women laughed heartily at the comment.

Tam didn't understand what was so funny about the dragon journeys, but she did learn that the question wasn't hers alone. She happened to ask it aloud, and she was surprised to learn that the older women were glad to be free of the men during summer, even though the sentiment was never publicly expressed.

Tam hesitated at the door to her home, wondering what mood her grandmother would be in. The old lady long outlived her generation, defying death as fervently as Marron defied any boy to best him, but she was thin and feeble-minded and couldn't dress or feed herself unaided. As soon as Tam was old enough to cope, Eesa put her in charge of caring for Gramma Harmi and tending to the old lady became part of Tam's responsibilities, along with looking out for her younger brother. Thankfully, Jaysin was looking after himself of late, and she seldom saw him, except in the morning, and when she returned in the evening. Jaysin disappeared during the day – Tam had no idea where he went – and Chasse played, explored, and focused on learning to be a dragonwarrior. Because they were boys, it was expected they would do these things. And she did the house chores, and looked after Gramma, because she was a girl, and she was expected to do those things.

'Is that you, child?' croaked Gramma Harmi from within the cottage.

Tam's irritation rose. The old woman persisted in calling her 'child'. Never once did she call her Tamesan, or Tam, which made her wonder if her grandmother could remember her name. She toyed with the idea of sneaking back up the mountain where she could sit alone and in peace. She could watch the sun set as the dragonship moored at the jetty, torchlights glittering on the water. That was how she imagined it would look. Then she could turn into an eagle, climb into the night sky, and circle above the merry revellers who were celebrating the dragonship's return and the close of summer. No one would know she was soaring overhead, a tiny shadow against the tapestry of stars. She would feel free. She would be free.

'Child?' the old lady's voice asked tremulously. 'Have you come to feed me?'

Tam pushed aside her daydream with a shrug, lifted the smooth door handle, and breezed into the darkening cottage, calling sweetly, 'Yes, Gramma, it's me, come to feed you.'

Three

The western sky was a patch of scarlet embers when the dragonship docked. Torches, teased by a fickle sea breeze that eluded the ship throughout the day, flickered along the jetty and threw glittering light across the dark water. People moved with purpose, calling for and catching the hawsers to lash the ship to its moorings, dragging the wooden gangplank into place to receive the disembarking Dragon Fang, Harbin's glorious warriors.

Tam pushed through the throng, aware of the collective anticipation of the women waiting to welcome their menfolk who were away from their hearths for ten long weeks. She missed her father, despite the fact that he was often surly and aloof when he was home, and she was keen to know if the dragon they pursued on this journey proved a tough adversary.

Scraping wood against wood, and a raucous cheer from the men aboard drew her attention to the ship, and as she pressed towards Eesa, who was foremost on the jetty to welcome her homecoming husband, Tam saw a dozen eager hands slide the gangplank over the dragonship's gunwales. Dark shapes swarmed at the edge of the light and Tam imagined them to be the frightening figures of her nightmares.

A large warrior stepped onto the gangplank and into the light, and Tam recognised his full greying beard and hair as the people let out a spontaneous cheer to welcome her father, Kevan, Dragon Head of Harbin. He lurched heavily off the ship and embraced Eesa in a hearty hug, ruffled Jaysin's hair, patted Chasse on the shoulder, and nodded to acknowledge Tam.

More cheers rose from the crowd as the dragonwarriors disembarked in Kevan's wake, accompanied by four initiate dragonwarriors wearing their battle armour and bearing war spears. Tam knew the young men. There was Harly, Karl's son; Kerik, son of Jon; the lanky and awkward Garret, whose father was killed by a dragon four years earlier; and Ion, who shared his father's name. All four tried to look stern for the occasion, but when their families greeted them with open and affectionate arms their fearsome facades melted into smiles and laughter.

To escape the crush of bodies, Tam moved away from her family to the jetty's furthest reach, and stood among the stacked fishing baskets and tackle, until the crowd gravitated shoreward and filed up the slope to the Long Hall. She could see her father's head and shoulders above the people around him. She went to follow, when she noticed a motionless figure at the foot of the gangplank staring into the dragonship's dark depths, as if held there by an invisible rope. Even in the dwindling light, Tam recognised the young woman, so she approached and said gently, 'Banni?'

Banni did not respond. Waves lapped against the jetty's pylons and the ship's hull, gradually subsuming the noise of the receding revellers.

'Banni, are you alright?' Tam asked gingerly. Banni stifled a sob, so Tam reached out to touch her shoulder.

'Where is he?' Banni asked the empty air. 'Where is my husband?'

Tam had no answer to her question. Jared did not come ashore with the others. Banni could not have missed him in the throng on the jetty, and he would have found her. Jared did not come home.

Banni's shoulder shook violently under Tam's hand, a sob escaped her chest, and the young woman collapsed onto the jetty planks. Hunched on her knees, Banni wept for her lost husband.

Tam knelt beside her, wanting to comfort her, but she felt awkward and confused, unsure of what to do or say. She'd seen women cry before, when their men did not return from the summer journey, but she never experienced the loss to someone close to her, so she did not know how

24

to react. Worst of all, she felt a need to cry, as if Banni's sorrow was her own. Tears welled in her eyes, and she hugged her friend, sharing her grief, while the dancing torches of the joyful home-comers disappeared into the Long Hall.

'We crept up to the dragon's lair and fanned out in a big circle. Everyone had a spear ready. When Salmon whistled, Kevan strode as bold as Varst from the bushes into the dragon's lair and yelled, "Who dares confront the Dragon Head of Harbin?"'

The audience in the Long Hall turned their admiration on Kevan, and he smiled and nodded to Chasse, as if affirming the truth of the tale.

Jon, the storyteller, paused for effect, and to take a mouthful of mead, and continued. 'The foul dragon heard the challenge and stirred. Its eyes opened, one at a time. Its teeth bristled, and its blue scales shone. With a deep-throated roar, and a flash of fire, it rose to the fight. But the Dragon Fang had planned well. As the beast showed itself, thinking it faced but a solitary warrior, a flight of Harbin spears darkened the morning sky and rained down on the beast. Some spears bounced harmlessly from its hide, and some missed their mark entirely –'

Jon paused to cast a shrewd wink at Theo, a dragonwarrior close to Kevan's age, and an outburst of friendly but derisive laughter greeted Jon's gesture. Theo lifted his fist in mock anger, replying, 'At least I hit something!'

'It has to be the deadest bush I've ever seen!' yelled Raven, and laughter echoed through the hall.

'It was a dangerous bush!' chimed in another warrior, and more laughter erupted.

'Tell the story!' Theo growled, keen to shift attention from his shortcoming in the adventure, and when he saw his two sons grinning up at him he cuffed both behind their ears, saying, 'We'll see who laughs when you grinning idiots face your first dragon.'

As the laughter subsided, Jon announced, 'Enough spears found their target. The dragon was sorely wounded. But it made one final attempt to attack the source of its anger, and mighty Kevan fought bravely to save himself from its dying wrath. Then Trask stepped forward and cut off its head, and the fight went out of the beast. The dragon curled up and died.' Applause and cheers greeted the statement. 'So, people of Harbin, the Dragon Fang has again conquered another of the foul beasts that stole away great Nakiades' beautiful treasure.'

Chorused approval greeted Jon's conclusion, and it was followed by congratulatory remarks, before individual warriors dropped into recounting fragments of the adventure and their part in it to family and companions.

Tam listened patiently, while Theo told Chasse for the third time how Kevan stood toe-to-toe with the dragon in its lair. She saw the long scar inflicted by the dragon's vicious claws on her father's arm when he proudly rolled up his sleeve to allow Eesa and friends to trace its puckered white path from biceps to wrist, while Theo artfully described the crimson blood that flowed freely from it during the battle. She stared absently at the small scar on her father's forehead, probably a legacy from the same battle, while her mind strayed from the tales of heroes to Banni and her lost husband.

Banni was not in the Long Hall. She retreated to her empty, cold, dark hut to deal with her grief. Tam walked with her as far as the door, but Banni said she would be alright and went inside alone, leaving Tam no choice but to go to the Long Hall.

When Tam first arrived, Chasse came to her, asking, 'Where have you been?'

'With Banni,' Tam replied. 'Why?'

'Father noticed you weren't here.'

'Jared didn't return,' Tam said.

Chasse shook his head, his expression saddened. 'I'm sorry. I didn't know. Those things aren't mentioned tonight.' He put his hand gently on his sister's shoulder and said, 'Come on. Father wants us all to be with him. He has done brave deeds.'

Tam followed her brother into the warmth and comradery of the Long Hall, but she could not forget Banni's sorrow.

In all the storytelling, Jared was unmentioned, as if the warrior never travelled on the summer journey, but Tam knew the sacred rule of the welcoming feast forbade naming the fallen. The feast was a time for happiness and joy, a moment for reunion and hope, so the names of those who fell before the dragon, or perished in the cruel seas, were taboo for that single night. There would be time for grief in the coming days when the dead would be honoured by everyone.

The ceremony for the dead, those summers that it was needed, was held five days after the dragonship's return. Family and friends of the fallen congregated with the Dragon Heart at Watersdrop to sing the Words of Passage, a prayer asking Varst to keep the souls safe from the great dragon Shaddho's maw as they journeyed through the dark realm of death to Varst's Eternal Paradise in the heart of the sun. Tam knew all this to be true, but Banni's grief still hung over her as the people around her celebrated the warriors' adventures.

Someone nudged Tam's kneecap. When she blinked and looked up at her father's solemn face, he directed where she should look with a subtle shift of his dark blue eyes, and he spoke kindly. 'It would seem my daughter has an admirer.'

Tam turned in the direction that her father indicated and saw Trask's family seated on the floor with several dragonwarriors, but no one was looking at her. Then she noticed Marron staring across the smoky space and, when he saw her looking, he smiled. She turned away.

Kevan nodded knowingly and patted Tam's knee, saying wisely, 'All things in their time, Tamesan. Trask's son will be a fine match for you.'

Tam lowered her eyes to stare at a half-eaten portion of bread, and blushed against her will, and she heard Theo say, 'Your young maiden glows with pleasure. You have an uncommon beauty ripening in your house, Kevan.' Kevan thanked Theo for the compliment, but Tam wished she hadn't blushed. She couldn't decide whether she was embarrassed by her father pointing out Marron to her, or angry because Marron was a not a boy she could be interested in. He was an arrogant bully, and his beating of Derin earlier in the day was sickening proof of his attitude. She had watched him swagger through the village for years. Even as a child, Marron dominated games and pushed other boys around, until they all followed him like sheep. He was cruel. He always teased the girls, but now that they were near adulthood the girls like Katris raved about his long dark hair and his muscles – although they were quick to remind themselves that the older dragonwarriors were more desirable. Still, of the boys nearing manhood, Marron was widely considered the best catch. Even though she spent much less time with Katris and her friends, she knew Katris openly hoped Marron would choose her for his wife when he became a dragonwarrior. She thought they were perfectly matched. As far as Tam was concerned, Katris could have him.

'Are you alright?' Chasse asked, as he leaned forward, his bright face filled with concern.

'I'm fine,' Tam replied. 'Thanks.' She chanced a quick glance across the hall at Marron to see, thankfully, that he was engrossed in another of his father's tales. She took a deep breath, and said to Eesa, who was listening to yet another variation of her husband's role in slaying the dragon, 'Should I see that Gramma is still alright?'

Eesa frowned at the interruption, hesitated, but said, 'Yes, of course, Tamesan. In all the excitement, I'd forgotten Harmi. Go.' She tilted her head towards the wall where a small body lay curled in sleep. 'Take Jaysin with you. I think he's had too much food and news tonight.'

Grateful to be excused from the smoke and noise in the Long Hall, Tam bade goodnight to her father and mother, and scooped up little Jaysin's sleeping form, conscious that his size and weight were making him almost too big to carry. As she made her way to the main door with Chasse accompanying her, Marron looked up, but she did not acknowledge him.

Chasse opened the door, and asked, 'Do you want me to come home with you?'

'No,' Tam answered. 'You'd disappoint Father if you left this early on the welcoming night. Stay. I know how to look after Gramma and Jaysin.'

Chasse smiled appreciatively as Tam stepped outside, and he closed the door and returned to the circle between Kevan and Theo.

The evening air was cold, and Tam's warm breath escaped in misty clouds as she held Jaysin in her arms and climbed the slope towards the bridge spanning Watersdrop. She stopped at the bridge to adjust her heavy sleeping bundle and gazed across the village.

A patch of silver moonlight chased shadows across the scattered ensemble of buildings. The yellow glow of the Long Hall filled the centre, and near the water's edge three tiny lantern lights wavered, village fisherman making their way home from the celebration.

She wondered what it was like to be a fisherman in Harbin. Some were dragonwarriors when they were younger who were forced by serious injury to abandon the summer journeys and remain home. Those men were sad and bitter when the dragonship sailed away, and they talked constantly of the old adventures, as if they longed for those times to return and dissolve the drudgery of their fishermen's lives. But there were others, like Amartl's husband, who chose to be fishermen. They never hunted dragons, and were never accorded the exalted status of dragonwarrior, and yet they enjoyed their work and their place in the village, taking pride in what they did and ignoring the condescending comments some dragonwarriors made about those men who stayed behind with the women and children. She would like to know why those men chose to be different. One day she would ask one.

A tiny point of light bobbed in the bay. A fisherman was still at his work. The ocean was a patchwork of light and dark, shining like beaten metal wherever the moon forced its beams through the clouded night sky, giving it a troubled, uncertain look, Tam thought, and she was suddenly afraid for the lone fisherman. She imagined the broad black wings of Shaddho, the great dragon of darkness who pursued Nakiades and Tam's ancestors into Harbin Bay, spreading across the face of the moon as the beast hunted for prey. And out there in the darkness, a solitary man went about his simple task, oblivious to the danger sweeping in around him.

She shivered and drew her eyes from the ocean to stare in the direction of Banni's lightless hut. *Is that how Banni feels now?* she wondered, *alone in a sea of darkness? And is Jared's soul somewhere out there, in the greater dark ocean called death, equally alone, frightened no one will sing the Words of Passage to bring him to the light of Varst's Eternal Paradise?* Sadness welled in her throat and tears formed in the corners of her eyes, a rising sensation of sadness she couldn't explain or understand. She hugged Jaysin's long body to her breast and hurried across the bridge to her home.

Four

Tam heard irritation in her mother's voice when Eesa replied, 'I have no idea where the old man is.'

'He is needed here!' Kevan insisted, banging his fist against the door jamb to emphasise his point. 'The Dragon Head wants him here.'

'You know, as well as I do, he is as easy to compel as wind on a windless day,' Eesa responded.

'It is unlike him not to come down from the mountain the first morning after the dragonship's return,' said Theo. 'He knows his skills with herbs will be needed. I should send one of my lads to fetch him.'

'No,' Kevan growled angrily. 'I am Dragon Head. I'll send for him, even though it infuriates me to do so.' He turned to Eesa and glanced at Tam who was feeding Gramma Harmi. 'As soon as the girl finishes with the old woman, send her to fetch the Herbal Man. I want him in the village today. There are men needing his healing and advice. Am I understood?'

'Yes, husband,' Eesa dutifully answered. 'She will go,' and she gave Tam a stern stare that warned Tam to be obedient or face terrible consequences.

Kevan beckoned to Chasse, who was loitering by the window, and said, 'You, lad, will come to the Warriors' Hall and see the dragon's treasure. Since you will be a man next summer, it's time you spent more time with the men.'

Eesa collected three pottery jars, after Kevan and Chasse left, and she glared at Tam, saying, 'You heard your father. Finish feeding Gramma and then go up to the Herbal Man's hut and bring him to the village. Bring him straight down, understand? No dilly-dallying or playing games on the mountainside, girl, or by Procra you will be sorry. Hear me?'

'Yes, Mother,' Tam replied, as she lifted another spoonful of gruel to her grandmother's lips.

'Make sure you do as your told. Your father is home again and he will not abide nonsense from a girl, especially his own daughter.'

Tam bit her lip. She desperately wanted to shout, 'Yes, Mother, I know! Father's word is law, and I'm only a girl, so it doesn't matter what I think, does it?' but instead she said, 'Yes, Mother, I'll bring the Herbal Man,' and she dutifully wiped the dribble from Gramma Harmi's chin with a piece of green cloth. Her grandmother gave her a crooked toothless grin.

'And when you get back, you can come down to help at the fish tables,' Eesa instructed, as she stepped through the doorway. 'If I'm not there, I will be in the Long Hall, cleaning and mending. You can come there to help.'

Tam watched her mother cross the bridge before she put down the half-empty bowl of gruel and cloth. 'Can I get anything else for you, Gramma?' she asked.

The old woman shook her head and mumbled, 'Little boys.'

Tam smiled at Gramma's comment, presuming she was thinking of Chasse and Jaysin. Her grandmother seldom kept track of conversations. She drifted from sleep, to feeding, to sleep, and when she spoke no one took notice because what she said was rarely connected to what was happening around her.

'That's all they are,' the old woman added, as Tam drew a light blanket over her legs.

'I'll be back later, Gramma,' Tam explained, and she straightened and headed for the door. 'Mother wants me to run another errand.'

'You be mindful of that dragon,' Gramma said firmly, as Tam closed the door.

There is no dragon on the mountain, Tam thought, as she headed for the bridge, and she wondered why Gramma Harmi held a dragon fixation.

On the far side of the bridge, Tam felt the weight of boredom and tiredness lift. Being sent to find the Herbal Man was at least an interesting task, although it wasn't the fetching of the old man that inspired her. She didn't cherish knocking at his hut and escorting him, alone, down Dragon Mountain. He was creepy. He lived in isolation, high on the mountain, even during the winter months when the slopes were locked under the weight of snow. He rarely visited the village, and his visits were customarily brief. He either came to barter for food and provisions, or to heal a gravely ill villager when requested. He wore a long dark cloak, as black as Shaddho's legendary hide, and he was incalculably old. Some villagers believed that he was even older than Gramma Harmi, although Tam doubted that was possible.

Adults in Harbin viewed the Herbal Man with distrust. No one knew anything of his origin. No one knew anything of his family. He had no wife, no children, and he lived alone on the mountain for as long as anyone could remember. No one knew his true name, so they called him the Herbal Man. Rumourmongers, like Sharmine and Marissa, claimed he was a servant of Shaddho, an evil man cursed to use his healing powers to atone for wicked misdeeds in his past. Tam never saw the logic in their tale, but others were willing to listen and believe. A few, like Amarti, believed the Herbal Man was being punished by Varst for a simple mistake, being forced to live alone and friendless until he died, or until he expunged his evil through good deeds.

For the children of Harbin, the Herbal Man was a vengeful demon. Parents warned naughty children that, if they didn't behave, the Herbal Man would come down from the mountain In the middle of the next storm and carry them away to his hut, where he would boil them in a vat, and feed them to beasts he kept locked in a cave beneath his bed. Tam remembered lying awake during a raging storm, rigid and terrified, when she was young, because her father threatened her with the Herbal Man's visitation. She didn't dare fall asleep for fear of being carried away. That's why village children screamed if the Herbal Man was called to treat their ailments and, if he did successfully cure them, they were left confused as to his true nature. Rather than develop their own beliefs about him though, most chose to listen to the village rumourmongers.

Tam never grew to loathe the Herbal Man like her peers. She witnessed what the old man could do with his herbs and broths when Chasse lay close to death six summers ago. Chasse contracted a strange malady that spread through the village after the dragonship's return, an illness that manifested as a dry feeling in the throat and morphed into a raging fever. Untreated victims died within four days. Two dragonwarriors and six villagers were the first to die because they refused to accept the Herbal Man's treatment, and the others who fell ill only allowed the Herbal Man to intervene after they saw him cure Chasse. Recovery for those who hesitated to accept treatment was slow, and some died despite the Herbal Man's efforts, but those who were treated early recovered quickly. Even though people were grateful for the Herbal Man's cure, many remained suspicious and distant because he did not save everyone. His response was to do the same. He chose to be secretive and aloof, and the fears and rumours remained uncontested.

Tam was happy to fetch the Herbal Man because she could spend more time on the mountain. It meant she didn't have to feed Gramma Harmi, or babysit Jaysin, or clean fish, or mend clothes, or mould pots or weave baskets, or do any of the endless, mindless tasks her mother set aside for her. It was early morning, and it would take until almost midday to reach the Herbal Man's hut; it would be mid-afternoon before she returned with him. She could enjoy most of the day without drudgery.

She spied Katris and a group of girls outside the Long Hall, but she headed through the pasture, away from the village, so they did not see her. She crossed foot-worn paths that led to outlying goatherd huts and climbed a wooden railing fence built to keep goats near the buildings at night. Crossing the wide pasture, she saw three youths driving goats out of a pen onto the hillside, each goat a splash of black, white and tan against the light green summer grass. She followed the tree line at the far side of the pasture, until she joined the path that led up the mountain to the Herbal Man's hut. Her goatskin boots and lower half of her skirt were damp from dew. She could have taken the main path from the village, but it was quicker to cut across the pasture, and she enjoyed walking through patches of long grass.

The lower section of the mountain path cut back across the lower slope in a lazy pattern, making it a leisurely walk between the tall conifers. She was in no hurry. Her mother warned her not to waste time, but she couldn't complain if Tam chose to walk slowly to avoid slipping. She watched for glimpses of the mountain wildlife she loved to study. She spied a rabbit, and the usual woodpeckers and jays flitted between branches. She saw a grey owl watching her and tensed when she heard a larger creature crunch through the undergrowth, but the unseen animal avoided her. She found plenty of scratchings and spoor and droppings, revealing that the forest was thickly populated, but the larger animals were either deeper in the woods or asleep in their lairs.

She stumbled upon three stray goats at one point. Even though the animals frequently wandered up the mountain, she knew the goat herders would be looking for them, so she decided that, if the animals were still there when she descended, she would drive them down to the pasture. There were bears on the mountain, and occasionally grey wolves, and goats were an easy meal. In the late days of autumn, driven by starvation, the larger predators sometimes came to the edge of the village to steal goats and chickens.

Tam saw wolves, from the safety of her village, on a warm evening two summers ago. A pack appeared at the edge of the goat pasture as the sun dipped into the western ocean. Lit be the last rays of golden light, the wolves skirted the tree line before melting into the forest.

Brown bears were more common. She watched two cubs playing near her mountain hideaway for most of a morning, last spring, until their mother lumbered out of the woods and led them away. Bears seemed harmless, their great shaggy brown coats looking soft and warm, but she knew the firm warning that all village children received to keep out of the woods and off the mountain, especially after dark when the bears roamed the forest.

After a while, the path made a definite upward turn, becoming steeper as it climbed the mountain. The ground was rockier, cliffs rose, and the trees appeared to cling desperately to the earth rather than grow firmly from it. Tam traversed this section of the path once before, last summer, when she accompanied Chasse, who was taking a message to the Herbal Man on their father's behalf. She remembered the path snaked between a series of rocky outcrops, before crossing a shallow, densely wooded plateau where the Herbal Man's hut lay.

She stopped halfway up the steepest section to clamber onto a gigantic outcrop of mossy granite boulders that erupted from the mountainside and tumbled over each other like excited wolf cubs. Her perch opened a view across the entire bay, and as the sun poked between the thin cloud layer it highlighted the vista and the sparkling deep blue ocean. She could see the forested peaks of Varst's Bluff and Nakiades' Watch on either side of Harbin Bay's entrance, Dragon's Mouth, and, directly below, Harbin nestled between the curve of ocean and forest. White gulls circled over the fishing huts and tables. Thin white lines of hearth-fire smoke trailed lazily skyward, and tiny figures moved on errands through the village. In contrast to the surrounding world, the people looked small, insignificant. She sat and soaked in the warmth of the mid-morning sunshine, enjoying being able to look over her world beyond reproach from an intrusive adult concerned with mundane matters. Finally, though, pricked by her conscience, she climbed down to the path and continued her task.

The sun was high overhead when she reached the plateau. As the path levelled, the foliage thickened and the trees huddled closer, as if thankful for a flat place where they could safely anchor their roots. The ground was damp underfoot and the soil rich. Tam could taste the increased humidity.

Last summer, when she reached this point with Chasse, Tam felt as if she had reached another world. The plateau hosted a lush garden where trees glistened with moss and lichen and broad-leaved ferns, some as tall as her father, grew abundantly between the trees. A profusion of colourful, exotic birds filled the air with chirruping and chatter and the clatter of their beating wings as they flew swiftly between the trunks, flashes of vibrant blues and reds and yellows. The lively garden fascinated her, but it was also eerie, because the plateau was unlike any other part of the mountain, or the village, as if it didn't belong to the world of Harbin. She dreamed of the forest several times, after her first visit. Always, in her dream, the forest was silent, full of expectation, as if awaiting a great event – caught in the moment between seeing and comprehending. It was a question waiting for an answer, an answer she did not have.

The path wound gently through the luxuriant forest, rising and falling where rivulets cut channels across the plateau. Above the tree canopy, the face of the upper mountain and its craggy peak loomed like a god. Even at the end of summer, snow clung doggedly to the peak, reminding everyone that winter would soon return to bury the world beneath its icy blanket. She tried to imagine the plateau forest deep in snow, the trees and ferns coated white, but the image eluded her, as if the concept did not belong here, and that thought only added depth to her sense of the pervading eeriness.

Tam paused at a rill and cupped her hands to scoop a mouthful of sparkling fresh water. The cool sensation awakened her thirst, so she drank three more mouthfuls before continuing.

Within a few paces, she reached a clearing on the crest of a rise, and at the far side of the clearing she saw the Herbal Man's hut, a structure so overgrown with creepers and moss that it almost merged into the forest. Obviously older than any hut in the village, its ramshackle appearance suggested that it was a chaotic construction of discarded wood and stone thrown together by a drunken lunatic. Tam believed that, if it wasn't for the myriad creepers and vines festooning the dilapidated hut, it would collapse.

The soft tinkling of wind chimes drifted on the faint breeze, a haunting melody of strange harmonies and erratic rhythms and discordant notes that pleased and jarred her senses, and her unease increased as she approached the hut. Fear that she couldn't quite control made her throat sticky and her legs weak, so she reminded herself the childhood nightmare stories were only make-believe. The Herbal Man didn't steal children or boil them in a vat. There wasn't a cave of horrors beneath his tumble-down hut. The Herbal Man healed Chasse, and her parents wouldn't send her on an errand up the mountain if the stories were true. She tried to laugh aside her nervousness, but she couldn't. The feeling that all wasn't right in that place persisted. She scolded herself for being silly.

The hut door was shut. She summoned her courage and knocked. No one answered. She waited. No one came to the door. She shuffled her feet and knocked again. Still no one answered. She thought of testing the door to see if it was locked but decided against it in case the Herbal Man was inside and mistook her uninvited entrance for rudeness. Instead, she ventured to a tiny window, partly obscured by creepers, on the near side of the hut, and peered through gaps in the shutters.

The interior was dark. She moved to a second window. Again, the interior was dark, but the new angle revealed thin rays of light filtering through the roof. She perceived the outline of a square table and part of a chair, but that was all. The hut was empty. The Herbal Man wasn't home.

She shrugged and retraced her steps across the clearing, considering what the situation meant. Her father would be infuriated to learn that the Herbal Man did not return with her.

At the clearing's edge, as she halted, deciding it might be prudent to wait in case the old man was nearby collecting herbs, she heard a noise in the foliage to her left. Someone groaned. Adrenalin pumped through her. She wanted to run, but she hesitated, straining to hear further sound. There was a second groan.

Curiosity overcame her fear. She warily picked her way between the huge ferns until she reached a gap where a stream cascaded over a pebble bed between two large trunks. A bare human foot protruded from behind one trunk. She crept to the other side of the moss-laden trunk and peered around. Spread-eagled on his back on the tiny stream bank, white hair flowing in the water, was the Herbal Man.

The unexpected discovery startled Tam. When she looked closer, she saw the old man's head rested on a rock, and there was dried blood on the rock and in the old man's hair. She slid down beside him to examine the extent of his injury and realised that the back of his head apparently struck the rock fiercely. The Herbal Man groaned again and rolled, tipping his face in the water, so she reached across and gently lifted his head out of the stream. As she did, the old man opened his eyes. 'It's alright,' she crooned. 'You're alright. I'll get you out of this.'

The old man's eyes widened, and she saw the intense grey hue within. His face creased into a painful smile, and he went to speak, but all that issued from his lips was a dry hiss.

'Don't talk,' Tam whispered. 'I'll need any strength you have left to help me get you out of here.'

Five

The Dragon Head strode across the open ground separating the Warriors' Hall and the Long Hall, and those who saw him knew that he was seething with anger.

'Eesa,' warned Janys, who was mending a rush basket near the entrance to the Long Hall. 'Your husband is coming, and he doesn't look happy.'

'Men!' Eesa cursed. She put down the length of sailcloth she was sewing and rose to meet Kevan.

He stood in the doorway, glowering like a storm cloud. 'Where is that girl?' he demanded.

'I take it she hasn't yet returned with the Herbal Man,' Eesa said, knowing that was certainly the reason for Kevan's dark mood.

'No, she has not,' he growled, 'and the day is slipping away.'

Eesa glanced up at the sun and was surprised to find it lower in the western sky than she expected. 'Perhaps he had a task to complete, and she was made to wait,' she suggested.

'When I give an order, I expect it to be obeyed,' he stated bluntly. 'If the Herbal Man disobeys me, that is one matter, but if that girl does not come back down in good time then it is an entirely different matter.'

'There is still time in the day,' Eesa responded, trying to placate her husband. 'Tamesan will return with the Herbal Man.'

'If he chooses to come,' Kevan grumbled. 'But I will still speak with the girl when she returns.' He grunted a greeting to Janys, turned on his heel, and stalked back to the Warriors' Hall to join the men cleaning their weapons and armour from the summer journey. Eesa watched until her husband disappeared into the Warriors' Hall, before she let out a deep sigh.

'Ten weeks is not nearly enough,' Janys remarked sardonically.

'That girl will drive me to madness,' said Eesa, as she squatted beside Janys. 'No matter what I get her to do, she finds a way to annoy her father.'

'Isn't that the way of girls?' Janys asked, grinning. 'They drive their fathers to distraction until they find a husband. My husband couldn't marry our Margret off to Heron's son quickly enough. All I remember at Procra's Feast was him saying how delighted he was to have her off his hands.'

Eesa laughed. She could see Kevan talking like Janys' husband, but it was not going to be so easy to marry Tamesan off. She was certainly growing into an uncommonly pretty girl, with her green eyes and flowing mane of red-gold hair likely to turn many a man's head, but she lacked a woman's grace. Her spirit was too flighty, too irresponsible, too fiery to make a man happy. Yet it appeared that Trask's son, Marron, was keenly interested in her. Even Kevan noticed. Perhaps Kevan and Trask were discussing the matter. It wasn't uncommon for fathers to arrange pairings, and a liaison between Kevan and Trask through the marriage of their children would strengthen Harbin. Marron was a strong, determined youth, and Eesa knew only a strong man could curb her daughter's fanciful ideas and wandering ways. It would be an unhappy pairing, initially, but Tamesan would learn to adjust. All women did. It was how things went.

'Tamesan will return shortly, Eesa,' said Janys. 'It's a long walk up and down the mountain for a girl.'

Eesa studied the sun's angle again. If Tamesan was foolishly wasting time gazing into the distance, or chasing birds and animals through the forest, like she too often did, she would be sorely punished by Kevan, of that Eesa was certain. As the leader of Harbin, he could ill afford people gossiping about his daughter's lack of respect for authority, or his weak discipline. Gossip would undermine his position. Besides, Tamesan was coming of age. Within two years she would be chosen to be a dragonwarrior's wife and accorded the status of a woman. It was time she started acting like one.

Getting the old man to his hut was not easy. Tam dragged him as carefully as she could up the slope between the trees and made him lean on her shoulder as she half-carried him across the clearing. Fortunately, he was not much taller than her, and surprisingly frail.

When she reached the hut, Tam discovered the door that she was reluctant to open was unlocked. She opened it and steered the old man inside. Her eyes adjusted to the gloom, and she spotted a dishevelled bed in the furthest corner of the room, so she manoeuvred the Herbal Man forward and eased him onto the bed. He groaned and moved his lips painfully, mouthing words, so she bent her ear close to his mouth.

'Water,' he gasped.

There were no water jugs in the room, but she located a dusty blue bowl and returned to the stream and, as she dipped the bowl into the water, she noticed broken pottery shards scattered along the stream bed. The old man must have been fetching water when he slipped and hit his head. She scooped a bowlful of water and hurried back.

In the hut, she gently nursed his head so that he could sip the water.

'Better,' the Herbal Man gasped, and he laid back. 'Thank you.'

'You have a nasty gash on the back of your head,' Tam informed him. 'Were you only getting water?'

'Yesterday – evening,' he whispered. 'I think – I – lost balance.'

Tam was astonished to learn that the Herbal Man lay by the stream for a day without help. 'You need that wound cleaned and bandaged,' she said. The old man did not answer.

Tam opened the entry door wide to let in the light and searched through the dusty and oddly useless collections of articles jumbled on the rickety wooden shelves until she found a flint and a rusty battered lantern. She located a near-empty paraffin container and topped up the lantern before she lit it. She placed the lantern close to the bed so that she could inspect the Herbal Man's head wound. Because the wound was immersed in the stream, it was relatively clean, although strands of hair were caught in the congealed mess around the cut.

Tam searched for a rag and a knife. On a low shelf that also apparently served as a bench, she found an old hunting knife, but she couldn't find rags, so she tore a strip from her hem that would, with cleaning, serve as a bandage. She located a pot, in which she could boil water, and set to organising a fire when she discovered a small pile of wood beside the cold hearth. Setting the wood in place in the hearth proved challenging because at the back of the space beneath the chimney was a small hole that dropped vertically in line with the chimney, but by carefully stacking the wood so that it didn't cover the hole she was able to light a fire. She went outside to fill the pot.

As she crossed the clearing, she realised it was late in the afternoon, but Tam figured that there was enough time to tend the old man's injury and descend the mountain before darkness settled. She couldn't leave him lying hurt and uncared for alone. It was sheer good fortune her father sent for him; otherwise no one might have stumbled upon him in the stream bed. She laughed at herself for being so afraid of an old man. The terrible childhood tales of the Herbal Man were cruel lies. He was no different to poor old Asmae or Gramma Harmi. He just needed someone to care for him.

When she lugged the heavy pot back to the hut, Tam was shocked to find the Herbal Man lying on the floor beside his bed, breathing hard and sweating profusely. 'What are you doing?' she cried and put down the pot.

'Have – have to – get – medicines,' the Herbal Man gasped. 'Down there.' He pointed vaguely at the floor near the small hearth, but all Tam could see was a dirty mat covering the floorboards. 'Down – there,' he repeated slowly, and collapsed.

Tam hauled him back onto the bed. She'd forgotten his clothes were damp from lying beside the stream all night and day, so she pulled a musty blanket over him for warmth and studied the mat that he pointed out. It was so faded and worn and dirty that the original weave and colours were indistinguishable.

The Herbal Man repeated, 'Down there.'

Why? she wondered. She nudged the mat aside with her foot to reveal a brass pull-ring and a faint square outline in the wooden planks – a trapdoor. The terrible horror stories about a cave beneath the Herbal Man's hut where monsters gobbled up children flooded her memory, and she hesitated, before she steeled her nerves and pulled on the ring. The trapdoor was surprisingly light and fluid to open. Wooden steps descended into darkness. She retrieved the lantern from beside the bed and, caught between curiosity and fear, she headed down.

The lantern revealed a space much larger than the cramped, dusty confines of the hovel, like a cross between a natural cave and a man-made cellar carved from the earth and rock. A large bench occupied the centre, and three lanterns hung from the ceiling. In the shadows beneath the bench were dozens of pottery urns. Shelves along two walls displayed multiple jars and containers, and a hearth with fresh cut wood piled before it was built into the third wall. She guessed the hearth accounted for the hole that hampered her efforts to build a fire upstairs, because sparks and embers were dropping infrequently into the fireplace. A carved wooden door sat to the left of the hearth. The fourth wall was bare rock, adorned with bunches of drying and dried plants and flowers hanging upside down from wooden hooks. The atmosphere of the entire place was of organisation and cleanliness, in stark contrast to the derelict hut above ground, and the Herbal Man was suddenly a deep mystery.

She investigated the jars and urns and discovered they were marked with strange etchings. Some contained powders, some liquids. A variety of strong and subtle fragrances teased her senses as she moved to the wooden door. The door was solid and polished, unlike any door in her village, and the handle was made from a shiny, white, cool and silky substance. She turned the handle and pushed the door open.

Her lantern illuminated a second chamber, smaller than the first. Lanterns hung from the ceiling, but the cavern's natural lines dominated and, if it wasn't for the furniture, it could have been a cave. More shelves were carved into the walls and lined with rectangular bundles and rolled portions of thin yellow material. A smaller table with a single chair sat beside a bed – a tidy bed, with a quilted maroon covering inlaid with gold filigree, more elegant than any bedding in Harbin. One odd rectangular bundle lay open on the table, together with a large feather, a small container of dark liquid, and a squat candle. Animal skins and woven rugs were scattered comfortably over the floor, giving the room a homely, welcoming air.

Two more doors led from the room. Tam tried the one directly opposite the entry, but it was firmly locked. The second door was unlocked and opened into a storeroom of food supplies. The Herbal Man was obviously prepared for winter. Deciding further exploration would have to wait, Tam withdrew to the first room and climbed the steps.

The Herbal Man had not moved. In fact, he'd fallen into a deep sleep, so Tam placed the water pot over the tiny fire to boil, hoping the pottery was fire-hardened, and she sat on the floor to wait. She understood why so much dust permeated the hut. It was a ruse, façade, but she was puzzled as to why the old man went to so much trouble to make it appear as if he was a poor hermit.

The water boiled, but Tam realised the pot was going to be too hot to lift from the hearth with her bare hands, so she descended to the lower chamber and found a large, thick square of green cloth hanging by the downstairs hearth, obviously left there for the purpose she required. Back in the hut, she lifted the pot from the fire and poured steaming water into the smaller bowl. She dropped the strip of cloth from her skirt into the water to rinse it, let it cool, and used it to dab at the congealed blood on the back of the Herbal Man's head, until the blood loosened. The cut was not long, but it was deep enough for Tam to believe that she could see a sliver of skull. She used the hunting knife to trim the old man's hair from around the injury.

When she was halfway done, the old man groaned and opened his eyes. 'Hold still,' Tam urged gently. 'I'm cleaning your wound.'

'Where – am I?' the Herbal Man asked. He seemed confused.

'In your old hut,' Tam informed him, and she cut away another hank of hair.

The old man squinted in the flickering lantern light. 'Who-?' he half-asked weakly.

'Tamesan,' she replied, hesitated, and added, 'Daughter of Kevan.'

The Herbal Man didn't seem to understand. 'Downstairs,' he said. 'My medicines.'

'I've seen,' she said, as she cleaned the outer edges of the wound with the damp cloth.

'You must get me downstairs. I need medicines,' the Herbal Man rasped, insistently.

'When I have finished cleaning away the mess,' Tam replied.

The old man sighed.

Moving the Herbal Man to the lower level was as difficult as dragging him from the stream, but Tam struggled gamely, until she laid him on the clean bed in the second chamber. The Herbal Man needed to get out of his dirty and damp garments, but despite having dressed and undressed Gramma Harmi and Jaysin many times Tam was embarrassed to do what she knew needed to be done for his health. She went to the storeroom and brought out a fresh set of clothes — a tunic, a pullover, breeches, a cloak — and laid them at the end of the bed. 'You can't stay in those clothes,' she said hesitantly.

'I need — medicine first,' the Herbal Man replied. 'In the — other — room. Bring me water — Callania Herb, Dewdrop Essence, and — the red Jenna Berry powder.'

Tam stared at him, but she did not understand what he meant. 'I'll look,' she promised lamely and left the room.

The containers on the shelves in the first chamber were an infuriating puzzle. Tam found a host of jars containing red powders, but nothing that looked like the blue Dewdrop flowers that she sometimes picked on the mountainside. She felt helpless, so she returned to confess that she couldn't find what he wanted and discovered him struggling feebly out of his damp clothes. There was no longer time for social propriety. She helped the Herbal Man Into drier garments.

Exhausted by the time he changed clothes, the Herbal Man collapsed on the bed and looked as if he was going to drift into sleep again, but he grimaced and asked, 'Can you read?'

'What do you mean?' Tam replied, baffled by the question.

'I thought not,' the Herbal Man said, shaking his head. 'No one in your village can.' He sighed, and drew a deep, shuddering breath, before saying, 'I want you to — bring some — things for me. Listen carefully.' He stopped, and for a moment Tam thought he was going to pass out, but he refocussed and gave his orders.

Tam diligently followed each laborious instruction, but she still brought five different jars of red powder to the Herbal Man before she found the one containing Jenna Berry powder. Dewdrop Essence was easier to identify.

The Herbal Man mixed the ingredients in water, drank it, and immediately suffered a severe coughing fit. 'Nasty,' he sputtered with distaste, 'but necessary.'

He described a crucible dish and a pair of tongs to hold it, which Tam found on the shelf under the long bench. She lit the fat candle beside the Herbal Man's bed and mixed the other two ingredients in water in the crucible, as instructed, taking care not to let the mixture boil. The Herbal Man slipped in and out of consciousness throughout the exercise, but his iron will kept him monitoring Tam's progress. Eventually, she created a foul-smelling mauve paste in the crucible.

'Let it – cool,' the Herbal Man wheezed.

Tam realised that he was succumbing to exhaustion because sweat beaded on his brow and he was shaking violently.

'You – must – you must smooth it – on the wound,' he stammered desperately and crumpled onto his pillow.

Tam panicked. She waved the crucible in the air to cool the paste as rapidly as possible, but when she stuck a finger in to test the temperature she nearly burned herself. She blew on the paste, but it took several minutes before it was cool enough to touch. As soon as it was, she scooped a gob of the mauve mixture and spread it over the back of the old man's head, covering the gash with a thick layer. It would be smeared all over the Herbal Man's pillow while he slept, but she hoped that it was thick enough to keep the wound covered. She rinsed the residue from her hands and pulled the quilted cover over the old man's sleeping form.

There was nothing else she could do for him. She needed to get home to tell her father the Herbal Man was gravely ill. Perhaps her mother would let her return tomorrow to see how the Herbal Man fared overnight. She shivered. *What if he dies?* she thought. *What if I come back and find his corpse?* She pushed the morbid idea aside, picked up the low-burning lantern and headed for the steps in the adjoining chamber.

The interior of the upstairs hut was darker than before and Tam realised why. It was early evening. She walked into the clearing and looked up at the twinkling sky. Her father and mother would be furious because she did not do as they asked. Perhaps Kevan was already on his way up the mountain, coming to drag his failure of a daughter home. She considered taking her chances and heading down the mountain, moving quickly so nothing ferocious could catch her. She listened, straining for approaching sound, but only heard the leaves rustling and whispering. *What if I slip in the darkness on the steeper section of the path? What if I stumble across a bear?* she pondered. Caught by indecision, Tam stood in the cold night air and gazed for a long time at the stars. Whatever she did would be wrong. Perhaps it would be better to wait for her father. At least she understood his anger. It was the least risk. She crept back into the hut.

The little hearth fire was long burned out. Tam glanced at the trapdoor. She could light a fire in the lower hearth and sleep by it. She was sure the Herbal Man wouldn't mind her using his wood. With the paraffin lantern light close to dying, she lit a fire in the first chamber, marvelling at how the Herbal Man built a chimney that rose through the fireplace in the hut above. It would give anyone observing the hut the impression that smoke was coming from within without disclosing the secret chambers.

Once she stabilised the fire, Tam climbed into the hut to retrieve the musty bedding and hastily arranged the tattered blankets before the downstairs hearth, and she curled up to sleep, trying to ignore her ravening hunger and overbearing sense of guilt for not going home. It was a long time before the comfort of sleep enfolded her.

Six

Tam stood before an old chipped and cracked wooden door that hung on one hinge at a crazy angle, threatening to fall. As she extended her fingers to grasp the shattered handle, the door swung open, freely and quietly. Blackness lay within. A breath of hot air rushed out and washed over her. Then she was inside, in the inky dark. The warmth was smothering. She was in danger, a terrible invisible danger, and fear clawed her gut. She wanted to run out, but she knew, without turning, the door no longer existed. She was trapped in darkness with an unnameable horror. Fear froze in her throat. She could not scream. Talons gripped her shoulder.

She jerked and opened her eyes.

'So, you're awake,' said a man's voice. 'Hungry?'

Tam rubbed her eyes and stared blearily at the Herbal Man. His hair was secured in a loose ponytail, and he wore a black cloak that looked too large for his frame. He held a steaming bowl in his outstretched hands.

'Gruel,' he announced. 'Hot and healthy.'

She accepted his offering and, after hesitation, during which the Herbal Man moved to another part of the chamber, Tam ate greedily. Behind her, the hearth burned brightly, flames illuminating the room and warming her back.

'I am very grateful for your help yesterday,' the Herbal Man said, when he approached. 'If you didn't find me, and stayed to mix the paste, I don't think I would be feeling well at all today. You did an excellent job on the wound.' He lifted his hand and gingerly patted the back of his head where the wound, and the hair she cut away, were masked by the ponytail.

Tam swallowed the last mouthful of her breakfast, before saying, 'My father sent me to fetch you to the village. The dragonship is back. Except now he will be angry with me for not going home last night.

'I'm sure he will be,' the Herbal Man agreed. 'But I will explain the circumstances, Tamesan, and he will appreciate what you've done.'

'You remembered my name?'

The Herbal Man smiled. 'You have a brother, Chasse, and a little brother, Jaysin. Your mother is Eesa, and you take care of your grandmother, Harmi. I know the names of everyone in Harbin.'

'How?' Tam blurted and blushed for her rude response.

'Names are important. I might not visit the village more than a dozen times in a year – often less – but I like to know who is there. You could call me nosy, but when you've lived as long as I have some things come naturally, names and people in my case.'

'I didn't mean to be so rude.'

'It's not rude to ask questions,' the old man reassured her. 'If you don't ask, you might never know.'

The Herbal Man's response surprised Tam because her mother regularly warned her to be less inquisitive and to accept what is. Encouraged, she felt compelled to ask another question, one that plagued her since discovering the Herbal Man's underground home. 'Why do you live down here?'

The Herbal Man coughed and said, 'I thought we would get to that point. You see, I have an important favour to ask.'

'What?'

'I would very much appreciate you saying nothing about these lower chambers to anyone else. No one in the village knows about them, and I prefer to keep it that way.'

'Why?'

'You do like to ask questions,' the Herbal Man noted, frowning. Tam feared that she overstepped the bounds of decency, but before she could offer another apology the Herbal Man grinned and continued. 'I can't explain why without telling you a long story, Tamesan, and, unfortunately, I don't have time to tell it. Your father and brother are already coming to fetch you, so we should meet them on the way down the mountain.'

That was it. The matter was closed, but the old man left her contemplating yet another question: how did he know her father was coming? Tam wanted an explanation, but she held her tongue. She shook out her makeshift bedding and set to straightening her long red hair with her fingers. 'You don't have a brush, do you?' she asked, when her fingers were caught in a mass of tangles.

The Herbal Man went to his bedroom and returned with a hairbrush, and Tam was astonished by its ornate beauty. The handle, carved from unusually soft, white wood, was covered with delicate reliefs of exotic birds and plants. She never saw such an exquisite hairbrush.

'Thank you,' she said, and set to work on the heavier tangles.

'You can wash your face and hands in the water bowl,' the Herbal Man offered. 'Then we must go. The sun is about to rise.'

While she finished brushing her hair, Tam watched the Herbal Man busily select containers from his shelves and store them in pockets within his black cloak. She rinsed her face, the cold water awakening her senses, and handed the brush to him as he went to climb the steps.

The Herbal Man waved his hand, saying, 'No. You may keep it.'

'But it's yours,' Tam insisted.

'Call it part of a small gift for helping me yesterday,' the Herbal Man replied. 'And perhaps a bribe to remind you not to tell anyone else about this place,' he added, with a sweep of his hand to indicate the lower chambers. 'As far as people should know, I live in the run-down little hut.'

'I won't tell anyone,' Tam promised, and she glanced down at the brush she clutched. 'I wouldn't have told anyone anyway, because you asked me not to,' she stressed, meeting his gaze, and she placed the brush back on a shelf. 'I would be asked where I got it from,' she explained.

The Herbal Man smiled appreciatively and led her upstairs.

The world was waking when they entered the forest. Birds chorused dawn songs and the sky was engaged in its ritual metamorphosis from black to grey to brief gold and into blue. Tam followed the Herbal Man's back, marvelling at the old man's speedy overnight recovery, but she observed that he walked slowly, tentatively, as if he was uncertain of his steps, which made her wonder how much illness remained.

On the downward path, at the point where the slope steepened, the Herbal Man paused and pointed towards the peak of Dragon Mountain. 'Look,' he said. Tam saw the first rays of the morning sun spreading across the sky, adding a yellow hue to the air and transforming the snow-capped peak into a golden mantle. 'Te-Amen-San,' he whispered.

Tam shivered at hearing the old words for her name. She'd heard the Dragon Heart and her mother use them, but they rolled so fluently from the Herbal Man's tongue it was as if his voice resonated in the core of her being. She stared at the widening glow in the eastern sky, caught in the childhood rapture that drew her to the roof of her home to watch the sunrise. She turned to ask if the Herbal Man knew what the words meant, but he was descending the path, so she fell into silent step behind.

The Herbal Man stopped three times on the steepest section. 'You should be resting,' Tam admonished.

'I can recuperate when we are in the village,' the Herbal Man replied. At the third stop, he withdrew a phial of blue liquid from within his cloak, uncorked it and swallowed a draught. The taste made him screw up his face and he coughed involuntarily.

'Is it really that bad?' Tam asked.

The Herbal Man grimaced, and said, 'It is. I've been trying to make it taste less foul for several years, but every time I do the mixture loses its curative potency.'

'What is it meant to do?'

'Clears infection from the lungs, mainly. Sometimes it reduces a fever, if it isn't too far advanced. I was told it is good for curing boils, if it's applied hot, but I doubt that.'

'Why?'

The Herbal Man cocked a bushy white eyebrow and looked at her. 'It would take too long to explain. Let's say the logic is flawed.'

'Could you teach me about it?' Tam asked.

The Herbal Man's expression hardened, and he studied Tam as if he was searching her face for something, a response that made her feel uncomfortable, but his face softened, and he said, 'Perhaps I could, if you are really willing to learn.'

Before she could declare that she was keen to learn the old man's craft, without seriously reflecting on what that might mean, Tam heard her father's booming voice, calling, 'Tamesan!' as he emerged from the rocks and trees with Chasse in tow.

'Now we meet with Kevan, the Dragon Head of Harbin,' the Herbal Man said, more to himself than to her, Tam observed.

Kevan climbed the short distance to confront the Herbal Man and Tam, and he dwarfed the old man as he glared at his daughter. 'Where in Shaddho's name have you been, girl?' he demanded.

'Your daughter has been taking good care of me,' the Herbal Man intervened. 'Thanks to her, I am alive.'

Kevan's anger altered to astonishment. 'What do you mean?' he asked, warily. Chasse approached Tam and winked.

'I fell, gathering water, two days ago,' the Herbal Man explained, and he told Kevan how Tam found and healed him. As he finished his explanation, the Herbal Man loosened his ponytail and bent forward to show Kevan the evidence of his injury.

Kevan studied the paste-covered wound and turned to Tam. 'Why didn't you come back down the mountain for help?' She heard his frustration. He came prepared to vent his anger and the Herbal Man denied his right to do so.

'If she left me,' the Herbal Man said, 'I would have died. Besides, by the time she did what was necessary, it was too dark to descend the mountain. You know how dangerous it can be.'

Kevan nodded appreciation before he gestured for everyone to follow, and he led the group down the mountain, travelling slowly to accommodate the Herbal Man's condition.

Walking with Tam, Chasse announced, 'I saw the dragon's hoard yesterday.'

'Much?' Tam asked.

'No,' he replied, unable to mask his disappointment. 'Some gold coins, a handful of gems, and a collection of weapons and armour. Most of the armour was damaged. The men said the dragon they killed was a small one. It didn't have time to acquire a true treasure cache.'

'I wonder how many dragons are left?' Tam queried, and added, 'I'd love to see a dragon.'

'I will, next summer!' Chasse declared.

'Yes. You will. But I won't,' Tam petulantly reminded him.

'I'll tell you all about him when we return. I'll bring you some treasure, Tam. I promise.'

'That's not the same,' she complained.

'I don't think you would really want to see a dragon,' Kevan interrupted sternly. 'They are ugly, greedy creatures that fly in the night, breathe fire, and delight in eating girls.'

Tam wanted to say, 'What has that to do with me seeing a dragon?' but she kept quiet, as was expected. Her father regularly reminded her that girls weren't meant to express opinions, especially about dragons. What she noticed however, was the questioning glance the Herbal Man gave her father while he was speaking, a look Kevan didn't see, but one that seemed to query his words, and that made Tam wonder what the Herbal Man found wrong with what her father said.

They entered Harbin mid-morning. Kevan directed Tam to go home while he took the Herbal Man and Chasse to the Warriors' Hall. Tam knew her mother would be waiting, and no doubt she would receive a reprimand for her tardiness. As she passed a pair of village women, she felt that they were staring at her, so she hurried to the bridge over Watersdrop, but Katris called her before she reached it.

Katris approached in the company of three girls. 'Your mother wants you in the Long Hall,' Katris announced, and her three companions giggled.

'What's so funny?' Tam asked.

Katris sent her companions a sly look, whispered, and they laughed.

'I asked you a question, Katris,' Tam said, irritation rising.

Katris stepped closer and asked, provocatively, 'We were wondering what he's like?'

'Who?'

'Your man.' The girls sniggered.

'I don't have a man,' Tam retorted, puzzled by Katris' absurd assertion. The girls broke into louder fits of laughter, so Tam started to walk on, tired of being a target for their obscure ridicule.

'We mean the dirty old Herbal Man you slept with last night,' Katris called after her.

The taunt halted Tam. She spun, seething with anger, but fought her emotion and responded calmly with, 'He is not a dirty old man.'

'Oh,' said Katris, with mock apology. 'Of course he's not.' She fought a smile and said, 'At least, not to you. But then he is the only man you're likely to get, so you wouldn't think of him as dirty, would you?'

Katris' sarcasm cut deep and, for the briefest instant, fighting blood rage, Tam almost charged Katris, but she controlled her compulsion. *Fighting resolves nothing*, she reminded herself, a conclusion she reached through watching the boys brawl over every issue. She bit her lip, and turned away, but Katris kept up her venomous attack.

'You're not even denying it?' Katris sneered. 'You do like him, don't you? Don't you, Tamesan of the dawn light? Oh, how disgusting!'

Tam sped up to leave the girls behind, ignoring their laugher as they followed her towards the Long Hall. For once, she would be glad to be with her mother – but she was puzzled as to why Katris was so intent on teasing her.

When Tam reached the Long Hall, she rushed inside, startling Eesa with her sudden entrance. 'Where in Procra's name have you been, child?' Eesa demanded. She dropped the rush basket she was weaving and stood to meet her daughter.

Tam caught her breath when Katris and her friends walked blithely into the hall, but they didn't look in Tam's direction as they took seats at the tables. 'Helping the Herbal Man,' Tam replied.

'All night?' Eesa asked. Someone sniggered, but when Eesa glanced at the girls they were all intent on weaving.

'He was hurt,' Tam explained, and she briefly outlined the previous day's events for her mother. Eesa asked the expected questions – Why didn't she come for help? Why didn't she come home before it got dark? – and she reminded Tam of her responsibilities to her father, and Gramma Harmi's needs, and she described how little Jaysin fretted for her.

Tam wanted to argue that the Herbal Man's life was more important under the circumstances, but she knew arguing was pointless, and she certainly didn't want to give Katris more fuel for teasing. Instead, she took the scolding and, when it was over, Eesa set her to smoothing rough edges of unfired pots that the women moulded during summer. Tam avoided the other girls, while she worked, but when everyone stopped for the midday meal she noticed they were whispering and giggling, and she was convinced it was at her expense. When Tam finished eating, Eesa sent her home to feed Gramma Harmi, after which she was to take a bowl of food to the men in the Warriors' Hall.

Relieved to be rid of the Long Hall, Tam walked briskly through the village, but when she reached her home she paused at the door because she heard voices within. At first, she thought her grandmother was talking to herself, as she often did, although her one-sided conversations were seldom intelligible, but the old woman was talking clearly and sensibly, and a quieter, deeper voice responded. Gramma was talking to a man. Unsure what to do, Tam listened.

'That was a long time ago,' Gramma said.

'It was only yesterday,' the man replied.

'To you, Eric, to you.' The old lady sighed. and Tam heard deep sadness in her grandmother's tone. 'Too many years have gone.'

'When I saw her early this morning, I thought it was you,' said the man. 'Same hair, same eyes lit by the morning sun. You haven't changed that much, Harmi. I can still see you.'

Tam recognised familiarity in the man's voice – the Herbal Man. She missed part of her grandmother's response, and only heard, '-as much anymore. It fades, Eric. Everything is fading.'

Her grandmother sobbed, so Tam coughed loudly and opened the door. In the half-lit room, her grandmother was hunched in her chair with the silhouette of the Herbal Man kneeling beside her, holding her hand, but he released his hold as Tam entered and stood slowly. Partly obscured in shadow, she thought that he appeared old and tired. 'Sorry,' Tam apologised. 'Mother sent me to feed Gramma. I thought I heard you talking.'

'We were,' the Herbal Man replied quietly,' but Harmi is very tired.' He looked down at Harmi, whose eyes were closed. 'I think she's already asleep,' he confided.

Tam walked past the Herbal Man and bent beside her grandmother. Harmi was fast asleep. As she smoothed a loose strand of white hair on her grandmother's forehead, she noticed a tiny teardrop in the corner of one closed eye, sparkling like a tiny jewel. She turned time to see the front door close. The Herbal Man was gone.

Seven

The Herbal Man remained in Harbin for four days. It was rare for him to spend long there, except in cases of extreme sickness, but he stayed because he was recovering from his injury. As a sign of respect, Kevan offered him the opportunity to sleep in the Warriors' Hall, but the Herbal Man declined, saying that he preferred solitude. Chasse told Tam that Kevan's offer met with significant dissension among the warriors, many of them reluctant to share their sleeping quarters with someone who never attained the formal status of manhood. Trask was especially critical of Kevan's gesture. The Herbal Man chose to stay in an abandoned fishing hut used to store tackle.

During each day, the Herbal Man treated villagers who were suffering minor ailments and saw to the more serious injuries of the returned dragonwarriors. He attended the ceremony at Watersdrop where the Dragon Heart sang the Words of Passage for Jared to speed his soul safely to Paradise. Tam observed that he stood apart from the crowd. Long-established rumours and lies made the people shun him, even when they needed and made use of his help, and he maintained a distance in accordance with their distrust. The Herbal Man was an outsider. Tam often felt like that, and only her respect for Banni's grief kept her in the crowd. She cried for Banni, and for Jared, and she cried for the Herbal Man, though she didn't understand why she cried for him.

The Herbal Man visited Gramma Harmi every day and gave her small doses of herbal medicines, and he instructed Tam on how and when to administer them during the approaching winter months when he would not be able to journey down the mountain. Every time the Herbal Man touched Gramma Harmi's arm or hand, she lit up with a smile that lingered long after he left, but Tam didn't catch them speaking in the way she did the first day.

The mystery of that intimate moment gnawed at her. She considered asking the Herbal Man straight out what happened, why Gramma Harmi was suddenly lucid, so like her old self again, why she responded as she did to his touch, but her questions remained unasked. The Herbal Man was busy attending to illness, and he was only ever alone when he retired in the evenings to his temporary quarters, and Tam was at home helping her mother.

Eesa kept Tam busy. The short autumn season was approaching and with it came two of Harbin's important festivals. The first was Procra's Dance, a fertility celebration in honour of Varst's goddess wife, Procra. On that night, dragonwarriors could choose partners from the eligible maidens. It was a night of dressing up, and of dancing, singing and drinking. It proclaimed the end of summer, and for the maidens of age the beginning of womanhood. Women were sewing new garments for the event to be held in a week's time. The Long Hall was full of gossip and speculation about who would be chosen by whom, and knowing smiles when names were considered.

Tam was still two summers from being eligible and she was glad. To be devoted to the beck and call of one man, satisfying his whims and lust, frightened her, but she listened on the outer edges to the idle chatter of the girls of age, and those who would be old enough the summer after, to learn the gossipy details of the approaching festival.

The most popular young men in the village were Kerik, Aaron and Sawl. Kerik was initiated into manhood that summer and, with dark, piercing eyes, the young women found him hauntingly attractive. Aaron was yet to choose a wife, despite reaching manhood three summers earlier, much to the disappointment of many girls because he was tall, handsome and strong, a perfect husband. Sawl's first wife died six summers past from the strange disease brought by the dragonship, and so he was free to choose again. Of the three, he was considered the least handsome, but he was a mature man who owned a well-kept cottage, and those features made him a good prospect.

Tam knew there were eleven single warriors in Harbin, four entering manhood, like Kerik, but there were only six eligible maidens, and four single women who lost husbands. The single women were not invited to dance in the celebration. If they were chosen again, the pairing would occur discreetly, at another time, and village life would continue as if the new pairing always existed.

The only women who could refuse a man's advances were those who were paired before. Maidens could not refuse a warrior's offer. It was a social tragedy not to be chosen, but it was a social disgrace to refuse. Old Asmae's isolated life was evidence of the latter. Everyone generally agreed that all six maidens would be husbanded this Procra's Dance because the odds were in their favour.

Tam persevered with cutting out and sewing, despite finding no pleasure in the tasks. She was creating a garment from the dark green material that her father brought home from the dragon's trove. When Chasse suggested it would match her green eyes and complement her golden-red hair, Tam teased him for making judgements about women's dresses, but she also thanked him sincerely for caring, and she warned him to never forget to be like that as a man.

When they found a spare moment together after one evening meal, Chasse proudly demonstrated the fighting techniques the dragonwarriors were teaching him. Tam initially feigned interest out of love for him, but her interest became genuine when he involved her in the action and they became embroiled in a rough-and-tumble play brawl.

'Easy, Tam,' Chasse warned, laughing as he disengaged from her attack. 'You're stronger than you think.'

'Girls can fight if they have to,' Tam asserted indignantly.

'Not most girls,' Chasse corrected. 'I think we played too many games together. None of the other girls would ever do this.'

'Have you asked any?' Tam teased, grinning.

'Not yet,' Chasse replied, mirroring Tam's grin. 'But I don't think I want to fight with any of them,' he jested.

Tam flicked back her tousled mass of hair and sat cross-legged on the ground. 'Who will you choose?' she suddenly asked.

Chasse stared, open-mouthed, and asked, 'What?'

'When it's your turn to choose at Procra's Dance, who will you choose?'

'I don't have to choose,' he answered. 'I'm still too young. Remember?' and he gave her a look suggesting he thought she'd lost her senses.

'Not this time,' she said. 'Next time.'

'I don't know. No one, probably.'

'Come on. You must like at least one of the girls. They're not all ugly,' Tam argued.

'Why do you want to know?' Chasse asked. Irritated by her question, he turned the question back on her. 'Who do you hope will choose you?'

'No one,' Tam answered flatly.

'You don't get a choice.'

'That's just it,' Tam replied, fixing him with a determined stare. 'I won't get a choice. That's why I hope no one will choose me – because I won't choose them.'

'What about Marron?' Chasse asked. He saw how Marron studied his sister. All the boys knew Marron wanted Tamesan. Of the girls in her age group, she was considered the prettiest, and she was the daughter of the Dragon Head, making her even more desirable, but he also knew most boys thought she was too headstrong, too aloof, to be a good wife. And because Marron was interested in her, no one else should be interested, unless they were willing to fight Marron first.

'What has he said?' Tam demanded, as she stood.

'Nothing,' Chasse replied hurriedly, aware he was annoying her. 'Just boys' talk. That's all. I only wondered what you thought of him.'

'He's rude, arrogant, self-centred, and a bully,' Tam announced. 'I wouldn't have him if he was the only boy left in Harbin.' She kicked a clump of grass out of the ground and walked towards the cliff that overlooked Watersdrop and Harbin Bay.

Chasse felt sorry for his sister. If Marron waited for her to come of age in two summers, she would have no choice but to accept him. That was how things went. Every boy knew that. Every girl knew that. It seemed that Tam was the only one who didn't want to be like everyone else. By the end of next summer, he would be a man, and he would have the right to choose a wife, if he wanted one. He hadn't made a choice yet. He liked Katris, but so did several other boys. Kerryn, the blond daughter of dragonwarrior Trent, was a nice girl, and she was the same age, but he honestly wasn't thinking about who his wife would be. There were more important matters to address, including a full winter of training to prepare for next summer's dragon hunt and initiation. He wasn't sure he understood why Tam even raised the subject of who he might choose.

Tam caught the Herbal Man crossing the bridge from her home, dressed in his dark cloak, and carrying a bundle of items he bartered for, or was given as payment for his healing work, during the four days in Harbin, and asked, 'You're leaving?'

'I am, Tamesan,' he told her. 'I feel much stronger, and I'm no longer needed here.'

'Did you see Gramma?'

The Herbal Man smiled at the note of curiosity in her voice. 'Yes, I saw Harmi. She's looking brighter today.'

'Did you chat again?'

The Herbal Man's eyes flickered slightly at her question, but his smile didn't waiver. 'I always talk to Harmi when I visit. She's a dear friend. We've known each other a long time, Tamesan, longer than most would remember in this village.'

Tam wanted to say, 'I heard you talking together on the first day. I heard you really talking,' but she held back, because something in the old man's gaze warned her to leave the matter alone. Instead, she asked, 'Can I visit you sometime?'

The Herbal Man's face registered genuine surprise. 'You are more than welcome, Tamesan. I would be honoured if you visited me,' and he added, 'As long as your father and mother approve.'

Tam wished he didn't say that, but he probably already knew they wouldn't let her go traipsing up the mountain whenever she wanted. Her mother would always find a menial task to tie her to the village. 'Remember what you said about teaching me about your herbs and things?' she asked. 'I'd like to learn about them.'

'I promise, if you visit, I'll teach you,' the Herbal Man replied. 'But now I must go home. There are important things to be done, even for an old man like me.'

'Don't go falling into any more creeks,' she joked.

He grinned. 'I won't, Tamesan.'

'And call me Tam, please.'

The Herbal Man nodded. 'May the child of the dawn light be blessed by the dragon,' he said, and he walked away.

As she watched the old man head for the mountain path, Tam contemplated his unusual parting words. She understood them, but the blessing seemed much older in origin and meaning, as if the Herbal Man spoke it from an ancient world.

In the evening, while she fed Gramma Harmi, Tam watched the old woman for a glimmer that indicated she was thinking more clearly, or at least remembered the Herbal Man's visit that afternoon, but Harmi gave no clues. She babbled briefly about gathering Snowpea buds, she held an imaginary conversation with someone named Claryssa, and she called Tam 'child', as always. Tam began to doubt that she overheard the conversation she stumbled upon the first afternoon the Herbal Man visited. She cleaned Gramma Harmi's chin, and wondered if, when she got old, she would have tufts of white hair growing on her face like her grandmother. She tucked Gramma Harmi into bed, said her goodnights to everyone, and went to the bedroom that she shared with Chasse and Jaysin.

Chasse was in the main room, talking to their father. Since the previous summer, Chasse always came to bed after Tam so that she could undress without him being there. There wasn't embarrassment — they always shared the same bedroom — but Chasse was acknowledging their encroaching adulthood and Tam appreciated his gesture. Jaysin, though, was awake, his eyes shining in the semi-darkness.

'Close your eyes,' Tam said softly. 'I want to get into bed.' The little boy obediently rolled over. Tam slid off her dress and under-tunic and put on her nightdress. She crossed to Jaysin's cramped bed space and bent to kiss her brother goodnight.

'Tam?' he asked.

'What?'

'Are the stories about the Herbal Man true?'

'What stories?'

'You know, about him taking little children away?'

Tam gently ruffled his hair, and said, quietly laughing, 'No, little mouse, they're not true.'

'Gramma says there's a dragon on the mountain,' Jaysin whispered.

'Gramma says lots of things. It's only called Dragon Mountain. There isn't a real dragon up there.'

'She says the Herbal Man keeps it.'

'Then it must be a very tiny dragon because he lives in a very tiny hut,'

Tam informed him.

'Gramma says she saw it once, when she was a little girl,' Jaysin persisted.

'It's a story, Jaysin. Gramma tells lots of stories. Now go to sleep. I'm tired.'

Jaysin fell silent.

Tam climbed beneath the skins and rough quilt of her bed and wriggled to get comfortable. She was tired, but she did not sleep. She listened to the murmuring voices in the main room. She heard her mother go to bed. Later, Chasse entered the bedroom and went to bed in silence, thinking she was asleep, but she could not sleep. Her mind was full of images of the Herbal Man's underground chambers, and the conversation she overheard between Gramma and the Herbal Man. His name was Eric, hers Harmi. His parting blessing to her repeated over and over in her mind. She could hear her father snoring. Harmi started mumbling in her sleep in the adjoining room. Tam strained to listen, but the words were garbled nonsense. She told Jaysin there was a dragon on the mountain. More nonsense. Jaysin listened too intently to Gramma's ravings.

When sleep finally came, Tam dreamed that she stood atop a mountain dressed in the green garment she was sewing for Procra's Dance, the sun rising in the east throwing the light of dawn in a golden arc across the sky. Gramma Harmi was looking up at her, waggling her finger as if she was warning Tam, and the Herbal Man appeared at Harmi's side, smiling. She could hear Jaysin shouting her name, but his voice was oddly overhead. She looked up, into the deepening blue sky, and saw a dragon flying towards her from the east, and Jaysin was clinging to its scaly back, laughing, really laughing, like he never laughed before. He was calling to her. She couldn't decipher his words, but she saw he was deliriously happy.

Eight

Her period started the morning of Procra's Dance. She woke feeling cramped and sore and she stayed in bed, until Chasse and Jaysin left and Eesa came looking for her. Her mother shook her head, and said, 'There's nothing for it. This is what being a woman brings. Blood and tears. And work. You'll learn to live with it, child. Clean up your bedding. There's little point you coming to help prepare the Long Hall today. I will send one of the girls here with something for you to do.'

'Not Katris,' Tam entreated.

Eesa frowned. 'Alright,' she agreed. 'I'll send another girl. Whatever is your reason, though? You were friends.'

'I don't want her to come here today,' Tam answered sullenly.

'Procra knows the mind of a girl,' Eesa said, sighing, as she gathered a pile of bedding from the boys' beds. 'And I was one once, Varst forbid. You and Katris used to be as close as barnacles on a boat.' She carried away her bundle, but she kept talking from the next room. 'There's no point lying around in there feeling sorry for yourself, Tamesan. You know what you must do. There are clean cloths by my bed, and plenty of water to boil to wash and keep yourself fresh, child. Hang the bedding outside to air, and make sure Gramma is comfortable and fed. You can sweep the floor, and by then someone will arrive with work from the Long Hall for tonight. Procra knows there's enough to do as it is.' As Tam climbed out of bed, Eesa appeared in the doorway with a concerned expression. She held out her arms and pulled Tam close. 'I'm sorry for you, girl,' she said. 'You don't need your bleeding on this day of all days. Let's hope the cycle of things will turn in your favour when your time to dance at the festival comes.'

Tam knew her mother was showing sympathy, but it only made the circumstance feel more awkward. For one thing, Tam didn't want to be ready for Procra's Dance in two summers' time. She didn't want to be 'chosen', like a sacrificial goat for Varst's Great Feast. For another, she was so much taller than Eesa that being hugged like a small child felt utterly absurd. Every aspect of the moment irritated her.

When her mother released her, Tam smiled weakly and said, 'I have to clean myself up first. I'll be fine.'

Eesa replied with an understanding smile and let Tam pass through to the main room before she collected a woven basket of items for her work in the Long Hall. She hurried out of the cottage, leaving her daughter alone.

When Tam was organised, she checked on Gramma Harmi. The old woman slept in the same room as Tam's parents, and this morning the room stank of stale urine, which meant the old lady wet her bed again. She did most nights. Harmi was fast asleep. Her bedding would have to be changed, but Tam decided to let her sleep a little longer to delay tackling that task. Instead, she took the pile of bedding that Eesa collected outside to hang on the Honeynut tree beside the cottage.

A fresh westerly breeze carried the smell of brine. The weather was changing. She hung the bedclothes and made her way to the clifftop. To her right, Watersdrop rushed over the cliff and thundered into the ocean twenty arm-spans below. The stream started deep in the mountains, beyond Dragon Mountain, and wound a narrow, tortuous course through gorges and over cataracts before sluicing onto the narrow strip of land at Harbin. Tam imagined it as like a dragonwarrior's life – rough, violent, short. That was the life lying ahead for her brother – a few short journeys into wild adventure and death. She corrected herself. That wasn't entirely true. Her father already lived a comparatively long time, all of thirty-six summers. He bore scars earned on his annual journeys, but he survived the violence and danger. Chasse could, too.

Dark clouds massing further out, over the great western ocean, warned that a small storm was coming. Though she was no weather expert, Tam guessed the storm would be brief, but it meant the Procra's Dance celebrations would be held in the Long Hall instead of around the customary bonfire. It didn't matter. She knew she could go to the celebrations if she wanted, but her period gave her an ideal excuse to stay away. She had a rare moment when she did have a choice.

She sat and stared at the heaving ocean. Waves surged against the base of the cliff, and she felt the powerful thud of each wave pass through the earth beneath her as it broke against the rocks. For every wave that rose and dissolved against the impassive cliff, another replaced it, over and over, day after day, year after year. The cliff didn't appear to change in her short lifetime, but she admired the waves' blind persistence and determination to break the cliff down. She felt an affinity with the ocean. Like it, she wanted to grow, expand, see more, do more, but there were cliffs hemming in her life, holding her in one place. She was too restless to accept the restraints, so she would keep pressing against them, pushing outward, moving, until the barriers eroded, the cliffs tumbled, and she was free.

'Tamesan?'

The voice, like the cry of a gull, broke through her reverie. She turned to see a younger girl, Alys, standing near the Honeynut tree, cradling a huge bundle of flowers. Tam rose to her feet, brushed down her long skirt, and approached.

'Your mother asked you to weave these into headbands and necklets for tonight,' Alys explained.

Tam took the bundle and thanked her. The girl smiled shyly and ran to the bridge, and Tam watched her retreat, thinking how lucky Alys was to be barely ten summers old and happy. So much was yet to change for her.

Inside the cottage, Tam spread the flowers on the floor and regarded them. Her mother sent yellow Summerflowers, a host of purple Frostpaws, large orange Field Banners, white Dragonspears, and a sprinkling of tiny blue Maidenbells. Tam loved the colour show. It seemed a pity to destroy the beautiful flowers for one night's celebration. As she bent to sort the flowers into smaller bunches for weaving, she heard Gramma Harmi coughing and remembered that she had to change the old woman's bedding and feed her. She sighed and straightened.

Tending to her grandmother's needs consumed a large portion of the morning. When Tam was finished, she propped Harmi in her favourite rickety old chair, rugged up against the cold air settling over the village as the weather changed, so the old woman could watch her arrange the flowers. As Tam expected, Harmi drifted in and out of sleep, blissfully ignorant of her granddaughter's labour, while Tam dutifully weaved colourful headbands and necklets. She held one headband up for Harmi's approval, and Harmi mumbled incomprehensibly, but Tam doubted her grandmother understood what was going on in front of her.

Thunder rumbled across the bay and reverberated against the mountain. The storm was sweeping in faster than anticipated and, as the light darkened, Tam found a lamp to enable her to continue her work. A lightning flash startled Harmi, and the old woman sat bolt upright and stared at the window. 'It's alright, Gramma,' Tam crooned soothingly. 'It's only a little storm.'

'Where's Eric?' Harmi asked. 'Is he here?'

'Who?' Tam asked and remembered that Eric was the Herbal Man's name. 'He's not here,' she said.

'A bolt of light,' Harmi said. 'There's a dragon there, you know.' She slumped in her chair and closed her eyes.

Tam rose and went to Harmi, but the old woman was asleep. She stroked her grandmother's hair and wondered why she was so obsessed with dragons. Tam knew who she meant, now, when she talked of Eric, but the other name she mentioned, Claryssa, was still a mystery. Harmi's mind was full of chaos and confusion. The wind gave a sharp burst of fury, a pause, and then heavy raindrops clunked on the shingle roof, heralding a downpour. The hissing rain set in.

Tam ran through the cottage, shutting the four sets of window shutters, before she mustered the available pots and placed them strategically to catch drips that would inevitably fall from the roof. Her father and mother, and even Chasse, used pitch to seal the roof leaks, but every downpour exposed new holes, new gaps, so she was well-versed in the ritual of placing and shifting pots.

She remembered the bedding. In a panic, she raced outside and salvaged the bedclothes from the Honeynut tree. The world was watery grey. Back inside, she threw the bedding down and assessed how wet it was. Saturated. Her mother would be angry. Tam cursed and set to stoking the hearth, and when the fire was blazing she dragged the table and chairs in front and hung the bedding to dry.

She returned to her flower weaving, occasionally glancing at the pots to ensure the leaks were being caught. Gramma was snoring. The musty odour of drying bedclothes slowly permeated the room.

The storm was brief, and no sooner did it end than Chasse blustered through the door, muddied, his nose bleeding. 'What happened?' Tam cried, jumping up to meet him.

'Nothing,' Chasse muttered, and he pushed past her to the bedroom.

Tam grabbed a damp rag and followed, and she found him seated on the floor. 'Chasse!' she demanded. 'Tell me what happened!'

'I was fighting, that's all,' he said. He took the rag and dabbed at his nose to clean away the blood.

'Who with?' Tam asked, and when Chasse didn't answer she repeated, with greater insistence, 'Who with?'

Chasse met her gaze, and she saw that he'd been crying. 'Marron,' he muttered.

'Why?'

'Because he says things that aren't true.'

'Like what?'

Chasse hit his clenched fist against the floor and swallowed, as if what he was about to say tasted sour. 'He said Father is too afraid to fight the dragons anymore. He said his father led the warriors against the dragon on the last trip, while our father stayed back on the ship like an old woman.'

'You know that's not true,' Tam argued. 'We all know it's not. We've heard the stories since the men returned. They spoke of his bravery and courage.'

'Marron says it's just his friends covering up what really happened. There are other men who tell a different story.'

'Have you heard anyone say anything like that?' Tam saw her brother's face cloud with anger, and he seemed less willing to answer her question. 'Chasse?' she prompted. 'Did they?'

'Yes,' he whispered hoarsely. 'I overheard them in the Warriors' Hall.'

Tam rocked back on her heels. Kevan was the Dragon Head, the most respected and feared warrior in Harbin. No one dared suggest he was anything but brave. Chasse's news astounded her. She squeezed his arm, and said quietly, 'It's gossip. See? Even men gossip.'

'It's not gossip!' Chasse shouted. 'I heard them say it!' He flung the damp cloth aside, shrugged away her, and buried his face in his hands.

'I'll get you some water,' Tam offered.

She retreated into the main room to give her brother a few moments alone, but as she filled a wooden goblet, she heard Harmi cough, and when she turned the old woman was looking straight at her.

'A man is a man,' Harmi rasped, waggling her head.

'What do you mean?' Tam asked, fascinated by her grandmother's statement.

'They all come to that,' Harmi announced. 'Eric showed me.'

'Gramma?' Tam appealed, approaching the old woman hunched in her chair. 'What do you mean?'

'A dragon knows these things.'

Until that remark, Tam thought Harmi understood what Chasse was saying, but Harmi was talking about dragons again. Tam patted her grandmother's hand and asked if she was hungry, but Harmi closed her eyes and went to sleep. Tam straightened her blanket.

When she took the water to Chasse, he was standing, staring into the hearth flames. 'Here,' Tam said, offering the goblet.

'Thanks,' Chasse said. He drank the water in a single gulp, returned the goblet to his sister, and headed for the door.

'Where are you going?' Tam asked.

'Back to the Warriors' Hall.'

'Won't Marron still be there?'

'We fought by the goat pens.'

'What if he's gone to the Warriors' Hall since?' Tam asked, but Chasse ignored her and closed the door in his wake.

Marron watched her carry the flower arrangements, between rain showers, to the Long Hall that afternoon. Tam was aware of him lounging against the wall of his father's hut, lazily twisting an old sword in his hands and drawing lines with the blade in the rain-softened earth, and she was surprised to see him alone. As soon as she noticed him, Tam made a sustained effort to avoid eye contact, but she felt his eyes following her down the path. His predatory air, a hunter's presence, made her uneasy, so she was relieved to reach the entry to the Long Hall.

Because of the weather change, the women reorganised to hold Procra's Dance inside and the Long Hall's interior was awash with colour and light. Fresh flowers and streamers of vividly dyed material festooned the wooden beams and walls and bright lanterns were hung at regular intervals, high enough to avoid the heads of the tallest men in Harbin. A bonfire-sized hearth, like the one traditionally lit for the mid-winter's Mad Wizard's Dance, was set up in the centre.

Eesa hurried to greet her daughter and took the colourful headbands and necklets from Tam's arms, complimenting her handiwork. 'Beautiful crafting, my girl. The girls will be proud to wear these, tonight. You have done well.' Pleased by her mother's praise, Tam smiled, so Eesa inquired, 'How are you feeling?'

'A little better,' Tam replied, 'but the cramps are still painful.'

Eesa's brow wrinkled with concern. 'It will be a shame to miss tonight's celebration.'

'I know,' Tam agreed, feigning disappointment, 'but it hurts too much. I would only be a burden.' She glanced around, keen to change the topic, saw only older women in the hall, and asked, 'Where are the others?'

'They've gone to Emma's hut to prepare for the Dance. It's getting late, and it will get dark quickly in this weather. I will take these flowers to them now.'

Tam saw Amarti and Sharmine staring, so she smiled weakly, maintaining her charade of illness for their benefit, and said to Eesa, 'I'll feed Gramma and Jaysin. That will save you time.'

'Thank you, child,' Eesa said, and she dismissed her daughter, but she watched Tamesan leave. Her daughter was grown so tall, so quickly. *The girl has so much potential*, she thought. *She will make a wonderful wife for any man in this village, but she's so frustrating at times, so unwilling to accept what is, what must be.* She shrugged, sighed, and wondered whether her own mother worried about her future as much as she worried about Tamesan's. Perhaps the common maternal concern was at the root of her frustration, the same challenge faced by every generation of mothers, as Varst and Procra designed in the greater scheme of life.

Nine

Bathing in the steaming hot springs was a pleasure, so Tam relaxed and let the warm water swirl around her, easing away the week's grime and weariness.

The springs were trapped in a jumble of rocks a short walk up the mountain. Village lore called them the Dragons' Cauldron and legend claimed they were formed when the great silver dragon spat at Nakiades and missed. Its vile fire cracked the rocks and water gushed out to fill the hollows, but the heat of the dragon's spittle was so fierce that it never cooled. Steam escaped from fissures on other sections of the mountain, but Dragon's Cauldron was the only site of hot springs.

Normally, Tam would be in the company of girls and women, but she started coming alone during the past summer and autumn, enjoying the solitude and peace.

She missed Procra's Dance, but she did not regret it. All six maidens were chosen, as everyone expected, and the night's revelry was joyful and long. Her father spent most of the following day sleeping off the effects of excessive mead drinking, and her mother was unusually quiet and sedate.

Chasse, however, was full of energy the morning after Procra's Dance. He bounced out of bed and left the cottage without sharing details of the night's events with Tam, much to her annoyance. She cornered him the following evening, and made him tell her what happened, especially the details of who paired with whom, but she felt he was concealing something from her. He never mentioned his fight with Marron. Tam pressed him on whether he danced with any girls, but he laughed and changed the subject, which only made her suspicious, and she guessed his reason for avoiding the matter.

Two days after Procra's Dance, Tam spied Chasse walking through the trees on the village outskirts with Kerryn. They held hands. Tam smiled and felt a possessive pang. She chided herself for her absurd emotional response. Chasse was nearly a man and he could choose any available girl when he was of age. Kerryn was friendly, and attractive, and she would be a good match for her brother. And yet Tam could not entirely dismiss her irritating jealousy. It ate at her for the rest of that day and she struggled to sleep, arguing with herself that she could neither judge nor deny Chasse's choice of a partner.

Lolling in the warm spring, she reflected on the changes in her brother's mood since pairing with Kerryn. He was more secretive, but he was also more confident. She ached to talk with him about his new relationship, but he seemed determined to keep his thoughts private. He was carefully, but deliberately, shutting her out of his life, and it hurt. Tam knew he wasn't deliberately trying to hurt her. It was just that he was so engrossed in getting to know Kerryn and coming to terms with what that meant for him that he had no time for his sister. *Perhaps*, Tam reasoned, *he is too embarrassed to discuss it with me*. She could force the discussion, but she loved him too much to bully him into it. She needed to trust that, when Chasse was ready, he would talk. She simply had to be patient.

The morning air was cool when Tam emerged from the water. She towelled and dressed, remembering Eesa wanted her home by midday, but there was enough spare time to walk the mountain, perhaps even to survey the world from her favourite eyrie. Time to spend alone, without the responsibilities forced onto her by her mother, was exceedingly precious and the forest was readying for winter. The deciduous trees were changing hue, washing the mountain slopes in shades of yellow, brown, red and orange between the conifers, and trees dropped their leaves, exposing stark limbs in mute warning that Blitzart would soon spread his icy breath over the world and climbing the mountain would no longer be possible.

Tam spotted a fuzzy-tailed squirrel scampering across the ground, carrying a large nut between its teeth. Like the squirrel, the villagers were preparing for winter. The last celebration of the Harbin year, Procra's Feast, was in three more weeks, a time when the villagers congregated to share and store food that would tide them through the winter. Each family would be invited to take a share from the collective produce. An additional portion was also stored in the Long Hall for emergency rations, and for the mid-winter Mad Wizard's Dance, or Blitzart's Feast as it was traditionally called. The mid-winter feast brought everyone together to break the winter confinement.

Tam crossed the path that led to the Herbal Man's residence and she slipped between the thin trunks of a stand of saplings, but as she entered a small clearing she heard a snort to her left. A furry brown muzzle emerged from the bushes, the bushes parted, and a mountain bear lumbered into the open. Tam froze. The bear took a hesitant step towards her, then sat back on its haunches, as if it didn't know what to do next.

Even on its haunches, the bear was as tall as Tam. She knew the horror stories about mountain bears. No one she knew was ever attacked by one, but there were village tales of how unfortunate individuals wandered into a bear's territory and were mercilessly torn asunder by the angry beasts. She watched the bear study her, tilting its heavy head left and right, as if analysing what it found. She considered making a dash into the trees. Or climbing onto the large granite rock to her left. The bear opened its mouth and growled and large white canines glistened with saliva. She wondered how hungry the bear might be.

Trying to keep calm, Tam eased her left foot towards the rock. The bear tilted its head and leaned forward. Tam eased her other foot towards the rock. The bear sniffed the air and grunted. Tam moved another step. The bear rocked forward and padded on all fours towards her. Tam bolted for the rock and clambered up, desperately hoping the bear couldn't reach her.

At the top, she spun, panting, to peer down at the creature. The bear was at the base, sniffing the ground. It reared onto its hind legs, lifting its muzzle towards her, and growled. Its teeth flashed and its sharp claws scratched the rock. Tam screamed.

'Don't do that,' commanded a voice. 'You're scaring the poor animal.' A figure in a dark robe stepped from the undergrowth, and the bear turned. Tam recognised the Herbal Man. He spoke in a strange language, and the bear cocked its brown head, as if listening, before dropping to all fours and ambling into the trees. 'There,' the Herbal Man said, as he approached the base of Tam's perch. 'He's gone. He wasn't going to eat you. He was curious. In fact, he was as nervous about meeting you, as you scared of him.'

'But he might have eaten me,' Tam argued, studying the claw marks on the rock. 'I've heard how bears attack people.'

'Wouldn't you, if a stranger with a spear intruded into your home?'

'Well, yes, but this is my home, and I don't have a spear.'

'Your home is the village,' the Herbal Man corrected. 'This forest is the bear's home. We are the intruders up here. It's up to us to respect his ways in his home.'

Tam slid down the rock. 'What did you say to the bear?'

'A simple thank you would suffice,' the Herbal Man replied, ignoring her question as he pretended to be offended by her lack of manners.

'Oh, I'm sorry. I meant to say thank you,' Tam apologised hurriedly. 'I was surprised by it all.'

'No injuries?' the Herbal Man inquired.

'None.'

'Then we best move on,' he said, turning to leave the clearing.

'Where are you going?' Tam asked.

'I'm stocking up on herbs. It will snow before the end of the week.'

'How do you know that?'

The Herbal Man glanced up at the grey clouds hanging overhead.

Tam looked up and smiled awkwardly at the obvious. 'Do you mind if I help you?' she asked. 'For a little while. My mother isn't expecting me back yet.'

The Herbal Man hesitated, considering her request, before replying, 'I see no harm in that. You're welcome to accompany me, Tamesan.'

Tam followed the Herbal Man on his foraging walk, pausing as he stooped to study a flower, or a plant, or a growth on a rock or tree. Sometimes he deviated from a narrow run to collect samples. She was fascinated by his methodical manner, the way that he traversed the mountain slope, choosing certain growths, rejecting others, all while he talked to her, telling her precisely what he chose and why it was useful.

'Do you know this flower?' he asked, holding a clutch of red blooms.

'Seleserin's Sorrow,' Tam replied, recognising them.

'Very good!' the Herbal Man declared. 'The flower is pretty, but not much use, except as a component for a dye, but the ragged leaves can be boiled to make an elixir that eats away warts, and it's a useful ingredient in other elixirs for curing skin ailments.' He scraped pale yellow fungus from the case of a clump of rocks, crying, 'Excellent!' and chortled, like an eager child. 'Rock Mould. There's little of it to be found this time of year. Soon, there will be none.' He packed the sample into a small leather bag and hung it on his laden leather belt. 'It can be worked into a paste that draws poison from the blood. There's not much call for it here, but I always have some on hand, just in case.'

As they walked, the Herbal Man taught Tam the essence of his trade. He explained how he searched for an enormous variety of plants on the mountainside, in valleys, and along the narrow strip of earth nestled at the foot of Dragon Mountain. Spring to early summer was the best season, because plant growth was luxurious, and he worked hardest in that period, collecting what he needed. But even in the dead heart of winter there were tiny fungi, and bitter, tough little plants, that battled for life in the snow and ice, and he sought them because they possessed greater qualities of strength and endurance than most plants. He explained the processes of drying, and powdering, and liquefying, and distillation, and measurement and dosages, until Tam was overwhelmed by the copious information.

'This way,' he urged at one point, and he led her into the gorge where Watersdrop streamed towards Harbin to show her his favourite herb. 'Mountain Blossom,' he said, holding up a small, damp white flower. 'It sometimes has red flowers, but mostly white.' Tam saw an occasional bloom drifting in Watersdrop near her home, but she never saw the whole plant. 'It only grows here, in this part of the gorge,' the Herbal Man explained. 'I don't know why. Other parts of the gorge have the same soil and water conditions, but this is the only place Mountain Blossoms grow. Only here.' He turned the delicate, thin petal flower in his fingers, studying it closely. 'I only ever pick a dozen or so when I come here. I'm afraid, if I pick more, the plants won't reproduce, and they'll die out. Herbalism isn't a case of ripping up what you need. You have to understand the balance of things, the way everything is bound together.'

'But why is this flower so special?' Tam asked.

The Herbal Man sat on a rock directly above the thundering cataract and looked at her with his piercing grey eyes as he explained. 'Every part of the Mountain Blossom is useful. The flower can be dried and crushed into a dye powder. It can also be mixed in water to make a tonic, which will help someone suffering from a fever, or tight chest complaints. If it is boiled in water, the vapours alleviate breathing difficulties. The leaves, eaten raw, are good food. Dried, the leaves can be burned and the aromatics they exude are relaxing.'

As she listened to the Herbal Man describe the various ways the mysterious little plant could be applied for herbal treatments, the roar of the angry water churning between the cliffs and over the rocks slipped into the background. He wasn't shouting, and she was mildly surprised at how easily he made himself heard as he described a world of things she never heard of. He stirred and fed her interest while the sun climbed through the morning sky.

The Herbal Man's prediction of early snow was accurate. The first light fall spiralled out of the low grey clouds at the end of the week and sent Harbin into restless activity. Eesa coordinated the girls and women in filling food pots with grains and nuts and seeds and preparing breads and cakes. The herdsmen mustered the goats and selected beasts to be slaughtered for meat. Plump chickens were rounded up. The fishermen hauled fresh catch ashore and set to filleting, drying and salting boxes of fish for storage. The warriors forayed into the forest to hunt game. The plans for Procra's Feast were brought forward and the village rumourmongers were predicting a long and bitter winter.

As was expected of all five boys approaching manhood the next summer, Chasse shifted his few possessions into the Warriors' Hall. During the autumn and winter months, the youths would live with the dragonwarriors to receive formal training that culminated in the dragonship journey. Tam helped her brother carry his gear and felt his excitement because, for the first time in days, he was chatting cheerfully.

'One last winter as a boy!' he shouted. 'This time next year I'll be a man!'

Tam smiled, but she didn't know what to say. She was never going to know how he felt – she was never going to be a man. She was never going to feel the exhilaration and impending freedom that he clearly felt. Next year, she was still going to be a girl, and the year after a woman, and neither role in the village brought freedom. When her mother and father stopped bossing her around, a husband would take their place. She would rather live like the Herbal Man, who came and went as he pleased. The whole mountain was his home. If only she could choose to live like that.

Tam left Chasse at the entrance to the Warriors' Hall because women never entered, unless invited to take food to the men or clean the Hall. Several times, she was seized with a desire to burst into the Warriors' Hall unannounced to break the traditional law, but she always curbed her urge. Her father would be so dishonoured by such an irresponsible act that he would be forced to treat her more harshly than he already did, and she hardly needed that.

Trapped in daily duties set by Eesa, Tam carried pots and kept the smaller village children amused while their mothers worked, but she managed to spend the early morning hours accompanying the Herbal Man on the mountain as he continued to hunt the last blooms and growths of the dying autumn, and she learned more of the old man's art and wisdom: how the plants and creatures were interdependent, working in harmony and balance.

'Men have too little respect for these things,' the Herbal Man told her. 'They fail to see beyond their greedy needs. The whole world is our garden to tend and nurture.'

His passion, his heartfelt observations, struck a resonant chord in Tam, because she felt these things when she spent time alone on the mountain. For the first time, someone was confirming what she believed.

'Can you remember this one?' the Herbal Man asked one morning. He held up a small, prickly plant.

'Lackweed,' Tam answered.

'Good,' he said. 'Is it useful?'

Tam wracked her brains, and replied, 'Only the roots. You dry them, boil them, and distil the liquid until there is a white – no, a green residue. That is then mixed with –' She hesitated, having forgotten what he taught her the previous day.

'With Snowbud juice,' the Herbal Man prompted.

'Of course,' Tam said quickly, 'Snowbud juice. It's good for wind in the body and headaches, isn't it?'

'Flatulence,' the Herbal Man said, grinning. 'Correct, Tamesan. You learn quickly.'

'What are you collecting tomorrow?' she asked.

As the Herbal Man heaved his sack onto his shoulder, he replied, 'I won't be coming down the mountain tomorrow, Tamesan.' He nodded at the sky and Tam looked up at the heavy grey clouds shrouding the peak of Dragon Mountain. 'The full winter snows will fall tonight.'

Tam was suddenly disappointed. She was enjoying learning the Herbal Man's trade, and it was far more interesting than being schooled in how to be a good village girl, but the old man was leaving, and he would be gone until the winter snows released their icy grip on the mountain. The same empty emotion that she felt when she escorted Chasse to the Warriors' Hall washed over her, and she did not know what to say.

The Herbal Man broke the silence. 'I have a favour to ask,' he said. He put down the sack and rummaged inside his cloak, until he produced a tiny drawstring dark leather pouch, which he handed to Tam. 'I would like you to give this to Harmi.'

'What is it?' Tam asked, accepting the pouch.

'Just something. A ring. She will understand when you give it to her,' the Herbal Man explained. 'Give it to her on the eve of Blitzart's Feast. Not before. And not while anyone else is near.'

'Why?' Tam asked. The gift was becoming a complex mystery.

'There are special reasons, but I cannot explain them to you,' he said. 'It's not that simple. I'm asking you to trust me. All I can tell you is that it is very important Harmi has this gift that night. Will you do this for me?'

Tam cupped the tiny pouch in her hand. She kept the secret of the Herbal Man's hut and his underground chambers and this would be no different, although her curiosity about the relationship between the Herbal Man and Gramma Harmi flared again. 'I'll keep it safe and give it to her as you've asked. It's the least I can do for teaching me about the herbs,' she promised and smiled.

The Herbal Man bowed his head in an unexpected show of respect and shouldered his sack again. 'I have enjoyed your company these past days, Tamesan,' he said. 'If you are willing to continue learning after this winter passes, I will teach you. Perhaps you can even learn how to read and write.'

Tam appreciated the sincerity of his offer, although she had no idea what he meant by learning to read and write. 'I will be waiting,' she said.

'May the dragon warm your winter!' the Herbal Man declared, and he turned and trudged into the trees.

Tam watched him, until he disappeared, before she descended the path to village. That night, exactly as the Herbal Man forecasted, winter's snow-white hand closed over Harbin.

Ten

'Are you coming?' Chasse called.

'Yes!' Tam yelled. She grabbed a coarse string bag that Eesa asked her to take, and a plate overloaded with steaming scones, kissed Gramma Harmi on the forehead, and closed the cottage door.

Chasse was stamping his feet on the cold earth in a vain effort to drive the biting chill out of his toes. His breath escaped in cloudy vapours.

'I'm ready!' she announced.

The world was coated with a white mantle and the heavy overhanging clouds threatened more snow. The early snowfall forced the villagers to hold Procra's Feast earlier than planned. As Chasse and Tam trudged the icy path over the bridge into the village, Tam spotted their little brother standing alone, near the Long Hall, watching other children embroiled in a snowball fight. It was obvious Jaysin desperately wanted to be included, but he made no attempt to join in the game. She wondered how she could help him, without interfering too much, but she had no easy answer. Jaysin's isolation was as complete as if he was an injured gull stranded on an islet in Harbin Bay.

Forcing her attention from her little brother, she saw people approaching the Long Hall, from all directions, carrying bundles of food to share at Procra's Feast. Her eyes were drawn to a familiar figure, the young widow Banni, bearing a food platter and dragging a sack behind her in the snow.

'Here, you lazy Chasse,' Tam said, shoving the scones and string bag into his arms, 'I'm going to help Banni,' and before Chasse could protest Tam bounded away across the snow. 'I'll carry the sack,' she offered, as she reached the young woman. Banni gratefully let her take it and they walked together to the Long Hall.

Inside the hall, Eesa and several women were receiving the bundles and platters of food and methodically sorting the goods into household bundles. The feast was laid on a row of trestle tables in the centre, and two fires were alight, one at either end of the Hall, warming the interior against the freezing winter. The sweet aroma of roasting meat permeated the air. Eesa directed Tam to help with sharing the food, and Tam obediently complied. This was one village tradition she considered important because winters were long and bitter at the foot of Dragon Mountain, and sharing food ensured no one starved.

A commotion drew everyone's attention to the ceremonial entrance of the Dragon Fang, led by the Dragon Head. Eesa ordered the women and girls to prepare spaces at the feast table for the Dragon Fang and the warriors took their seats. Married dragonwarriors left a seat to their left for their women. Next, the eldest boys were called to sit. Eesa sat beside Kevan, and the wives followed her lead. Men who were not dragonwarriors took places away from the table, closest to the door. The remaining women and girls could sit where spaces in the Long Hall remained, but only after they served the people at the table.

As everyone settled, the door opened again and the Dragon Heart entered, wearing his grey bear cloak, and an ornate ceremonial head-dress stylised in the image of a dragon claw. Children swarmed around him until Sharmine and Amarti shooed them away. The Dragon Heart paraded around the table, rhythmically shaking a handful of reeds as he chanted the traditional song to begin Procra's Feast. Tam mouthed the words as she listened. Every child in Harbin knew the song and sang it playing games. Parents sang the song to calm babies during the dark winter nights. The lyrics spoke of the seasonal cycles, of winter's arrival and Blitzart's ascent, of warm hearths and ice-covered water, the contrasts in Harbin's world.

Procession finished, the Dragon Heart stood at the head of the table with Kevan to his left and Trask seated to his right, and he cast a discerning eye over the food, nodding appreciatively. He selected a leg of roasted pigeon, and loudly pronounced, 'Almighty Varst would be greatly pleased with gentle Procra's offering set today before the children of Nakiades. Be joyful and eat, my children!' Formal blessing done, he heartily bit into the pigeon leg, the annual gesture inviting the men to take their first portion of food.

Tam took drinks to the people at the table, but she filled Kevan's goblet first as a mark of respect for her father. He smiled, and broke convention by handing her a slice of roasted meat while she was still serving. Eesa glared, but she knew better than to make an issue of his impropriety. Tam moved along the table, pouring wine, until she heard someone call. She turned to discover Marron holding out his goblet. 'Tamesan, fetch me some mead,' he said. She reached for his goblet, but when she grasped it he deliberately stroked her fingers. She retracted her hand and retreated to the hearth where a jug of mead was warming beside the coals.

As she stooped to pour mead into Marron's goblet, she heard another voice. 'Give me the goblet, Tamesan.' She looked up to see Katris holding out her hand. 'I'll take it to Marron.' Tam passed the goblet to her without comment, but Katris' eyes narrowed, and she said, spitefully, 'Don't think you have any chance with Marron, because you don't.' She whirled and carried the goblet to Marron.

Katris' vindictiveness unsettled Tam, but she was glad not to have to serve Marron. His unwanted attention and constant staring were making her increasingly uncomfortable. Katris could have him. She continued serving drinks and sweetmeats to the men, and laughed at Chasse's efforts to act aloof, like a man, when she served him. At first, he was miffed by her mocking, but he relaxed and teased her in turn.

As the feast wore on, the single women and girls found places at the table and shared in the meal. Tam squeezed between Banni and a girl named Fay and engaged in idle chatter about weaving and babies and cooking, until Banni unexpectedly announced that she was pregnant. Tam didn't know whether to be happy for Banni because of the impending child, or sad because she lost her husband, Jared, and would have to raise the child alone.

'Aren't you happy for me?' Banni asked, seeing Tam's bewilderment.

'Yes!' Tam blurted. 'Of course I am. It's –' she started to explain, but she reconsidered her intention and stopped.

'I know what you're thinking,' Banni said, her smile tightening, 'but it means I haven't completely lost Jared, Tamesan. I have part of him here,' she explained, pointing at her belly, 'within me. This will be our son, and I will name him after his father.'

Tam smiled, and hugged Banni, thinking perhaps it might not be so hard for the young woman. She had a purpose, a link with her husband, she had happiness, so she immersed herself in Banni's joy and helped her share the news around the table. The only nagging thoughts she retained was whether Banni considered that the coming child might be a girl.

The afternoon's feasting glowed with warmth and contentment, and the plentiful stores of food to share boded well for the coming winter. When word spread that the snow was falling heavily, families rose to leave, collecting their allotted food rations and paying respects to the Dragon Head as they departed. The numbers steadily decreased, but for those who remained eating, drinking, and talking, the Long Hall's cosy and comfortable atmosphere was enjoyable, until a sudden outburst of angry voices startled everyone. Tam saw her father, Kevan, and Trask rise and confront each other.

'Take back your words!' Kevan roared.

'When you admit the truth everyone already knows!' Trask shouted.

'I have nothing to admit! I am the Dragon Head!'

Trask clenched his fists and leaned closer to Kevan. 'I say you are no longer fit to hold that title! I say it's time for a stronger leader, a real man, a warrior who is not afraid to fight!'

Kevan reddened with fury as he snarled, 'You are a fool, Trask! I lead this village and my word is law! You mock tradition with this accusation!'

'You mock our traditions with your cowardice!' Trask retorted and spat.

Kevan's right arm shot out and he grabbed Trask by the throat, and Trask grappled with Kevan's arm. Some of the Dragon Fang rose.

'Stop!' bellowed the Dragon Heart. 'How dare you desecrate Procra's sacred feast!'

Both men ignored his plea as they wrestled, but five older warriors pushed forward and wrenched Kevan and Trask apart.

'Enough!' Theo ordered, holding Kevan's left arm. 'This is neither the place nor time to dispute this matter. You're squabbling like little boys!'

Trask strained against the pinning arms, but then relaxed, accepting the futility of his resistance. Kevan, however, shrugged off those who loosely held him and stormed from the Long Hall.

'See?' Trask shouted in Kevan's wake. 'You want him as your leader? You want someone who runs from a fight to lead the Dragon Fang?'

'Enough of your mouth!' Theo growled.

Trask gave Theo a piercing glare before spitting on the floor and resuming his seat. He lifted his mead goblet, and said sardonically, 'Here's to the Dragon Head. May he live long and prosper.' He drank the mead before his stunned audience.

Despite the tense situation, Eesa remained calm. She rose from her seat and went to help the last family groups collect food. Tam left the table to help her mother, followed by Banni, Fay and several women, until only a handful of men remained at the table with Trask, drinking. When the last family withdrew, Eesa dismissed the girls and women.

Tam waited outside for Eesa. The snow was falling heavily in the grey afternoon light and it was cold, and she looked in the direction of the Warriors' Hall, thinking of her brother. Tam would only see Chasse on rare occasions over the winter. He left the Hall before the altercation between Trask and their father, and for that she was glad. Kevan's confrontation with Trask shocked her. Even though she knew there was ill-feeling between the two men, especially since Chasse disclosed the situation after his fight with Marron, she didn't imagine it was as bitter as it was expressed in the Long Hall, and she was astonished to see it flare so publicly. The Dragon Head was the most powerful man in the village, and anyone defying his law, under any circumstance, was liable to harsh judgement and punishment. Yet Trask seemed intent on publicly opposing her father, obviously undeterred by the traditional threat. *Why?* she wondered. What so rankled Trask about her father that he was willing to risk humiliation and ostracism?

Eesa emerged from the Long Hall carrying a bundle of goods and closed the door behind her. 'There was no need to wait, girl,' she said, as she handed the bundle to Tam. 'I hoped you would go home to check on Gramma.'

'I wanted to make sure you were safe,' Tam replied.

Eesa stared at her daughter, and asked, 'What in Procra's name do you mean by that?'

'I mean with Trask and Father arguing.'

'Tsh!' Eesa exclaimed. 'They're men. They argue all the time.'

'About Father's right to be the Dragon Head?'

'About everything,' said Eesa. 'They argue about who has the quickest hand, the sharpest spear, the biggest nose. They spend all their lives trying to prove one is better than the other. That's what men do.'

'But it seemed so serious,' Tam insisted, unconvinced by her mother's explanation.

'Men think everything they do is serious, girl,' Eesa replied, 'and the argument you witnessed was serious. But it was a mead argument. Trask drank too much. Men say stupid things when they're drunk. They tell you they will love you forever, swear to Varst that they killed a dragon with their bare hands, and claim that they can tame the oceans. Tomorrow, this will all be forgotten. Believe me, girl, I've seen it all before, and you will see plenty of the same when you are a woman. Now, let's get home before this snow buries us where we stand.'

Tam hoisted her burden and trudged through the snow beside her mother. Although Eesa emphasised that the incident was trivial, Tam was not convinced because it was the first time she witnessed a clash between two important dragonwarriors. Her mother's tone lacked credibility because she was friendlier than normal, as if she needed Tam to accept her word despite what she witnessed and by the time she reached her home Tam was less certain than ever that things were normal in her village.

The snow fell relentlessly for five days. Although it wasn't an unusual length of time for snowfall in Harbin, it arrived earlier than normal and the bitterly cold temperature kept everyone indoors. When Tam peered through the shutters, she saw the village rapidly disappearing beneath swirling snow drifts that were reaching window ledges and blocking doors. Even the acute angle of the shingled roofs failed to prevent many huts and cottages appearing as little white hillocks in the landscape. Only the larger structures of the Warriors' Hall and the Long Hall retained semblances of their selves.

Locked in the cottage, Eesa kept Tam busy to occupy the hours. There were clothes to wash and sew, baskets to weave, utensils to craft and repair, foodstuffs to bake, Gramma to care for, the fire to tend. After setting her daughter to work, Eesa started separate tasks to while away the time.

Kevan spent the time whittling wood into animal shapes, honing his great war-axe, eating, drinking and sleeping, but he was morose being confined with his family and unable to join the men in the Warriors' Hall. He tried to teach Jaysin the art of whittling, but the child was too young to stay interested and possessed an acute aversion to the sharp whittling blade, which only added to Kevan's aggravation.

'The child is a changeling,' he complained to Eesa, the third afternoon that he unsuccessfully tried to engage Jaysin in the manly art of whittling.

'Patience, husband,' Eesa crooned. 'Patience. The child will learn when he is ready.'

'Varst's wrath he'll be ready!' Kevan snarled, and he threw the whittling knife at the hearth, the blade point burying precisely in a chunk of wood. 'The boy is weak! He will never learn!' Jaysin skulked into his bedroom. Tam left feeding Gramma Harmi and followed Jaysin. 'And don't go mothering him!' Kevan warned in her wake. 'He already has too much girl in him!'

Jaysin lay face down on his bedding and Tam thought he was crying, but when she placed her hand on his shoulder he sighed. 'I think Father is frustrated at being cooped up, Jaysin,' she said softly. 'You know how he gets.'

'What's a changeling?' Jaysin asked.

'I don't know,' Tam replied. 'It doesn't mean anything.'

'Yes, it does. I heard an old lady say it behind my back once. She said I must be a changeling. Father says it. I want to know what it means.'

Tam knew the meaning of the term, but she didn't have the heart to explain to her little brother how cruel his father was being to him. Legends and folk tales sometimes mentioned changelings – demon children swapped for human babies. Changelings were strange, mysterious, and brought disaster to the families affected. 'It doesn't matter what it means,' she reassured him.

'Tam?'

'Yes, Jaysin?'

'Why am I so different?'

His candid question caught Tam unprepared. 'You aren't different, Jaysin,' she said awkwardly.

'Yes, I am. I know I am.'

'How?'

'I don't know,' he murmured into his bedclothes. Then he sighed again, rolled over and sat up, his big eyes full of appeal and sorrow. 'You know how,' Jaysin said quietly. 'I don't know what the other children do. I mean, I do know, but what they do doesn't interest me. I don't like how everything is about fighting and chasing. Why are all games like that, Tam?'

'That's how games are,' she replied, but Jaysin's question touched a memory of how she felt.

'But they don't have to be like that. Aren't there better games we could play, games that aren't about hurting others?'

'Are you worried about the others teasing you?' she asked.

'No,' Jaysin said, and corrected himself with, 'a little. But I don't care about that. I mean, it's not only me they pick on. They pick on others, and that's why I don't want to play with them. They have to pick on someone all the time. They always want to hurt someone.'

Eesa called Tam from the main room. 'Mother wants me,' Tam said. 'Are you coming out?'

'No. He'll only give me dirty looks,' Jaysin said, and sighed as he buried his head back into his bedclothes.

Tam discovered Eesa with potatoes for her to peel when she returned to the main room. She set to the task, rinsing the potatoes in a bowl of cold water, but she noticed that her father was peering anxiously out of the window, watching the falling snow. She knew all he wanted was to retreat to the haven of the Warriors' Hall to be among the men in an environment he understood. He was never comfortable in his home. He acted as though he was under threat, as if he feared his family would not obey him, or would weaken his stature as a man, which is why he sustained his stern, overbearing presence.

Tam scraped skins from the potatoes and contemplated her little brother's dilemma. He was very different from the other children, even, she believed, from herself. A misfit in Harbin's culture because he abhorred violence, he could never be a dragonwarrior, but it was a disgrace for the Dragon Head to have a son unwilling to follow the traditional path. There was no logical reason for Jaysin to be like he was. *Perhaps he is a changeling*, she mused, as she sliced potatoes into a fresh bowl, but she scolded herself for thinking cruelly. Jaysin was Jaysin, and she loved him the more for being so different.

Eleven

By the time a break in the snowfall finally came, Harbin was buried. Families clambered through windows to clear drifts from their doorways and scrape the weight from their roofs, and the dragonwarriors and initiates emerged from the Warriors' Hall to help where help was needed. The last place to be uncovered was Asmae's cottage on the outskirts, and despite her cottage being totally buried the old woman survived.

Chasse returned to help his family and Tam was glad to see him. 'So, what's it like being locked up with the men?' she asked, as they scooped snow from a window ledge. 'What do you do all day?'

'There's no fun,' Chasse replied. 'We clean and polish things. We have to polish every link in the chain corselets, sharpen every blade, and work oil deep into every piece of leather the men find.'

'What else?'

'There is nothing else.' Chasse flicked a scoop of snow over his shoulder. 'Oh, and we have to sit every day and night and learn verses from the old legends about Nakiades and the dragons, and we have to memorise the stories about dragonship adventures. It's all boring.'

'It must be important. Otherwise, why would they make you do it?'

'I think they make us do it because there's nothing else to do. No one's teaching us how to hunt or fight or kill a dragon yet. No one's even mentioned it. You're probably having more excitement here.'

Tam snorted contemptuously, and said, 'I hardly think so. Nothing changes. I look after Gramma and do everything Mother tells me to do, Father whittles wooden figures and mopes around like a bear in a cage, and Jaysin just mopes. I miss having you here to talk to or to fight with.'

Chasse scooped a handful of snow and tipped it on her head, saying with a grin, 'So, you miss that, do you?'

'Yes!' Tam cried, laughing, and she retaliated with a handful of snow. Within moments, they were pitching snowballs at each other, using the Honeynut tree as a shield, until Eesa intervened and ordered them to get on with their task.

The following day, blue patches appeared in the sky, so Tam worked quickly to complete her morning list of duties. Once she dressed Gramma and comfortably seated her in her favourite chair, she left the cottage and headed for the hot springs, hoping no one else was foolish enough to bathe in the Dragon's Cauldron on such a cold day. The cottage's confined spaces, and the sweaty work shifting snow, made her long for a dip in the soothing waters.

The absence of footprints in the snow on the path confirmed that no one was ahead of her, and when she reached the springs she stood and silently watched the spiralling steam. Winter held a special fascination in this place. Thermal rocks kept the snow several paces from the water's edge and she admired the stark beauty of the ice-bound trees and rocks enclosing the Dragon's Cauldron. If the weather suited, Harbin women and girls would bathe the morning before Blitzart's Feast. Tam intended to bathe no matter what that day's weather was like. She would come early, and leave early, and that way she could avoid Katris' snide comments.

She stripped off her clothes, slipped into the water, and let the wonderful warmth rush over her skin. As she adjusted to the temperature, she shifted to the centre of the pool and, savouring the serenity, her mind drifted.

Katris was incredibly jealous of Marron's attention to her. Perhaps that explained why Katris no longer liked her. She would tell Katris that Marron was all hers because she was not interested in him – that might change her attitude. Maybe.

Chasse was going to choose Kerryn next summer, after he returned from his initiation journey as a dragonwarrior. She knew because he hinted his intentions to her the previous day when they were shifting snow. Chasse and Kerryn both came of age next summer and it wasn't unusual for a new dragonwarrior to choose a wife from women his age. Some chose older women, though most waited three or four summers before taking partners and beginning families. Chasse would be a good husband. He was sensible and caring. He would treat Kerryn respectfully, and, consequently, she would have more freedom than most women. If Tam decided to accept a husband, he would have to be like her brother — but there was no one quite like Chasse in the village, no one she could think of, at least.

She wondered what the Herbal Man was doing, alone in the winter. She remembered the ring that she was meant to pass to her grandmother on the evening of Blitzart's Feast. She carefully stored the pouch with the ring in a crack in her bedroom wall where no one would find it, but she wondered why it was so important and what the connection was between her grandmother and the Herbal Man.

'Hello, Tamesan.'

Startled by the intruding voice, Tam faltered in the water, before looking to her left where Marron sat on a smooth rock by the pool. Three boys stood behind him, grinning at her.

'Isn't it a bit cold to be swimming?' Marron asked with mock concern, the boys sniggering behind him.

'Would you mind going away?' Tam requested calmly, although she glanced uneasily across the pool to where her clothes were strewn on the rocks.

'Why?' Marron asked. 'We were admiring the view. It is quite beautiful.'

Tam shifted her arms to cover her breasts. 'Please, Marron. You know it's not right to be here when a girl is bathing,' she tried to reason.

'We're as surprised as you are,' he replied to the delight of his appreciative audience.

'Marron,' she said, her tone shifting to a warning.

Marron's eyebrows rose, but his dark eyes remained fixed on her, as he said, 'I will go, but only if you tell me how much you want me.'

'I don't want you!' Tam snapped, green eyes flashing angrily.

'Then I will stay here,' Marron declared, and he pretended to make himself comfortable on the rock.

'Marron!'

'Your eyes flare when you get angry,' he said. 'They look prettier like that.' The watching boys laughed and mocked him, but politely, in case he took offence. Marron was not someone they wanted to upset.

Tam turned her back and drifted closer to the opposite bank, nearer her clothes, deciding whether it was worth getting out and dressing, ignoring the ogling boys. She could wait them out. The water was pleasantly warm, and if it was cold enough in the open air they might give up and move on.

'All you have to do is admit you want me, Tamesan. Then we will leave you alone,' Marron offered again.

'I don't want you, Marron,' Tam reasserted.

'But next summer I can choose to have you.'

'I won't be old enough!'

'Then the summer after. I can wait. I want you.'

'Wait as long as you want,' she retorted. 'Even if you were the last man in Harbin, I wouldn't have you. I don't want you.' The boys oohed in the background, taunting her.

'You won't have a choice, Tamesan,' Marron said arrogantly. 'I will choose because I will be a man, and I will choose you.'

'Why don't you choose someone else, like Katris? She wants you. Choose her,' Tam entreated.

Marron smiled maliciously, making Tam feel more vulnerable. 'I know

Katris wants me,' he admitted. 'That's why I don't want her. She's too eager, too easy. But you, you are different. You're beautiful. Your father is the Dragon Head. You're the most desirable girl in Harbin. Every dragonwarrior says so. But only I will have you. I will choose you.'

'You won't!' Tam cried vehemently. 'I won't go with you! Hear me? Take your creepy friends with you and go away!'

'Not until you say you want me,' Marron calmly repeated.

'Marron!' another voice called, and everyone turned to see Chasse emerging from the trees, waving, accompanied by two more youths. Chasse started to speak, but he stopped when he saw Tam in the pool. 'What are you doing here?' he asked, unable to mask his surprise.

'I was bathing,' Tam replied. 'At least I was until these boys barged in.'

Chasse looked to Marron for an explanation, but Marron shrugged and said, 'Your sister was telling us how she was waiting for me to choose her for my wife when she comes of age.'

'I was not,' Tam countered. 'I asked him to leave, and he won't.'

'If she's bathing, we shouldn't even be here,' Chasse affirmed, directing his comment to Marron. 'Theo sent me to fetch you back to the Warriors' Hall.' He turned to Tam, and added, with a smile, 'We'll leave you to yourself, Tam.'

'She hasn't answered my request, yet,' Marron objected. 'I'm not leaving until she does.'

'What request?' Chasse asked.

'None of your business,' Marron replied. 'Run back to Theo.'

'I think you can leave my sister alone,' Chasse warned.

Marron stood on his rock. 'Who's going to make me do that? You?'

'If I must,' Chasse replied.

'Chasse, don't,' Tam pleaded. She saw the brewing violence and she didn't want her brother to get hurt like he did the last time he fought Marron.

'Better listen to your sister,' Marron taunted. 'She knows you shouldn't fight her man.' He swaggered around the edge of the hot springs towards Chasse.

'I'm not looking for a fight,' Chasse stated calmly. 'I don't think it's right to be here when a girl is bathing in the Cauldron.'

Marron came within an arm's length of Chasse and said, sneering, 'You mean you don't want to fight because you're as gutless as your father.'

Tam went to protest, but Chasse leaped and took Marron down in a heap in the snow. The other boys raced forward for a better view.

'Stop them!' Tam screamed, but she knew her words were futile. The boys loved to watch a fight, and they were urging the combatants on.

Marron and Chasse wrestled furiously a moment and fell apart. Marron was first to his feet. 'When you're ready to fight like a man,' he challenged.

Chasse struggled out of the snow, a cut bleeding above his eye. 'Try me, fish breath,' he snarled.

Marron lunged, but his move was too confident, because Chasse read it, dodged, brought his arm around and smacked him across the back of his head, sending the youth sprawling face forward. He rolled to his feet, spat, and scowled, 'Lucky hit! Now we get serious.'

Tam watched them circle clumsily in the snow. Marron feinted with his left, but again Chasse anticipated what was coming and ducked a swinging right hand. He sidestepped and gave Marron a stinging blow across his left ear. Marron roared and charged. Chasse stepped back to fend off the frenzied attack, but his ankles sank in a small snowdrift and as he faltered Marron hit him full on, and the pair collapsed in a flurry of arms and legs, and spraying snow. In the chaotic struggle, Marron used his greater bulk and strength to lever himself onto Chasse's back and, to Tam's horror, he pushed Chasse's face into the soft snow. Chasse writhed vainly to escape.

'Stop!' Tam screamed. 'You'll smother him!'

Marron laughed, looked at her, and said, 'Tell me you want me.'

'No!' she yelled defiantly. Marron pressed down on Chasse's head.

'Don't!' she screamed.

'I'll let him up,' Marron offered, 'if you declare to everyone here that you want to be my woman.'

Tam felt rage rising and she wished she was strong enough to fight for her brother and save him from humiliation.

Marron wrenched Chasse's head up, let him desperately suck in a mouthful of air, before pushing his face back into the freezing snow. 'That's his last gasp, unless you admit what you feel for me, Tamesan,' Marron said emotionlessly.

Tam looked to the five boys watching the proceedings for assistance, but even though Chasse's companions' distaste for Marron's behaviour was evident in their expressions she knew her plea was in vain. Marron's friends were relishing the unfolding action. Chasse kept struggling against the weight on his back. 'Alright,' she capitulated. Her brother's life was more important than a handful of words.

'Alright what?' Marron asked.

Tam hesitated. She could rush Marron. She wouldn't be able to overpower him, but her effort might be enough to allow Chasse to alter the situation. *No*, she realised. *It wouldn't work.* 'What you said,' she muttered reluctantly, avoiding an open declaration for Marron.

Marron shook his head and pushed harder on Chasse. 'You have to say you want me. We all need to hear it.'

'I want you,' she replied hurriedly, in the belief that saying it quickly would lessen its import. 'Now let my brother go.'

Marron lifted Chasse's head to let him gasp another breath. 'Tam-' he sputtered, but Marron forced his face into the snow before he could finish what he tried to say.

'Let him up!' Tam demanded. 'I said what you wanted to hear.'

'One more thing,' Marron said. He glanced at the small audience who were waiting expectantly to hear what he intended. 'Come out of the water.'

Despite the water's heat, Tam felt as if ice trickled down her spine. 'That wasn't part of it,' she objected.

'Your poor brother is feeling very cold around his head,' Marron goaded.

Tam saw the other boys watching her like hungry wolves outside the Long Hall on a feast night. 'Are you all going to stand there and let him do this?' she implored. No one moved. Chasse kicked violently, but ineffectually. She drew a deep breath, climbed out of the pool, and wrapped her arms around her body for modesty.

'Lift your arms,' Marron ordered. She sneered at him, but she obeyed. Chasse needed her help. 'Now that is pretty,' Marron remarked, and he wrenched Chasse's face out of the hollow in the snow. 'Look at how pretty your sister is,' he said. 'Now you see why I have to have her.' He looked at the other boys, and grinned when he saw how fixated they were on Tam. 'You all heard her say that she wants only me, didn't you?' His three friends nodded. The other two boys looked away. 'Good,' he said. 'Make sure you all remember it.' He turned to Tam and said, 'Remember it, Tamesan. You are Marron's woman. From today onward, everyone in the village will know you belong to me. And don't worry, because I will treat you as kindly as any great warrior treats his beautiful woman.'

'Let Chasse up,' Tam insisted, shivering.

'After you dress,' Marron replied. He glared at the other youths, and said, 'Where are your manners? My woman is dressing. Go back to the village.' All five obediently slunk into the trees. 'And you shouldn't be looking either,' he added, and he pushed Chasse's head down. Tam gasped, but Marron said, 'Don't worry. He can breathe. I'm not holding his head all the way down.'

'Do you have to do this?' Tam asked, as she quickly towelled her limbs.

'It's for my pleasure,' Marron replied casually.

She dressed rapidly, refusing to look at Marron, and as soon as she was ready she demanded, 'Let my brother up!'

'Of course,' Marron acceded. He pushed up but kept sufficient pressure on Chasse to prevent him getting up quickly. As Chasse began to rise, Marron kicked him solidly in the ribs, sending him rolling onto the snow, clutching his side.

'You had no need to do that!' Tam yelled, kneeling beside her gasping brother.

'If I didn't, he might stupidly attack me as I walked away, and a great warrior leaves his enemy no chance for retaliation,' Marron nonchalantly explained. 'And you wouldn't want any harm to come to me, would you, Tamesan?' he added, smirking. He brushed snow from his leather leggings, and sauntered through the trees towards the village, laughing as he disappeared.

Twelve

Infuriated by Marron's attack on Chasse and his humiliation of her, Tam wanted to tell her father immediately, but Chasse begged her not to speak to anyone about the incident. 'Why?' she asked, when Chasse refused to go with her to find Kevan.

'It won't change anything,' he muttered disconsolately.

'Chasse, he can't keep doing what he's doing,' Tam argued.

'You don't understand,' he said, and sighed.

'What don't I understand? That he's cruel? That he bullies people?'

'He wasn't bullying anyone. It was a fight. He won. I lost. That's all anyone will see.'

'He could have killed you.'

'But he didn't, Tam,' Chasse countered. 'It's no good you trying to say anything about it. How can I hold my head up as a man if you keep trying to protect me? Or if you get Father involved? I must face Marron on my own, man to man. You know that's how it is.'

Tam understood what was eating her brother. Marron questioned his manhood, denigrated Chasse in front of five other boys, and Chasse needed to prove his inner strength by accepting Marron's challenge. It was a stupid attitude, she believed, driven by Chasse's sense of honour. 'Then what about what he did to me?' she pleaded, trying a different tack to spur him into action.

Chasse lifted his face, and his pale blue eyes met Tam's steady gaze, but he turned away, mumbling, 'He had no cause to do that.'

'Then let me tell Father what he did to me,' Tam implored. 'I won't even mention the fight.' Chasse was silent, his eyes fixed on a point in front of his feet. 'Chasse?' she queried.

'Tam – I can't,' he answered reluctantly, and he swallowed, as if the words were bitter.

'Why not?'

Chasse glared at her. 'See? You don't understand. It's not that simple anymore.'

Tam opened her mouth to argue, but Chasse turned and sprinted towards the village centre. She let him go. Chasse was heading for the Warriors' Hall, driven by his desire to prove himself, but what choice was she left? If she said nothing about the incident, Marron would get away with his injustices. If she did speak up, she risked humiliating her brother further, and she felt that he had already suffered enough to make him question his place in the rank of men.

But she couldn't bear the thought of Marron gloating triumphantly over them. He forced her to say that she wanted him, but that was the least of her concern, because the words meant absolutely nothing to her. She loathed him. If it came to him choosing her, she would refuse him. There would be an uproar, and her father and mother would be furious with her for defying tradition and law, but even enforced, marriage-less isolation, like old Asmae endured, would be preferable to being Marron's wife. She knew Marron would treat her with less respect than the herdsmen offered their goats. The social suffering from denying him would be less than the lifetime suffering of accepting him.

What most frustrated Tam was that he attacked them so viciously and nothing was going to be done about it. There would be no justice. Chasse was trapped by his principles, the principles that men forged to bind themselves for centuries, and he could not sanction her telling the truth. It wasn't fair. Silence was wrong, but speaking out was risky. Tam kicked her foot through a small mound of snow, making it puff in an angry cloud, and headed home.

The temporary break in the wintry weather freed Kevan from his home-imposed isolation, so he spent every possible moment in the Warriors' Hall, including staying overnight three nights. Chasse avoided Tam, keeping to the Warriors' Hall like his father. Tam was employed by Eesa in mending and making, but for once she appreciated the work because it kept her from dwelling constantly on Marron's attack.

To break the monotony of her labour, when no one could hear, Tam recited the Herbal Man's lessons, memorising the various uses of plants, plants she took for granted, or ignored, or never knew existed. The Herbal Man understood and showed her a world and an interest beyond the traditional confines of Harbin, and she was fascinated and wanted to be immersed in it.

Three days after the Dragon's Cauldron incident, Eesa took Tam to the Long Hall where the women were meeting to clean, prepare and smoke a haul of fish caught by a stroke of fortune during the lull in wintry weather. By working together, they could share the spoils with their families.

Tam saw Banni busy at one basket, so she found a long scaling knife and sat beside her, and the pair chatted as they worked, mainly about Banni's coming child and clothing she was making for the arrival. Tam felt, for the first time in ages, that she was coping with the menial role women were expected to fill in Harbin.

Tam was made aware of Katris' presence when the dark-haired girl slapped a half-gutted fish on the bench before Tam and said, 'You didn't scale this one right.'

Tam looked up and Katris' dark eyes narrowed. 'I'll redo it now,' Tam conceded and reached for the fish.

Katris snatched the fish away, snarling, 'Don't touch my fish!'

'Then why did you put it down in front of me? Tam asked, aware others were staring.

'You take everything that isn't yours!' Katris accused spitefully.

Tam straightened, puzzled, and asked, 'What is your problem?'

Katris dropped the fish in her lap, and yelled, 'You! You're the problem! You think because you're the Dragon Head's daughter that you can have anything you want!'

'Katris, get on with your work,' Banni said.

'You shut up!' Katris snapped. 'This is nothing to do with you!'

Tam heard several intakes of breath from the women. It was unacceptable for a girl not come of age to speak rudely to a woman in public. Banni, however, seemed unperturbed. 'If I have something to say to a girl, I will say it,' she said firmly. 'Remember who you are, and where you are.'

Katris pulled a face at Banni and spat at Tam. Tam rose, seething with anger, scaling knife in her hand, and one of Katris' companions grabbed Katris' arm and urged, 'Come away, that's enough, Katris. Everyone is watching. Even Eesa.'

'Good!' Katris declared brazenly. 'Let them watch!' She raised her voice, and said, 'Let everyone know Tamesan thinks she is so much better than the rest of us that she takes a man before it's her time of choosing! Don't deny it, Tamesan!' Katris challenged. 'All the men know already! Why shouldn't we?'

Katris' accusation stunned Tam. She was aware of a startled gasp from one woman and the murmur of astonished voices in the Long Hall, and she saw Eesa rise and approach. 'You don't know what you're talking about,' Tam replied.

'Yes I do!' Katris screamed. 'I know because it's Marron you're taking! You're stealing Marron from me!' She grabbed Tam's tunic and went to slap Tam's face, but Tam lashed out and knocked Katris backward. The dark-haired girl collapsed into a pile of buckets, and fish heads and guts cascaded over her. The accident shocked several women and girls, but others, Banni included, grinned at Katris' misfortune.

Tam started to apologise, but Eesa grabbed her arm and spun her around, saying, 'You, girl, go straight home at once!' When Tam looked like she was going to object, Eesa cut her short and dragged her towards the door. Humiliated by her mother's action, Tam shook free and marched out of the Long Hall in disgust and defiance, ignoring Katris' sobbing and the stares of women on her way to the door.

Outside, Tam clenched her fists in rage and screamed at the grey sky. The only way Katris would even know about the encounter at the Dragon's Cauldron was from Marron. She was certain the other boys wouldn't have mentioned it, except among themselves, but Marron would have gone out of his way to ensure Katris knew what transpired, at least his version of it. He broke through Tam's defences, wounded her dignity at the hot springs, and now he was deliberately twisting the knife. He was heartless. He was using Tam to torment Katris, while he forced his will on her. She hated him.

Tam kicked the snow and started walking, but the situation nagged her. She was certain Eesa would listen to Katris' side of the story after what happened in the Long Hall. What chance did she have? If she told the truth, Eesa would demand to know why she didn't tell her about the incident straightaway, and Chasse would be angry at her for exposing his humiliation at Marron's hands. If she didn't tell the truth, her mother would see her, at best, as a presumptuous child meddling too early with boys; at worst, as a slut interfering with Katris' chances of pairing with Marron. She would have to endure the harsh criticism of the entire village. The situation was becoming so unfair.

'Look who's here,' a voice said, as Tam passed the Warriors' Hall. She knew it was Marron. She ignored him and walked on, but he thrust out his hand and caught her arm. 'Why are you ignoring me?' he asked in a frighteningly gentle manner.

'Let go!' Tam yelled, wrenching her arm free and glaring. He wore a reproachful expression that might have disarmed her, if he was anyone else, but on Marron it looked vulgar. 'Gloat and tell lies as much as you want, but I will tell everyone what you really did,' she threatened.

Marron shrugged. 'Tell people what you want, Tamesan. It's your word against mine.' His eyes narrowed and he leaned closer. 'But don't expect me to feel sorry for your brother when I make him look like a complete idiot because of your stories.'

'It's not a story, Marron, and you know it.'

'Do I?' he asked, feigning surprise. 'I can ask Aaron, or Hale, or Jared. They will say it happened exactly like I say it happened. They were there.'

'So were Tass and Evan,' Tam reminded him.

'Were they?' he asked. He flexed his biceps and cracked a knuckle in his fingers as he pressed one fist into the palm of his other hand. 'I think you might find that they will say they weren't anywhere near the Dragon's Cauldron. That's what they will say, if you ask them. Even your precious brother doesn't know anything about the incident. You seem to be making it all up, Tamesan.'

Overwhelmed by the enormity of his lie, Tam stared at the wall beyond his shoulder for what felt like an eternity, unable to move, unable to speak. He had trapped her again. The blood fury welling within exploded, and she lashed out, swinging her arms, kicking wildly, all feeling, all sense of control lost. She hit and punched and kicked, until someone pinned her arms and pulled her away, big hands gripping like iron manacles. A man's voice ordered her to stop, but she struggled vehemently against his hold, only snapping into awareness when her mother's voice broke through her rage.

'You have a hellcat for a daughter,' the man said. 'The lad is lucky she's not a boy.'

'I wish she was a boy,' Eesa replied bitterly. 'She would be less of a problem that way.'

Tam felt the heavy hands release her, but she focussed on Marron, who was leaning against the Warriors' Hall, his hand against the side of his mouth. A trickle of red ran over his fingers, but he forced a smile, despite his hurt.

'You, girl,' Eesa said. Tam shifted her attention to her mother's bulky figure. 'I told you to go home. Now do as I say.' Tam saw three warriors in the doorway looking at her. The man who took hold of her was Theo, her father's friend, and he was studying her with a serious frown. 'Go!' Eesa ordered. Tam turned on her heel and stalked towards Watersdrop, her angry mother following in her wake.

The winter storm sweeping over Harbin could not match the storm raging in Tam's home. She weathered Eesa's diatribe about appropriate public behaviour, a woman's expected manners, the limited rights of girls, bathing alone, fighting, and responsibilities, until it seemed her mother was never going to let up.

When Tam was eventually allowed to speak, she told Eesa that she knew Katris was jealous, but she was adamant that nothing existed between Marron and herself. Her statement of innocence did not appear to appease her mother. Eesa ordered Tam to explain clearly what Katris meant when she said that Tam had pledged herself to Marron. Tam emphatically denied making any pledge to Marron, but Eesa commenced to lecture her about the correct behaviour of girls around young men.

Forced to listen, Tam was grateful for the howl of the wind driving sleet and snow in from the western ocean, keeping Chasse and Kevan locked in the Warriors' Hall and away from home. She pitied Jaysin, lying awake in the adjoining bedroom, listening to Eesa's incessant castigation of his sister. He was frightened whenever people raised their voices. On the other hand, asleep in Eesa's room, Tam knew Gramma Harmi was oblivious to the whole affair.

When Eesa tired of upbraiding her errant daughter, Tam retreated to her bedroom. She dragged on her bedclothes and climbed into her bedding, but she could not sleep. She listened to the whistling winds, her mind swirling with emotion and thoughts from the day's events.

In the embracing darkness, she thought she heard a whimper from Jaysin, so she crawled across to investigate and found him crying. 'What's wrong?' she whispered, but he didn't answer, and he kept sobbing quietly. She cradled the boy in her arms and crooned, 'It's alright,' as she gently rocked him, 'It's alright,' while the storm rose in tempo, hammering against the walls of Harbin's homes.

Thirteen

Men and boys were gathering at the jetty. The storms came and went for more than three weeks, but the last storm damaged the dragonship and the men were taking advantage of the lull in the weather to repair what they could. Heavy clouds burdened the sky, warning yet another storm and heavier snowfalls were brewing.

On Harbin's outskirts, herdsmen were busily bracing the roofs and walls of the animal shelters, so Eesa sent Tam and three girls with Banni to lend assistance. The women raked manure from the shelters and packed it in small bricks to fuel hearth fires. Herdsman Galt sent two girls back to the village to borrow grain containers from the Long Hall's winter store to bolster the animal feed bins. He asked Banni to organise a meal for the herdsmen, and set Tam and the remaining girl, Serene, to fetching armfuls of twigs from the forest to serve as fresh flooring in the animal shelters.

Serene was two summers younger than Tam and a chatterbox, and she talked all the way to the forest edge about different wild animals she saw on the pastures, and how frightened she was during the last storm. While Tam appreciated the company, she wondered if Serene ever tired of talking. It wasn't until they entered the forest that she noticed the girl was silent, and when she saw Serene's brown eyes were wide and fearful she asked, 'What's the matter?'

'I don't like it here,' Serene whispered.

'Why? Nothing's going to hurt you.'

'What about the wolves?'

Tam laughed, remembering what the Herbal Man told her after her encounter with the bear. 'The wolves are more scared of you.'

'I don't like it,' Serene said. 'I never come up here.'

Tam sighed. 'How about I load you with wood here, and you take it to Galt. I'll go a bit further for some more while you head back.'

'Aren't you scared?' the girl asked.

'Of the forest? No,' Tam replied, smiling. 'I love coming here.' She collected twigs protruding from the snow and hanging from branches, and piled them in Serene's trembling arms, aware the girl was watching her as if she was a strange and incredibly brave creature for being unafraid of the forest. When Serene's arms were laden, Tam sent the girl back to the animal enclosures, while she climbed higher.

Glad to be alone, Tam took her time. The fresh air and wood-gathering exercise was a pleasant change from being cooped up with Eesa, Jaysin and Gramma Harmi. Even the cold mountain air was refreshing, although she constantly rubbed her hands together to keep her blood circulating. As she stooped and tugged at sticks, she imagined how difficult it was for the Herbal Man to find herbs in the thick winter snow. He said he searched in mid-winter for the hardiest plants, but she saw nothing living in the bleak spaces between trees. Curious, she laid down her load of twigs and scraped away the powdery snow at the base of a tree. She reasoned in other seasons plants sheltered between large tree roots so perhaps that was how winter herbs survived beneath the snowy mantle.

The scrunch of approaching footsteps startled her, and she turned to discover Marron staring at her. He held a spear in one hand and a brown leather sack in the other. 'What are you doing here?' she asked, full of suspicion.

'I might ask you the same question,' he replied.

'I'm gathering flooring,' she said, rising.

'And I'm hunting squirrels,' he replied, 'although what I see now is far more interesting.'

'Galt is expecting me,' she said, as she bent to scoop up her bundle of twigs.

Marron took blocked her path, saying, 'You don't need to leave yet.'

'I'm already late,' she said, glaring fiercely.

'A little longer won't hurt,' he argued, grinning. 'You wouldn't want to disappoint your man.'

He took a step towards her, but she stepped back, scanning the landscape for Marron's friends. No one was visible. Anywhere. 'Don't do this,' she warned. 'I told you I don't want you. Do you understand what I'm saying? I don't want you.'

Marron's eyes glinted in the weak daylight and he bounced the spear in his hand. He wore the menacing, overconfident smile he always wore when he was certain that he was in complete control of a situation. 'All I want is a kiss,' he said.

The mountain air suddenly seemed still to Tam. Yielding a kiss to Marron was dangerous, heralding a greater demand, and he would take her yielding as confirmation of her subservience. She weighed her options for escape, and said, 'No.'

'A kiss, Tamesan. One kiss,' he appealed. 'Even you can do that much for me.' He reached for her shoulders, but she flung her bundle of twigs in his face and bolted. Marron dropped his spear and sprinted after her.

Her first reaction was to run, anywhere, but a few paces on she realised that she was heading up the slope, and she knew there was no safety in that direction. Her only hope was to reach Galt or another herdsman. She veered left and bounded across the face of the slope, dodging trees and skirting the rocky outcrops protruding from the snow. She could hear Marron pursuing her, but she dared not look back because the snow underfoot hid treacherous obstacles. She re-crossed her earlier tracks, paused, and thought better of following them back down because she meandered erratically as she collected wood. She deviated right and scrambled over a low snow ridge before she finally checked where her pursuer was. He was calling her name. She chose a direction and shut out his voice with the wind in her ears as she dashed across a tiny clearing into thicker forest. She knew if she could make it to the pasture, the herdsmen would see and hear her and Marron wouldn't risk chasing her there.

She turned at a copse and headed straight down the slope, chancing a glance over her shoulder to see how close Marron was. She couldn't see him. She'd probably lost him, but she wasn't stopping until she reached the open ground, so she continued her descent.

Then her heart sank. Between her and the forest edge, a figure moved. Marron. He second-guessed her escape plan and cut off the direct route out of the forest. And he spotted her and was climbing towards her.

She assessed her options. She knew the quick paths and short cuts nearer her favourite hideaway. If she could beat Marron to the rocks there, she knew she could lose him and make it safely to the village. She sucked in her breath and doubled back on her tracks.

She held the initial advantage, running across the slope while Marron was forced to climb, but her advantage rapidly diminished. The snow hindered her and she wasn't used to running like this. Her legs were tiring. Marron closed the distance, and she could hear him panting for breath. Before long, she could hear his boots crushing the snow. But she could also see the rocks. A few more paces and she would have a real chance. She pushed herself.

Too late. Marron caught her quicker than she anticipated. She dodged his clumsy lunge, but his hands caught the hem of her skirt and he dragged her into the snow. She screamed and kicked, and heard Marron grunt as her foot connected, but she didn't break his hold. She struggled as he pinned her legs, and he clambered onto her, sitting astride her stomach, and clamping her thrashing arms in his hands. She screamed again. 'Stop!' he demanded. She screamed louder, her voice echoing across the mountain, but a stinging slap across her cheek was accompanied by Marron yelling, 'I said stop it!' The slap shocked Tam into silence. She stared up at him. His weight was hurting her. 'That's better,' he said. 'Now we can share the kiss you promised me.'

She was about to protest that she didn't promise anything when she realised he was already leaning down to kiss her. She lashed out with the hand he released to slap her and dug her rough fingernails into his face.

Marron howled and clutched his cheek with both hands, and she seized her chance to roll left. Caught off balance, Marron toppled into the snow.

Tam thrashed, kicked and scrambled to her feet as he tried to grab her again, and ran. She heard him yell as she fled, but she didn't know what he yelled, or whether he took after her. She only wanted to make it to her home. She ignored her throbbing legs and ran on sheer fear down the mountainside towards Watersdrop.

'I want the truth, girl. I don't want any foolish lies.'

Tam stared at her father. Kevan was watching her closely as he awaited her reply. Eesa stood behind him. She looked tired. 'What I said is what happened,' Tam explained resolutely. 'Marron chased and attacked me. I got away.'

'And the cuts on his face?'

'I scratched him to get him off me.' She saw her father shake his head slightly. 'It's true, Father,' she insisted. 'I swear it's true.'

'That's not what he says happened,' Kevan said. 'He said you attacked him.'

'Why would I attack him?' she cried. 'He's lying.'

'Why did you go off alone?'

'Serene was too scared to go into the forest to fetch wood, so I sent her back. I got wood by myself.'

Kevan rubbed his grey beard, and asked, 'Why were you so long about it?'

She needed to be truthful. Her father didn't approve of her time-wasting and daydreaming, but that wasn't the issue. 'I like walking in the forest,' she confessed.

'But you were supposed to be gathering wood for Galt,' Kevan growled.

'I did.'

'What happened to it?'

Kevan's barrage of questions was irritating her. The fate of the wood was irrelevant, but he was treating it like it was a mistake that she made. 'I dropped it when Marron attacked me.'

'You threw it at him, you mean.'

She met his steady gaze. 'Yes. I threw it at him. It's all I had to defend myself with when he tried to grab me.'

'Marron says that's how you cut his face.'

Tam was stunned by the accusation. Marron twisted the story into a different one in the Warriors' Hall in his effort to lie his way out of the circumstances. 'No,' she said. 'That's not what happened. I scratched his face with my nails.'

'So, you did attack him.'

'No!' Tam snapped, frustrated that her father seemed determined to make her the guilty party. 'Aren't you listening?' she implored. 'He attacked me!'

'Did he hurt you?'

'Yes!'

'Show me where.'

'He didn't leave any marks on me.'

'You said he hurt you,' Kevan reminded her. He lifted a sceptical eyebrow.

'He did hurt me,' she insisted, confused by the turn of argument.

'How?' Kevan asked, adding before she could answer, 'He's the one with all the cuts. What did he do to you?'

'He chased me,' she replied, and she realised how weak her accusation sounded. 'He tried to kiss me.'

Her father shook his head again, and said, 'Marron says you walked up to him and threw the sticks in his face because you saw him looking at Katris.'

'Not true!' Tam asserted.

'So, you didn't throw the sticks in his face.'

'Yes, I did!' she screamed. 'But not for why he said I did!'

Kevan let out a heavy sigh and ran his hand through his mass of hair. 'Make up your mind, girl. Either you attacked him, or you didn't.'

Tam felt as trapped in her father's words as she was on the mountainside with Marron breathing heavily on her. She threw up her hands in despair, and said, 'You're turning it all around. Why? Why are you trying to make me the bad person in this? What do you want me to say? I'm telling you the truth and you don't even want to hear it!'

'Talking to me like that isn't going to help, Tamesan,' Kevan warned.

'But you're making me sound like a liar, and I'm not.'

'Why did you attack Katris in the Long Hall?'

Tam caught her breath at the unexpected question, and glanced at Eesa, before replying, 'She accused me of taking Marron from her.'

'I thought Marron wanted you.'

'He does,' she said, and she thought there was finally a chance to make her father see reason. 'He tells everyone that. But I don't want him.'

'Why not?'

'Because he's cruel. He's always bragging and fighting.'

'He's a strong young man,' Kevan replied. 'Trask's son can be no different.'

His defence of Marron angered her. 'He's a liar,' she argued. 'He bullies everyone. And he won't leave me alone.'

'Every young man is persistent when he thinks he's found the woman he wants,' Eesa remarked, as she stepped forward beside Kevan.

'You should feel honoured that he's chosen you,' Kevan added. 'Yet all you do is humiliate him.'

'Humiliate him?' Tam gasped. 'That's all he ever does to everyone else. Ask the other boys what he does. Ask Derin.'

'The other boys respect him, Tamesan,' Kevan replied. 'Every boy in the village listens to what he has to say. He will be a leader one day, perhaps even Dragon Head.'

'He terrorises them!' Tam countered, astonished at her father's naiveté. 'They don't respect him, they fear him!'

'A leader has to be strong, and feared,' Kevan stated. 'He will be a dragonwarrior next summer, and you are privileged to be sought after by such a fine young man.'

'Why do you think Katris and the others are so envious of you?' Eesa added.

'They don't envy me,' Tam retorted. 'They hate me. And they can have him!'

'If you keep treating him like you do, they may end up with him,' Eesa cautioned. 'And it will be your loss, girl.'

'My loss?' Tam sputtered, exasperated. 'How can I lose what I don't want? I hate him! Hear me? I hate him!'

'If Trask's son chooses to pair with my daughter, you will accept him with grace and honour,' Kevan pronounced, mustering his authoritative tone.

'No!' Tam screeched. 'I would rather be married to a goat than with Marron!'

Kevan glared with fierce determination, the expression Tam imagined her father holding when facing a dragon, the look of a man prepared to kill to get what he wanted. 'You will do as your father and the Dragon Head of Harbin orders, child!' he snarled. 'Do you hear me?' When she held her silence, he demanded, 'Answer me respectfully!'

Tam understood she would be best to obey. She took a short breath, and muttered, 'Yes, Father.'

'By Varst's eternal fires, I want it clearer than that, girl!' he roared. 'Say it louder!'

'Yes, Father,' she repeated, but she kept her eyes lowered so that her father could not see the rage and defiance and fear burning in her heart. She hated him for beating her down.

'Good,' Kevan announced. 'And that's the last I want to hear of this behaviour. Hear me?'

'Yes, Father.'

'See to your grandmother,' he ordered, before he turned to Eesa to say, 'I have work for you in the Warriors' Hall before it gets dark. There's another storm coming, so we must get the work done now.'

Tam waited in obedient silence for her parents to leave, but when the door closed she slumped to the floor, desolate, and burst into tears. It was wrong, all so terribly wrong. Marron caused all the trouble and yet she was getting all the blame. He was arrogant and ruthless, but everyone saw those faults as his strongest qualities. She came home seeking help and was made to look like the troublemaker. Why? Why were her parents defending him? Why couldn't they see what was happening? The worst was her parents believed that Marron should be her husband when she came of age. They had already decided. They intended to force her to live with the person she most hated. Why? Why weren't they willing to listen to her?

A sudden wind gust hit the cottage and the door swung open. Tam wiped her eyes and stood to close the door, but she heard her grandmother stir in the adjoining bedroom, where Kevan moved her before he began his inquisition of Tam about Marron's injuries.

Tam went to the bedroom door and stuck her head around the corner, asking, 'What is it Gramma?' but she didn't expect an answer. The old woman seemed to be lost ever deeper inside herself this winter. Tam overheard Eesa in the Long Hall telling Amarti this winter would most likely be Gramma Harmi's last, and the thought saddened Tam. She couldn't imagine the cottage without her grandmother's presence.

'I thought I heard Eric,' Harmi said with unusual clarity. 'Tell him I'll be ready soon.'

'Eric isn't here, Gramma,' Tam explained gently. 'It was the wind.' She pulled a shawl over her grandmother's shoulders.

'He will be here,' Harmi confidently replied. 'I heard the dragon.'

Tam shook her head in despair. Eric. Dragons. Her grandmother lived in another world, a twilight world. Perhaps she was lucky to be there. There were no Marrons or parents, no menial tasks, no barriers, no demands. Why were her parents so determined to make her do the very things she didn't want to do? She was never going to accept Marron. She was not going to be yet another woman serving the dragonwarriors. There had to be more to life. Choices. What were her choices?

Another gust of wind shook the cottage and broke her thoughts. It was getting darker. The storm was closing in, so Jaysin would come home, Eesa would return from the Warriors' Hall soon, and Tam would be trapped again inside the cottage. She'd seen Jaysin creep out the door when Kevan's anger rose, and she wondered to where her little brother escaped. She was sure he had a private hiding place like her. Everything in the village was cruel. No one accepted Jaysin, either, because he didn't want to do what the other little boys did, so how would her parents treat him when he reached his coming of age? He was never going to be a dragonwarrior. He hated violence.

She wrapped herself in a cloak against the falling temperature, lit a lantern, and stoked the hearth, but her frustration and anger continued to boil. She would never marry Marron. Never. If her parents were bent on forcing her to marry him, she needed to make her own choices. She rummaged through the pots in the main room and filled a small bag with foodstuffs. She grabbed another cloak, a lined leather one, and pulled it over her other clothes, before she checked outside. No one was on the bridge, and Eesa wasn't yet coming up the path from the Warriors' Hall. She could slip away, unnoticed, before the storm settled, and find solace on the mountain. She could even seek shelter with the Herbal Man.

Then she remembered her promise. The mid-winter feast was less than a fortnight away. She darted into her room to retrieve the small pouch containing the ring that the Herbal Man wanted passed to her grandmother and carried it to Harmi. Tam loosened the drawstring, shook the pouch, and a spider-web-thin glittering amber band fell into her palm. It looked so fragile, so exquisitely delicate, that she was afraid she would crush it, but when she put experimental pressure on the band it felt stronger than any she ever held. She gently lifted her grandmother's hand and brought the ring towards the old woman's middle finger. Outside, the wind whipped into a frenzy and rattled the wooden shutters. Tam hesitated, glancing apprehensively at the window.

'Eric?' Harmi rasped. Her eyes snapped open, startling Tam, and she fixed her gaze on the window. 'Eric?' she repeated. 'Is that you?'

'It's me, Gramma,' Tam said, soothingly pressing her grandmother's hand. 'Just me, and the wind.'

Harmi focused on Tam and smiled. 'Tamesan,' she whispered, 'sweet Tamesan,' and she closed her eyes.

Tam looked at the ring poised before Harmi's finger, and in her mind she could hear the Herbal Man reminding her, 'Give it to Harmi only on the night of Blitzart's Feast. Not before.' The words suddenly carried greater meaning, a warning. What would happen if she gave Harmi the ring ahead of time? Did it matter? Circumstances were changed and she couldn't be here for Blitzart's Feast, not anymore. She brought the ring closer, but the wind surged again and howled around the cottage, the front door flew open, and a cloud of snowflakes swirled in.

Jaysin stood in the doorway, staring at her. 'What are you doing?' he asked, in a soft piping voice.

She cupped the ring in her hand, lowered Harmi's hand, and replied,

'Talking to Gramma. Where have you been?'

'Out,' Jaysin said. He stepped into the room, and asked, 'What's in your hand?'

'Close the door,' she ordered.

He closed the door, turned back and asked, 'What were you holding?'

'Nothing.'

'Yes, you were,' he accused. 'You had something. It was a ring or something.'

He caught her, but Jaysin seldom argued so she was sure she could bluff him. But another possibility presented itself. It was a risk, but there was no time left for alternatives with the storm sweeping in. 'It's a ring,' she confessed, opening her hand. 'It's a gift for Gramma, a special gift.'

Jaysin solemnly studied the thin amber band on his sister's palm. 'Are you giving it to Gramma?'

'I am – or I was,' she replied, correcting herself as she formulated her plan.

'Why?'

'Because the Herbal Man asked me to give it to Gramma.'

'Why?'

'Why doesn't matter. It's, well, I was going to give it to her, but then I remembered the Herbal Man said that I wasn't supposed to give it to her until Blitzart's Feast.'

'Why does she have to have it then?'

So many questions, she thought. *Am I this painful?* 'I don't know,' she said. 'All I do know is that she has to have it only on that night. She can't have it before then.' She kept assessing her plan as she explained. 'Except now I won't be able to give it to her like I promised.'

'Why not?' Jaysin asked.

She thought quickly. 'Um, well, because Mother said she wants me to help her prepare the feast and to clean up afterward. I won't get a chance to spend time with Gramma.'

'How will you give her the ring then?'

'That's what I was going to ask,' Tam quickly proposed. 'Could you give the ring to Gramma on Blitzart's Feast if I forget – or if I'm too busy?'

Jaysin's eyes lit with fervent hope. 'Can I?' he asked. 'I mean, if you're working, you'd let me?'

'Of course I'd let you,' she assured him. 'But it's a very special secret. You can't tell anyone, not even Father or Mother.'

'I can do it,' he eagerly agreed. 'That's easy.'

Tam rolled the amber ring between her fingers, hoping the Herbal Man would approve of her decision. She didn't understand the ring's purpose, but she made a promise, and promises were meant to be kept. 'Here,' she said. She slipped the ring back into the pouch and pressed it into Jaysin's tiny hand. 'You have to promise to keep this safe and tell no one else about it. If I'm not here to give it to Gramma on Blitzart's Feast night, you must. You mustn't ever forget. Promise?'

'I promise,' he said, his nine-year-old face set in serious conviction.

Tam ruffled her little brother's mop of auburn hair and asked him to hide the pouch securely in his bedroom. As he left, she leaned closer to Harmi and whispered, 'The Herbal Man said the ring was for you, Gramma. I was meant to give it to you, but I won't be able to anymore. Jaysin will do it. I know he will.' She wondered if her grandmother knew what was happening, but the old woman was dozing quietly.

Tam sighed, but as she did Harmi opened her eyes and muttered, 'I knew he would come this time. She made him promise. Dragons never forget.'

Tam straightened and stared at her grandmother, expecting her to speak further, but Harmi's head nodded slightly, her eyes closed, and she fell asleep. Tam watched her for a moment before she lifted Harmi's hand, kissed it softly, and backed quietly out of the room.

She felt guilty for leaving Harmi like this. It might be the last time they spent together. She wanted to go back into the room to cuddle her grandmother, to tell her she loved her, but if she didn't leave now Eesa would return and then she could never leave. She picked up the gear she dropped by the door and opened it.

'Where are you going, Tamesan?' Jaysin called.

She held up her food sack, and said, 'Mother wants me to take this to the Long Hall.'

'But there's a big storm coming.'

'I know,' she replied, 'which is why you have to stay inside. I'll be back quickly with Mother. You can stir up the hearth and have it ready for us. Can you do that?' Jaysin nodded. Tam scuffed his hair again and urged him to close the door after her, saying, 'I'll see you soon. Whatever happens, don't forget our promise.'

'I won't forget,' he replied as the door closed.

Tam wrapped her leather overcoat around her body and hurried over the bridge in the biting cold wind and darkening world. She looked in the direction of the Long Hall and saw people filing out, fanning towards their homes, so rather than following the regular path which would take her past the Hall she cut behind several buildings and followed the lip of Watersdrop gorge, until she reached the tree line. As she began to climb the lower slopes, the first flakes of the looming snowstorm spiralled to earth.

Fourteen

A halo of white light expanded until it filled the whole world. In the light, coming towards her, was a man with white hair and a beard. He walked with a staff in his left hand and she thought she knew him. He smiled. She opened her eyes. Everything was crisp, white. Then she remembered. Snow. She was face down in snow. But the snow was warm and dry. Had she lost all sense of feeling?

The storm swept in faster than she anticipated. She followed Watersdrop gorge as far as possible from the village before she cut back across the face of the mountain to find the path to the Herbal Man's home. As she traversed the slope, the wind whipped at the trees, and sleet and snow swirled around her menacingly, until she could barely see ten steps ahead. She struggled through the snow, determined to reach her goal, but when she reached the path darkness swallowed the world and the wind howled mercilessly over the mountain like a tortured soul. She sweated from fighting against the wind and snow and the sweat froze on her brow and the tip of her nose. Even with two cloaks over her winter clothes, she felt brutally cold.

'Where are you going?' someone called. Marron's face appeared. He was laughing. 'I will have you,' he said, grinning, and he reached for her. She tried to scream, but fear locked her voice and rooted her legs to the spot. Marron's hands encircled her and her heart pounded with terror.

'It's alright,' the gentle voice crooned. 'You will be alright.'

The mountain was invisible. She bent forward, feeling the rocks and snow with her hands, trying to decipher where she was in relation to the path, but it was too difficult. She was lost. She was so very, very cold. The freezing storm was burying her and she was overwhelmed by an inexorable desire to lie down in the darkness and sleep.

'Te-Amen-San, the dawn's light,' the gentle voice whispered. The cold faded. The pain eased. Her fingers, her feet, her hands, her arms were numb. 'Te-Amen-San,' said the voice through the darkness.

And then the light appeared, a dot, far away at first and faint, but it grew, and it grew until it washed over her, enfolded her within its radiance, and the man's voice called to her, called her by her real name, the old name given to her at birth.

Her only hope was to go up. If she went up, there was a chance she was headed in the right direction. She would climb. It was the only way out of the confusion. She had to climb.

'You will be alright,' a voice whispered. 'Drink this.'

The gentle, familiar voice came and went. She swore her eyes were open, but she was locked in darkness like ice. She couldn't even feel the vessel being held to her lips, only knew that it was there because she felt liquid trickling down her throat. She was cold, oh so cold, but the liquid spread through her veins like fire.

Her first impressions were of white fabric and warmth. She blinked.

'How are you feeling?'

She turned her face up from the pillow and saw the Herbal Man. A lantern flickered on a small table to her right. 'Where am I?' she asked groggily.

'In my home,' he replied. 'Are you hungry?'

Tam recognised the room as she considered his question. She was in the Herbal Man's bedroom and bed. A faint voice within asked, *How did I get here*? but it was a distant voice, and she held no interest in the answer. 'Yes,' she murmured sleepily.

'Good,' the Herbal Man said. 'I'll bring you warm broth.' He shifted out of sight.

Tam had no energy, and the bed was big and comfortable, so she lay on her side, listening to the Herbal Man's activity in the adjoining room, and stared at the lantern's flickering yellow flame. When the Herbal Man returned and knelt beside the bed, holding a bowl of steaming broth, Tam rolled onto her back and sat up. 'I feel so weak,' she confessed.

'I can feed you if you want,' the old man kindly offered.

'Thank you,' Tam said, 'but I'll try first.' She wrapped her hands around the warm bowl, breathed in the enticing aroma, and lifted the green broth to her lips, pausing to ask, 'What's it made from?'

'Legumes,' the Herbal Man replied. 'Mountain potato mainly.'

'It tastes good,' Tam pronounced after sampling a mouthful. She blew on the broth to cool it and sipped, and between sips she asked, 'How did I get here?'

'By luck,' the Herbal Man said.

'I can't remember much,' Tam murmured hesitantly. 'There was a light.'

'I found you. You were lying in the snow.'

'There was a storm.'

'There still is a storm,' the Herbal Man said. 'A big one. It's been blowing in from the north for five days.'

Tam paused and stared at him. 'Have I been asleep for five days?'

'Mainly,' he replied. 'You were sick, Tamesan.'

When Tam finished the broth, the Herbal Man took the empty bowl to the next chamber and returned with a small yellow cup. 'Drink this,' he instructed.

Tam studied the blue liquid in the cup, and asked, 'Is this Dewdrop Elixir?'

'Yes,' the Herbal Man confirmed. 'You remembered.'

She screwed up her nose in disgust, also remembering his reaction when he took the medicine. She braced herself and drank. It was awful! The instant the foul elixir ran down her throat she wanted to spit it out. She gagged and coughed, and swore, 'Procra's mercy! It's horrible!' As she pushed away the half-empty cup, she realised the Herbal Man was laughing and she was shocked by his reaction. Then the absurdity of the moment struck her and she laughed as well. 'It really is so horrible,' she sputtered as she regained her breath and composure.

The old man nodded. 'I think it's the worst remedy I've created,' he admitted, 'but it is incredibly effective.' He nudged the cup towards her.

'You don't mean I have to finish it?' she asked pensively.

'It won't work otherwise.'

'All of it?'

'All of it.'

She briefly thought it might be better to be sick, but the Herbal Man was watching so she knew she must drink the liquid. She took a deep breath, lifted the cup and quickly drained it. Grimacing, she put the cup down and muttered, 'Goat dung would taste sweeter.'

The medicine made her drowsy and while she drifted through bouts of wakefulness and sleep the Herbal Man came and went, bringing her water and more broth. Slowly, she felt her strength returning.

When she asked if she could get out of bed, the Herbal Man brought her a fresh robe and a cloak and left her to dress in peace.

Tam was amazed by the robe's intricacy and delicacy. Maroon in hue, it was woven through with silver and gold thread forming a dragon motif that ran across the back and extended over the left shoulder, and the cuffs and collar were embroidered with symbolic flames. She never saw such craft, nor held material so soft, liquid to her touch. It raised goose bumps on her skin when she slipped it on and it fitted exceedingly well, as if it was tailored for her.

The cloak was as equally unusual, and unlike the rustic animal hides or common rough weave in Harbin the cloak was made from soft, thick grey thread that was lightweight and tightly woven. The Herbal Man also left her a pair of goatskin boots, with fur on the inside like those traditionally worn by the dragonwarriors in winter. She slipped her feet into them and dutifully tidied the bed quilt before leaving the room.

She found the Herbal Man hunched over the bench at the centre of the main room, etching coloured dye into the wax of a candle, creating equidistant rings along the candle's length. A similarly marked candle burned on the nearby cluttered benchtop. 'What are you doing?' she asked, studying his handiwork.

'Creating a clock,' he replied, without diverting his attention from the candle. 'Do the clothes fit?'

'Perfectly,' she responded. 'What is the robe made from?'

'Silk.' He glanced up and noticed Tam's puzzled expression, so he explained. 'It's a special thread made by a very special insect.'

'Oh,' she murmured, no less confused by his explanation. 'What's a clock?'

The Herbal Man completed colouring the final ring and held up the candle for her inspection. 'This is a clock,' he announced. 'See the rings? When the candle burns, the wax melts at roughly the same speed to each ring. Of course, it must be protected from the wind, and other factors that might slow down or speed up the rate of melting, to keep it accurate. I've measured the time it takes for a candle to burn from top to bottom, and that's a half a day. Two candles take a full day to burn. So, when the candle melts to this line,' he said, pointing to a red line, 'I know it's the middle of the day, or the middle of the night, depending on when I lit the candle.'

'Why do you need a clock?'

The Herbal Man smiled and walked across the room to stir the contents of a small jar bubbling over another, larger candle, as he answered her question. 'Many things I do must be completed in a specific timeframe. A clock helps me break the day into parts, not only morning, midday, afternoon, evening. Each candle has ten rings, so each day has twenty candle rings of time. If something takes two candle rings to do, I can accurately measure that. I can even estimate half candle ring time, giving me up to forty moments in each full day.' He paused to lift the steaming jar from over the candle.

'What's that?' she asked.

'A special herbal liquid,' he replied. 'I boiled the leaves and roots of a Goatnut plant to extract it. This is an essential ingredient in an elixir called Arthur's Cure. The elixir is meant to soothe sore throats and ease bad tempers, according to the Apothecary's Compendium, but its real value is as a drying agent on festering wounds.' He chuckled to himself, before continuing. 'I only found out its true properties when I accidentally spilt some of it on a bad cut on my finger.' He lifted his finger and stared as if he could still see the fresh wound. 'That was a long time ago, of course.' He pointed to another object on a shelf behind her. 'See that?'

She looked at a device shaped in the parody of a woman's body, going from a large bowl at the top, through a slender waist to another large bowl at the base. It was made of a shiny, clear substance, like frozen water, clasped within a metal frame. Heaped in the bottom was clean yellow sand. Two smaller versions sat beside the first.

'They're called timing glasses. Some people call them hour glasses.

They're clocks, like the candles, only they can measure time in much smaller quantities, and they're less affected by the vagaries of wind and fire.'

She listened patiently to the lecture on clocks and their functions. The Herbal Man obviously needed them for his work, but she couldn't see an immediate application for the devices in Harbin, except perhaps the candles might help people measure the days trapped inside during winter storms. She tired quickly, but she forced herself to listen because the Herbal Man was an enigma, describing things and places she'd never heard of beyond Harbin's confines, a larger world she'd only glimpsed in the dragonwarriors' stories and ballads. 'Where is Ilyastral?' she interrupted at one point.

'Was,' the Herbal Man corrected. 'It was a city built in the forests of Janiya, but it no longer exists.'

'Why not?'

'Barbarians destroyed it.'

'Why?'

'Greed, mainly. Ilyastral was a cultural centre for artists, musicians, poets, philosophers, but it also owned a lot of gold, and the gold attracted the wrong people. One day an army came, killed the people, took the gold and tore down the city, and for good measure they torched the forest. All that remained of Ilyastral were ashes and legends.'

'But that's wrong,' Tam complained. She had no idea what poets and philosophers were, but her sense of justice was affronted by the city's wanton destruction.

'It might be wrong,' he agreed, 'but, sadly, that's the way of the world. The greedy and powerful prey on everyone else. It even happens in Harbin.'

'What do you mean?'

The Herbal Man hesitated, before saying, 'That's how some things are. But now it's time for sleeping.' He indicated that she should return to bed, and concluded with, 'Tomorrow, we will see what the weather brings. For now, you need more rest.'

She let him bundle her back to the bedroom, but her curiosity burned as to what he meant about Harbin, especially who he thought was greedy and preying on others. When she broached the topic, he avoided a straight answer with, 'Some things are best left alone.' He offered for her to have a candle clock by her bed, which she readily accepted, but she was dissatisfied he evaded her question.

As she undressed and climbed into bed, she speculated on who could be labelled a 'barbarian' in Harbin, someone capable of destroying a place like Ilyastral. Her first choice was Marron. He held the potential to pillage and burn beautiful things, but she doubted the old man was referring to him because the Herbal Man wouldn't know what Marron had been doing. It couldn't be anyone in the Dragon Fang. The warriors fought dragons, bringing treasures to everyone from the hoards, and what they did was traditional and honourable beyond reproach. So, to whom was the old man referring?

The conundrum teased her as she snuggled into the bedclothes. The Herbal Man was full of puzzles, more puzzles than answers, and she needed the answers. She tried to reason through all possibilities as she lay staring at the candle clock flame, but the combination of exhaustion, the dancing flame and the bed's cosiness rapidly drew her into a deep, restful sleep.

Fifteen

'This is the symbol for the sound "ah",' he explained as he demonstrated. 'If the sound "ah" is written as part of a word, this is how it is written. If you see this symbol, you know how it should be spoken.' He rewrote the symbol slowly, so that Tam could grasp the pattern and process before he handed her the quill. 'Now practise,' he instructed. He observed her stumble through her first effort, giving advice on how to improve her technique and the shape, before he moved to work on a different project.

Tam hunched over the parchment and scratched at it, painstakingly copying the flow and curl of the "ah" letter. It was the eighteenth symbol he taught her, learning them at the rate of five per day, and he expected her to remember the order of the symbols in a list he called an "alphabet." There were thirty-two symbols to learn. She was already memorising whole words from the labels affixed to the abundant pots and jars on the shelves and she understood it was how the Herbal Man identified pots and jars that looked identical, even though they contained different powders.

As far as she knew, no one in Harbin could read or write, and yet everyone went about their lives without needing either, so she wondered what the real use was for reading and writing. Learning the skills was tedious, repetitive, as bad as her mother teaching her how to weave baskets, or gut fish, and she only persevered because the skills were new to her and she had nothing else to do while the weather outside the Herbal Man's underground hideaway remained foul.

The storm was still raging after nine days. The Herbal Man told her the weather deteriorated since her arrival, and she gathered from his unspoken emotion that the storm was worse than he was accustomed to. He previously warned there was no point attempting to leave via the trapdoor into the old hut because snowdrifts buried the building and caused the roof to collapse, so she was curious how he knew what the conditions outside were like, given that he apparently never left the underground shelter.

'How will we get out?' she asked.

'There are other ways,' he said.

She was yet to see any, but perhaps there were doors she hadn't discovered. The compensation for being confined in the Herbal Man's underground home was that it was constantly warm, tolerable even when the hearth wasn't alight. If she was weathering the storm in her home, she would be huddling with her mother and Jaysin by the hearth, rugged up under worn blankets to keep out the bitter cold.

'Tomorrow night is Blitzart's Feast,' the Herbal Man announced when he checked to see how Tam was progressing with her writing. As he stood beside her to critically appraise her letter formation, he asked, 'What did you do with the ring?'

Tam looked up and saw the shadow of concern on his brow. 'I gave it to Jaysin and made him promise he would give it to Gramma if I couldn't,' she tentatively explained.

'When did you give it to Jaysin?'

'Before I left. I didn't know what else to do. I wasn't sure what I was going to do, or where I was going to be. I didn't want to break the promise I made to you.'

The Herbal Man frowned and moved away a couple of paces, scratching his beard meditatively. 'Are you certain Jaysin will remember?' he asked.

'I made him promise,' was all Tam could offer in reply. She suddenly felt annoyed with herself for running away from home and leaving such an important responsibility in the hand of her little brother. Her decision was too hasty, too selfish. 'I nearly put the ring on her finger before – before I came here,' she admitted.

'I'm glad you didn't,' he said sternly, still frowning. 'It would have not been the right time. These things can only be done when the time is right.'

'I don't understand,' she said.

'How was Harmi before you left?' he asked, ignoring Tam's comment, but his tone softened.

'She was sleeping, although she woke when a gust of wind rattled everything.'

'Ah,' he said, nodding. 'Did she say anything?'

Tam shook her head. 'Not really?'

'Nothing at all?'

She wondered why he was so concerned with what her grandmother said. Harmi's last utterings were embarrassing to repeat. 'She only mumbled something about dragons never forgetting,' she confessed shyly, and she quickly qualified it with, 'But she always babbles about dragons.'

'Does she?' the Herbal Man asked, and a faint smile flickered on his face, but he suppressed it with a solemn expression and said, 'I wish you told me this before.'

'You didn't ask.'

The Herbal Man nodded and held out his hand for the quill. 'Now you can learn the letter "th",' he said, and he scribed the new symbol on the parchment.

Tam sighed and returned to the lesson, but the mystery of the ring and the Herbal Man's response to her grandmother's ramblings plagued her mind throughout the afternoon and into the evening, until sleep discovered her.

The Herbal Man seemed chirpier than usual when Tam woke the next morning. As she dressed in a silver silk robe, she heard him singing a ballad in the adjoining study, and when she emerged he was dancing around the bench holding a couple of jars.

'Good morning, Tamesan!' he sang. 'Breakfast is waiting in the cooking pot. Eat up. I have work for you this morning.' He danced past her into the bedroom and closed the door.

Bemused, Tam scooped a ladle of warm cereal from the pot, and as she ate she tried to guess why the Herbal Man was so happy.

He returned as she finished eating, carrying a wooden pail. 'Finished?' he inquired, and answered his own question with, 'Good!' He produced a set of keys on a large metal key ring, singled out a brass key, and said, 'Take this key and go through the door in the bedroom. This key opens another door on the left side of the corridor. Fetch a fresh bucket of milk.' He smiled as he handed Tam the pail. Surprised by his jocular mood and the request, she hesitated, so he prompted, 'Go on. If we're going to celebrate Blitzart's Feast, we should do so in style,' and he added, 'Take a lantern too.'

Inquisitiveness piqued, Tam took the keys and pail, picked up a lantern, and left the study. She had already wondered what lay beyond the locked door in the bedroom and now she was going to find out. If she was fetching milk, then she reasoned the door led outside, perhaps to a goat pen. She didn't consider the Herbal Man might keep animals. If she was fetching goat milk, it also meant the storm must have abated.

Tam opened the door leading from the bedroom and discovered a narrow corridor, cutting deeper into the mountain rock, as the Herbal Man said there would be. Several paces in, however, she found three doors, not one. There was a door to the left, but also another to the right, and one in the end of the corridor. She held up the lantern to study all three and then tried the handles. All three were locked.

Her curiosity tingled. She had the keys. She had time because goat milking wasn't a quick task. She looked back along the corridor to see if the Herbal Man was following, but the corridor was empty. She put down the lantern and fumbled with the keys, trying each one in the central door lock, but oddly none fitted. When she repeated the process on the right door, she found one that did fit. She unlocked it, collected the lantern and opened the door.

The space was dark, but as she took a step into it the feeble yellow lantern light seemed to leap outward and splash across the chamber, exploding into a rainbow of colours as it touched and radiated from myriad multifaceted crystals embedded in the walls and ceiling. Tam was so dazzled by the sudden and vivid display of green, red, blue and gold light that she almost dropped the lantern, but she steadied and squinted until her eyes adjusted to take in the details.

The entire ceiling was a mass of crystals, as was the wall to her right. The wall crystals were smooth and flat, but those in the ceiling were jagged and protruded in acute angles. The curved wall directly ahead glowed with a dark golden hue, and it was tessellated like the rocks at the base of the cliffs at Watersdrop. To her left, the wall was filled with volumes of the objects that she knew the Herbal Man called books, neatly stacked in shelves, so many she couldn't even estimate the number. The chamber's centre was occupied by a stone pedestal and a large circular mat covered the floor.

She tentatively crept forward until she could see that the top of the pedestal was hollowed into a shallow bowl containing a shimmering liquid. The pattern on the mat at her feet perfectly imitated the light and face of the full moon, as if the moon had fallen onto the floor of this strange room.

She sensed movement and a shiver thrilled through her spine. She looked at the golden wall. *I'm not meant to be in here*, she reminded herself, so she cautiously backed out of the chamber, closed and locked the door, and sighed with relief. *Fear made me imagine it*, she silently told herself. *The idea is absurd*. Yet, in the briefest instant, she thought the golden wall moved – as if it breathed. She trembled at the notion and chided herself for being foolish. The chamber's crystal light shimmered so erratically anything would appear to be moving. 'Walls don't breathe,' she whispered. She examined the keys and selected the brass one to unlock the left door.

The chamber she entered had a low ceiling and reeked of goat. Her lantern twisted shadows on the cavern walls, giving the space an eerie aspect and eyes glittered at the edge of the light. 'Come on,' she crooned. 'Come on.' One animal took a wary step towards her, but the other shadows waited timidly. 'Come on,' Tam crooned again and she held out her free hand.

Reassured by her voice and gesture, the first goat approached, nose lifted in expectation of a food reward, and the others came into the light. She had no food, but she rubbed the proffered muzzles as she moved among the herd, feeling for the nannies with swollen udders.

When she found the first, Tam squatted to milking and was pleased with the way the nanny accepted her touch. In Harbin, every girl knew how to milk goats. It was part of the growing into womanhood process, as important as learning how to sew and cook, and she enjoyed it more than most tasks because of the animal's closeness and trust.

As she milked the Herbal Man's goats, she became aware of a cold breeze in the cavern, so when she finished the third animal, the pail half full, she lifted the container out of the goats' reach, took up the lantern and searched for the source. She discovered a narrow cleft behind a thick stack of stalactites at the rear of the cavern that opened into a low tunnel. She dropped to her hands and knees and crawled along the downward slope. Rising wind threatened to extinguish the lantern, so she pushed it aside to retrieve on her return and continued into the darkness.

A short distance on, the tunnel levelled, and her fingers sank into wet snow. She scrambled through the entrance into a dark, cold, wild world where the winter storm was as ferocious as ever. Wet, shaking from the chill, she retreated into the tunnel, retrieved the lantern, and crawled to the goat cavern, grateful to be embraced by its warmth. The animals had a wonderful refuge, better than the wooden shelters their kin shared on the outskirts of Harbin. She collected the pail of goat's milk, locked the door, and hurried along the corridor towards the comforting light of the Herbal Man's chambers.

'Wonderful!' the Herbal Man cried when she entered the study. She expected him to ask why she was soaked, but he took the pail, declaring, 'Today, there will be no formal reading or writing lessons or work! Today, we prepare dishes for Blitzart's Feast!' He glanced at her again and said, 'Best wash and change your clothes.'

'Why do they call it the Mad Wizards' Dance?' she asked, as she filled a pot to warm water over the hearth.

The Herbal Man paused, as if considering alternative answers, before he smiled, and said, 'A long time ago, Tamesan, there lived people called wizards. They always held an annual meeting, this time of year, and all the wizards journeyed from their homes to attend. At the gathering, after the formal business was completed, they would challenge each other to out-trick one another, and so the gatherings were mostly for playing practical jokes and laughing. People who weren't wizards, who saw and heard the events, called them mad, and in time the annual gathering was called the Mad Wizards' Dance. Actually, the Mad Wizards' Dance lasted two weeks.'

'I thought the celebration was always called Blitzart's Feast?'

'Dragon's fire, no!' he exclaimed. 'It was called the Mad Wizards' Dance long before your ancestors settled in Harbin, but your ancestors had no wizards, and Blitzart's breath lies heavy in this part of the world, so they changed the name.'

Tam dipped her hands in the warm water and began to wash her forearms. 'Tell me about the wizards,' she urged.

'Ah,' he muttered, and shook his head. 'Wizards. Now that's not an easy story to tell. When you can read for yourself, I'll show you the books that will tell you a great deal about them.'

'But what did they do?' she asked.

The old man shuffled through a pile of parchments on the benchtop as he spoke. 'Wizards mainly studied things. They were people who studied the stars, the earth, animals, plants, water, people. They studied patterns and laws, ideas and philosophies. What they didn't already know, they wanted to learn. They met to share knowledge and consider issues, parted and met again. They wanted to know everything about everything.'

Tam bathed her legs and feet and listened while the Herbal Man explained how wizards travelled many lands, acquiring mysterious knowledge and arts, and how great kings and queens sought them, and employed them, and even bowed to them because they knew more than any living person. His words washed over as she left the study to change her robe, and she listened through the door, amused that he kept talking even when she wasn't immediately near him. He was still relating his tale when she emerged and began organising cooking utensils, but she interrupted when he mentioned dragons.

'What did you say?' she asked.

The Herbal Man blinked, and repeated, 'They were dependent on them.'

'Before that,' she prompted.

He scratched his head. 'Each one had a dragon, but they're all gone now?'

'Yes,' she said. 'What do you mean by "they're all gone now"?'

'Exactly what I said,' he answered, nonplussed.

'Do you mean there are no more dragons, or no more wizards?'

'There are no more of either,' he replied. 'Dragons and wizards were mutually dependent. What one thought, so did the other. What one felt, the other felt. Two lives, one essence. So, when the last wizard died, so did the last dragon.'

'But there are dragons,' Tam contended.

'Not in this world.' The Herbal Man saw Tam's bewildered expression and said, 'It's a legend, nothing more, a story about wizards and why we call it the Mad Wizards' Dance.' He pointed at a shelf, changing topic, and asked, 'Have you cooked with exotic herbs?'

The day dissolved in a flurry of cooking, subverting Tam's inquisitive questions about wizards and dragons. Cooking with Eesa and the women in Harbin was a boring chore, but the Herbal Man introduced her to a fascinating and new range of herbal recipes. Every time he returned from his storeroom, he brought a new culinary wonder, an ingredient to alter the flavour, the smell and the colour of the food. Among all the food, she noted there wasn't a shred of meat, a fact that surprised her because goat, poultry and game meats were at the centre of Harbin celebrations.

When Tam mentioned the absence of meat, the Herbal Man laughed and said, 'The forest garden provides all the food I ever need. Why would I kill living creatures to eat meat?'

The concept of a meatless diet fascinated Tam, and she pondered its ramifications as they worked.

By evening, according to a candle clock, the preparation was done. The hearth fire was roaring, and across the Herbal Man's bench was spread a banquet worthy of ten people. They cleaned the dishes and cutlery used in the preparation, and then the Herbal Man cried, 'To the feast! Let the madmen dance away the night!'

Tam was worried that her appetite would be diminished by working all day with the food, but the moment she tasted the first dish her hunger returned with vengeance, and she ate heartily.

When they ate their fill, the Herbal Man excused himself from the room, but he returned carrying two large golden goblets. He polished them with his sleeve, until they shone, held them up to glisten in the light, and said, grinning, 'Real dragon's gold!' He passed a goblet to Tam, went to the hearth, collected a pot he left mulling at the edge, returned and poured a white steaming liquid into Tam's goblet before filling his own. 'Honey milk,' he explained, as she sniffed the sweet aroma. 'In the kingdom of Hatua, it is called the nectar of the gods, fit only for royalty to drink. Poor people caught drinking it are beheaded in the marketplace.' He sipped and indicated that Tam should do likewise.

Her stomach full, a warm fire raging in the hearth, her head fuzzy with honey milk, Tam struggled to stay awake. She drifted to the floor on the rug lying before the hearth and listened to the Herbal Man's voice fade in and out as he told a tale of a young wizard with an equally young dragon companion. The pair were notorious for constantly getting into scrapes with the law and with the rulers of the land. If there was an ending to the story, she didn't care. Somewhere along the journey she slipped into another realm, a world full of soft edges and contentment, and the comfortable blanket of sleep.

Tam woke, confused, to a world glowing red, until she realised the hue came from dying embers in the hearth. She was still on the hearth rug, but the lanterns were out and a solitary candle clock flickered in the far corner. She shivered as she sat up, even though the chamber was cosy. There was no sign of the Herbal Man, not even in his makeshift bed in the study. She crept into the bed chamber, but the bed was empty. Despite her extraordinary weariness, a buzzing curiosity as to where the old man was infested her thoughts.

Tam approached the door that led deeper into the mountain, fumbled in the dark for the handle, and eased the door open. Light from the crystal chamber spilled into the corridor from the right-side doorway, and a sudden chill knifed through her. She shook her head to clear her mind, and to test if she was awake, or merely caught in a vivid dream. It seemed real. Summoning her courage, she crept through the darkness towards the light. Closer, she heard a voice – no – two voices. She recognised the Herbal Man's voice, and the woman's voice was uncannily familiar.

'And then you wouldn't believe it,' the Herbal Man said, and laughed, and so did the woman.

'Eric, you teased me until I cried,' the woman replied. 'There's no such thing, I said, no such thing.'

'Claryssa was terribly upset,' the Herbal Man declared. 'Dragons have immense pride, you know.'

'So I learned,' admitted the woman. 'Procra bless her.'

Tam knew the woman was her grandmother. Her voice was the same as she remembered hearing it the day the Herbal Man visited Harmi in the village. Somehow, despite the storm, her grandmother was in the chamber. She burst in, expecting to see Harmi, but the light within was so intense she was momentarily blinded. 'Gramma!' she cried excitedly.

As her eyes adjusted, she saw the Herbal Man shrouded in flowing white robes, bent over the pedestal, staring into the shining water, and the vivid light radiating from the surrounding crystals seemed to flow through him. He lifted his head at the sound of her cry, and stared, at first with surprise, and then with profound sadness. Astonished by the vision, she felt weak at her knees, and as she stumbled forward the image filling her mind was of a great golden eye gazing at her from the far wall.

Sixteen

The Herbal Man encouraged Tam to laboriously transcribe texts every morning while he worked with herbs and chemicals or read books from his library. Every afternoon, he made her read short passages to him and memorise specific words and phrases. His teachings originally held her interest because they were new, different, but she was becoming bored by the repetition. The only compensation was that the Herbal Man seemed to anticipate the point at which she was about to tell him she'd had enough, because he would interrupt whatever task she was doing and give her an entirely different one, like marking candle clocks or mixing an elixir.

Tam resented that he left the cleaning jobs to her. She made the beds, washed the cooking and experiment utensils, and tidied the workspace at the end of every day. She fetched goats' milk in the morning and fed the goats every night, and she had no free time to herself. She felt as trapped in mundane work with the Herbal Man as she did with her mother in Harbin.

Every time Tam entered the corridor to work with the goats, she passed the chamber door and it teased her memory. She was unsure what she witnessed on Blitzart's Feast eve. It was indistinct, a half-remembered dream. She thought she heard Gramma Harmi's voice and saw the Herbal Man immersed in bright light – or was she confusing it with her memory from when he found her in the snow?

She planned to return to the chamber the night following Blitzart's Feast to refresh her memory, but the Herbal Man annoyingly removed the door key from the key ring. Because everything was fuzzy in her mind, she held back from asking him directly about the night, but she hoped that he would mention it, thereby giving her an avenue for asking questions. He didn't. His only reference was the morning after, when she woke with a vague headache and dizziness, and he simply asked if she enjoyed the meal. He also said that he carried her to the bed because she fell asleep on the hearth rug, but he didn't mention the crystal chamber. Only the key's removal gave her assurance that what she thought she witnessed did happen. But she did have one vivid memory – the golden eye in the end wall.

Eight days after Blitzart's Feast, the Herbal Man woke Tam with news that the storm was over. 'Put on warm clothes and come outside,' he invited. 'Time for fresh air.'

She dressed and followed him into the corridor, but instead of entering the goat cave, as she anticipated, the old man pulled a key ring from his robe and unlocked the centre door. He swung it open, lifted his lantern, and said, 'Through you go.'

The corridor widened and branched into three arched openings, and the lantern exposed an array of intricately carved leering goblin faces above the portals. The central arch led straight into the mountain and the right dropped into the mountain's depths, but the Herbal Man led Tam to the left, a steeply rising stone stairway. 'Where do the other tunnels go?' she asked as they ascended.

'Down and in,' he cryptically replied.

'Exactly where?' she persisted, annoyed by his inadequate answer.

He chuckled, before saying, 'Ask your questions when we get outside. I'll answer what I can answer then.'

She wanted to protest, but she acquiesced, and she determined to pursue the questions gnawing at her when they emerged on the mountainside, especially questions about the crystal cave.

The stairway zig-zagged up four flights before levelling in a large, oval cavern, worn so smooth that the walls and ceiling glistened in the lantern light. A portion of the rear wall was blackened by soot and a hollow in the floor by the wall seemed to have served as a fire pit. The rest of the walls were decorated with line drawings.

Tam approached one drawing and identified a bear and an animal with horns protruding from its muzzle. Smaller human figures with spears clustered around the horned animal.

'Interesting, aren't they?' the Herbal Man observed as he joined her. 'These drawings are older than anyone knows.'

'Who drew them?' Tam asked.

'Probably a tribal arm of the Dawn People.'

'Who are the Dawn People?'

'The first people who lived in the lands,' said the Herbal Man. 'They are given different names in different places, but mostly it's what they are called. I was surprised to find their art in a cave this far north when I arrived, because they preferred to live in warmer lands, but perhaps it was warmer here in the past.'

'It's always been cold here,' Tam asserted.

'In your time, and even in Nakiades' time,' the Herbal Man agreed. 'Perhaps even for a long time before. But not always, Tamesan. Nothing is for always, except the Eternal Laws, and change is an Eternal Law. There are philosophers who argue that change may be the only Eternal Law.'

She listened, but she decided he was rambling again. He frequently spoke of philosophers and laws when he broached odd ideas, ideas that raised more questions to plague her mind. She was contemplating what he meant by an "Eternal Law" when he tugged her arm.

'Come on,' he urged. 'There's sunshine outside and we should be in it.'

Tam followed the Herbal Man through the large cavern, past an immense pile of bones, into a short tunnel and then outside, but she was so accustomed to the gloom and lantern light in the Herbal Man's underground retreat that the daylight dazzled her.

The bright blue sky was pocked with puffy white clouds and the sun shone defiantly. She stood on a broad ledge on the face of Dragon Mountain, higher than she ever ventured, and she could see out to the endless expanse of the great western ocean. The world was a vista of white and blue – water, sky, snow and clouds. She could not see Harbin buried beneath the white mantle of winter at the base of the mountain. She sucked in the brittle fresh air and its purity stung her throat. 'It's beautiful,' she murmured.

'A rare morning,' the Herbal Man agreed. 'If I was religious, I would be praising the gods for this moment.'

'What do you mean "if you were religious"?'

The Herbal Man chuckled and scratched his head, looked at her and asked, 'Do you know what religion is?'

She shook her head.

'Ah,' he exhaled. 'How do I explain this?' He shook his head, before saying, 'Religion is to do with gods and goddesses.'

'Do you mean you don't believe in Varst or Procra?' she ventured.

He tilted his head with a pained expression. 'I do, in a way, and in another way I don't.'

'That doesn't make sense.'

'It's not as silly as it might sound,' he proposed. 'The dragons are like gods and goddesses to your people, but I don't believe beings exist like Varst or Procra, or Shaddho. There's no logic to their existence. The old wizards studied and researched and argued over the religious concept of gods for thousands of years, but not one of them could prove their existence.'

'But Procra made all of this,' Tam argued, spreading her arms grandly to embrace the world. 'And great Varst breathed life into everything. He brought the dragons into existence.'

'Is that what you believe, Tamesan?'

'Yes.'

'Ah,' he breathed again, pausing before continuing. 'Then, for you,

Varst is real. Procra is real. They are real because you believe in them.'

'Then why don't you believe in them if they exist?'

The Herbal Man smiled vaguely. 'Tamesan, do you believe in The One Eternal Being?'

'Who?'

'The people of the Karmin Empire believe in The One Eternal Being. He, or she – no one knows for certain which gender, if either – is their god. The One Eternal Being creates all and destroys all: Maker and Unmaker. Do you believe in The One Eternal Being?'

'No,' Tam replied. 'I've never heard of it.'

'Precisely. And the Karmin have never heard of Varst or Procra. Just as the Weremouth Tribes, with their two thousand gods and goddesses, have never heard of The One Eternal Being.'

'That's ridiculous!' Tam exclaimed. 'How can there be two thousand gods and goddesses?'

'Why not? Who is to say your belief is any more valid than theirs? Have you ever seen Varst?'

Tam hesitated, before reluctantly admitting, 'Well, no. But I know he's real.'

'You have faith, as most religions call it. And it is the basis for all religions. Because you believe something, it must be true.'

'Then why don't you believe?'

'What you believe is true for you. What I believe is true for me. The universe is full of individual truths.'

The old man talks in endless, confusing riddles, she decided, but Tam persisted by asking, 'Are they the "universal truths" you mentioned before?'

'Some say they are, and some say they are not.'

'And you?' she pressed, determined to get a straight answer.

The Herbal Man squatted on a granite rock jutting from the snow and stared into the middle distance. 'I think the gods, whoever believes in them, have their uses; some good, some bad. I believe in the belief in gods, but I do not believe in the gods themselves. They are a universal truth containing no truth.'

His answer was no answer for Tam, so she stared into the hazy blue distance to see what he was studying, but the world was void of any meaning beyond light, colour and the cold. Silence settled between the pair on the mountain, until Tam broke it by reminding him, 'You said you would answer my questions when we got outside.'

The Herbal Man turned his head and replied, 'I did. What do you want to ask?'

She had so many unanswered questions, so many unsolved puzzles since meeting the Herbal Man, that she paused, wondering what to ask first. She wanted to avoid offending him, remembering that every time she asked important questions at home either her mother scolded her for being disrespectful or her father dismissed the question as unimportant. There was also the issue that the Herbal Man always answered in frustrating riddles and all she wanted were plain answers. 'Were you talking with Gramma Harmi on Blitzart's Feast?' she asked.

The Herbal Man stared at her, his grey eyes shining in the brittle daylight, his face emotionless, and Tam felt that she had asked a foolish, inappropriate question. She meant to qualify it by admitting that she thought she dreamed it, so she started to apologise, but the Herbal Man cut her off. 'Yes. I spoke with Harmi.'

His admission startled Tam, not only because it confirmed what she believed she heard, but also because it opened the path to many more questions concerning the crystal cave.

'Do you want to know how it was possible, how I could speak to Harmi when we are here and she is still in Harbin?' he asked.

She nodded.

'The ring and the Seeing Waters,' the Herbal Man explained. 'The ring I sent to Harmi is a conduit, and you'll be pleased to know Jaysin kept his promise. He is a rare child.'

Tam's mind whirled with questions – *What are the Seeing Waters*? *How can a ring help the Herbal Man and Harmi talk to each other*? – and each question raised a fresh crop of new questions. *Where to start*? she wondered. 'You told me there used to be wizards,' she said, 'so why aren't there any left?'

The Herbal Man cocked his bushy white eyebrow, as if he didn't expect that question, cleared his throat, and replied, 'People grew suspicious and envious of them. Kings and emperors were threatened by their power. Religious leaders were angered by their questioning of beliefs. Ordinary people were frightened of their dragons. So laws were passed to dissuade wizards from living in the great cities to prevent them influencing masses of people, and their universities, schools and libraries were either pulled down or turned into barracks for soldiers. They were encouraged to adopt low profiles and live in isolation.'

'Why didn't they protest?'

'Some did,' he replied. 'Some petitioned the rulers for leniency. Some organised protest marches through the streets. Some barricaded themselves in the universities and libraries and refused to leave. The irony was that most wizards preferred to live in isolation outside the cities because they could concentrate on their research without regular or noisy interruptions. Only a minority exerted power and influence in the cities, the hungry ones, the ones whose research led into the Dark Arts. They believed in gods and goddesses, and demons and devils, and they tried to make them real in different ways. Because their aims were financial and political, they protested loudest against the new laws and they plotted and carried out violent, evil acts against those who stood in their way, but their actions only served to make wizards hated more than ever. New laws were issued in many countries banning wizardry altogether. Wizards were outlawed, hunted, hanged and burned at the stake, whether they were peaceful or not.'

'Didn't they resist?' Tam asked.

'Yes. Some did. There were wars and battles in different lands. The most decisive was a battle in the Hayge Valley, aptly named the Massacre of Dragons. It was a long and bloody battle between the Emperor Jorg of Ilrympia and the Confederation of Wizards. Both armies were evenly matched, until the wizards were betrayed by one of their own.'

'What did the traitor do?' Tam asked, intrigued by the tale.

'Ethan – he was the traitor – was offered freedom and glory if he helped Jorg defeat the dragons, so he drugged his fellow wizards at dinnertime and put them in a deep sleep. The Emperor's soldiers crept into the camp and cut off the wizards' heads.'

'And the dragons?'

The Herbal Man cast her a meaningful look.

'They died because the wizards died,' Tam corrected, remembering what she learned. 'What happened to Ethan?'

The Herbal Man snorted contemptuously. 'Jorg let him and his dragon live in the Imperial capital for a year and a day after the Massacre, and then Ethan was killed in the same way. It was crude justice, really.'

'What happened to the wizards who didn't fight?'

'They fled into the wildernesses. Many were hunted down and slain in the early years. Those who found isolated strongholds and refuges outlived several generations of their enemies, but they eventually grew old and died.'

'All of them?'

'Yes.'

Tam took a deep breath because the Herbal Man's answer contradicted what she knew to be true. 'If all the wizards died, how come there are still dragons?'

'There are no more dragons, Tamesan,' he refuted. 'The last observed dragon disappeared more than two hundred years ago.'

'I know it's not true and so do you,' she argued. 'The Dragon Fang kill dragons every summer. There are lots of dragons left.'

The Herbal Man shook his head and stared into the horizon again. 'Some things are best left alone, Tamesan,' he warned. 'If you believe there are dragons to be hunted, then there are dragons.'

'What is that supposed to mean?' she demanded.

'I've told you what I know. It is the truth as I believe it to be. I know there are no more wizards, and without wizards there cannot be dragons. Among wizards, it was a kind of universal law. Perhaps it is wrong. Perhaps it's only true for me because I believe it.'

'Like I believe Varst exists?'

The Herbal Man nodded appreciatively, saying, 'You learn quickly.'

'But I know there are dragons,' she insisted.

'Have you seen one?'

'No,' she admitted. 'But my father has. And so have the dragonwarriors. They've all seen dragons.'

'Then we believe different truths, Tamesan. Some argue truth is an indisputable concept, but I've always contended that truth is a matter of perception. It's not a bad thing. Remember, I think religious beliefs produce much good, even though I do not hold those beliefs as being true for me. I guess it means that you have to say dragons still exist – for you,' the Herbal Man concluded.

'Have you seen a dragon?' Tam asked.

The Herbal Man allowed a wry smile to play along his mouth, as he replied, 'I have.' He clasped his arms and stood. 'It is getting too cold to stay out here, philosophising on religion and world history. I think warm broth is in order, and then we'll come outside again to collect a batch of herbs while the weather remains pleasant. You have a lot yet to learn, my young friend, and this winter is nearly done.'

Seventeen

Chasse adjusted his balance, shifted his grip on his blunt point-heavy spear and watched Derin's hips for movement for a clue as to his next move.

'Watch his left shoulder, boy,' Theo growled.

'Be patient,' warned another voice.

The youths circled, heeding advice, as voices urged them to engage.

'Come on! This isn't a dance festival!'

'Take him, Derin! Take him now!'

'Go low, Chasse! Hit him low!'

Chasse enjoyed fighting when it was a game, but this was more than a game for the initiates. All winter they lived in the Warriors' Hall, learning how to care for their weapons and armour, learning how to fight, learning how to obey experienced warriors like Theo, or Trask or Kevan, but winter's hard training was ending, and the spring melt was underway. Soon summer and the dragonship would carry them south to adventures and manhood.

They were also learning how to earn status among the dragonwarriors – the better a warrior fought, the higher the warrior's status. Marron established himself as the best of the initiates because he fought hardest, and what he sometimes lacked in technique he compensated for with bloodlust and strength.

Only Chasse came close to beating Marron among the initiates, but it was because Chasse was motivated by a slow-burning hatred spawned by Marron's deliberate humiliation of his sister and himself. *One day*, he decided, *I will turn the tables*. Inspired by the thought, Chasse feinted forward and low, then swung his spear high towards Derin's left shoulder. Derin dodged, stepped right, and brought the shaft of his spear across the back of Chasse's unprotected legs with a resounding whack. Chasse yelped and leapt back, barely escaping Derin's second swing, the shaft whistling past his left ear. He spun to meet the stabbing attack he anticipated would follow, but Derin surprised him by viciously kicking his knee. Knocked off-balance, Chasse barely blocked a flurry of blows, and when Derin feinted high he made a mistake to block, allowing Derin to stab him solidly in the sternum. The blow sent Chasse reeling into the circle of spectators amid a rousing cheer.

'Derin is the victor!' Theo announced, and he stepped forward to clap his big hand on Derin's shoulder.

The herdsman's son grinned proudly and offered to help Chasse to his feet as a show of respect which Chasse graciously accepted. Losing was embarrassing, but Chasse considered Derin to be a good friend and a worthy opponent.

Two new combatants stepped into the circle, older dragonwarriors eager to hone their skills, and Chasse was about to settle against the wall with Derin to watch the fight when a young boy burst through the main door. The boy went straight to Kevan, spoke, and the reaction on his father's weathered face warned Chasse that something was amiss. He pushed to his feet, rubbing the bruising on his chest as he watched Kevan speak to Theo, and when Kevan strode towards the door he gestured to Chasse, ordering, 'Come with me.'

Chasse half-jogged to keep pace with his father, with no opportunity to ask what happened, as Kevan headed for their home. They crossed the surging water of Watersdrop, fed by the fresh snowmelt from Dragon Mountain, and Eesa met them at the cottage door. A tacit message passed between the adults, before Chasse followed his father inside where he was astonished to see his sister, Tamesan, standing by the table. He heard Kevan swallow, before he asked, 'Where have you been?'

'With the Herbal Man,' Tam replied.

Chasse's attention was caught by movement in the room's darker corner. Sitting in Gramma Harmi's favourite chair was a familiar white-haired, dark-robed figure, and Kevan, also aware of the Herbal Man's presence, turned to him for an explanation.

The Herbal Man rose and said, 'I found her in the snow on the mountain. It was lucky I was caught out in the storm or else she might not have been so fortunate. As it was, she nearly died from exposure.'

'Why didn't you let us know?' Kevan demanded, but he knew the storm buried the mountain and the village beneath deep snow, making the paths impassable, so he waved the Herbal Man aside before he could reply, by saying, 'It's a foolish question and I apologise – but this vision of a daughter that we believed was devoured by Blitzart's cold maw overwhelms me. I – I am caught between joy and astonishment. I should be making you welcome for what you have done.'

Chasse watched his father stumble through his emotions, having never seen him so confused, and he saw Tam come forward and embrace their father. Kevan winced, but his reaction was fleeting, and he enfolded his daughter in his arms. 'Procra has indeed blessed this child,' he said, and he glanced at Eesa, who was leaning against the door frame, softly crying.

The Herbal Man refused to stay in Harbin, despite Kevan and Eesa's offers. He visited individuals who requested treatment for minor ailments before he left the village on the pretext of being busy. Tam heard from a fisherman that he was seen near the jetty talking to her little brother, Jaysin, and the last time she saw him he was speaking with Kevan on the village outskirts. She knew he was saddened by Harmi's death during the winter, as she was, and she guessed he couldn't stay in the place where she lived. She cried in the night, after she heard the news from Eesa, angry with herself for leaving her grandmother and sad to have missed singing the Words of Passage for Gramma Harmi.

Tam spent her first day in the village with Chasse. He was keen to hear her adventurous tale; of being lost in the storm, of being rescued in a halo of shining light. She explained what she could of her lessons with the Herbal Man and she scratched words in the earth to demonstrate her budding writing skill. Chasse was impressed with the writing, although he saw no purpose to it.

She couldn't tell Chasse about the Herbal Man's underground home or the tunnels in the mountain, because the Herbal Man wanted those matters kept secret. When she pressed the Herbal Man for his reasons, he answered, 'I am a simple herbalist and a hermit, Tamesan. That's how your world knows me and that is how it should stay. I ask you to keep this secret and in exchange I will teach you my trade.'

She respected his request, reminding herself that, even if he was eccentric, he was a healer who helped many people in Harbin, but her knowledge of the ring and the Seeing Waters made her wary of trusting him completely, and fuelled her determination to unravel his mysteries.

Tam observed the changes in her older brother who was coming from spending the winter weeks in the Warriors' Hall. He was taller, his arm and chest muscles were more defined, he possessed more bulk overall, and she saw the man emerging from the gangly youth, and this made him partly a stranger to her. He told her about his training and what he was learning, and she could hear his enthusiasm. He explained how Marron had already gained status among the dragonwarriors, and how Kevan and Trask constantly bickered over the Dragon Fang leadership. He gave her sketchy detail of the struggles that villagers endured during the excessive snowfalls and constant storms, and how Sharmine and her crones predicted Blitzart's revenge on Nakiades' children with a long, cruel winter.

'And you know Gramma died in her sleep during Blitzart's Feast,'

Chasse said. 'Mother said Gramma was unusually happy on Blitzart's Feast eve, brighter than she'd been for many years.'

Tam nodded, but she immediately thought of what happened between the Herbal Man and her grandmother, and asked, 'Did anything odd happen?'

Chasse met her gaze, and replied, 'Yes.' He paused for her to explain why she asked her question, but she waited for him to continue, so he said, 'The storm kept everyone inside, so there was only Mother, Gramma and Jaysin home. Mother swore that, later in the night after they were all meant to be asleep, she heard Gramma talking to someone in the main room, but when she went to the room she found Gramma sitting in her favourite chair, quite dead.'

'Did she say who she thought Gramma was talking to?'

'No,' Chasse replied. 'Why would you ask?'

'I thought Mother might have said.'

Chasse shook his head. 'She didn't say who it was. Jaysin was upset. He still is. Mother coaxed him to eat, and now he keeps even more to himself than ever.'

'I missed her passing,' Tam said forlornly.

'We held a ceremony at Watersdrop during a break in the storm. She wasn't the only one we sang the Words of Passage for. Marc died. There was a little stillborn baby. And old Asmae. She froze to death.' Chasse looked at Tam. 'We buried you, too. We thought you froze to death on the mountain.'

'I'm sorry,' she said.

'Everyone searched for you. The Dragon Fang even searched during the storm. Everyone knew no one could survive on the mountain in foul weather, but Mother wouldn't let the Dragon Heart sing the Words of Passage until she was certain you were dead. In the end, we held a small memorial.' He grinned, and added, 'Even Katris cried.'

'I don't believe it,' Tam said.

'The only people who didn't believe you were dead from the outset were Mother and Jaysin, and Gramma, before she died. Father and I wished you were somehow alive, but we didn't believe it was possible. Mother told me Gramma kept mumbling before Blitzart's Feast that you were safe with Eric and Claryssa, and –'

'I was!' Tam declared, her eyes wide in understanding.

'Sorry?' Chasse queried.

'Eric, Tam explained. 'The Herbal Man. His name is Eric.'

Astonished, Chasse asked, 'Are you saying Gramma knew where you were?'

Tam hesitated. The idea was absurd. 'No,' she muttered, and corrected herself. 'I mean, yes. I know it doesn't make sense, but Gramma was right.'

'But how could she know? Did you tell her where you were going?'

'I don't think I told her anything. It's probably a coincidence. She was always talking about Eric and Claryssa, and probably said it to Mother. I didn't meet anyone named Claryssa, so perhaps it was Gramma being Gramma,' she suggested.

Chasse appeared to accept her explanation because the alternative was illogical, but the event plagued Tam after their conversation, and she rued forgetting to ask the Herbal Man about his relationship with Gramma Harmi. The fragments aggregating in her mind were forming a fascinating picture with endless possibilities.

Late in the afternoon, Chasse returned to the Warriors' Hall, leaving Tam to help Eesa prepare food. Eesa could not contain her joy at her daughter's miraculous return. 'Your father is organising a feast to celebrate your return, and the entire village is attending,' she announced.

'But I don't want a feast,' Tam protested.

'Tush,' Eesa said, and she handed Tam a knife for preparing vegetables, before she began kneading dough on the table.

'I missed you,' Jaysin declared, hugging Tam's waist, and he clung to her as if he never intended to let her go. When Eesa went outside to collect eggs, Jaysin said, 'I was scared, Tamesan, but I gave Gramma the ring like I promised and she told me you were safe.'

Tam hugged her little brother, saying, 'I missed you too, Jaysin, but Gramma was right, wasn't she?'

The boy nodded and looked up with his dark eyes, and Tam felt her little brother knew Harmi better than anyone in her family. She guessed at her grandmother's secrets, but Jaysin accepted them for what they were. 'I miss Gramma,' he muttered.

Whether it was his sorrowful expression, or her own loss surfacing, tears welled in her eyes. Gramma Harmi was gone, snatched by Shaddho, the Death Dragon. Unable to hold back her grief, she hugged Jaysin to her and cried.

The people of Harbin flocked to the Long Hall. Denied Blitzart's Feast by the remorseless winter, the spring Celebration of Fler, called five days early by the Dragon Heart, was warmly welcomed, and news of Tamesan's miraculous return buoyed their spirits. It was fitting, many said, that Kevan's daughter should return for the spring feast held in honour of Procra's daughter, Fler, who symbolised rebirth, and Sharmine and her friends said it was a sign from almighty Varst that the people of Harbin were blessed and would prosper.

Tam felt terribly self-conscious sitting between her father and the Dragon Heart at the head table in the Long Hall, because people entering the hall stared at her as if she was a spirit. She wanted them to speak to her to show that nothing was changed, but no one came close enough to speak, and she wasn't allowed to leave her seat. She made a minor protest when Banni entered, but the Dragon Heart restrained Tam, leaving Banni to stare like the others before she took her seat among the single women at the furthest table from the front.

'Patience, child,' the Dragon Heart said quietly. 'Tonight, you must keep your place. You are a gift from the gods, a sign of their power and presence. The people see this is true and know you for it. It would be wrong to trivialise the moment with womanly emotions. Be what is ordained by Varst and Procra. You make your father and mother very proud.' Held by his hand on her arm, and his words, Tam reluctantly acquiesced.

The Hall quickly filled, and the women served the warm meal from stock stored over the winter. Dressed in his best chain mail, links burnished to shine in the torch and firelight, Kevan the Dragon Head rose to welcome everyone to the Celebration of Fler and when he called on the Dragon Heart, the lore keeper stood, regaled in his green, yellow and white robes and traditional goat's horn and feather head-dress, and made the formal introductory vows.

As he finished, the Dragon Heart put his hand on Tam's shoulder and motioned for her to stand beside him. He smiled at her before he bowed his head in an act of obeisance reserved for the Dragon Head, and he began his speech with passion.

'It has been a bitter winter, my friends. Great Blitzart's icy breath blew longer and more fiercely than anyone alive can remember, until all the land was frozen. Some were called to journey across the darkness to Varst's Eternal Paradise. This we have all seen and shared. Perhaps it is punishment for a wrong we have unwittingly committed. Perhaps it was Blitzart's futile attempt to be avenged on the children of Nakiades. It has been a harsh trial for us all, and the sorest trial was inflicted on the family of the Dragon Head. We sang the Words of Passage for the mother and the daughter of Kevan, this past winter, and great sorrow lingered in the Dragon Head's home. But the gods are just. Harmi lived a long life, longer than any in living memory, a full seventy summers and then some. She was blessed by Procra, who gives birth to all life, and taken mercifully by Shaddho, without struggle or pain. The gods are just. They are merciful beyond all reckoning. For, when it seemed they were cruel and vindictive for leading the girl, Tamesan, from her home into the teeth of Blitzart's storm, they were orchestrating an event far greater, more miraculous than we could have foreseen. For here is Kevan's daughter among us again, brought back alive from the Winter Dragon's clutches, delivered to us as a gift of trust, a sign that we, the children of Nakiades, the people of Harbin, are many times blessed by Varst, by Procra, and by their children. We have seen death and rebirth, the terror and the beauty, the mystery of life, the eternal cycle. Praise be to Varst. Praise be to Procra, to Ecg and to Fler. They led us through the bitter winter of death to show us the promise of life eternal. Let us accept their gifts of food tonight, and the promise through the return of Tamesan, the child who is the Dawn's Light, and know in our hearts that we are truly blessed.'

Eighteen

Tam was furious. The Celebration of Fler was a total disaster. The Dragon Heart and her father made her appear greater than she was. They lied. To everyone. She wasn't saved or delivered by the gods. The Herbal Man deserved the accolades, not Varst or Procra.

When she raised the matter at home, Eesa told her to keep the truth to herself and Kevan refused to discuss it. The Dragon Heart, however, was willing to talk to her. He took her aside when she told him that she was unhappy with being set up as a gift from the gods, and he said, 'You are more than a gift from the gods, Tamesan. You are an inspiration and strengthener.'

'How?' she asked.

'The people believe Varst is their protector, and they are happier because of the knowledge. Did you see their faces last night? Did you see the effect of your amazing survival on them?'

'All I saw were people staring at me, even my friends, as if I was a strange creature. No one spoke to me after the feast. I feel as if I can't see anyone because of it.'

'Because you are someone very special now,' he affirmed.

'A lie isn't special.'

The Dragon Heart leaned closer, and said, 'Sometimes a lie is more special than the truth, Tamesan. Can you tell me that you have never lied to help someone feel better?'

She hesitated, knowing he was right, but she said, 'No. But I've never lied like this.'

'No,' the Dragon Heart agreed, 'never like this. Because this is not an ordinary lie. It is a special truth that will bring the people of Harbin together. Not only do they see Varst's hand protecting them, they also see your father is a blessed warrior, the man Varst chose to be the Dragon Head, the man to lead them against the dragons again this summer. It strengthens Harbin. It makes the Dragon Fang mighty again.'

'But I know the truth,' she objected.

'And what truth is that, Tamesan?'

'I was rescued by the Herbal Man. He cared for me and brought me safely home.'

The Dragon Heart shook his head, and said, 'He may have done that, but he was acting as an instrument of Varst's wishes. How did he manage to stumble upon you in the middle of a howling snowstorm? It was no accident. An old man in the storm would have perished as easily as you almost did. He found you because he was protected from Blitzart's icy breath by Varst. Varst led you both to safety. That is the truth.'

'But-,' she started and stopped. The Dragon Heart was arguing exactly as the Herbal Man did on Dragon Mountain, meaning there was no compromise possible. She knew the truth, but the Dragon Heart's interpretation made her question what she believed. She was sure the Herbal Man rescued her, but how did he find her in a raging storm? How did a skinny and bowed old man carry her halfway up the mountain?

'The gods have blessed you, child,' the Dragon Heart reassured her, with a kindly touch on her shoulder. 'You are alive when you should be dead. You are tall and beautiful, and the daughter of the Dragon Head of Harbin. When it comes to the time of your choosing, what warrior would not give everything he has to call you his wife? Few women have been blessed with so much, and none have been returned to their family as mercifully as you have been returned to yours. Be thankful to the gods for what you have been given, and trust what is happening because it is for the good of all Harbin.'

And the matter ended, because the Dragon Heart excused himself to attend to other matters. Watching the man head into the village, Tam felt she had no choice other than to accept the tale being spread through the village of the gods delivering her from harm.

Tam expected Eesa would set her to work immediately the first day after the Celebration of Fler, so she went to the Long Hall and offered to help the women clean the mess from the feasting, but the women told her she wasn't needed. When she asked where her mother was, Layni said she was at the fishermen's tables.

Tam walked to the shore where Eesa and Amarti, and several more women, were cleaning the morning catch. The women greeted Tam with a great deal of fuss, questioning her about the Herbal Man's home and what it was like to spend winter on the mountain, and they all remarked how blessed she was to have survived, but Tam felt emptiness in their welcome, as if she was a stranger among them. She set to scaling a fish, but Eesa stayed her hand, saying, 'No need, girl. You don't have to work today.'

At a loss, as she put aside the knife, she asked, 'Has anyone seen Banni?'

'The younger women are bathing in the Dragon's Cauldron,' Eesa replied. 'You could join them.'

Set free of duty to work, Tam thanked her mother before heading through the village towards the hot springs. She noted that the dragonwarriors, including Marron, were busily training on the goat pasture, and she shivered at the memory of his bullying as she skirted the pasture and hurried up the slope.

Banni and four others were soaking in the steaming water when she reached them, and they greeted Tam cheerfully. 'Come in,' Banni invited, smiling.

'Thanks, but I'll stay here,' Tam replied. She eased onto a rock at the water's edge and answered a barrage of questions about her adventure and her miraculous survival. She responded with careful details, but she was acutely aware that the only question no one asked was why she ran to the mountain in the first place. Not even her family asked the question since her return, as if no one wanted to know what drove her to the mountain.

Conversation swung to Banni's approaching baby, and Tam saw her belly was appreciably swollen over winter, although Banni assured her that she still had one full moon cycle of pregnancy to go. Tam was happy for Banni as the group engaged in chatter about motherhood without a man, but she felt as distanced from the young women in the pool as she did from her mother and women in the village.

When the bathers began to emerge from the Dragon's Cauldron, Tam rose, excused herself on the pretence of work, and returned to the village outskirts.

She paused in a stand of trees near the goat pasture to watch the dragonwarriors practising a manoeuvre requiring them to maintain a protective circle while trainers harassed them with wooden spears and swords. Her father and Theo stood apart from the melee group, observing the action. She spotted Chasse's red hair among the defenders, and Marron's dark, athletic figure at the centre. Theo bellowed a set of instructions and the younger warriors separated from the group to begin fighting among themselves. The rules of the new mock battle were unclear to her, but she studied her brother and saw how much skill he had gained over winter. He moved with confidence and grace, beating down opponents as they confronted him, even Theo, who stepped in as the energy of the battle waned.

She anticipated Chasse and Marron would fight, but they stayed apart. Like Chasse, Marron also fought with fluid efficiency, but his attacks were ruthless, deadly, and three opponents retreated, holding their arms in pain. Whereas Chasse fought with clear awareness that his opponents were friends, Marron revelled in every vicious blow he dealt and was delighted by every howl of pain he drew from his foes. The bully was growing hungrier as he fed on his victims.

She skirted the pasture, and she avoided Katris and her peers when she re-entered the village, imagining her public elevation during the Celebration of Fler would only make Katris hate her more. Chasse's revelation that Katris cried when the Dragon Heart sang the Words of Passage for Tam's spirit did not surprise her – Katris had sentiment – but she doubted her return would make Katris happy. Moreover, Tam saw Marron studying her throughout the night of the feast, and Katris was eyeing them both. The Dragon Heart was right. More than ever, because of events, Tam would be sought as a prize by the dragonwarriors, and Marron would be more determined to win her. And it would inflame Katris' jealousy.

Tam wandered the fringes for part of the day, and filled her time helping Derin's father herd goats, but she was drawn to her favourite place, so she climbed the lower slopes to the smooth rock where she sat and gazed at the bay, remembering the mysteries the Herbal Man unfolded for her in his hidden retreat. Alone, she pondered the irony that she came home and yet she felt further from home than ever.

She descended as dusk fell and found her father waiting for her outside the cottage. He ushered her in, and her mother was sitting at the table. A lantern burned at the table's centre. Kevan sent Jaysin to his bedroom and indicated for Tam to sit, while he remained standing, an imposing figure in the low-ceilinged room. 'Are you happy to be home?' he asked.

'Yes, Father,' Tam replied, wondering what her father was leading to.

'Your mother and I are happy you are home,' he said, and he coughed to clear his throat, a sign Tam recognised always preceded her father's important statements. 'We know why you ran away, Tamesan.'

'We are also glad you were returned to us,' Eesa added.

'It is not easy to be a woman,' Kevan continued. He glanced at Eesa who nodded. 'You already know more about it than I do,' he conceded. 'A woman's lot is work and more work. A woman must not only bear her own burdens, but also the burdens of her husband and children. Even as a man, I know this much. It has always been so.'

'Your father understands the important role women play in this village,' Eesa affirmed. The women of Harbin are its backbone and its soul.' She looked at her husband and added, 'No man will deny it.'

'It is true,' Kevan agreed. 'The women are Harbin's strength. Without them, there would be no home for the Dragon Fang, no sons to become dragonwarriors, no memories of Nakiades, no future, no Harbin.' He paused and ran his hand through his long mane of greying hair, leaned forward, and said, 'I am thrice blessed in you, my daughter. First, you are beautiful, like your mother. Second, you are strong and healthy. And third because you have stared into the face of Blitzart's fury and returned unharmed. When you come of age in one more summer, you will be the rarest woman in Harbin for all these reasons.'

Tam heard the echo of the Dragon Heart's voice in her father's words and guessed what he was leading to. She was caught in a web spun before winter, and it grew stronger with her return. Her heart sank, but she feigned an outward show of respect.

'The daughter of the Dragon Head has greater responsibility than any other girl in the village,' her father was saying, as she returned her attention to him. 'You were born into a position of highest honour, a position coveted by every girl in Harbin, and it is time for you to accept your responsibility by being ready for what your future holds.'

'Trask's son is a handsome young man,' Eesa offered gently.

'His show of interest in you has been clumsy,' Kevan admitted, 'but he is learning what is right and what is wrong for a man to do. If he chooses you to be his wife when you come of age, you will also do what is right for a woman.'

'Your father does not mean to be unkind, child,' Eesa intervened. 'He only wants you to understand what is right and for you to be happy in accepting it.'

'There are traditions,' Kevan reminded Tam. 'We are all bound by them. Coming of age is not simply a measure of how many summers we have lived. It is also measured by what we understand and how we act.'

'We want you to receive the honour and respect that you deserve when you become a woman,' said Eesa.

'Do you understand?' Kevan asked.

The silence awaiting Tam's response hung above her like a threatening blade. *What choice do I have*? she thought. 'Can I visit the Herbal Man?' she asked.

Unprepared for her question, Kevan shot Eesa a searching glance as he scratched his chin. 'That is another matter,' he replied.

'But what is the answer?' Tam asked.

Kevan shifted his weight and walked around the table, away from Tam. He stopped, put his big hands on the table and leaned forward to stare Tam directly in the eyes. 'Did he ask you to be his – what was his word for it?'

'Apprentice,' Eesa reminded him.

Kevan glanced at her before fixing Tam with a stern gaze. 'Did he ask you?'

Tam shook her head, puzzled by her father's line of inquiry, and replied, 'No.'

'Just as well,' Kevan said, straightening up. 'What he proposed to me when he brought you down from the mountain is not appropriate for you.'

'What did he propose?' Tam asked, confused but curious.

Kevan threw another glance at Eesa, before he said, 'I see no harm in you knowing, because you will see why the notion is foolish. When we spoke, he offered to teach you his skills in herbalism and healing. I'm sure it was a kind gesture, made in good faith, but it is not a thing a Harbin woman would want to contemplate, especially a young woman close to coming of age who has more pressing matters to learn. I thanked him, but I told him you would not be considering his offer.'

'You would have too little time to learn his strange ways,' Eesa claimed. 'A husband especially would not want his young wife dallying across the mountain slopes with an old man.'

'It is not a young woman's place,' Kevan asserted. 'Perhaps an older woman, or one without a husband or children, would suit the Herbal Man's needs better. You understand?'

'Can I still visit him?' Tam persisted.

Kevan's eyes widened in disbelief, and when he realised Tam was awaiting an answer he threw his arms up in exasperation, moaning, 'By Varst's holy fires I have tried! Must I endure this?'

'Be patient, husband,' Eesa said. 'The girl's question is not difficult to answer.' Kevan glared, but Eesa ignored him, turned to her daughter and said in a bemused tone, 'Why would a young woman want to share her time with an old man?'

'He teaches me,' Tam replied.

'See?' Kevan growled. 'Already he meddles.'

'Hush,' Eesa warned Kevan, and asked, 'What does he teach you?'

'How to read and write. How to recognise which plants are useful for healing and what has to be done to make them useful.'

Kevan shook his head in disapproval. 'These things are wasted on you. What use are they to you?'

'I can learn to do for the village what he does. I can teach others too.'

'No!' Kevan declared. 'My daughter will not be lured away from her responsibilities by the meddler. You will not be his apprentice and that is final.'

'Can I still visit him?' Tam repeated doggedly.

Kevan swore another oath and smashed his fist against the table, bellowing, 'Are you deaf? What have I told you?'

Frustration threatened to overwhelm Tam, but she calmed her anger and held back her tears to say, 'You said I cannot be the Herbal Man's apprentice, and I accept your decision, Father. I am only asking to visit him, sometimes, when there is time. It is the least I can do to honour him for saving my life. I thought you would be pleased to see that I have learned to honour those to whom a life is owed.'

Kevan sucked in his breath. His daughter was calling on a foremost principle of the Dragon Fang code: honour. Warriors died for honour. Honour was linked with uncompromising respect. It forged courage and loyalty and determined the worth of a man. He looked at Eesa and saw she was nodding slowly. His daughter was right. If she visited the Herbal Man, everyone in the village would see that the Dragon Head and his family honoured debts owed to others, regardless of station in the community. He looked at Tam sternly and said, 'As a mark of respect, you can visit him, briefly, when your mother decides it is convenient. But there will be no sneaking off to the mountain, and there will be no apprenticeship. You will accept your village responsibilities exactly as all women do. And I warn you. Do not disobey me.'

Nineteen

The days of spring swung through passing rains and streaming sunshine, and the snow blanket quickly melted, sending fresh streams cascading down the mountain gorges. The men hauled the great dragonship from the water to scrape barnacles from the hull and caulk its leaking seams, while the women repaired the red sail and renewed the ropes. Fishermen cast their nets and lines into the bountiful ocean and the herdsmen managed their flocks sprinkled with new-born. Children revelled in their release from winter's white prison, playing and exploring Harbin. Banni gave birth to a baby girl and named her Jara in memory of her dead husband, and the villagers revelled in the news. Tam visited Banni regularly, marvelling at Jara's cherubic face and tiny fingers and toes, and helping her friend with chores, and the village women pitched in to make sure Banni was not left alone.

For Tam, life settled into its traditional cycle of washing, cleaning, mending, supervising children, preparing fish. She quietly accepted her duties, focussing on doing them well, and listened politely to the women's conversations when she worked with them. She tolerated Katris' presence, aware of the brooding enmity between them, even though Katris ignored her. Tam knew any attempt to appease Katris would be futile because neither had control over Marron's desires. He would choose whomever he wanted, because he would be a man and they would be available young women. And it was equally possible he might choose someone entirely different when the time came.

When Tam could find time, she practised the knowledge and skills revealed to her by the Herbal Man. She wandered the forest fringe searching for herbs, identifying them as best she could, reciting their properties and uses. She searched the village for a quill, ink and parchment, but no one understood what she wanted. She fashioned a quill from seagull feathers, and used tar and Bloodberry sap as ink, with limited success, but she could not find an equivalent substance for parchment. Eventually, she resorted to using a stick to scratch letters and words in the earth. She amused the children under her supervision by teaching them how to draw letters from the Herbal Man's alphabet.

Tam taught Jaysin everything she remembered. He was keen to learn and quickly copied what she taught him. For the first time, she saw her little brother hungering to learn, happy as he mastered the shape of letters and read aloud words that she created, but he was disappointed when she told him she had reached her limit of knowledge. He pestered her for more, and when she could not offer more, he withdrew further from the company of others to practise writing his name and what he remembered of the alphabet. Tam marvelled at her little brother's new obsession.

The villagers began preparing for the next event on the Harbin calendar, the Feast of Ecg, where initiate dragonwarriors were presented with their armour and weapons. Tam assisted in decorating the Warriors' Hall, which involved cleaning the interior thoroughly and hanging shields and spears on the walls. She longed to see her brother initiated, but the Feast of Ecg was a male-only event, with the exception that the mothers of the new warriors could lay out the banquet, but they had to leave before the ceremony commenced.

On the night of the feast, after she finished serving food, Eesa returned to the cottage and boasted to Tam how fine Chasse appeared, seated with the men at the long table in the hall.

'Your brother is sitting side-by-side with your father,' Essa said, smiling with motherly pride. 'They are handsome and strong men, Tamesan. We are very lucky. Our world is prosperous and in balance.'

Tam felt a pang of envy for Chasse, but she was happy that he was becoming a man.

A week after the Feast of Ecg, the warrior Symon was accidentally killed as the men hauled the dragonship back into the water. A log for rolling the ship forward jammed on a rock, the hull heeled over, and Symon wasn't quick enough to scramble to safety. Crushed beneath the ship, he was dead by the time the men lifted the weight from him. The subdued dragonwarriors carried Symon's body to his wife, Ashlee, and withdrew to the Warriors' Hall to mourn their dead comrade.

When Eesa and Amarti were summoned to Ashlee's hut by the Dragon Heart to prepare the corpse, Eesa insisted that Tam accompany her.

'There is a time for everything, Tamesan,' she explained as they walked. 'You know more about the living than the dead, but now it is time that you learned about caring for the dead. This is something women do better than men.'

Banni, nursing Jara, and several women were waiting outside Ashlee's hut, and Banni spoke as Eesa and Tam reached her. 'Ashlee will not see us,' she explained. 'She says she wants to be left alone with her husband.'

Eesa placed her hand on Banni's shoulder, and said, 'Then do as she asks. You wanted to be left alone when you lost Jared. In time, she will want to talk, but for now go back to your work.'

Banni and her companions asked Eesa to tell Ashlee how sad they were for her loss before they withdrew, leaving Eesa, Amarti and Tam to enter the hut.

As she put her hand on the door, Eesa paused and said, 'I think I should go in alone, first. This is not easy for Ashlee.'

'That would be wise,' Amarti agreed. 'The girl and I will wait until you call us in.'

Eesa nodded, quietly entered, and closed the door.

Tam and Amarti waited for a long time. They heard Ashlee sobbing, and once she screamed, 'Get out! Leave me alone!', a cry that startled

Tam.

'She does not mean it, girl,' Amarti told her. 'It is the anger and fear she is feeling. It will pass.'

'Perhaps we should leave her alone, like Mother said,' Tam suggested.

'No,' Amarti replied. 'Grief is necessary, but we must never let it overwhelm us. Death is part of life, as my old mother used to say, Procra guard her spirit. I was no older than eight summers when my father drowned, and my mother missed him sorely. But she told me then it was how the world went. She said, "Remember we are blessed with every moment of happiness, and those are the moments we must remember when we lose a friend, or a husband, or a child to Shaddho's dark passing." I have never forgotten her words. When she died, Varst keep her in Paradise, twelve summers past if my memory serves well, I said those words over her burial mound and at Watersdrop. When I think of her, and even the little I remember of my father, I think only of the happy moments. They keep the dragon grief in its place.'

Amarti's advice surprised Tam because she always thought of her as the 'tough little crab' that her name implied, and she was undoubtedly tough, being a fisherman's wife and sharing his hard work, but she was also someone else within her shell, someone softer, wiser. What Amarti said was true. When Tam thought of Gramma Harmi, she pictured the good moments, the living moments as Amarti's mother called them.

Ashlee's hut was silent for a long time before Eesa opened the door and beckoned Amarti and Tam to join her. As Tam entered the darkened room, she felt trepidation, despite Amarti's advice. Slivers of light angled across the space revealing overturned furniture and Symon's corpse on the floor in the centre. She spied Ashlee huddled against the wall in the corner, staring blindly, unaware of her three visitors.

'We need more light,' Eesa said, quietly. 'Tamesan, kindle the hearth.'

Relieved to be given a task, Tam exited via the rear door and found a lean-to housing Ashlee's firewood. She gathered an armful and returned inside to lay the wood in the cold hearth. Amarti lit a lamp and joined Eesa kneeling beside the corpse, while Tam started the fire. Tam glanced at Ashlee, but the young woman hadn't moved.

'Warm the water until it is steaming, Tamesan. Don't let it boil,' Eesa instructed. 'It's in the bowl to your right.'

Tam placed the bowl on a crude metal stand designed to suspend containers above the hearth fire, and when the water was steaming she used a heavy cloth to protect her hands to carry the bowl to Eesa. Eesa and Amarti stripped away Symon's clothing in readiness and they dipped cloths into the water and gently sponged the body, cleaning away dirt and blood. Tam stared at Symon's face, noting death's discoloration, but because he had no head injury he looked as though he was asleep, and the care Eesa and Amarti were applying as they washed him enhanced the illusion.

Eesa paused when Ashlee started sobbing, and said, 'I think it's time she got some fresh air. Tamesan?'

Tam crossed to Ashlee and squatted before her, but she was at a loss what to say. Finally, she gently put a hand on Ashlee's arm and asked, 'Do you want to come outside?'

When Ashlee didn't respond, Tam felt awkward, and wondered what else she could say, until Ashlee wiped her arm across her face, pushed clumsily to her feet, and stumbled across the room and out the door.

'Go with her, child,' Eesa urged.

Outside, Tam caught up with Ashlee, who was heading for the northern end of the village, and walked beside her. The pair walked in silence along the curve of Harbin Bay, towards Varst's Bluff, until they reached the second stream that ran into the ocean, Meltsparkle. Unlike Watersdrop plummeting as a waterfall into the bay, Meltsparkle cascaded down a gentler slope through a conglomeration of boulders. Above the stream reared the cliffs and steep slopes of Varst's Bluff, impossible to climb, except via the leg called Nakiades' Watch that jutted into the bay.

Ashlee scrambled across a narrow channel of rushing water onto a large boulder, and sat, knees tucked beneath her chin, staring across the bay's dark blue water. Tam hesitated on the bank. There was enough room for two people on the boulder, but she was uncertain whether Ashlee would accept company. She plucked up her courage and traversed the slippery boulders to sit beside the grieving woman.

They sat in silence a long time, Tam patiently watching the ocean rise and fall while she waited for a sign from Ashlee that she might be willing to talk. White and grey sea birds wheeled around the cliffs and across the ocean swell, riding the fickle spring air currents, as the sun drifted in and out of the clouds, sending shadows scampering across the water and land in endless pursuit. Tam remembered sharing the same emptiness with Banni the night the dragonship returned without her husband and she understood how Ashlee must feel. Despite the beauty of the spring day surrounding her, with Symon dead she knew Ashlee gazed on an empty world.

'He wanted a son.'

Ashlee's quiet statement startled Tam. She looked at Ashlee, but the young woman kept staring seaward.

'I could only give him two girls,' Ashlee continued. 'He wanted a son and I gave him girls. Two dead girls.' She fought back a sob, but it escaped as a choking cry above the tumbling water. 'He wanted a son and now he has nothing.' She smashed her fist against the rock, but she did not cry. Tam touched Ashlee's fist to comfort her, but the grief-stricken woman turned swollen eyes on Tam and sneered, saying, 'Why are you here, daughter of Eesa? What was my husband to you?'

Unsettled by Ashlee's anger, Tam started to say, 'A dragonwarrior-' as testimony of Symon's status in Harbin, but Ashlee angrily cut across her.

'A pillager! A rapist! A slayer of children!' she screamed. 'A killer and a coward!' She burst into tears, finishing with, 'All wasted! All wasted!'

Ashlee's bitter, passionate outburst against her dead husband shocked

Tam. She drew a breath and tried to coax the woman into a calmer state by saying, 'Your husband was a dragon slayer. Everyone in Harbin knows.'

'No one knows!' Ashlee howled. 'No one knows anything! It's a lie, one horrible, big lie! All of it! And it killed my husband! It killed him as sure as that stupid ship!' She sobbed and drew a deeper breath, before she stared through tear-stained eyes at Tam and said, 'They tell us they go to hunt dragons, but they don't! There are no dragons! Do you know that, daughter of Eesa? There are no dragons!' She sobbed again, caught her breath, her mouth twisting with contempt, and snarled, 'Don't waste your pity on me, little girl. It doesn't matter. I don't care anymore. Nothing matters any more. Leave me alone. Do you hear me? Leave me alone!'

Tam didn't argue with the murderous glitter in Ashlee's eyes. She scrambled off of the boulder and back to the bank, where she hesitated, looking at Ashlee, but the woman was staring out to sea again, seemingly oblivious to the capricious breeze toying with her dark mass of hair. Tam wished she could take away Ashlee's pain. She never saw someone so maddened. Shivering, she clutched her arms to her breast, and she retraced the path to the hut where Eesa and Amarti were attending Symon's corpse.

That night, and several nights thereafter, Tam struggled to sleep restfully. Ashlee haunted her dreams. Sometimes, Tam dreamed that she stood on Nakiades' Watch, watching the dragonship drift on the ocean. Symon stood on the dragonship's prow, the way her father normally stood there, tall, clean, silent. And then a dragon swept out of the sky with a long wailing cry before it belched fire over the ship. Every time, in the dream, as it rose, the dragon turned towards Tam and its visage became a twisted reptilian version of Ashlee's face, with one golden eye staring at her. And the dragon screamed, 'It's all a lie! A lie! There are no dragons!' before it vanished.

In another dream, she stood beside Chasse on the dragonship, with Symon lying beneath a white shroud at their feet. And Ashlee appeared before them, screaming 'Killer! Child-slayer!' Tam recognised Ashlee, but Chasse hurled his spear at her as she screamed, 'It's a lie!', and Tam could do nothing but watch in horror.

She woke from her dreams, gasping for air, and then she comforted Jaysin who was woken by her cries.

The Words of Passage for Symon were sung five days after his burial. Ashlee stood silently staring over Watersdrop throughout the ceremony, refusing comfort from the women who were her friends, speaking to no one. She returned alone to her hut and she continued to refuse visitors in the days after.

A week after the ceremony, on the eve of Varst's Great Feast heralding the beginning of summer and the departure of the Dragon Fang, a fisherman recovered Ashlee's body from the rocks at the base of Watersdrop. Kevan ordered the Great Feast to be postponed for one day while the villagers mourned the tragedy.

Twenty

Varst's Great Feast was the highest event in the Harbin calendar. The women gathered fresh spring berries and nuts and blended them into sweetmeats, baked and decorated cakes and bread, and the men slaughtered and prepared fattened goats and chickens. The Long Hall was furnished with a central table, embellished to symbolise the dragonship for the Dragon Fang, and surrounding tables were set up for the common folk. Eesa directed the younger women, Tam included, to construct a pseudo-dragon from goatskin, feathers and dried grass. The dragon was to be paraded before the village assembly in the Long Hall before being ritualistically 'killed' by the initiate warriors. The young warriors spent the entire day attiring themselves in their new armour to ensure they looked handsome, strong and fearsome as they prepared for the summer journey into manhood.

Tam's spirit was buoyed by the busy time preparing for the feast and the night's celebration. There was an enormous bounty of food and mead, and endless dancing and singing. The women and girls laughed at the initiates parading before a very drunken dragon borne by Theo and four senior warriors, and when the young warriors moved in for the ceremonial kill the disoriented dragon lost balance and collapsed in a chaotic heap to riotous laughter and applause. Promises were made, oaths sworn, and the Dragon Heart offered a series of prayers to Varst the Almighty, to his bountiful wife, Procra, to their warrior son, Ecg, and to their beautiful daughter, Fler. The villagers sang traditional ballads about the voyage of Nakiades and the summer journeys of the great dragon, Arkamroth, and shared stories of past adventures as they ate and drank, and Tam was swept along by all the merriment, happier than she felt for a long time.

As the night drew to its close and the dragonwarriors made their ceremonial farewell, Tam was overcome by a deep sadness bringing her to tears. Chasse, so tall, so handsome in his shining armour, was leaving. The brother she loved was going away and would never return. In his place would be a new Chasse, a stranger she already glimpsed since winter's end. He would return as a young man, a man who travelled on the dragonship and knew the glory of battle with a dragon. She cried, and looked around shamefully, fearing others saw her tears amid the celebration's pride and happiness, but she saw that she was not alone in her sorrow. Other women were crying too – mothers, wives, daughters, sisters – all feeling their impending loss, sharing their hopes and fears for the men who were sailing away. Tam felt a hand on her shoulder and turned to Eesa and her mother smiled and hugged her as the men marched from the Long Hall.

The tide and breeze called the Dragon Fang to the ship well before the sun rose above the mountains, and the womenfolk and children huddled on the jetty in the grey pre-dawn light. Farewells were shared; hugs, kisses, promises and tears exchanged. Kevan reminded Tam to look after her mother before he hugged Eesa and said, gruffly, 'Do not worry. How many summers now have I done this?'

'Too many,' Eesa replied. 'You be careful.'

'There isn't a dragon smart enough to better me,' Kevan boasted.

'It's just as well dragons aren't very smart,' Theo quipped from behind Kevan. He looked past Kevan's shoulder and winked at Tam as they all laughed.

Chasse kissed Eesa and stood before Tam to ask, 'How do I look?'

'Handsome,' she replied. They stared at each other awkwardly while others bustled around them, until Tam leaned forward to kiss her brother's cheek. 'Take care,' she said. He grinned sheepishly and nodded, and then he turned and boarded the ship.

Kevan mounted the prow, as was tradition, the Dragon Head bravely leading the Dragon Fang, his eyes fixed resolutely on the distant dark gap between Nakiades' Watch and White Eagle Ledge, and Theo gave the order to cast off. Tam searched for Chasse among the dark cluster of figures on the ship and saw him waving to someone else in the crowd on the jetty. She guessed it was Kerryn, and she wondered if her brother would choose Kerryn for his wife when he returned. Everything was changing again.

Theo ordered the men to take up the oars and row, and the wooden oars slid noisily over the gunwales into the water. At that moment, Tam noticed Marron looking up at her. The semi-darkness hid his expression, but his eyes glittered with light from a lantern on the jetty. She looked away. His attention was the last thing she wanted. Instead, she focussed on her father's tall, solid figure as the ship slid from the jetty. The summer journey was underway.

At the summit of the steepest climb, where the mountain path levelled onto the plateau, Tam halted to catch her breath, and she took in the magnificent view of Harbin Bay's deep blue harbour and mountain sentinels. Far out on the western ocean, a small rain squall scudded southward and she wondered if it would reach the dragonship. Closer to Harbin, though, the sky was clear blue, as if the gods were keeping the early summer rain away.

With Kevan gone three days on the dragonship, Eesa relented and allowed Tam to visit the Herbal Man. Her mother seemed more relaxed in her mood towards Tam, but Tam assumed it was due to Eesa being too busy overseeing the affairs of the village to be overly watchful of her daughter. Before she left, Tam found Jaysin tracing alphabet letters in the earth behind the cottage. She informed him that she was going up the mountain, and said, 'If you need mother, she's teaching the girls basket weaving in the Long Hall. I'll be back before sunset.'

Tam wanted to see the Herbal Man. He hadn't visited the village since he returned her, and she wondered if his absence was due to Kevan telling him that Tam could not be his apprentice. She was still angry at her father's decision and, while she deliberately played dutiful daughter when her father was home, she used every opportunity to revise the skills the Herbal Man had already taught her. She was frustrated practising writing without parchment or texts and she wanted to learn more. As boring as the Herbal Man's lessons sometimes were during the long winter, she relished how different they were from anything she could learn in Harbin, and she knew that, if she persevered, she would have skills no one else possessed. She could be useful to the village by helping to teach and heal, and the Herbal Man was old so she could take his place when he was no longer able to do those things.

She had other reasons for seeking him. Questions plagued her. She wanted to know what was in the crystal chamber, and how he managed to speak to Harmi on Blitzart's Eve. She also wondered if he could explain why Ashlee echoed his statement that there were no dragons. Questions without answers – and she was sure the Herbal Man knew the answers.

She wound through the plateau's rich forest, breathing in the cool, fresh air and smiling at the coloured butterflies flitting across the ferns. The forest's air of mystery reflected every aspect of the Herbal Man. The first time she passed through, she marvelled how the forest was a world of its own on the mountain, full of greater life and vitality than any area around Harbin, although under the crushing weight of midwinter snow it was the same.

When she entered the small clearing where the Herbal Man's decoy hut lay, she was astonished to find the hut relatively secure and tidy, because it was partially collapsed under the snow when the Herbal Man took her home. She assumed he wouldn't bother repairing it beyond a rudimentary fix because it was a blind to his underground quarters, but as she approached she realised that he had put significant effort into rebuilding the structure. It retained its rustic, rough appearance, a hut built by a poorly skilled layman, but it looked homely, more lived in than the first time she visited. Fresh kindling was piled beside the front door and smoke drifted from the stone chimney. Tam knocked, half-expecting an answer, but when no one appeared she wondered how the Herbal Man knew when he did have visitors to the makeshift hut.

She tried the door, but it was locked, so she went to a side window and peered through the partly open shutters. The interior was tidier than she remembered. The bed was made, the table and chairs orderly, and the only aberration was the fireless smoke drifting from the hearth. The source fire, as she knew, burned a level below in the Herbal Man's underground study.

She considered her options. The Herbal Man might be on the slopes searching for herbs. She didn't sight him on the ascent, but the mountain was vast. She could search for the goat cave and enter the underground sanctuary that way. Or she could climb through the window and enter via the trapdoor. She chose the third, confident that he wouldn't object to her letting herself in.

She forced the wooden shutters wider and squeezed through. The floor was recently swept, and the decrepit and faded rug with the incomprehensible design hiding the trapdoor was clean. She lifted it aside to uncover the trapdoor ring and knocked on the wooden boards politely, to announce her presence. When there was no answer, she knocked again. The lack of response suggested the Herbal Man was most likely outside, foraging, and if he was she had little chance of finding him. She decided to open the trapdoor and enter because it was possible he was deeper in his hideaway and didn't hear her knocking.

The customary books lay open on the bench, and a candle clock burned in the study and a lantern lit the bedroom, but the Herbal Man wasn't in his study or his bedroom. The lantern indicated he couldn't be too far away. She checked the storeroom, before she noticed the door to the inner corridor was ajar. Perhaps he was with the goats. She opened the door and stepped through.

As she approached the end of the corridor, she saw the door to the crystal room was open. She hesitated, remembering snatches of her experience on Blitzart's Feast, but then she drew a deep breath and entered. The crystal chamber was dark, except for a pale orange glow along the base of the far wall and the golden tessellated structure wasn't visible. Curiosity aroused, she walked cautiously around the pedestal supporting the shallow bowl of water, and as she came closer she realised the wall was an opening from which the glow emanated. She took the last steps warily, nervously, and when she peered over the edge she gasped.

The floor she stood on dropped several spans to a lower level that opened into a huge cavern. The walls were curved and smooth, like the cavern of the Dawn People that the Herbal Man showed her, but this space was so much larger and the walls were stained with multicoloured streams of rock. The soft orange glow radiated from an apricot ball floating an arm's span below the ceiling. She saw the Herbal Man near the centre, in white and gold robes, his long white hair flowing grandly over his shoulders, but what amazed her most was the creature curled before him. Huge, with golden scales on a lizard body, a long raking tail curled around it and along the edge of the chamber, delicate bat-like wings folded along its back, the creature lay before the Herbal Man expectantly, obediently, its great golden eyes fixed adoringly on him.

Tam had never seen a dragon. She heard warriors tell tales of the dark, or red or green scaled winged creatures sweeping through the sky, breathing fire on unfortunate victims, ripping apart villagers with their scythe-like talons and teeth like spears, and she knew they were mindless, voracious reptiles striking fear into the hearts of Harbin people and igniting vengeance in the minds of the dragonwarriors. Now, she was staring down on a dragon, a monster from Nakiades' legend, and her fear struggled with fascination. She was rooted, caught like a mesmerised mouse under the stare of the death cat, unable to speak, unable to run, so awesome was the vision. The dragon was real. It lived in the mountain above her home. The Herbal Man was talking to it as if it was nothing more than one of Galt's goats. And it was terrifyingly beautiful.

Her mind full of confusion and wonder, she gazed into the chamber and understood why the wall disappeared. It was never a wall. The tessellated pattern on the curved wall she saw was the dragon's flank pressed against the chamber, and the golden eye she glimpsed on Blitzart's Feast was the dragon's eye. She shivered.

And then the dragon stared straight at her. Fighting a swirling rush of vertigo, she focussed. She wasn't dreaming. There was a dragon. And it was looking at her with deep, liquid golden eyes. The Herbal Man was staring at her too. Terror outstripped her fascination, and she was seized by an irresistible desire to run to safety, to escape the living nightmare.

'Te-Amen-San,' a profound voice whispered. 'Eswyllyion fay, Te-Amen-San. Ilya ta-est.'

Tam's fear melted, smoothed away by the voice. She heard her name in the strange words. The voice was speaking in the old tongue, the language of Nakiades' ancient homeland, words only the Dragon Heart knew.

'Eswyllyion fay, Te-Amen-San. Do not be afraid.'

The dragon stared up at her with eyes glowing like languid pools of fire, and she was no longer afraid.

Twenty-One

'She won't hurt you,' the Herbal Man promised.

Tam wasn't so sure. Even standing beside the Herbal Man on the upper level, she found the dragon's presence unnerving. She eyed the dragon's protruding fangs. A golden eye blinked and she suppressed a shiver.

'Perhaps you will feel better if we retire to the study,' the Herbal Man suggested.

'No,' Tam responded, gathering her courage to take her gaze from the dragon. 'Here is fine.'

'As you wish,' the old man said. 'Watch your eyes a moment.' The Herbal Man passed his hand over a small crystal embedded in the wall and it instantly pulsed with brilliant white light, setting every crystal in the ceiling ablaze and lighting the chamber.

The shift from amber to white light momentarily hurt Tam's eyes, so she rubbed them until they adjusted. 'How did you do that?' she asked.

'Simple art,' the Herbal Man replied. 'The ignis crystal in the wall has a self-generating structure that responds to touch because it is fundamentally unstable. The light it produces when it is activated is reflected in the Lumin gems embedded in the ceiling.'

The concept that light could be created without the need to strike a flint fascinated Tam, but she didn't understand the Herbal Man's explanation. She nodded, and said apologetically, 'I didn't mean to sneak in. I came to visit -'

'It doesn't matter, Tamesan,' the Herbal Man cut in, as he waved aside her apology. 'What has happened has happened and I am not concerned that it has. In fact,' he added, smiling, 'I think it is the right time for it to happen.'

Bewildered, Tam asked, 'For what to happen?'

'For you to meet Claryssa.'

Tam turned to stare at the dragon. 'The dragon is Claryssa?' she blurted.

'Yes,' the Herbal Man replied. 'At least that is her pet name. Her real name is Ke-Ly'aar-Ees-Arshem-Var-Del. It means "She Who Shines Like Gold." Claryssa is easier to say, though not as beautiful.'

'You mean Gramma Harmi really did know about you and Claryssa?'

The Herbal Man grinned. 'Of course Harmi knew. She visited us.'

'How?' Tam asked. 'She could hardly move around the cottage.'

'It was a long time ago, Tamesan,' he explained, sadly. 'A very long time ago. Harmi was hardly much older than you are when she first came here.'

'Harmi wasn't really my grandmother,' was she?' Tam asked, suddenly understanding one of the anomalies in her family. 'She was my great-grandmother, wasn't she?'

'She was,' the Herbal Man confirmed. 'I thought you knew.'

'No. Chasse and Jaysin and I only ever called her Gramma. Father and Mother never told us any different.'

The Herbal Man nodded, as if her explanation made sense. 'Harmi brought your father up from when he was very young,' he told Tam. 'His mother and father both died when he was only about three or four summers old, if I remember correctly. That's why you never knew your father's parents, your grandparents.'

'How did they die?'

'There was a fever in the village. Half the people came down ill. Some recovered. Others died. Your grandparents were among those who did not recover. Harmi's husband, Leith, also died and Harmi was terribly upset. She took a long time to get over her grief, but she took in Kevan and raised him as if her was her son. I think there are very few people left in Harbin who would remember.'

'Why is it a secret?'

'It isn't a secret, Tamesan,' the Herbal Man corrected. 'Simply a sadness.'

Tam cast another sidelong glance at the dragon watching them. 'How did Gramma meet you and Claryssa?' she asked.

The Herbal Man smiled faintly, recalling a fond moment, before he replied. 'In the same way I met you, Tamesan. Like you, she loved to walk the mountain.' He chuckled quietly. 'She had long red hair and the same green eyes as you, and when I saw you last summer I thought Harmi had magically returned. It was uncanny. She was always in trouble for avoiding women's work, and she stole away from the village to the mountain so often that her father threatened to chain her up in the Long Hall.'

'Did he?' Tam asked.

'No,' the old man answered, chuckling again. 'Not quite, although he banned her from coming up here.'

'But how did you meet?'

'By accident.' The Herbal Man turned to gaze into the dragon's chamber. 'No one in Harbin knew I lived up here. People sometimes climbed the mountain, warriors mainly, but I had no hut back then, only these caves, and no one found them. That was how Claryssa and I both wanted to live. Peacefully. Securely. The world of people was too cruel to us, and we were getting older, too old to be concerned with petty day-to-day routines of people. Hidden up here, Claryssa and I could live without interference.' He smiled and shook his head. 'But then I saw Harmi and I knew she was different. She didn't see me the first time. I stayed out of sight, but she was beautiful and I was struck by her beauty. I must have watched her a dozen times without her knowing. She was the most beautiful woman I'd ever seen.'

'Why didn't you introduce yourself?' Tam suggested.

'I couldn't.' The Herbal Man looked at Tam, and sadness marked his face. 'Not at first. I was already an old man, and I didn't think a young woman as beautiful as Harmi would want to know an old recluse like me. And I was afraid that, if I spoke to her, she would tell others in the village, and Claryssa and I would not be safe and we would have to move on.'

'So why did it change?'

The Herbal Man laughed softly. 'I was careless,' he said and shook his head. 'Like I was careless this morning and you walked in. It will be our undoing, one day.' He returned his gaze to the dragon chamber, but his eyes seemed to be viewing a scene that Tam could not see. 'It was a beautiful, warm summer's morning, so I crept down to bathe in Watersdrop. There's a pool trapped high in the gorge, further up than Harbin villagers venture, and I always went there because I was sure it was a safe place. I was wrong, of course, because, while I was bathing in the morning, I heard a voice, and when I looked up it was your great-grandmother. She was standing on a rock, laughing.'

'Why would Gramma laugh at you?' Tam asked.

The Herbal Man turned to Tam, and said, 'She wasn't laughing at me. Harmi was always happy, always smiling and laughing. She loved being alive, especially on the mountain. She felt happy and free.'

'That's why I come here,' Tam admitted. 'It's the only place I can go to be me. I don't have to be a girl, or the Dragon Head's daughter. I can be myself.'

'You are undoubtedly Harmi's great-grand-daughter in spirit,' the Herbal Man said, and he chuckled. 'Ah, but I miss her.'

'So, what did Gramma do after she saw you?'

'It was all rather embarrassing,' he confessed, and he appeared to blush. 'You see, I was, well, I was undressed, and from where I came it was impolite to be seen naked by anyone, especially a woman. But Harmi wasn't the least offended by my — what's the correct saying? — um, my indecency. And because I had no intention to emerge from the water, she sat down, as comfortable as you like, and asked me to explain who I was. I had no choice, but to do so.'

Tam imagined the moment and knew she would have done the same, but she stifled her laughter to avoid offending the Herbal Man and persisted with her questions. 'How did Gramma meet Claryssa?'

The Herbal Man stroked his beard, before answering. 'I took a chance, as I have with you. Harmi kept my secret as I asked, and she kept visiting, and she made me realise how lonely my life had become. Not that Claryssa isn't good company,' he said, smiling apologetically at the dragon. Claryssa blinked and her tail twitched. 'But Claryssa and I are inextricably bound, and we think and feel the same things. We've lived together for a very long time. It was nice to have someone else to share time with.'

'You talk to the dragon?' Tam asked, amazed by the possibility.

'Of course,' he asserted indignantly. 'Why not?'

'I didn't mean to be rude. It's just I thought dragons were-'

She hesitated, but the Herbal Man added, 'Animals?' She nodded. 'Far from it, Tamesan,' he said. 'All things considered, dragons are the wisest, most intelligent beings in the world. They know things human minds barely guess at.'

'Do you use the ancient language – to talk to the dragon, I mean?'

'Claryssa and I don't talk as you think of it. We share our thoughts. If she wants me to know something, she thinks it into my mind and I do the same.'

'In words?'

'No. It would be too complicated and clumsy. We share a mixture of images and feelings. Wizards have tried describing how we communicate for a long time, but no one has yet successfully explained it. It exists. And I think dragons understand it better than our human minds can.'

'How did Gramma meet Claryssa?' Tam asked, determined to get all her answers while the Herbal Man was candidly talkative.

'I brought her here,' he confided. 'Somehow, I knew I could trust her, and she was the first person in a very long time I felt I could trust. Besides, time for me was growing shorter. I needed an apprentice to inherit from me.'

'Why didn't you choose a wife?' Tam asked. 'You could have had a son of your own to inherit your skills.'

'A son isn't necessary to inherit. A daughter would do as well,' the Herbal Man explained. 'And I did marry, Tamesan. Twice. The first time, I was very young. I was living in Yssaria. It's a very long way from here. In fact, the country may not even exist now. The world changes so much in a wizard's lifetime.' He paused, as if assembling his memory, before saying, 'Her name was Eunice. She was about your age, but men did not choose a wife in Yssaria like they do in Harbin. The parents of the girl select a husband they deem suitable. The man could only refuse if he was a soldier, or if he was of higher rank than the girl. Eunice was higher rank than I, so when her parents told my master that they chose me for Eunice's husband I had to accept.'

'Were you happy?' Tam asked.

The Herbal Man smiled at Tam's concern, and said, 'I didn't mind, Tamesan. I was young, and marriage to a pretty girl from a wealthy family was a dream come true. We had seven children.'

'Seven?' Tam gasped. 'Where are they now?'

'There was a war. I was away from home, serving Prince Alund when the Asharkaan Empire invaded Yssaria. The Asharkaan cavalry pillaged my family's town, Gathis, and put every living person to death. Even babies.'

The shadow of sadness on the old man's face upset Tam. 'I'm sorry,' she said. 'I didn't mean to pry.'

'I don't mind, Tamesan,' he reassured her. 'I still grieve for them, but it was a very long time ago, and grieving does not restore the past.'

'And your second marriage?' Tam asked.

The Herbal Man drew a deep breath before he continued. 'My second marriage came when I was High Wizard to the Queen of Marigan. I was much older then, and I'd seen the Asharkaan Empire rise and fall. Queen

Lela insisted that her High Wizard be married to an important lady and so she arranged a wedding with Lady Elisabet Tomoy, whose family owned almost a quarter of the kingdom's holdings. There was no courtship or exchange of vows before the ceremony. I hardly knew the woman. On our wedding day, she told me that she did not want to live with an old man, and that she intended to keep her lovers. I told her I was sorry because the marriage was not my choice either. In hindsight, I should never have been so honest. It made her even more bitter.'

'It must have been terrible for you,' said Tam, imagining being forced to accept Marron if he liked her as little as she liked him.

'It was terrible for us both,' the Herbal Man conceded. 'We kept a public façade for the Queen, but we went our separate ways whenever we could. She spent her time with her court friends and I – well, I was studying too much. Claryssa and I had so much to teach each other.' He paused again, and a wry smile graced his lips. 'It was ironically amusing because Elisabet became jealous of Claryssa.'

'And you had no children,' Tam concluded.

'We did, actually,' he admitted. He shook his head, sighed, and said, 'Don't ask me how these things happen. It would be improper of me to explain. But Elisabet and I had two children, a boy and a girl. The boy, Mark, grew up to be a soldier, I think. I never saw him after he turned eight. You see, boys born into the Middle Classes, and some of the Higher Classes, were taken from their families aged eight to live in the public military barracks where they learned to be soldiers. I thought it was a barbaric practice, I still do, but Mark was taken, and Elisabet was proud to mother a soldier for the kingdom.'

'What happened to the girl?'

'Jennet was sacrificed on the Holy Altar to the Goddess Ite,' he replied, bitterly.

Tam couldn't disguise her shock. 'Sacrificed? You mean like goats are sacrificed at Varst's Great Feast?'

'Probably,' the Herbal Man muttered, and he shuffled his feet as he shifted his gaze to the shimmering water in the pedestal. 'Elisabet arranged it all. To be chosen as a sacrificial virgin for the annual ceremony was the highest honour in Marigan. Families of the sacrificial virgins were feted throughout the kingdom and lifted to a new social rank, second only to the Werelords who owned enormous tracts of land. It provided a lifetime annuity, allowing the family to live very comfortably.'

'But you said Elísabet's family were already landowners,' Tam argued.

The Herbal Man nodded. 'Yes. Her father was already a Werelord. But Elisabet's family were ambitious and having a second Werelord in the family made them wealthier and more powerful. Jennet was a lucrative sacrifice.'

'Couldn't you stop it?'

'I tried, Tamesan, but it wasn't easy,' he said, and shrugged. 'I wasn't fighting the Queen or Elisabet. I was fighting a whole social order and a history. Marigans believe sacrificial virgins enter Ite's Eternal Realm where they serve the Goddess as handmaidens. Even Jennet believed it. She didn't want me to interfere. I had no choice.'

'What happened to Elisabet?'

'I outlived her,' he replied, soberly. 'After Jennet's sacrifice, she held sufficient status to do as she pleased, and we saw very little of one another. I went to her funeral, out of respect, but I felt no loss. Then the world changed again, and wizards were outlawed, like I told you before. Claryssa and I had to leave the kingdom and we spent many years wandering, searching for a safe place to settle. Finally, we arrived here.'

'Did you ever ask Gramma to be your apprentice?'

The Herbal Man chuckled quietly, and said, 'Almost, but I knew the time wasn't quite right. And something else happened, something I only learned by chance, but in answer to your question, no, I didn't ask her.'

Tam's curiosity flared. 'Did she tell the others about you? Is that why you didn't ask her?'

The Herbal Man laughed, and replied, 'No. Well, not exactly. Circumstances made us break our secret. Harmi's mother, your great-great grandmother, became so ill that everybody in the village believed she was dying. Harmi was very upset. As much as she fought with her mother, she still loved her dearly. She asked if I knew a remedy. She felt ashamed to ask, because she knew that, if I helped, I would be giving away my secret existence here, but she wanted to save her mother's life. What could I do?' he asked, raising his eyebrows in mock exasperation. 'I loved Harmi. I couldn't let her watch her mother die, especially when I knew I might be able to prevent it. So, I went down to the village with her, and attended her mother, and recognised the fever she had. With Harmi's help, I found local herbs to create an elixir to bring down her mother's temperature and improve her chances of survival. And it did.'

'But then everyone knew that you lived here,' Tam said. 'What did they say?'

'Most were amazed. A few were suspicious. Harmi concocted a story that I was washed ashore from a shipwreck and I was trekking across the mountains around Harbin Bay, searching for help, when she found me wandering on Dragon Mountain. It was an utterly absurd tale, but everyone accepted it, and the Dragon Head of the time invited me to live in the village. I declined, of course, because of Claryssa and my hideaway, and I kept up a charade as a grumpy old man who preferred a hermit's life. I built the decoy hut on the plateau and pretended it was my home, and that's how things remained.'

'And Gramma?'

'Harmi visited when she could. She couldn't come as often as she wanted because people knew who I was, after helping cure her mother. Then her father intervened and she stopped coming altogether.'

'But you saved her mother's life? Why would her father stop her?'

'He wasn't ungrateful, Tamesan. Circumstances changed, as I said. Harmi came of age and Leith chose her for his wife. It was no longer right for her to visit me.'

Tam saw the parallels with her own life and argued, 'But you were friends.'

The Herbal Man shook his head and explained, 'Village gossip. People spread cruel rumours when a married woman is seen frequenting the company of another man, even one as old as I was then. Her father could not let it happen to Harmi, or Leith for that matter, and neither could I.'

Tam understood. Katris' barbs against her stuck deep, even though they were lies. People were believing the cruel comments. 'So Gramma never came here again?'

The Herbal Man shifted his weight from one foot to the other. 'No,' he said. 'Not here. We saw each other discreetly when I visited the village, when I needed supplies or was invited to tend the ill. I was with her when Leith was sick with the plague. It was a terribly sad time.'

Tam heard the catch in his voice and saw tears pooling in his eyes. He wiped them away and in the awkward silence Tam regretted asking her questions. She was about to apologise when the Herbal Man slumped forward and barely managed to catch his balance on the lip of the pedestal. Dragon scales scraped against the rock and Tam saw Claryssa's golden eyes gazing into the crystal chamber. 'Are you alright?' Tam asked as she reached to help the old man.

'I am weary, Tamesan,' he replied, as he straightened, and in the crystal light she saw the deep lines furrowing his face. 'It's Claryssa who is unwell. I've been up with her most of the night.'

'What's wrong with her?' Tam asked, turning towards the dragon.

'She's old, Tamesan, old and tired,' he replied. 'Dragons live a very long time, longer than most humans can imagine, but even dragon clocks eventually burn out. Age is her illness.'

'Is she dying?' Tam whispered, turning to the Herbal Man.

'We are all dying,' the Herbal Man answered in his cryptic manner, and he continued with, 'You've asked all the questions, this morning. Before I ask you to return to Harbin so that I can continue to attend to Claryssa and perhaps catch up on sleep, I have a question for you. Are you willing to be my apprentice?'

His question caught Tam unprepared. She remembered her father's emphatic denial of the Herbal Man's offer. 'Why do you ask me?' she cautiously inquired. 'You know my father's answer.'

'Because Claryssa chose you,' the Herbal Man informed her. Tam turned to the dragon and saw the golden eyes staring at her. 'And I agree with her choice,' he continued. 'You are intelligent, compassionate, a free spirit, and you're willing to learn. You have all the right qualities.'

'But you already asked my father,' she reminded him.

'It is not your father I am asking, Tamesan,' the Herbal Man stressed. 'I am asking you. And you must make your decision. No one else can.'

No one in Harbin dared disobey the Dragon Head, but Tam was willing to defy her father when it came to doing something she desperately wanted. 'What must I do as your apprentice?' she asked, overwhelmed by the turn of events.

'What you are already doing,' he replied. 'Learn. Ask. Try. Claryssa has accepted you. Dragons understand humans far better than humans understand themselves. We do not offer you this burden lightly. We are offering you the gift of our total lives' work.'

Tam looked from the Herbal Man to the dragon and back to the old man. She stood in a crystal chamber unlike any space she dreamed could exist. She was standing so close to a real dragon that she could hear its scales shift as it breathed. She was talking to a wizard who made light appear from gems, a man who lived longer than anyone could possibly live, travelled further than anyone could hope to travel, and seen more people and places than anyone would wish to see. The same dragon that her Gramma babbled about for years, without anyone understanding the truth, was choosing her to be the wizard's apprentice. Gramma Harmi knew the truth and she knew it all along. Everyone else, not Harmi, was mad.

And now the wizard wanted Tam to accept his inheritance. What choice did she have? What answer could she offer that wouldn't offend either her father or the Herbal Man? She understood that she was being offered a chance at freedom from the monotony of Harbin and the slavery of a dragonwarrior woman's life. If she accepted, she might break her shackles and become what she dreamed she could be. She had one chance to be free. And it was offered by a dragon.

Twenty-Two

Warm summer weeks drifted through their annual cycles. The mornings were crisp and fresh, full of blue sky and sunshine, and the nights cool and calm. Having endured the harshest winter in memory, now the people of Harbin enjoyed a stable summer, punctuated twice by heavy rainstorms. Fishermen slept away the days, their work confined to early mornings before dawn and late afternoons until after dusk. The women, children and men who remained in Harbin found time on their hands, despite Eesa's efforts to create work, and the people were happy.

The relaxed lifestyle was a blessing for Tam because it gave her ample opportunity to commence her apprenticeship in earnest with the Herbal Man. To allay Eesa's mistrust, the Herbal Man visited the village as often as Tam went up the mountain, but Eesa still confronted him on his first visit.

'By Procra, you have cheek, interfering like this,' she snarled, stepping into his path.

The Herbal Man bowed his head respectfully, and replied, 'I mean no one harm.'

'You know very well my husband's decision on this matter. The Dragon Head's decisions are law,' Eesa warned, placing her hands on her hips.

'Tamesan is very talented,' the Herbal Man replied, 'and I am a very old man. I am nearly too old to do what I do best, and it would be a shame not to leave someone in Harbin to carry on my healing work. Your daughter has a rare feeling for the art.'

'That does not appease my husband's decision,' Eesa insisted.

'No,' he agreed. 'It does not. Kevan is the wise and rightful leader of

Harbin when he is present, but what harm can come from Tamesan learning from me while the Dragon Fang are away? By the time Kevan returns, what I want to teach Tamesan this year will be done. He may rethink his decision when he sees what she can do for his people.'

'You are asking me to lie to my husband, and encourage my daughter to lie to her father,' Eesa flatly accused.

'Who is lying?' the Herbal Man calmly asked. 'I will teach Tamesan, but she will not be my apprentice. A true apprentice would live with his or her master, but I will come to Harbin to teach Tam, and I will ensure she does not shirk the daily work you require. The discipline will be good for her. Surely you agree?'

His offer appealed to Eesa because Tamesan was certainly not a disciplined girl and the lazy summer exacerbated that flaw in her, but Eesa knew that Kevan forbade an apprenticeship. 'I cannot go against my husband's word,' she argued.

'Who is Dragon Head while Kevan sails in the dragonship?'

Eesa's eyes narrowed, suspecting the old man was playing a game. 'Kevan is,' she answered.

'On the dragonship with the Dragon Fang,' the Herbal Man agreed, 'but what about in the village? Who leads while he is away?'

'I do.'

'Can you make decisions in his absence?'

'Yes.'

'Then you can decide whether Tamesan can learn from me,' the Herbal Man concluded. 'Kevan said Tamesan cannot be my apprentice. You and I must obey his decision. But he did not say I cannot visit and teach Tamesan. That is now your decision to make.'

Eesa felt trapped between reason and duty. The Herbal Man was right. Technically, she was not countermanding Kevan's decision. Besides, she saw no harm in what he offered. 'I will allow Tamesan to learn from you,' she decided, but she qualified her answer with, 'but only if you visit

Harbin, and only after she has completed her daily tasks. Am I understood?'

'Eesa is the true leader in Harbin,' the Herbal Man responded, with a gracious smile.

Eesa blushed at the undisguised flattery, checked herself, and said, 'When Kevan returns, the lessons are to end, unless he changes his mind.'

'I understand,' the Herbal Man sombrely affirmed. When Eesa excused herself and walked away, he smiled and went to find Tam.

The Herbal Man insisted that Tam continue to learn reading and writing. 'If you can read,' he told her, 'every mystery, every recorded truth, will open to you. Most people learn about the world through their own experiences, and it is all they ever know, but reading gives you access to other people's experiences and lets you see the world through their eyes and words to see and feel things you might never experience for yourself.' He also expanded her knowledge of herbalism as they walked the mountainside, showing her the summer plants and revealing their medicinal uses.

Tam discovered Jaysin shadowing the Herbal Man on his visits and, when he refused to go when she ordered him to play, she told the Herbal Man, 'He also wants to learn reading and writing.'

The Herbal Man's bushy white eyebrows lifted, and he beckoned for Jaysin to approach. When the shy boy reached him, the Herbal Man bent forward and asked, 'Has Tamesan shown you any of the alphabet letters?' Jaysin nodded. The Herbal Man handed him a stick and said, 'Draw what you know.' With painstaking accuracy, Jaysin drew every letter that Tam taught him, and the Herbal Man nodded appreciatively when Jaysin finished. Turning to Tamesan, he said, 'Very good. It seems that there are two of you who learn quickly.' He squatted before Jaysin to study the boy's forlorn face. Dark eyes stared back. 'Would you like to learn more?' the Herbal Man asked. Jaysin nodded. The Herbal Man rubbed his beard, as if deciding, before he said, 'I think it will be fine for you to stay for the lessons.' He met Jaysin's gaze with a serious frown. 'You must practise everything I show and tell you, and you must do whatever your sister tells you to do when I am not here. Do we have an agreement?' Jaysin nodded emphatically, as if he was determined to show the Herbal Man he would do anything to be involved in the lessons. 'Good,' the Herbal Man pronounced, and he straightened. 'We have work to do.' As the Herbal Man turned away, Tam was sure she saw a faint smile flutter across her little brother's mouth.

The Herbal Man's agreement with Eesa restricted Tam to four visits up the mountain. 'A small price to pay in exchange for learning,' he assured Tam, but she had a new reason for climbing the mountain – Claryssa. After her first encounter, fascination overcame her ancestral fear of Nakiades' ancient enemy, and she wheedled opportunities from the Herbal Man's instructions on how to use his alchemy equipment to study Claryssa's golden form while the dragon slept.

'Why does she sleep so much?' Tam asked on her second visit.

'Her age,' the Herbal Man replied. 'The weight of so many years. She's tired now. Dragons do spend a lot of time sleeping when they are young, but they sleep then because they are growing rapidly. Claryssa sleeps now because there is so little energy left in her body.'

'How much longer will she live?'

'I don't know, Tamesan, but I fear her time is growing short. She knows it herself. There's a wizard legend saying that dragons know exactly when they are going to die. Claryssa hasn't revealed a time to me, but she knows her time is coming. She feels it.'

And you feel it too, Tam thought. She heard the melancholy in the old man's voice and remembered that the lives of dragons and wizards were inseparably bound.

The lessons became complex as the summer weeks passed and, although Tam tried to absorb everything the Herbal Man shared, it seemed too much in such a short time. The dragonship was returning within days and her father would be home. She knew he would be angry when he learned how lenient Eesa was concerning the Herbal Man's influence on Tam. Eesa said as much to Tam in the evenings. She knew her father never changed his mind once he made his decision because he believed only weak men backed down, and he justified his philosophy on the predication that men worthy of respect never made stupid decisions, so Tam learned as efficiently as she could while there was time.

On her fourth visit, she asked, 'How do you control the dragon?'

The Herbal Man looked up from a scroll, and said, 'I wondered how long it would take for you to ask that question.' He laughed as he finished.

'What's so funny?' Tam asked.

Seeing her irritation, the Herbal Man ceased laughing and apologised. 'Sorry, Tamesan. The question is a fair one, a good one. I only laughed because it's the question leading to the answer that all apprentices want to hear from their wizard masters.'

'And what's that?'

He peered at her in disbelief and his intense scrutiny unnerved her. He shook his head as he settled on a stool at the bench in his study and he studied her again, before saying quietly, 'Sit down, Tamesan.' She sat, and the Herbal Man fixed his gaze squarely on her, before he asked, 'Do you know what magic is?'

She shook her head. 'I've never heard of it.'

Her response appeared to surprise the Herbal Man because he hesitated before continuing. 'I'd forgotten how isolated Harbin is.' He tapped the bench with his fingers and Tam noticed that his fingernails were long. 'Tamesan, in the world beyond Harbin, a long time ago, perhaps even before Nakiades led your people to settle in this wilderness, wizards were revered and sought by kings and queens and emperors to solve their problems.'

'I remember you said that,' she said.

'Good. But I omitted a detail which I took for granted that you would already know.' He ceased drumming his fingers. 'I told you why wizards fell from favour.'

'People feared their dragons and the kings and queens thought they were becoming too powerful.'

'Correct,' he said with an approving smile. 'A wizard's power has two sources. A wizard has the power of knowledge. I have shared that key with you. But there is a second source. It's called magic.'

'What is magic?' Tam asked.

'It's an indescribable force, an energy, an ability, and a burden, all wrapped up in one thing. Magic is the power to do almost anything you want.'

'Like what?' she asked. 'I don't understand.'

'Like this,' he said. He snapped his fingers and a small green flame appeared and danced on his fingertips.

Tam gasped with wonder, squeaking, 'How did you do it?'

'Magic,' he answered. 'Wizards could fly, make themselves invisible, heal with a touch, tear down walls, stop armies. With the right knowledge, and a dragon, no one was more powerful than a wizard.'

'But where does magic come from?'

'An excellent question, Tamesan,' said the Herbal Man. 'Most apprentices want to start using magic immediately, instead of wanting to understand it, and they are inevitably disappointed when their masters tell them that, first, they must understand the source of magic. You see, to understand a thing, you must first know its source.' He blew on his fingers. The flame disappeared. 'Wizards have studied the source of magic almost as long as there have been dragons, and what they discovered, too late to save themselves from history, was that the source is related directly to the dragons. Magic is a gift from the dragons.' He paused, and corrected himself, saying, 'No. That's not entirely true. It's not a gift. It's a burden.'

The Herbal Man rose from his stool and paced the floor of the study as he continued his explanation. 'Dragons are different from every other creature. Somehow, their bodies and psyches create vast energy reservoirs, wild forces that dragons have learned to harness to enable them to fly and breathe fire and cast spells. A wizard named Tarran traced the energy source back to an ancient legend of a meteor falling to earth called the Genesis Stone, but her research ended there, and no one knows how the two are linked. What we do know is that, once a dragon chooses a human to become its attendant wizard, the two meld into one. The dragon shares its energy with the wizard and activates the wizard's mental and psychic energy. The wizard then has to learn how to tap into the dragon's vast energy store and use it without losing control of it.'

'But why would a wizard want to use a dragon's energy field?' Tam asked, bewildered by the Herbal Man's theories.

'To create magic,' he replied.

'How?'

'Ah,' he breathed out, and pulled at his beard. 'It is not a simple question to answer. You see, dragons and wizards aren't the only things to have energy reservoirs or fields. Everything in this world has an individual energy field, an aura as colleagues called the phenomenon. The art of magic is to identify, harness and manipulate energy fields. Some aura, like those surrounding most people, are weak. Other fields, like those surrounding the four elements of earth, fire, air and water, are vast reservoirs. Alone, a wizard can create minor magic, like hypnotic spells, trivial illusions and trifling healings. Coupled with a dragon, however, a wizard's magic becomes exponentially greater. The dragon provides potency and the wizard provides control.'

The Herbal Man's explanation made Tam's mind swirl in confusion, but she asked, 'What happens when the wizard loses control?'

'If it happens,' the Herbal Man replied, 'the wizard can destroy both the dragon and themself. At the very least, the wizard would bring great harm to them both. Dragons usually prevent it happening, though.'

'How?'

'They are highly intelligent, as I've said, and they intercept dangerous outpourings of magic that might or would jeopardise their safety.'

'Always?'

The Herbal Man hesitated, his gaze firmly on Tam, and replied, 'No. Not always. Sometimes there is a need to take a risk. I've heard tales of it happening.'

'What happened?'

'I know too little of the details to relate now. Perhaps you will read those tales in my library.'

Tam swallowed, her mouth feeling unnaturally dry, but she summoned her courage to ask, 'Will you teach me how to use magic?'

The Herbal Man shook his head, saying, 'No. I can't teach you. But I will teach you how to learn about it so that you can teach yourself. You see, without a dragon of your own, there will be no magic for you to use.'

Despite the Herbal Man's answer that he could not teach her to use magic so long as she never had a dragon to work with her, Tam continued to contemplate his theory. Claryssa obviously paired for life with him, and so they shared an aura of magic. What they could do because of their shared magic she couldn't guess at, but one consequence was longevity because, from the matter of his tales, they clearly lived a very long life together. She was curious as to why the Dragon Fang and her father never mentioned encountering wizards or magic in their dragon-hunting adventure, and she wondered if the dragons to the south were searching for wizard partners to adopt. If she could travel south on the dragonship, next summer, she might find a dragon willing to accept her. She laughed at the absurdity of her idea. Even if her father agreed to let her travel with the Dragon Fang – and she knew it would never happen in her lifetime – and even if she managed to find a dragon, it would most likely eat her before she could introduce herself.

The Herbal Man was training her to heal and teach the people in

Harbin. The magic he spoke of was beyond her reach, a talent to which she might aspire in a different world under different circumstances. Harbin's limitations on her exceeded even what the Herbal Man imagined, but she was content with learning to be a good herbalist and healer. It was a preferable alternative to the Harbin lifestyle offered to other girls.

The sea-watcher's horn echoed from White Eagle's Ledge across Harbin Bay late one summer afternoon, signalling the dragonship's return. Tam put down the scrap of weaving she was adjusting for Banni and followed the women, her mother included, out of the Long Hall.

Outside, she stood with everyone and strained to see the blood red sail at the bay's entrance. A stiff westerly breeze was carrying the dragonship swiftly to its mooring, so Eesa issued orders for the women to prepare for the ship's arrival. The dragonwarrior heroes were returning – husbands, fathers, brothers and sons of Harbin – and Tam savoured the village's anticipation and swelling excitement.

Eesa sent Tam to the shore to assist Amarti with cleaning fish for the homecoming banquet. Last summer, Tam was set the duty as punishment for her tardiness, but this time she accepted the task as a sign of Eesa's trust in her to help Eesa's old friend do the job properly. Tam understood the summer and the Herbal Man's lessons altered her relationship with her mother for the better. She was confident Eesa understood her need to learn more than the standard duties of girls in the village, and, in turn, Tam felt she better understood her mother's role and responsibilities.

Tam smiled when she took up the gutting knife that Amarti handed to her. *Perhaps*, she considered as she started working, *it's part of the secret in reaching adulthood – learning to understand each other's points of view*. Enthused by the bustling activity sparked by the dragonship's return, she sang a Harbin fishing ballad as she cut through the fish bellies.

The dragonship swept across the harbour faster than anticipated and Tam and Amarti stopped cleaning fish to watch its approach. With the great red sail fully rigged, the ship raced towards the shore, but Tam noticed discrepancies in what she expected to see. The wind blew from the stern, but the ship heeled to port far more than it should and the sail was tattered, partially torn from the upper spar, rents marring its face. Fear flickered in her mind, and when she turned to Amarti she saw that the old fisherwoman mirrored her concern. Wordless, they rose from the cleaning tables and hurried to the jetty.

Other villagers were gravitating to the shore and Tam saw the herdsmen running down from the goat pasture. People clustered on the jetty and watched with increasing trepidation as the dragonship bore down on them, seemingly going too fast to stop, but at the last moment a warrior shouted, the red sail dropped with a clatter, and the ship swung to slide beside the jetty.

As the belaying ropes were tossed out, a woman screamed and a mournful cry rose. Caught at the back of the crowd, Tam pushed forward to see what caused the sudden outburst of anguish and gaped in astonishment. The ship's watery bilge was crimson and flooded with dragonwarrior corpses, bodies and limbs caked with blood, and her father sat among them, cradling Theo's shaggy blond head, weeping. Half the Dragon Fang had not come home this summer.

Twenty-Three

'Amarti! Bring all the clean cloth you can find! Banni! Take five girls and prepare a bedding space in the Long Hall! Galt! Find poles and oars to make stretchers for the wounded! Don't stand there! These men need our help now!'

Having stirred the stunned villagers into action, Eesa boarded the listing ship and clambered towards her husband.

Kevan lifted sorrowful eyes as she reached him and stared blankly, murmuring, 'Theo walks the shadowed path. I could do nothing.'

Eesa kneeled and wrapped him in her arms.

Tam spied Chasse on the stern, staring into the water. He was so still that Tam feared her brother was badly hurt, but before she could respond to her fear Chasse climbed unaided onto the jetty. She pushed past people to reach him, hugged him fiercely, and whispered, 'Thank Procra you are safe.' He stiffened in her embrace, so she released him, asking, 'What's wrong?' as she studied his face.

'Nothing,' he grunted. 'I have to help the others.' He turned away from Tam and climbed into the ship, where he began tying down ropes as if the task suddenly assumed great importance.

Tam watched her brother from the jetty, puzzled by what had changed him, but when she heard her name called she turned her attention to her father. Kevan had a bloodied bandage tied over his left shoulder, another masked part of his head, and a third wrapped his left calf and Tam understood from the carnage that the dragon the dragonwarriors encountered gave a grave and costly fight.

Eesa and Jon were helping Kevan stand, and Eesa was signalling to

Tam, yelling, 'Fetch the Herbal Man, child! None of his excuses! Tell him what you've seen and bring him down, even if you have to carry him! Go! Hurry!'

Tam ran and walked and scrambled up the mountain, but by the time she reached the Herbal Man's abode, exhausted, the sun was slipping below the western horizon and Dragon Mountain was swathed in grey. She caught her breath and knocked at the hut. As usual, no one answered, so she climbed through the window, opened the trapdoor and descended. She found the Herbal Man in his study.

'Sorry for the rude intrusion,' Tam apologised, 'but Mother wants you to come down immediately. The dragonship is back and there are a lot of injured warriors. It's terrible.'

'Are your father and brother hurt?' he asked.

'Father is badly hurt,' she explained. 'Chasse seems alright.'

'Then we best hurry,' he said. 'Gather those ointment jars on the shelf there,' he indicated, 'and the herb bag on the hook.'

A short while later, Tam and the Herbal Man began the descent to Harbin, but capricious clouds hid the fragment of moon and made the path dangerous. 'This will be useful,' said the Herbal Man, waving his walking staff, and when he muttered a dozen arcane words the staff radiated a bright glow. 'There,' he said. 'We can continue.'

Tam recognised the light. 'It's the light you used to find me in the snow.'

'It has its uses,' the Herbal Man said. 'Wind and rain can't affect it. Quite practical, really.'

'Is this magic?'

The Herbal Man chuckled and sighed, before replying, 'A very small example. Unfortunately, it's about all I have left.'

'What do you mean?' Tam asked.

'Too many questions, Tamesan. There are men dying. We have to hurry,' he reminded her, and he led the way briskly down the mountain path.

On the village outskirts, the Herbal Man extinguished the staff light and produced a small lantern from under his cloak. 'We'll proceed with this,' he said, as he fumbled with his tinderbox to light the wick. 'It would be difficult to explain the staff.' Lantern burning, the pair crossed the goat pasture, heading for the Long Hall.

A dozen lanterns and torches illuminated the Long Hall, throwing angular, flickering shadows across the wall and floor, where Eesa and several women attended to the injured warriors. Tam led the Herbal Man to Eesa, who straightened, frowning, as they reached her.

'You took too long!' she berated. 'Vetch died!'

'I am sorry to hear the news,' the Herbal Man replied, bowing his head. 'I will work where I am most needed.'

'See to Kevan,' Eesa ordered. She turned to Tam and said, 'Help Amarti in the Warriors' Hall. She's preparing a small meal for the men who are not in here.'

Tam went to obey her mother, but the Herbal Man intervened. 'With your permission, Eesa, but I would rather Tamesan remained here to help me. She knows enough of the healing art to be useful, and I need someone who can mix pastes and apply poultices while I work.'

Eesa glared, but she shrugged and replied, 'If that is what you wish. I put responsibility for what happens here in your hands, Herbal Man. I will help Amarti. Tamesan will stay here.'

'Thank you,' the Herbal Man responded, and he beckoned Tam to follow him.

As Eesa asked, he went to inspect Kevan's wounds first, but the Dragon Head waved him aside, saying gruffly, 'My wounds need little attention. There are others here more in need of your healing than me. See to them.' The Herbal Man bowed his head respectfully, but as he went to move Kevan grabbed his arm and held tight as he said, 'You have the lives of the Dragon Fang in your hands tonight. Do not fail them.'

The Herbal Man glanced down at the hand gripping his arm, before he looked Kevan directly in the eyes, and replied firmly, 'I will do all I can do. That is all I can promise.' He maintained his steady gaze until Kevan released his grip, and then he walked away with Tam in tow. Tam saw her father's eyes following her.

Her father included, Tam counted fifteen dragonwarriors needing healing. Most of the ugly injuries would heal with care. Ion had a nasty gash running across his upper cheek to his brow and it had taken his right eye. Keegan had a hole punched through his chest, but the gods mercifully protected him from major internal organ damage and infection.

Of the fifteen in the Long Hall, four were in critical states. Frankton, one of the oldest dragonwarriors, was unconscious and pale from excessive blood loss, and Jon told the Herbal Man that Frankton was in that state for at least four days. Frankton's wife, Nyssa, kneeled beside him on the floor, keeping vigil.

Adrian received a vicious blow that left a dent in the top right of his head and the wound was infected. He drooled and he babbled incomprehensibly, so his companions tied him up to prevent him hurting himself, or anyone else.

Fallan was in his death throes. The wound in his knee was a small puncture, but it was so badly infected that poison was running wild through his veins and the Herbal Man said he would die before midnight. His wife, Arien, sobbed at the foot of his bedding for a while before she left the Long Hall.

The fourth was Marron. Tam was shocked to find him lying among the critically injured, and her dislike for him was submerged beneath sympathy when she saw his fractured right arm, smashed in three places, a jagged bone piercing the skin below his elbow.

The Herbal Man squatted to inspect Marron's arm while Trask explained how he tried to keep the wound clean on the homeward journey. 'You will make my son well again,' Trask concluded.

The Herbal Man rose, shaking his head slowly. 'It's a very bad break,' he conceded. 'The poison is already in his arm. I cannot promise it will mend.'

'But I kept it clean,' Trask insisted, his anger rising.

'You did well,' the Herbal Man assured him. 'But it is a very bad break.'

Trask grabbed the Herbal Man's cloak and wrenched the old man closer, snarling, 'He is my only son! Understand me? My only son! You will make him better again or I will kill you!'

Tam reached for Trask's arm, but Jon pulled her gently aside before he put his hand on Trask's shoulder. 'Let the Herbal Man do what he's been called here to do,' he said calmly. 'He will do what he can for your son. He's promised you. But Marron's life is not in the Herbal Man's hands. It is in Varst's. He, not the Herbal Man, will determine if your son lives or dies.'

Trask gave Jon a murderous look and grunted to show his frustration as he released the Herbal Man's cloak, before saying, 'Be sure you do all you can, old man. I will be watching.' He spat on the ground and stalked to the door.

'Thank you,' the Herbal Man said to Jon, who nodded. 'I'd best get to work.'

He set Tam the task of cleaning Marron's arm with a pungent disinfectant, while he searched in his bag of phials and jars. Marron was sleeping, but the instant Tam touched his arm with the damp cloth he jerked awake and screamed and turned his gaze on her. She cringed. His eyes were dark, wide and wild.

'Make him drink this,' the Herbal Man said. He handed Tam a goblet of watery green liquid, but when she offered it to Marron, Marron refused to drink and kept staring at her.

'You must drink this,' Tam coaxed. Marron ignored her plea, but he tried to move his injured arm and cried in pain. Tam squeezed his left hand and offered the goblet again. 'Please drink,' she begged. 'It will ease the pain.' Reluctantly, Marron acquiesced and accepted the goblet. He took a sip, and then a deeper draught, and he stared at Tam again, his eyes still wide and wild, but they slowly glazed over and he slipped into unconsciousness. Tam turned to the Herbal Man.

'The potion has put him into a very deep sleep,' the Herbal Man explained. 'It's called Jasmine's Green Cloud, made from the powder of a plant you won't find locally, Tamesan, but I've always kept a large supply. Lucky I have. It will make the next part much easier.'

'What next part?' Tam asked, as she tentatively recommenced bathing Marron's relaxed arm.

'I have to reset the bones. If they're left like this, he will not have an arm worth using. Wash away every scrap of dried blood and dirt, especially where it is infected. And smear plenty of Becchrin's Cure over every section of broken skin,' he added. 'I will see to some of the others while you do it.'

Tam tried to avoid looking at the bone jutting from Marron's arm as she cleaned his wounds, and she wondered how he received so brutal an injury, and how the Dragon Fang came to be so badly defeated. Perhaps the dragon ambushed them. Perhaps it was harder to kill than ever before. Perhaps it was bigger than previous dragons. She pictured a creature Claryssa's size lurking in wait for the Dragon Fang, but for all her size she was old and lethargic, and Tam couldn't imagine Claryssa being a match for the dragonwarriors. Perhaps younger dragons were more ferocious. Perhaps the dragonwarriors were attacked by more than one dragon.

When the Herbal Man returned, he asked if Tam wanted to watch him reset Marron's bones. 'It's not a pleasant business,' he warned. 'If, at any stage, you feel you cannot watch, go. I will understand.'

'I'll stay,' she said.

He began, and Tam winced for Marron several times as the Herbal Man probed and twisted the young man's arm. She felt queasy and nearly passed out when the Herbal Man forced the broken bone beneath the skin, but she watched the entire operation and helped tightly bind the arm at the completion.

'You are very brave,' the Herbal Man announced as he tied off the bandage. 'The first time I saw this done I ran from the tent to be sick. You have a stronger stomach for this work than I have.'

Tam accepted his compliment silently, but it did not quell her hidden distress, and she took several deep breaths to calm herself before she offered to attend to another warrior's needs. When she did, the Herbal Man directed her to her father.

Kevan watched Tam approach, and she read questioning distrust in his eyes, emotion bordering on anger, but she pushed aside her personal feelings and smiled when she reached him, asking, 'Can I inspect the wound on your head please?'

'I see my daughter disobeyed my instructions,' he murmured, as he bent forward.

'You bathed these wounds in seawater, Father?' she inquired, refusing to argue with him.

'Yes,' he answered.

She was relieved that he acquiesced so easily, though it left her curious as to why. She assumed he was tired and sore. She unwrapped the bandage and assessed the wound. A chunk of hair and flesh was missing from the top of his head and his greying hair was matted with dried blood. 'I must clean this wound, Father,' she informed him. 'Then I will do the same for your other wounds. We have to avoid infection.'

Kevan sat patiently while Tam efficiently bathed his wounds, applied ointment, and re-bandaged them, but she could sense his uneasy mood. Apart from the necessary exchanges to hasten the process, neither Kevan nor Tam spoke, but she knew there would be a time for argument over her lessons with the Herbal Man. Yet, as she finished the final dressing, she was aware of a change in her father's demeanour. He looked at her through exhausted eyes with a glimmer of pride and acceptance, and he mumbled, 'Thank you, Tamesan. It feels better.'

'You need rest, Father,' she urged. 'There is a bed beside you. Sleep here tonight.' She helped him to lie down and she made him as comfortable as she could, and in a matter of moments Kevan was asleep.

Eesa brought warm broth to the Herbal Man and Tam shortly after. 'How is your father?' she asked Tam.

'Sleeping,' Tam replied.

'Kevan will recover,' the Herbal Man said. 'He is lucky.'

Eesa walked among the injured, speaking to those who were awake, and she knelt beside Kevan's sleeping form a while before she left the Long Hall to continue working with the other women, but she paused in the doorway and nodded to Tam before she exited. Eesa returned before midnight and sat beside Kevan's bed to keep vigil.

Tam assisted the Herbal Man throughout the long night, responding to the needs and cries of injured warriors. At times, individuals jerked awake, screaming, and Tam went to them and spoke soothingly until they closed their eyes. After the first two men woke, howling in anguish, she asked the Herbal Man, 'Why do they do that?'

'They have seen things more terrible than they wished to see,' he replied. 'This summer has dearly cost the Dragon Fang.'

Fallan died shortly after midnight. Eesa sent Tam to fetch Arien, but when Tam reached Arien's hut she refused to go to the Long Hall.

'What can I do?' she asked, her face smeared with tear stains, her eyes large and exhausted. 'I will come in the morning.' Tam relayed Arien's reply to Eesa.

'Everyone grieves in their own way,' Eesa said, and she leaned her head against Kevan's bed, dismissing her daughter.

Frankton died before dawn. He sat up, staring vacantly in the torchlight, exhaled heavily, and toppled to his left. The Herbal Man asked Tam to help lay Frankton back in his bedding, before he pulled the top sheet over Frankton's face, and said, 'His wife can come when the village wakes.'

'He isn't married,' Tam replied. 'He has no family.'

The Herbal Man shook his head, and murmured, 'In death, we are truly alone.' He sat on a chair and said to Tam, 'You should sleep. It's almost morning.'

'I can sleep later,' she said. She heard Jakon murmuring and took a water jug to him and, when he finished drinking and slipped back to sleep, Tam moved among the warriors, mopping perspiration from fevered brows, adjusting blankets and checking breathing. She sat beside Marron, who was squirming in a bad dream, and made sure he didn't move his injured arm excessively. She felt pity for him. The summer journey was violent and cruel. When he settled into a calmer slumber, she continued circulating until the last lantern burned out, replaced by a sickly grey dawn light filtering through the wall cracks and door. Tam sat at the foot of Kevan's bed and closed her eyes.

Exhausted by the night's long battle, the Herbal Man rose from his chair and shuffled between the makeshift bed spaces, checking his patients. When he reached Kevan's bed, he found Eesa seated with her head lying on her husband's arm, and Tam curled on the floor at the foot of Kevan's bed, fast asleep.

Twenty-Four

Harbin mourned. Not since the plague, before most living people were born, had the village suffered so great a tragedy. The Dragon Fang, pride and heart of Harbin, was torn apart. Of sixty-three warriors on the summer expedition, including five initiates, thirty-five returned, and fifteen of those were injured, four badly so. Twenty-six dragonwarriors lay dead in a land to the south. Theo and Vetch died on the homebound journey. Frankston and Fallan died the first night back in in Harbin, and several under the Herbal Man's care were walking perilously close to the path of shadows. Only twenty escaped the fierce and bloody journey unscathed, save minor wounds and bruises.

The Dragon Heart sat with the mourners throughout the morning after the ship's arrival, helping them pray for their men's spirits to find the path to Varst's Eternal Paradise. The Harbin women bore the greatest impact of the misadventure. Mothers, wives, sisters and daughters were caught in the numbing web of loss, and the women whose men returned, Eesa among them, did what they could to comfort the devastated families.

Of all who suffered, everyone's heart went out for Carmel. She lost her husband, Daren, her brother, Make, and her son, Leon, who was an initiate. Women came to her cottage to be with her, even those who bore their own loss, and each consoled the other in grief.

Tam woke late, cold and stiff from lying on the Long Hall's floor. As she sat up, the Herbal Man knelt beside her, holding a cup of steaming goat's milk. 'Energy,' he said, smiling. 'Drink it. You worked hard last night.' She looked around guiltily, aware that she fell asleep and wasted most of the morning, but the Herbal Man read her thoughts and said, 'Relax and drink,

Tamesan. Your mother and I let you sleep. You must sleep when you have to.'

'What about you?' Tam asked, concerned. 'Have you slept yet?'

The Herbal Man waggled his head, chuckling, and said, 'The older you get the less sleep you need, and I am so old I doubt I will ever need to sleep again.' He pulled a silly face, making Tam laugh, and when she caught her breath she sipped at the warm milk.

'Thank you,' she said.

'Thank you,' he replied. Tam looked across the hall and saw her father was sleeping. 'He will mend quickly,' the Herbal Man reassured her.

'I should find Chasse,' she said.

'Help me check the wounds and bandaging, and then you can find Chasse. But be careful what you say to him,' the Herbal Man warned gently. 'He has been through the same events as all these men, and he may not be ready to talk about what happened.'

Tam helped as the Herbal Man asked and then left the hall to find her brother. He was not at the Warriors' Hall as she expected. Jon told her Chasse went home, and the news brightened her hopes that her brother was coping with his experiences. She crossed the Watersdrop bridge, but Chasse wasn't at home. Neither were Eesa or Jaysin.

Concerned, Tam walked to the side of the cottage to stand under the Honeynut tree and spied her brothers sitting side-by-side on the cliff overlooking Watersdrop, both staring silently across the bay. She pulled a twig from the tree and joined them, and she stood beside Chasse, respecting his silence, until Jaysin rose and ran towards the village without speaking.

Startled, Tam asked, 'What was that about?'

Chasse kept staring silently seaward.

Tam sat beside her brother, and said, 'Father is sleeping.' When Chasse did not respond, she continued, feeling she should keep the dreadful silence at arm's length. 'I cleaned and dressed his wounds. I think he was surprised that I could do it. The Herbal Man taught me healing skills over summer.'

'Did anyone die last night?'

Stunned by Chasse's blunt question, Tam hesitated, hoping that he would say something else to divert her answer, but when he kept staring silently into the distance she swallowed and replied, 'Fallan. And Frankston. Nothing could be done for them.'

'No,' Chasse muttered. 'Nothing.'

Tam was at a loss. Chasse's mood resembled Ashlee's despair on the rocks at Meltsparkle, and she felt afraid for him. She put her hand on his shoulder and he flinched at her touch, but when he didn't complain she took his passive acceptance as encouragement and wrapped her arm across his shoulders, surprised at how broad he was becoming.

Chasse's shoulders shook and he pushed aside her arm, snapping, 'Don't mother me!'

His rejection startled Tam, and she suddenly realised that Chasse was severing what remained of their affectionate bond. 'I'm sorry-', she started to say, but Chasse abruptly stood.

'I'm going up the mountain, alone,' he said, warning Tam in his tone not to follow, before he stalked away, past the cottage.

After Tam watched her brother leave, she stood on Watersdrop cliff for a long time, contemplating why he left without wanting to share tales about the summer expedition or the disaster. A veil of sorrow had fallen across her village, and Chasse was suffering like all the warriors. Unable to fathom how to respond to her brother's turmoil, Tam returned to the Long Hall to continue aiding the Herbal Man.

Relatives of the injured men were congregating in the Long Hall, mainly women, but Trask was kneeling beside Marron's bedding, talking to his son. Tam spotted the Herbal Man asleep in a corner, but he opened his eyes as she leaned over to check on him. 'I'm sorry,' she whispered. 'I didn't mean to disturb you.'

'No harm,' he replied and stretched his arms. 'I've lain here too long as it is. There is work to do.' He stood slowly, stretching his back and legs, and said, 'The man, Edgar, is suffering from a strange ailment he must have contracted on the homeward journey. I need handfuls of the purple fungi your people call Seleserin's Table. Can you find some for me?'

'I know where there is plenty,' Tam replied.

'Good. When you return, I'll show you how to make an elixir called Danso's Breathing Drink. But you must hurry. The quicker we can make the elixir, the quicker Edgar will recover.'

Tam left the Hall and crossed the goat pasture into the forest where she collected bunches of the purple fungi. When she headed back, she met her mother as she entered the village.

'Where are you going?' Eesa inquired. Tam explained her task. 'When the Herbal Man has shown you what to do,' Eesa continued, 'can you go home and prepare a meal for us? I'll get some other women to cook food for the men in the Warriors' Hall tonight, and for the sick in the Long Hall. I need to spend time with your father.'

Tam entered the Long Hall and gave the fungi to the Herbal Man. His preparation of the medicinal elixir, while instructing Tam, was efficient and easy, and once the elixir was administered to Edgar Tam explained her mother's request and excused herself.

Evening was settling across Harbin, painting the western sky pastel shades of apricot, grey and dark blue, as Tam hurried home. Jaysin would be hungry and irritable, but she had time to organise the evening meal because Eesa was still in the village.

When she reached the bridge over Watersdrop, she turned to look over the village and she saw her mother entering the Long Hall to visit Kevan. For all their faults, she knew that her parents loved each other, and the knowledge gave her an inner warmth. Near the water's edge, a group of children played in the twilight, and the forlorn wreck of the dragonship swayed idly by the jetty. A solitary woman sat on the end of the jetty, staring seaward. The distance was too great for Tam to identify the mourner, but her heart ached for the lonely woman. Heartache burdened everyone, and Tam understood that the wounds from the summer journey would take a long time to heal. The rest of Harbin was empty. Even the bay was empty of fishing boats. The only other visible life were goats grazing in the outer pasture on the forest fringe, oblivious to their masters' sorrow. Harbin was melting into darkness.

The Dragon Heart led a long ceremony at Watersdrop to sing the Words of Passage for Harbin's thirty-three dead dragonwarriors. Five of the seriously injured died in the days after the ship's return. After Frankton and Fallan, Denys, Patrick and Adrian succumbed to infections, despite all that the Herbal Man could do, and each new death tightened the grip of grief on the village.

Tam continued to help in the Long Hall as often as she could, and she witnessed the impact of each death on the Herbal Man. He worked tirelessly, desperate to save the chronically ill warriors, and when one died he seemed stunned and exhausted by the loss, as if he truly believed he had the power to save each of them.

She also heard whispering discontent brewing in the village as people began suggesting that the Herbal Man was to blame for the deaths. Distrust of the Herbal Man in Harbin ran deep. Some whispered he was a servant of Shaddho, that he was cursed and the men he touched were marked for death. The lies and accusations riled her, but, because they were only whispered insinuations, she knew she could do or say nothing, so she focussed on helping the Herbal Man and being his friend.

Kevan left the Long Hall on the fourth day because, like six other patients, his wounds healed quickly. Due to the Herbal Man's treatment, with Tam's help, and the help of the women who assisted in the Long Hall, most of the men made rapid recoveries. Bandaged, some limping and heavily bruised, they honoured their dead companions at the Words of Passage ceremony and returned to their families' care. Kevan insisted on speaking briefly at the ceremony to pay his final respect to his lost companion, Theo, before he was borne to his cottage to recuperate.

Only one warrior remained critically ill after ten days – Marron. He appeared to grow stronger for several days after the Herbal Man reset his arm, and even Trask's distrust diminished by the Words of Passage ceremony, but the Herbal Man and Tam returned to the Long Hall to discover Marron groaning and sweating profusely. A quick inspection of the injury confirmed the Herbal Man's worst fear.

'The infection is deep,' he concluded, bitterly.

'What happens now?' Tam asked.

'We have to work quickly. He must drink draughts of Acton's Curative, but if the poison is too deep it will not be good for the young man.'

Whatever residue of hatred Tam retained was subsumed by her concern for his life. She asked, 'Will he die?'

The Herbal Man frowned as he replied, 'No, Tamesan, I will not let it happen. But we must stop the infection spreading. Fetch boiling water please.'

Tam organised the water and stood beside the Herbal Man while he bathed Marron's wounds. She looked up when she heard the Long Hall door open and she saw Trask enter.

'Is it time my son came home?' Trask asked, as he approached the bed, but when he saw Marron's condition he swore and demanded, 'Explain this! What in Varst's name have you done?'

'The infection has worsened,' the Herbal Man replied.

'You are meant to be making him better, not worse!' Trask snarled.

'We're doing everything we can,' Tam said.

Trask turned to her. 'You speak when I talk to you,' he warned, glaring.

'The girl means well,' the Herbal Man said.

'You make my son better immediately or I will kill you!' Trask yelled at the Herbal Man, before he turned and stormed to the door, muttering, 'Anyone who trusts the shoddy work of old men who think sucking a plant makes a man better should be condemned to endless torment.' He paused, glared at the Herbal Man and said, 'My son will be well in the morning, or you will be dead. I swear!' He slammed the door on exiting.

Marron's condition worsened as the evening progressed, despite the Herbal Man creating three separate elixirs and applying a new ointment. Tam accepted the Herbal Man's offer to sleep after midnight, but when she woke before dawn she found the Herbal Man sitting beside Marron's bed shaking his head slowly. Marron was groaning weakly, rivers of perspiration pouring from his skin.

'What's happening?' Tam whispered as she crouched beside the old man.

'The infection in his arm is too deep. It's coursing through his body. The curatives are having no effect.'

Tam sucked in her breath. 'Now what?'

The Herbal Man lifted his face and in the lantern by the bed he looked haggard, his grey eyes sad and sunken. To Tam, he looked older than ever. 'Unless I remove the source of infection, he will die,' he answered slowly, but before Tam could ask what he meant to do he said, 'Bring your father. At once. There can be no excuses. Every moment wasted carries Marron closer to death. Go.'

Tam leapt to her feet, bolted from the Long Hall, and sprinted up the slope and across the bridge to her cottage as the first morning rays set fire to Dragon Mountain's snow-capped peak. She burst into her parent's bedroom and urged her father to go to the Long Hall.

'Your father is still unwell!' Eesa complained. 'Let him sleep.'

'Marron is dying,' Tam told them. 'The Herbal Man says Father must come!'

'What can your-', Eesa started to say.

'Enough!' Kevan interrupted gruffly. 'I will come. Help me, girl.'

Despite Kevan's injured leg hampering their speed, Tam helped her father reach the Long Hall in a relatively short time. The Herbal Man met them at the door, and he directed Kevan to a chair, describing Marron's condition as they crossed the hall.

'But how can I help?' Kevan asked, looking down at Marron.

'There is only one thing I can do, now, to save his life,' the Herbal Man explained. 'And even if I do that thing, there is still a chance he might die. I need you to speak to Trask.'

'But what is it you intend to do?' Kevan asked.

The Herbal Man paused, before replying, 'Amputate his arm.'

Trask burst into the Long Hall carrying a spear, followed by five men looking as if they were trying to summon courage to stop the enraged warrior. A woman washing bandages near the door screamed and Tam looked up. Seeing the twisted mask of hatred on Trask's face as he raised his spear, she turned to warn the Herbal Man, but the Herbal Man was already at Marron's bed facing the angry father.

'Get your Varst-forsaken filthy hands away from my son!' Trask bellowed. Kevan's bulk appeared in the doorway. Behind him, a crowd formed.

'Put down the spear,' the Herbal Man calmly requested.

'In Varst's hell I wILl!' Trask roared, and he bent his arm to hurl the spear, but as he went to launch it Kevan grabbed the tail. Trask whirled to see who dared to interfere, and when he recognised the Dragon Head he swore and snarled, 'This does not concern you! Your son is whole! Go back to your home with your family while I teach this meddling fool what it feels like to be struck by a warrior's wrath!'

'You are the fool,' Kevan said in a level tone. 'This is not how a warrior behaves. You lack courage.'

'Courage?' Trask howled. 'Courage? To do what? Stand aside while a doddering old man maims my only son? You call it courage?' He spat at Kevan's feet. 'Your kind of courage can rot in the eternal fires!' He spun and strode towards the Herbal Man, grabbed the old man's cloak and threw him roughly against the wall. The Herbal Man grunted as the breath was knocked from his frail body and he crumpled to the floor like a rag doll. Trask hauled him to his feet, lifting him from the floor, and pinned him against the wall. 'Forget the butchering, you worthless bag of dragon dung!' he growled. 'When I'm finished with you, there won't be enough to feed the fish!' Trask raised his heavy fist, but something thwacked across the back of his wrist, drawing his attention from the old man. He turned to discover Tam holding a broom handle menacingly. 'Back in your place, girl!' he jeered, and he made a backhanded swipe at her, but she ducked and rapped the broom handle smartly across his nose. Trask howled with pain and released the Herbal Man to grab his stinging nose. 'Little she-dragon!' he yelled, and he squared up to confront Tam, but in her place stood Kevan and several warriors.

'That is enough, Trask!' Kevan warned. 'Act like a man. You are a dragonwarrior, a member of the Dragon Fang –'

'A plague on your stinking words!' Trask cried. 'No one will butcher my son!'

'Then he will die,' Tam said in a thin, sad voice.

Trask's defiant eyes rested on her. 'He will die if I let that piece of dragon dung touch him!' he rasped, pointing at the Herbal Man, who was struggling to his feet.

'The Herbal Man is doing more for Marron than you are,' Tam retorted.

Trask's eyes flared with rage and he took a step towards her, but Kevan stepped into his path. 'Touch my daughter, Trask –' he growled, deliberately leaving the threat unfinished. The other dragonwarriors drew rank beside the Dragon Head.

Trask clenched his fists and turned to the Herbal Man, who politely bowed his head, and said, 'Tamesan is right. Your son is dying, and he will die because the infection is too deep. And you are right. What I offer to try to save him is not without great risk. But it is all I have now.'

'Wretched butcher!' Trask roared, and he lunged for the Herbal Man, but several strong hands grappled him and pulled him back.

'Take him to the Warriors' Hall and keep him there,' Kevan ordered. He waited until Trask's head was lifted so that he could look his adversary in the face. Trask's eyes burned with hatred. 'If you have to use ropes to keep him in the hall, do so,' Kevan instructed, while he locked gazes with Trask. 'But, if he is man enough, you won't need to rope him like an animal.'

The men restraining Trask escorted him from the Long Hall, but as Trask reached the door he screamed, 'You are dead, old man! Hear me? Dead! No man harms my son and lives! No man! You are dead!'

Kevan waited until Trask's cries subsided before he turned to the onlookers and said, 'Go back to your chores and whatever you have to do. The Long Hall is closed. The Herbal Man has important work. Leave us to help him with what must be done.' The crowd of warriors, women and children shuffled out of the hall, and Kevan shut the door in their wake, leaving the Herbal Man, Tam, the Dragon Heart, the woman, Astra, who was cleaning bandages, and himself. Kevan cast a cursory glance at Tam before addressing the Herbal Man. 'Jon is coming. He has what you asked for.'

'Thank you,' the Herbal Man replied. 'This is not something I want to do.'

'We understand,' said the Dragon Heart, who was staring at the pale, sweat-soaked youth stretched on a bed of pain. 'Too often Varst directs us to do things we do not want to do, but we are merely his servants.'

The Herbal Man smiled wanly and then turned to Tam. 'I need a lot of boiling water, as much as you can make. And I need one lot of it by the bed, in a container large enough to take an axe head.'

Tam set to work boiling water, but she noticed her father talking with urgency to the Herbal Man. Then the Herbal Man beckoned to her. He leaned forward and said, 'The last time I said this to you, I was setting the young man's arm. This time I have to take his arm away.' He paused, judging Tam's reaction to his statement, making certain she understood what was about to happen. 'This is a terrible thing I have to do, but I have to do it to save his life. There is no need for you to be here. There is no shame in not wanting to see this. If you want to go, say so. Everyone will understand.'

Tam looked at her father. His craggy face was as tired and drawn as the Herbal Man's face, but his eyes were asking her to leave. Perhaps he believed this was not the right place for a girl. Perhaps he was concerned for her over what was about to transpire. Perhaps it was both. What was about to happen to Marron was terrifying to imagine. She saw anger and fear in Trask's face as he was dragged from the hall. Men were afraid of the thing she would witness if she stayed. But the Herbal Man was making it her decision, and it meant she would be responsible for what she chose to do. She felt ready. She looked back at the Herbal Man and shook her head. 'I will stay,' she announced quietly.

Twenty-Five

'He took his arm, didn't he?'

Tam sat beside her brother on Watersdrop cliff and studied his expression. It was hard, angry. She sensed the same air of ingratitude in Chasse that was infecting others in Harbin, turning them against the Herbal Man for amputating Marron's arm, and it disappointed her. 'He had to,' she answered. 'Marron would have died if he didn't.'

'I'd rather be dead than live with one arm,' Chasse muttered.

'Don't say that,' Tam chastised. 'Being dead is forever. Nothing is as bad as being dead.'

'Being useless is worse than being dead,' he retorted. 'What's Marron going to do with one arm? He can't be a dragonwarrior.'

'He could be a fisherman,' Tam suggested.

'How can he pull in lines or nets with one arm when they're heavy and slippery?'

'He could be a herdsman, or a sea-watcher on White Eagle Ledge.'

'Marron?' Chasse asked, and he snorted. 'Marron lives to be a dragonwarrior. He won't accept anything less.'

Tam knew Chasse's statement was true. Marron would not cope. He dedicated his life to becoming a dragonwarrior. 'He proved himself,' she offered. 'The dragon took his arm, but at least he fought it.' An ironic snigger escaped Chasse's lips. 'Why do you laugh like that?' she asked.

'It's nothing,' Chasse replied.

'No,' she argued. 'It wasn't nothing. Why did you do it?'

'Because I felt like it!' he snapped. 'Do I have to explain everything to you?'

229

His angry reaction startled her. Since his return, he was negative, sour, distant, as if the happy brother who sailed away was lost somewhere in the south, replaced by a bitter, secretive stranger. His response roused her determination to know why. 'I want to know what's going on, Chasse. Why are you so angry?'

'There's nothing to talk about,' Chasse replied sulkily.

'Were you with Marron when he was injured?'

Her change of tack caught him off guard. 'Yes,' he answered, and then he scrambled to cover himself with, 'I meant no. I wasn't with him.'

'You didn't see the dragon?'

Chasse glared at her. 'Of course I saw the dragon.'

'What did it look like?'

'Why do you want to know?'

'I've never seen a dragon,' Tam explained, although the image of Claryssa flashed through her thoughts. 'I've only heard stories and legends. I want to know what they're really like.'

Chasse knitted his eyebrows and he seemed confused, reluctant to answer. He took a deep breath and said, 'It was big and, sort of, er – I don't know, sort of black. It breathed lots of fire.'

'Anything else?'

'What do you mean?'

'I mean did it have scales, or large golden eyes, or wings?'

Chasse stared at her as he said, 'Yes. All of that.'

'Oh,' Tam sighed, disappointed with her brother's lack of interest in describing the dragon. To her, he seemed unsure of what to say, so she asked, 'Were you scared?'

Anger flickered across his face. 'Of course I was scared, Tam. You would be too, if you saw a dragon.'

I was terrified when I first saw Claryssa, she thought. *If only you knew what I know.* She blinked to change her thought and asked, 'Why didn't you see what happened to Marron?'

'It was dark, and there was a lot of fighting and noise and confusion,' Chasse irritably replied.

'Did the dragon ambush the Dragon Fang?'

Chasse hesitated before he answered. 'Yes. It wasn't where we expected it to be. No one expected it. We were preparing to sleep in our camp after disembarking, and suddenly there was a lot of noise and fighting and we had to get back to the ship. That's why I didn't see how Marron broke his arm. Now do you understand?'

Tam nodded. His explanation also revealed why Chasse was so moody. He never had a chance to fight the dragon, which meant he also probably didn't feel as though he'd become a dragonwarrior. 'You don't actually have to fight a dragon to be a brave warrior,' she offered in consolation. 'I think you are very brave.'

Chasse's eyes widened and then narrowed with suspicion. 'What do you mean?' he asked.

'What I said,' Tam replied. 'You've been on a dragon hunt. It makes you a dragonwarrior like the others, even like Father. And there's always next time. You have a lifetime of journeys ahead now.'

'I'm never going again.'

Chasse's blunt statement stunned her. She studied his face again, but he was staring into the middle distance, and she was reminded of the same faraway sorrow she'd seen in Ashlee's eyes, the look of despair. She knew there was a greater secret troubling her brother, and she knew she needed to unravel it to save him. She needed to know the truth. She couldn't bear to see Chasse so tormented. 'Why not?' she asked gently.

'I have my reasons,' Chasse muttered, and he got to his feet.

'Where are you going?'

'For a walk.'

'I'll come with you,' Tam offered, rising.

'No!' Chasse snarled. 'I want to walk alone.'

'You haven't told me everything,' she argued. 'You haven't told me why you don't want to go next summer. What happened?'

'Leave it alone, Tam,' he warned, eyes glittering with anger.

'I won't leave it alone, as you put it!' she declared defiantly. 'I want the truth. What really happened, Chasse?'

'Leave me alone, please,' Chasse begged. 'I want to be left alone.' He turned and ran for the hillside.

Chasse's sudden escape frustrated Tam – and then memories of Ashlee came to mind. She chased Tam away when Tam asked to talk and then killed herself. Tam wasn't letting that happen to her brother. Spurred by fear, she ran after him and caught him on a forested slope above Watersdrop gorge. He was climbing onto a rocky perch, but when he spied Tam he started to slide down. 'No!' she yelled. 'Don't run away! I'll run after you!'

He swore, and cried, 'I don't want to talk about it! Do you hear me? It's nothing to do with you!'

'It's everything to do with me,' she argued, as she approached. 'You are my brother. That makes it to do with me.'

'Tam, you don't understand.'

'I want to understand,' she implored. 'You have to tell me.'

Chasse moved to the edge of the gorge to gaze into its depths and Tam stood beside him. Watersdrop churned, swirled and foamed over the rocks, and Tam imagined the tormented water mirroring the swollen torrent of confusion in her brother's mind.

'Talk to me, Chasse,' she pleaded.

'I can't, Tam,' Chasse replied, his face scarred with frustration.

'I'll listen,' she urged. 'I won't judge.'

'No,' he said. 'You don't understand. I know you will listen. It's not that. I'm not allowed to talk to you.'

'What do you mean?'

Chasse swallowed, and said, 'I can't tell you the truth. It's the Dragonwarriors' Oath. They make us swear it on the ship once we're at sea. We promise not to say anything about the journeys to anyone else in the village.'

'I don't understand,' Tam admitted. 'Do you mean you have to keep everything a secret?'

'Yes,' he said, and he shook his head miserably. 'It's a secret. It's a terrible lie.'

'But the men share all their stories at the feasts,' she argued. 'What's the secret?'

Chasse cursed and kicked a stone into the gorge. It rattled against the rocks but never made it to the water.

'What's the secret?' Tam persisted.

'The lie,' Chasse replied reluctantly. 'The secret is the lie.'

Her brother spoke like the Herbal Man, talking in riddles. *The secret is the lie*? 'I don't understand,' she repeated.

'I said you wouldn't understand.'

'Then explain it to me,' she urged.

'I'm not allowed to.'

Tam grabbed Chasse's arm, and said, 'I won't tell anyone else, Chasse. You know I won't. I can keep secrets. I'll keep this one.'

'But I can't tell you, Tam. I can't. I've sworn the Oath. I'll be punished if I tell you,' he emphasised passionately.

'Punished? By who?'

'The Dragon's Wrath.'

Tam paused. The Dragon's Wrath was invoked when matters of law or disputes required resolution in Harbin: a special meeting between her father as Dragon Head, the Dragon Heart, and three experienced and wise men chosen from the Dragon Fang. 'How would they punish you?' she asked.

'I don't know,' Chasse muttered. 'No one explained that part.'

'Chasse,' she insisted, 'I promise you I won't tell anyone. You can't keep this locked inside. It's not good for you. Believe me, I know. You've got to tell me. Please.'

Chasse ran his hand through his red hair and sighed. He turned and took three steps along the edge of the gorge and stared up at the mountain. Tam watched her brother, afraid he was deciding to lock her out of his world, and sad that she failed to get him to open to her. Then he turned. His face was twisted with anger and sorrow, and tears glittered in his eyes. 'They lied to us, Tam!' he cried. 'They lied!' A wrenching sob burst from his chest.

Stung with compassion, Tam moved towards her brother, but Chasse turned and scrambled up the rocks. 'Chasse!' she screamed. 'Chasse, come back!', but he climbed until he cleared the rocks and disappeared into the forest, leaving Tam standing above the thundering gorge.

'He said they lied. What did he mean?'

The Herbal Man studied Tam's face as he always did when he contemplated an important answer. He stroked his beard, cleared his throat, and said, 'You are right to be concerned for your brother. He carries an enormous burden. Perhaps –' He faltered as if he was uncertain what to say, before continuing. 'Perhaps it's time you knew.'

'Knew what?' she asked, tiring of the riddles.

'Come with me, Tamesan,' the Herbal Man instructed.

'Where are we going?'

'No more questions. It's time to watch and listen. You can ask your questions afterwards.'

The Herbal Man ushered Tam into his hut, down the trapdoor ladder, and through to the crystal chamber. He waved his hand and light flooded the space, reflecting off of Claryssa's golden scales on the far wall as it did the first time Tam visited the chamber. She stared at the dragon's flank, remembering her shock when she learned what the wall was.

'Tamesan,' the Herbal Man interrupted. 'Stand at the Seeing Waters,' he directed, indicating the pedestal.

Tam approached and gazed into the shallow pool in the pedestal's circular head. Amber light danced in the watery reflection.

'I must have Claryssa's help with this,' the Herbal Man said, and he began chanting in an ancient language, unfamiliar to Tam, until she recognised Claryssa's full title — Ke-Ly'aar-Ees-Ar — in the incomprehensible words. She heard a gigantic intake of breath, and the dragon's scales heaved and shuddered as Claryssa shifted her bulk, until her massive head and great golden eyes peered into the chamber. The Herbal Man spoke softly to the dragon in the ancient tongue, before he turned to Tam and said, 'Claryssa agrees I should show you the truth. She says you are ready.' Tam looked at the dragon, unable to read expression in the reptilian face. 'I will stand with you, Tamesan,' the Herbal Man said. 'Claryssa and I will bring the Seeing Waters to life for you. What you witness in them is the truth. The Waters cannot lie. Remember it. What you see has happened exactly as you see it. Understand, also, Tamesan, the truth is often far more painful than we want it to be.'

As Tam watched, her surroundings dimmed as if every light source at the periphery of her vision was extinguished, until she stood with the Herbal Man in a circle of light surrounded by darkness. The water held her gaze as it lost its amber luminosity and became a dark well, black, foreboding.

Tam sensed movement, shadows flitting across the well, figures, a line of men. Warriors. Creeping through a forest in the night. One figure was tall, solid, familiar, reminding her of her father. Another beside him could be Theo. They crouched in the bushes, watching a flickering fire throw light across indistinct buildings. People were gathered at the fire, strangers, some eating, talking, singing. Men, women and children, families celebrating at a communal fire. The scene made Tam content, reminding her of Harbin feasts.

Until a woman screamed and pointed at a man beside her. A spear jutted from his chest. He staggered like a drunk at Varst's Great Feast and pitched forward into the fire. As sparks erupted, and others screamed, the warriors leapt from the bushes and charged into the scene, flailing their swords and axes with bloody abandon. Despite the efforts of the men at the fire to fend them off with swords and firebrands, the attacking horde swept over, hacking indiscriminately at anyone in their way. Everywhere there were strangely familiar faces distorted by masks of anger, terror and the flames of the dying bonfire. The surrounding buildings erupted in flames, lighting the night, exposing dark figures running to and fro with torches, touching them to every flammable object. Men with bloodied faces dragged the bodies of their mutilated victims onto the bonfire, and the blaze grew higher and higher, spreading more light across the carnage.

At the centre, one man stood apart, his beard and hair shining gold in the light of the funeral pyre, a big man, strong, determined, and as the firelight expanded it lit his face and Tam saw it was her father. Around Kevan, the Dragon Fang celebrated the spoils of their butchery and destruction.

'It's not true!' she protested. 'It can't be true!'

'The Seeing Waters never lie, Tamesan,' the Herbal Man gently reminded her. 'Besides, Claryssa and I have no reason to lie to you.'

'But they were killing people. People,' she repeated, as if convincing herself. 'Why would they do that? Why? They're supposed to be hunting dragons.'

The Herbal Man shook his head, and asked sadly, 'Would hunting dragons make it any different?'

'Yes,' Tam said. 'It would. That's what they're supposed to do. That's why the legend of Nakiades exists. The dragons have to be hunted.'

'Why, Tamesan? For vengeance? Is that why dragon hunting matters to your people? The men sail away every year to exact revenge for someone who died four hundred years ago. Isn't it rather stupid?'

'No!' she cried. And then she paused. Every belief of her village, every foundation value of Harbin was being questioned. Hunting dragons because belief in a legend says that is what should be done suddenly did look stupid to her. But her father, and his father, and now Chasse, belonged to the tradition. The dragon hunt made boys into men. 'But why people?' she asked, exasperated. 'What did they do wrong? Were they hiding a dragon?'

'Those people did nothing wrong, Tamesan,' the Herbal Man said. 'At least nothing more than what you or your people do in Harbin. They weren't hiding a dragon. They happened to be in the wrong place when the Dragon Fang came hunting.'

'But why people? Why kill the children?'

'Because there are no dragons left, Tamesan,' the Herbal Man stated. 'There haven't been dragons for more than a hundred years. Men wiped them out. They killed every wizard and every dragon.'

'But you're a wizard,' Tam pointed out. 'And there's Claryssa.'

'Yes,' he agreed. 'We are still here. But only because we've been very lucky. We ran away when the hunting and the wars started. We're the last of our kind, the last dragon and the last wizard.' His voice faltered as he added, 'Except we are both so old that we are shadows of what we were.'

'Couldn't there be others who escaped like you did?' Tam suggested.

'No. There are no others,' said the Herbal Man. 'The Seeing Waters showed Claryssa and me what happened a long time ago. All our friends and colleagues are dead. The Harbin Dragon Fang have never seen a dragon, not even when your great-great-great grandfather sailed on the dragonship.'

Tam looked up and met Claryssa's gaze and saw immense sadness in the dragon's eyes. 'Then what Ashlee said was true,' she murmured. 'And Chasse. Chasse knows it's all a big lie. That's what he meant. Every summer journey is a lie.' She hung her head and stared at the crystal water in the pedestal.

The Herbal Man gently placed his hand on Tam's shoulder. 'I'm sorry it is like this,' he said, 'but I think you would have learned the truth very soon anyway.'

'Do you know what happened to the Dragon Fang this summer?' she asked despondently.

The Herbal Man nodded. 'We have seen. Do you want to see?'

Tam shook her head, and whispered, 'No. I've seen enough brutality. Just tell me.'

'The Dragon Fang of Harbin have become too well-known to the villagers living to the south. Your people preyed on them too long. The southern people united in their complaints to the Karudar Marfek, a powerful ruler to the east, and she finally accepted that the Dragon Fang's annual intrusions were destabilising the western regions of her Empire and disrupting its economy. She ordered her generals to destroy the Dragon Fang. By sheer luck, the Dragon Fang avoided the soldiers for almost five years, but this summer they blundered into an ambush when they attacked a village that they thought was unprotected. Under the circumstances, the Dragon Fang got off lightly. The men of Harbin are good warriors, but they are no match for trained Imperial soldiers.'

'I still don't understand why my father and the others want to attack people. It doesn't make sense.' Tam said. She struggled with the Herbal Man's revelation because what had always been right in her world was suddenly terribly wrong.

'They have their reasons, Tamesan,' the Herbal Man replied. 'All men have reasons for what they do, no matter how senseless their actions appear to be to others. The men of Harbin need to prove their manhood, prove they are descendants of Nakiades – brave, strong, adventurous.

They can't imitate Nakiades' fabled adventure by fishing, or herding goats, or doing the mundane matters of village life. They are victims of Nakiades' legacy. And since there are no dragons left to fight, which would be the ultimate adventure for them, they make do with a lesser enemy. Other people. It satisfies their need.'

'But surely they know what they are doing is wrong?'

'Of course they do. At least, most of them do,' said the Herbal Man. 'That's why they never tell anyone outside the Dragon Fang what they are doing. They swear the Oath. They all carry and share the guilt, even the men who no longer sail on the ship because of injury or age. Young Marron will carry the guilt for the rest of his life. A dragon didn't maul his arm. It was crushed during the Dragon Fang's desperate retreat. But no one will tell the village. Neither will Chasse. Your brother was made to swear the Oath and now his hands are marked with blood. He may not like what it means, but he will never break the Oath. To do so would mean sacrificing the title of manhood that he has been waiting to don his entire life and to live in shame. Keeping the secret, living the lie: it is what being a man means in Harbin. It's the heart of the tradition.'

'Chasse said he won't go next summer,' Tam announced in Chasse's defence.

'He will,' the Herbal Man said. 'By next summer, he will have adjusted to the darker side of his manhood, and when the dragonship is ready he will also be ready. Chasse is not the first Harbin warrior to feel guilty after his initiate journey and he won't be the last. It's all part of the cycle spawned by Nakiades' legend.'

'Won't the Imperial soldiers be waiting?'

'Perhaps. Perhaps not. Governments change their policies as readily as the wind changes direction. Next year is quite some time away, the southern coastline is very long, and the Dragon Fang are a very small raiding party. Chances are, next year they'll find a village that hasn't heard of them. It's a big world, Tamesan, a very big world.'

Tam glanced at the Seeing Waters in the pedestal. The world was bigger and uglier than she ever imagined and the Herbal Man showed her things she wished she never saw. But she knew the wish was absurd. All the Herbal Man did was open her eyes and show her the truth. He showed why Chasse was changed, the horrible secret he was forced to conceal. He showed her the cause of the terrible sorrow that scarred Ashlee and led her to kill herself.

She wondered how other people would react if she exposed the secret? How would the women, the wives, mothers, daughters, sisters of the dragonwarriors react? Ashlee knew the truth. She wondered how many more women knew where the dragonwarriors went every summer, and knew what they did? Were the children the only ones who didn't know? Was knowing the truth what really separated childhood from adulthood – knowing the ugly lie at the heart of Harbin? The people were living a lie, an enormous lie that kept them together as a group but threatened to tear them apart individually. Where, then, did knowing the truth leave her?

Twenty-Six

Tam stood at the centre of a world without dragons. A world with dragons held its share of darkness and terror, but it also had reason and order. The legend of Nakiades, the story the people shared to bind them to their past and present to ensure they were not forgotten by the future, lay at the heart of the world. Now, it was lost to Tam. She stood at the centre of an empty alien world made of half-truths and lies.

The Dragon Festival traditionally following the dragonship's return was forgotten while the people bore the brunt of their sorrow and buried the dead. Tam helped wherever she was needed by preparing food for those trapped in the deepest grief, caring for recovering warriors, and listening to those people who simply needed to talk to cope with their loss.

The Herbal Man's visits diminished and then ceased. On his last visit, he told Tam, 'My work is done. The rest is manageable by you and the others.'

'You're still needed,' Tam argued.

'No,' he replied. 'Besides, I'm no longer welcome. Trask has fermented too much ill-feeling and it's better for everyone that I stay away.'

'But Father ordered Trask to stay in the Warriors' Hall when you are here,' Tam told him.

'Marron's father swore a blood oath on his spear to kill me for crippling his son,' the Herbal Man said. 'You know as well as I do that it means Trask will do whatever he needs to do to fulfil his oath. I cannot come here again.'

'But what if he comes after you?'

The Herbal Man smiled faintly as he replied, 'I have nothing to fear,

Tamesan. Marron's father will not harm me outside Harbin. He has a reputation to uphold in the village in keeping his blood oath, but if I am not around the matter is moot. You know what to do, now. I am returning to my solitude.'

'I will visit,' Tam promised.

'We'll see what your father has to say,' the Herbal Man said. 'Take care, Tamesan.'

Marron's amputation healed quickly, but once he could get out of bed he disappeared into the Warriors' Hall with his father and refused to see anyone. He avoided the women when they took food to the men by hiding in the darkest corner of the hall. Tam attempted to speak to him on a visit, but Trask brusquely intervened. 'Daughter of the Dragon Head,' he said, 'you have no right to meddle with my son.' He reached for her arm, but Jon intervened.

'This way, young Tamesan. I need your help over here,' Jon said as he steered Tam away from Trask, and when they were far enough from Trask he added, 'Do not go near Marron again, please. It's not safe to do so.'

'I was only –'

Jon cut her off. 'I know you mean good, Tamesan, but Trask and Marron are not themselves. I will ask your father to release you from duties at the Warriors' Hall, at least until Trask is sensible again. You were with the old man when he took Marron's arm and they have not yet forgiven you.'

'We saved Marron's life,' Tam argued.

'We know, Tamesan, but Trask and Marron have yet to see what it means.' Jon looked her in the eye. 'Please, I ask you, stay away.'

At home, in the evening, after talking with Kevan, Eesa reinforced Jon's request. 'There is plenty to do elsewhere,' she said. 'Time is a great healer. We must give them time. For now, stay away from Trask and Marron.'

Tam accepted her parents' request, but she soon faced a separate threat – from Katris. During the summer weeks while the Dragon Fang were away the girls easily avoided each other. Tam was busy learning from the Herbal Man, while Katris and her friends learned how to be good village women and prospective wives. The dragonship's return, and the loss of her father on the tragic expedition, plunged Katris into deep mourning. Marron's grievous injury added to her woes. Distraught, Katris locked herself indoors, praying to Varst and Procra to guide her father's lost spirit and to heal Marron. When Katris heard that the Herbal Man removed Marron's arm, she screamed her anguish into the night and wept for the mutilation of her love. In a few short days, she lost her father and the man she wanted as her husband. Her dreams were haunted by the spectre of a one-armed man proudly displaying his catch of fish to impress her, but she did not want to be a fisherwoman. She hated scaling and gutting fish. She hated milking goats. What could a crippled man offer her? The man of her dreams, Marron, was as dead as her father.

When Katris learned that Tam was present when the Herbal Man amputated Marron's arm, she found a focus for her pain and loss, a target she could hate. She speculated, in her sorrow, that Tam deliberately let Marron's arm become infected because she was jealous and afraid that Marron would choose Katris over her, and so Katris concluded that Tam made the Herbal Man take Marron's arm out of spite.

Three days after Marron's operation, Katris confronted Tam as she was carrying washing to the Long Hall with her mother and loosed her venom. 'Dragon bitch!' she screamed. 'It was you! You did it! You made him do it!'

Flustered, rendered speechless by the ferocity of Katris' attack, Tam clutched the washing basket she was carrying, and stared, open-mouthed, until several girls pulled Katris away.

Eesa took Tam's arm and drew her on towards the Long Hall. 'That one has gone strange,' Eesa confided as they entered the hall. 'Some do not take grief well.'

'What did she mean, saying I did it?' Tam asked, grappling with the import of Katris' attack. 'What did I do?'

'It is nothing, girl,' Eesa assured her. 'It will pass.'

Eesa was wrong. Katris harangued Tam at every opportunity, thereafter, swearing at her, calling her names and accusing her of complicity in crippling Marron. Tam spoke to her mother, hoping Eesa could find a solution to the situation. 'She blames me for Marron losing his arm,' Tam said.

'I will talk to the girl,' Eesa promised, 'but it won't be easy. If she blames you, while she is angry I doubt she will listen to reason.'

'I cared for Marron,' Tam said. 'I cleaned his arm and bandaged it. I helped the Herbal Man try to save Marron's arm. Where was Katris when we were doing that? How can she blame me?'

'Believe me, Tamesan, others are trying to make Katris see sense, but she does not want to listen. If it gets worse, and I fear it will, I will order her to stay home until she can be reasonable.'

Tam was dissatisfied with the idea that Katris could end up like Trask – a prisoner in the village – because it would give her another reason for hating Tam. 'Leave her alone, then,' Tam begged. 'It may be better if you don't speak to her. She'll only think I am behind it.'

'As you choose,' Eesa said, and the matter was closed.

Then came the stone-throwing.

Early one morning, as Tam walked with Jaysin to the goat pasture to collect a pail of milk, Katris emerged from behind a hut and hurled a stone, hitting Tam above the right eye. Tam collapsed, clutching her forehead, and lay motionless on the path, while Katris fled.

Jaysin thought his sister was dead until Tam sat up, groggily, and dabbed at a trickle of blood. 'Are you alright?' Jaysin asked, eyes wide with shock.

'I'm fine, little brother,' Tam replied, and she was aware of Jaysin's intense interest in the blood and her cut. She was about to comment when she noticed a group of women approaching, so she scrambled to her feet and said, 'Don't say anything about this to Mother, or anyone, please. Mother would get too angry with Katris if she knew.'

'But she tried to kill you,' Jaysin argued, still staring at the wound.

'She didn't try to kill me,' she corrected. 'She tried to scare me.'

'But why?'

'She thinks I hurt Marron.'

'That's silly,' Jaysin declared, frowning. 'We all know you helped him.'

Tam ruffled Jaysin's hair and said, 'I know you know the truth and that's important to me. Come on. Mother expects us to be back with the milk.' She urged Jaysin forward and kept her hand over her forehead as she greeted the women with their burdens of milk, but her mind whirled with concern. Katris' attack was premeditated and violent and it made her worry how far Katris might go for vengeance. She had to find a way to make Katris accept the truth, or face having to completely and permanently avoid Katris. The latter option was impossible in Harbin.

Finding an opportunity to talk to Chasse also proved difficult. Since running from her on the mountain, he kept his distance, hiding like Marron in the Warriors' Hall, but the painful truth the Herbal Man revealed gave Tam a connection with Chasse's anguish and why he suffered, so she was more determined than ever to speak with him.

Tam sought her father's assistance to intercede by convincing Chasse to meet with her, but Kevan returned with sorry news. 'Chasse has made his decision,' he informed her. 'He does not want to see you.' He offered no explanation for Chasse's answer.

'Please ask him again,' she pleaded.

Kevan frowned, and growled, 'Chasse is a man, now. He has made his decision and you will respect it. He does not have to come to you if he chooses not to.'

'But he's my brother,' Tam insisted.

'He is a dragonwarrior first,' Kevan retorted. 'I will not try to change his mind on this trivial matter.'

Tam wanted to argue that the matter was not trivial, but she knew the argument would be futile. Her father was not the least interested in her needs. She was a girl. Chasse was a man. The gulf between the two positions was greater than the distance between the mountain peaks above the village and the shoreline. But she was resolved to find a way to let Chasse know that she knew the truth and that she understood his dilemma, so she went about her duties while keeping a watchful eye on the Warriors' Hall, hoping an opportunity to follow her brother would arise if he ventured out.

Two days later, Tam saw Chasse leave the Warriors' Hall alone and walk quickly along the path leading to Meltsparkle. She delivered the basket of sharpened knives she was taking to Amarti, excused herself from helping to prepare fish on the pretext of having a task to perform at home, and headed for the northern end of Harbin.

Meltsparkle stream cascaded over the water-smoothed rocks, sending fine mist into the air and creating a shimmering rainbow in the mid-morning light. Tam surveyed the rocks, but when she did not see Chasse she wondered if she inadvertently missed him, or if he turned off the path and headed higher up the mountain. She decided he might have ventured deeper into the gorge and so she began to pick a path across the slippery rocks.

Narrower than Watersdrop, and steeper, Meltsparkle's water churned through the gorge at a greater velocity, making passage treacherous in the lower reaches, and impossible higher up. Tam had never fully explored the gorge because she preferred to wander the southern side of the mountain, above Watersdrop. After clambering and slipping across the rocks for several paces, she considered turning back because the cliffs rose in steep, angular blocks on either side, and she doubted that Chasse would climb into Meltsparkle beyond this point.

She reassessed the situation and remembered there was a ledge in an alcove a short distance ahead, hidden by a massive boulder in the stream.

It was the furthest she ever ventured into the gorge, and there was a slim chance that Chasse found it. Tam slid down from the rocks and edged around the boulder, the stream surging at her ankles, foaming as it forced a way under the massive obstruction. As she reached the outer edge of the boulder, the raging water rising to her thighs threatened to pull her in, but she used the strength in her wrists and fingers to stay upright and, with a concerted effort, she hauled herself around and clambered onto the ledge beyond. Chasse sat in the alcove, frowning at her.

Tam crawled across the glistening rock to her brother, shook her damp hair and sat cross-legged beside him. While she waited for him to speak, she appreciated Meltsparkle's rugged beauty. Soft spray, drifting above the turbulent stream, created colourful rainbow fragments and enhanced the natural hues in the rocks – greys, carmines and sepias of trapped sediments. Light glittered on the water and shadows flitted across the higher rocks like brief sorrow. Tam wondered what Chasse was dwelling on. She sensed he was uncomfortable with her presence and she felt that she needed to initiate the conversation or he would leave. She was also afraid that, if she did speak, he would leave anyway, but she had waited too long not to speak to him.

'I know the truth,' she finally announced.

Chasse looked up but remained silent. He glanced at the water, and back at Tam and she realised that he couldn't hear her above the roar of the water.

She drew in her breath, and repeated loudly, 'I know the truth!' Chasse lifted an eyebrow. 'About the dragons!' she added. Chasse stiffened, his face registering a trace of fear, but Tam continued. 'I know the dragonwarriors don't hunt dragons. They hunt people. I know what happened on your journey.'

Chasse suddenly looked like a rabbit in the forest cornered by a wolf. He shifted his weight and started to push to his feet, but Tam grabbed his arms to hold him down.

'Don't go! Please don't!' she pleaded. 'I know the truth, and I want you to know that I know. Don't you understand? I know what happened. I know why you're so angry inside.'

Chasse tried to break her hold, and she was frightened he would succeed, but he suddenly acquiesced and collapsed on the ledge, sighing. He hung his head forlornly, and muttered something, but the words were drowned by the thundering water.

Tam put a hand under his chin and lifted it so that she could see his face. His eyes were red. 'I didn't hear you,' she said apologetically.

'I asked how you found out,' Chasse murmured.

'The Herbal Man,' Tam replied. She would tell him the truth. After all, how could she expect him to be honest with her if she wasn't honest with him? 'He showed me what happens.'

Astonished by Tam's revelation, Chasse frowned in disbelief and asked, 'What are you saying? How could he show you what happened?'

'The Herbal Man is a wizard, Chasse. He uses the Seeing Waters to show him the truth,' she explained.

Chasse pulled away and snorted. 'Are you mocking me, sister?'

Tam shifted to look at him eye to eye, and said, 'I'm telling you the truth. If I'm not, then how would I know the Dragon Fang was ambushed by Imperial soldiers? How could I know Marron's arm was crushed between the dragonship and another ship's hull that attacked as you tried to escape?' She saw realisation spreading across Chasse's face and continued. 'I know there are no dragons, Chasse. I know the Dragon Fang preys on villagers. The Herbal Man showed me the truth.' Chasse's expression registered increasing shock and dismay. 'You see?' she asked, trying to ease the pain on his face. 'You don't need to hide what happened from me. I understand what you meant when you said it was all a lie. I know what you mean. I understand.'

Chasse started shaking, his face melting into a mask of grief, and tears glinted in his eyes. He shuddered, groaned, and cried, 'Oh, in all Varst's hells, Tam, what have I done? What have I done?' He shuddered again as a convulsive sob wracked his body. 'What have I done?'

Tam embraced him and he did not resist, and she cradled her brother as he poured out his disillusionment and grief above the tumultuous waters of Meltsparkle gorge.

When Chasse finally caught his breath, he eased out of Tam's embrace and wiped his face. 'There's so much to explain,' he said.

'I will listen,' Tam promised, and she took his hand in hers.

Chasse nodded, and reluctantly, slowly, he revealed how the summer unveiled the Dragon Fang for him. 'We trained how to fight, how to best strike an enemy,' he explained. 'No one mentioned fighting dragons in the training. It was all about killing enemies, other people. I didn't question it. We've done it ever since we could play fight with sticks.' He described the dragonwarrior rituals and rules, and the Dragonwarriors' Oath. 'We were a day's sailing out of Harbin when Jon called us initiates together. We stood at the centre of a circle of the Dragon Fang, and our father, the Dragon Head, stood on a crate before us and made us swear the Oath. We were to never tell anyone the truth of what happens on a journey. We were to agree to tell the same story as everyone else when we returned. We were made to swear to keep the truth from everyone, even our families, even to never talk about it among ourselves. We were warned that breaking the Oath meant immediate expulsion from the Dragon Fang and possibly exile from Harbin. Of course, we were confused. What was there not to talk about after a successful dragon hunt? But we all swore the Oath.' He shook his head, before saying, 'And we learnt the truth a day later, when we were told what the target for the journey was this summer. All the tales that we used to hear around the hearths, all the talk of dragons at the feasts, they were all half-truths. Dragon is the name the Dragon Fang give to the villages they pillage. When the men brag about cutting off the dragon's head, they mean it in exactly the same way we would mean it. They kill the village leader, a man like our father, the

Dragon Head. See? They aren't lying. They aren't telling the truth. The treasures they bring home? They steal it from ordinary people, like you and me, like everyone in Harbin. They kill them and take what they own, and come back in triumph, and brag about the dragons they killed. But there were never any dragons. Ever!'

Chasse dropped his head again, but Tam said, 'You're not the only person with secrets, Chasse. I've had to keep some too. No one else knows the Herbal Man is a wizard with a secret hideaway on the mountain, but I can tell you the truth about him because I trust you. I've always trusted you.' Chasse looked up and met Tam's steady gaze. 'So, I will trust you with the biggest secret of all,' she said, and she paused, before adding, 'There is a dragon, Chasse. I've seen it.'

Chasse's jaw dropped. He blinked, struggling to comprehend Tam's admission, and gasped, 'Where?'

'In the mountain. Her name is Claryssa. She is the Herbal Man's companion.'

'A real dragon?' Chasse asked in disbelief. 'Are you sure?'

'I've seen her,' Tam answered with pride. 'She's very old, but she's magnificent. She has enormous golden eyes,' she said, and then she described the dragon in minute detail.

The sharing of secrets, beautiful and dark, full of promise and despair, trust and betrayal, in the gorge above Meltsparkle renewed the childhood bond between Tam and Chasse, but they understood that they would never see the world through childlike eyes again. Their childhood belief, the fabric at the heart of Harbin, was shattered forever by the strange and cruel experiences of the past summer. They had tasted the reality of adulthood and were irrevocably changed by its bitter-sweet nectar.

Twenty-Seven

The sun was yet to light Dragon Mountain peak when Tam led Chasse across the goat pasture to the tree line. She convinced him to climb the mountain with her, but only after great difficulty. Chasse was struggling with the enormity of the truth about what lay at the core of Harbin culture.

'A dragon on the mountain above us, and yet the Dragon Fang have been hunting people all this time, not knowing the dragon was always there,' Chasse said, as they started climbing the path.

'I know,' Tam replied. 'The Herbal Man used a term – ironic, I think – meaning what we know or do is the opposite to what it is. He thinks it's almost somewhere between amusing and tragic.'

'There's nothing funny about it,' Chasse retorted. 'Everyone keeps the lie. They know it's a lie and yet they keep pretending,' he said, shaking his head. 'Even Father, our own father, has lied to us, all along. What else have they been lying about?'

'We can ask the Herbal Man,' Tam suggested, rounding rock.

'He's the biggest liar of all,' Chasse accused. 'He's been hiding a dragon on the mountain.'

Tam stopped to face Chasse. 'He had to,' she argued. 'Or else people would find them and kill them.'

'Sorry,' Chasse offered, shrugging. 'I don't know who to trust anymore.'

'You can trust me,' Tam reminded him. 'Come on. I'm in enough trouble already.' She turned and continued up the path between the trees and rocks.

'Mother wanted you to help with preparing for Procra's Dance,' Chasse reminded her.

'Exactly,' she replied, without faltering in her ascent. 'I understand why. She wants the feast to be a grief-breaker. We never held the Dragon Festival, not with what's happened.'

'She wants me to choose a wife,' Chasse said. 'That's her real reason. But it's cruel because there should have been five of us choosing and now there's only me, and everyone else will be angry because I came back and others didn't.'

'And Marron,' Tam said. 'He can choose.'

Chasse snorted, saying, 'Marron won't come out of the Warriors' Hall. He speaks to none of us, no one except his father. He won't be choosing anyone.'

Tam didn't answer. She felt great pity for Marron and she remembered how Eesa told her that she believed the gods were unnaturally cruel to the young man.

'There are people in the village who blame the Herbal Man for Marron being alive,' Eesa said. 'They say Varst chose Marron to walk the dark journey through the shadows to Eternal Paradise, but the Herbal Man interfered.'

'He saved Marron,' Tam reasoned.

'I know, girl,' Eesa said, 'but others say the Herbal Man consigned Marron to hell with one arm.'

Tam knew her mother was siding slowly with the growing view that the Herbal Man was an ill-omen, a pariah. Eesa did not condone bitterness towards other people, but she was also a leader who was sensitive to popular opinion.

'It might be wise to keep away from the old man,' Eesa advised Tam, and Tam knew that her mother's reason for making her responsible for the Long Hall decorations, instead of an older woman, was to make it difficult for Tam to visit the Herbal Man. 'You are becoming a woman,'

Eesa told her, 'and a woman must be trustworthy and reliable. Grown women are too busy to dabble in trivialities like you have with the Herbal Man. Time to outgrow your girlish ways.'

'You know Trask is determined to take revenge,' Chasse said, breaking into Tam's reverie.

'But Father has given him strict instructions,' Tam replied over her shoulder.

'Trask isn't stupid, Tam,' Chasse remarked. 'He knows he can't act alone, so he's playing on the sympathies of the others.'

Tam stopped to face her brother. 'What do you mean?'

'They're angry, Tam. They want to blame someone for what's happened. Trask is telling everyone that the debacle is the Herbal Man's fault.'

'How could it be his fault?'

'It doesn't matter,' Chasse said. 'Trask is blaming him, and everyone is believing Trask. He's telling them we should climb the mountain and get rid of the old man once and for all.'

'Even Father?'

Chasse shook his head. 'No. Father opposes the plan.'

Tam nodded, but as she turned to continue climbing she said, 'We need to warn the Herbal Man.'

'Father won't let it happen,' Chasse argued.

Tam stopped and turned to him again, saying, 'Father is one man and Trask isn't afraid of him. We need to hurry.'

Tam increased her pace, driven by her churning thoughts. *Am I betraying the Herbal Man? I can still tell Chasse the dragon is a lie. No*, she corrected. *I can't. Chasse has been lied to by too many people, and I need to prove to him there is truth in the world.* She was certain the lies and knowing about them was what killed Ashlee in the end. Ashlee had no one to trust, no one to believe or turn to for truth. *I can at least stop the lies for my brother and myself*, she decided. *It's the first step to changing our world*. For her, Harbin was confusion and mystery, like the roiling waters in Meltsparkle gorge, and the Herbal Man was the only rock of truth in the swirling turmoil.

At the unexpected sound of approaching voices and footsteps, Katris slid from the broad tree bough and melted into the dew-dampened green foliage beside the path. She anticipated ambushing Tamesan alone because the disgusting Dragon Head's daughter was always sneaking up the mountain to the dirty old Herbal Man's hut, but someone else was accompanying her.

Katris had lain in wait each day for four days for the opportunity to punish Tamesan for what she did to Marron. Her grandfather's ornate whalebone dagger was wedged in her belt, the wickedly sharp blade honed on the whetstone of her hatred, and her initial plan was to kill Tamesan swiftly, but each morning that she waited she entertained unpleasant alternatives. She could wound Tamesan, cripple her, and leave her to bleed agonisingly to death. She could cut out her tongue and eyes. She could maim her arm so that it would need to be amputated like Marron's. She could lacerate her face so badly that no man would look at her. Tamesan was far too pretty and far too proud, and without her pretty face she would be no one in Harbin without a husband. Katris liked the last alternative. She would disfigure Tamesan's face.

Crouched in the bushes, Katris waited for the walkers to pass. Her fingers tightened on her dagger hilt as she saw Tamesan's outline in the dull light, excited that the gods brought the wicked enemy to her, but she hesitated when she saw the solid bulk of a young man behind her target. She would be foolish to attack Tamesan with a witness, especially a man who would most likely defend Tamesan. When she recognised Chasse, Katris' hand slid restlessly over the dagger's pommel, and she silently cursed her luck while she waited for the pair to climb past and disappear among the trees and rocks.

Spurred by curiosity as to where Tamesan and Chasse were headed, and goaded by her frustration, Katris crept from her hiding place to peer up the rugged, twisting pathway, until she was certain the brother and sister would not see her trailing them, and she started to climb after them.

The higher sections of the mountain path were new territory for Katris because her friends and she had no cause to explore, and she stayed close to the village, except for the aberrant period in her life when she naively considered Tamesan a friend. She only came higher than usual the past few days because she was driven by grief and revenge, but this time she would see where Tamesan and her brother were going. It might lead to a better place for her to set a trap for the one she hated.

'Hello?' Tam tentatively called at the door to the old hut. When there was no answer, she turned to Chasse and asked him to wait while she checked inside. She forced open a window shutter, to Chasse's surprise, and climbed through. A moment later, she opened the front door and announced, 'He's not here.'

'Now what?' Chasse asked, unable to hide his disappointment.

'He'll be around. He's probably collecting herbs. We can wait.'

Chasse spun on his heels to survey the plateau, and said, 'When I came up here to give the Herbal Man messages for Father, I always felt this place was odd, like it didn't quite belong on the mountain.'

'Uhuh,' Tam responded. 'Everything is fresh, and there are so many different plants growing in this small flat area. I still feel it's odd. I think it has to do with his magic.'

'What is magic?' Chasse asked.

Tam stared at Chasse and pulled a face, replying, 'I'm not sure I know what it is. The Herbal Man explained it over summer, but it's incredibly complicated.'

'Tell me what he told you.'

'I'll try,' she said. 'It's knowing that there are energy fields around all things, and all things are interrelated through the energy fields. Magic is the ability to manipulate the energy fields to make things work or change them.' She continued explaining what she remembered, but she was acutely aware of Chasse's growing confusion as she described the legend of the Genesis Stone and the relationship between wizards and dragons, so she cut the explanation to a brief synopsis and switched to telling her brother the background story to the Herbal Man. His interest lifted as she described the world beyond the mountain wall encircling Harbin, and his response shifted between disbelief and delight as she talked of kings and queens and great cities. While Tam talked, the morning sun crept across the cloudy sky and was already directly overhead.

'I don't think he's coming back, Tam,' Chasse said, glancing up at the sky. 'We better go back down. You're in enough trouble with Mother as it is.'

'I'm not concerned about it anymore. I'm old enough to make my own decisions,' she declared quietly.'

'You've always been old enough to make your own decisions,' Chasse chided, smirking. 'It's why you are unique.'

'Where did you get that word from?' Tam asked.

'Unique?' he queried. 'I heard Sharmine use it about you when she was talking to Mother. I've always remembered it.'

'But what does it mean?'

'It means you are remarkable, the only one of your kind,' announced a voice from within the hut. Tam and Chasse turned to see the Herbal Man emerging.

'I thought you weren't in,' Tam uttered in surprise. 'I looked.'

The Herbal Man laughed and winked at Chasse as he replied, 'I probably wasn't in when you looked, Tamesan, but you should remember there are other ways in and out of my home.'

Tam blushed at her forgetfulness, recovered, and said, 'I brought Chasse to see you.'

'I can see,' the Herbal Man observed with a wry grin beneath his flowing white beard.

'No,' Tam amended, 'I mean I told him everything. The truth.' She lowered her gaze in apology.

'I know,' the Herbal Man informed her.

'You do?' Tam exclaimed, her eyes widening.

'Of course I know,' he said, and he turned to Chasse, who shifted his stance uncomfortably in the old man's presence. 'I expected you to tell your brother. It's the right thing to do.'

Tam felt relief surge through her body. 'I told him about Claryssa, too,' she said.

The Herbal Man nodded, and beckoned for the pair to follow him inside, saying, 'Chasse best meet her, then. Come on.'

Chasse glanced apprehensively at Tam, who smiled and said, 'She is beautiful, Chasse, truly magnificent. You'll see. She is nothing like you've imagined a dragon to be.'

Katris watched Chasse and Tamesan enter the Herbal Man's hut, annoyed that the pair waited so long for the old man, and it seemed they were going to be with him even longer. Hidden in a thicket, she strained to overhear the conversation between the three in front of the hut, but she wasn't close enough, so she was no wiser as to what Chasse and Tamesan were doing. The sun was at midday, and she knew she should be helping prepare for Procra's Feast, but curiosity urged her to creep to the hut.

A dozen heart-thumping moments later, she pressed against the wall, listening. To her surprise, the interior was silent. She gathered courage and peered through a crack in a wooden shutter and discovered the hut was empty. Fascinated, she moved to the door and tried the handle and found it unlocked. She cautiously opened the door, expecting someone to challenge her entry, but no one did. She studied the walls, looking for a door, and admonished herself for wasting time because all the walls were exterior. She checked the hearth in case it concealed an exit, and saw the space was dirty, disused with an odd, narrow hole under the grate at its centre.

Three people had vanished. The impossibility made her shiver. Warily, she backed towards the door, but her heel caught an uneven board in the wooden floor and she stumbled. The dilapidated rug pulled back with her foot and exposed a section jutting above the other boards. Katris steadied herself and inspected the segment, recognising a trapdoor not fully pulled shut. She lay on the floor and listened, and when she was satisfied the area beneath the trapdoor was silent she eased it open until she could see steps descending into a lighted space.

Blood pounded in her ears. She pulled the dagger from her belt and measured its weight. She'd never played with a dagger, and for once wished she was a boy who would have been trained to use a weapon. She didn't need to descend, but desperate curiosity dragged her down the steps despite her fear.

She found two connecting chambers. The first, cluttered with an odd array of items, was lit by a strange candle painted with red lines, and second was a bedroom, lit by a lantern hanging on the wall. A partially open door leading from the bedroom revealed a dark passage and at the end of the passage a doorway glowed on the right wall.

Katris crept along the passage, mesmerised by the light, until she heard voices emanating from the lit doorway. She recognised Tamesan's voice. Pleased to have tracked her quarry, Katris edged to the doorway, but she was ready to retreat if anyone saw her.

In the space beyond the door, she heard the Herbal Man speaking gibberish, and the light brightened momentarily and dimmed, setting Katris on edge, but no one came to the door. Heart beating fiercely, Katris leaned around the jamb and peered in.

The Herbal Man, Tamesan and Chasse stood five paces into the chamber, backs to Katris, facing a horror beyond her worst imaginings. Katris had never seen a dragon, but she knew all the tales and legends, and the reptilian head with golden orbs for eyes, protruding curved yellow fangs, and scaly snout staring back at the three in the room could only be such a creature.

Fear gripped Katris' stomach and threatened to turn her legs to water. She'd seen too much for mere curiosity's sake. She forced her eyes from the vision and eased into the security of darkness, and the moment the darkness enveloped her she bolted. She ran through the chambers and scrambled up the steps, pursued by the knowledge that the most terrible of Varst's creatures was nesting in the mountain above her home, and by the time she burst out of the Herbal Man's false hut Katris was running in blind terror from her darkest childhood nightmare.

Twenty-Eight

'What's happening?' Tam asked, as Chasse and she reached the edge of the goat pasture and saw people crowding the entrance to the Long Hall.

'Something important,' Chasse replied. 'We best find out.'

They hurried across the pasture in the late afternoon, Chasse still enraptured by his first meeting with Claryssa. Tam smiled as they jogged together, glad that she shared the secret of the Herbal Man's awesome companion with her brother to show him that he could trust her, no matter the circumstances.

They reached the Long Hall as the last people squeezed through the door and waited in the crowd to see what was underway. Tam saw the dragonwarrior, Jon, who closed the door behind the last people, staring as if he was astonished to see Chasse and her. Chasse noticed too and asked Jon, 'What's going on?'

'I thought the two of you would know,' Jon replied.

Tam cast a quizzical glance at Chasse, as she asked, 'Know what?'

'Listen,' Jon directed, as he turned to look over the crowd. The buzz of voices quietened.

'I'm going forward,' Tam said to Chasse.

Chasse tried to grab his sister's arm, sensing from Jon's odd expression that something was not quite right and that it concerned them, but Tam moved too quickly and Jon gripped Chasse's arm, shaking his head, saying, 'Stay here. This is not where you should be.'

Tam pushed through the throng until she could clearly see the focus of everyone's attention. Her father, Kevan, faced Trask, anger smouldering in their faces, and between them stood Katris, her pale face framed by her shining long dark hair. Katris looked afraid, but her body leaned towards Trask, away from Kevan. Tam spied her mother, Eesa, with Amarti and a group of village women, but as she started to move towards them Trask's voice erupted, haranguing the villagers.

'All of you! Listen to me! Your lives are in great danger!'

'Hold your tongue, Trask!' Kevan bellowed, taking a step towards his adversary. 'You speak out of turn!'

'I'll speak as I wish!' Trask retorted. 'We don't need to hear your excuses! We want to hear the truth!'

'Let the girl speak!' a voice shouted from the left, chorused by more in the crowd. 'Let the girl speak!'

'Hear them?' Trask asked, sneering at Kevan. 'Let the girl tell everyone what she told us. They have a right to hear!'

People cheered Trask's statement, but Kevan looked vexed, and Tam knew he did not want Katris to speak. She wondered if he was stopping her because she was a girl. Kevan looked past Trask at the Dragon Head, who nodded affirmation to Trask's challenge, so he swallowed and said, 'The girl can speak,' but he added angrily, 'I do not believe what she says.'

All eyes focused on Katris, and her face whitened as if she wanted to run from the massed attention. Tam felt pity for her, and she wished she knew what was wrong so that she could help Katris.

'Go on, girl,' Trask urged. 'Tell everyone what you've seen. Tell them the truth.'

Katris started shaking, and hesitated, as if the words stuck in her throat.

'Speak!' Trask ordered. 'Tell us what you saw.'

Katris stared blindly, opened her mouth, and nothing emerged. She swallowed to control her nerves, and said in a harsh whisper, 'There is a dragon on the mountain.'

Complete silence immediately followed Katris' revelation, but fear ripped through Tam's spine and then a babble of voices erupted, filling the hall, all questioning the news that a dragon lived on Dragon Mountain.

'Quiet!' Trask bellowed above the cacophony. 'Listen to the girl!' The frantic conversations ceased. Everyone stared at Katris. 'Go on,' Trask prompted.

Katris shifted nervously and glanced fearfully at Kevan, who glared fiercely in return. 'I saw the Herbal Man, and Chasse, and Tamesan,' she announced. 'They were talking to it. It lives in the Herbal Man's home.'

Gasps of surprise and shock echoed through the hall, but Leshan the fisherman called out, 'Must be a small dragon if it lives in the Herbal Man's place!'

Leshan's sarcasm raised a spatter of laughter, but Trask cut it short, scowling, 'Quiet! Let the girl explain!' He turned to Katris. 'Tell them what you saw.'

Katris' face flushed at being mocked. She looked in Leshan's direction and said, 'There is a cave under the Herbal Man's hut, a huge cave. The dragon lives there. That's where I saw them all.'

Voices rose again and Tam saw Eesa stare in amazement at Kevan, who stiffened and gave Trask a murderous look, an expression that Tam knew came when her father was infuriated beyond reason.

'What have you to say, Dragon Head?' Trask challenged over the din. People quietened to hear Kevan's answer.

'The girl is obviously mad,' Kevan said. 'How can there be a dragon on the mountain? How has it stayed hidden all this time? Why have we never seen it before?'

'I'm not mad!' Katris screamed. 'I saw it! I followed them up the mountain and I saw it!'

'Where are your son and daughter?' Trask jeered. 'Why are they not here?'

'I am here,' Tam announced, and she stepped out of the crowd. Her heart raced and she felt sick, but she needed to stop the furore.

Startled by her unanticipated presence, Trask gathered his wits and demanded, 'Where were you today when your mother was looking for you?'

Tam looked at Eesa and saw her mother's despair. 'I was —' she began and paused, contemplating what to say. Lying would compromise her principles. Telling the truth would condemn Chasse and herself, and Claryssa and the Herbal Man. But Harbin was already too full of lies. 'I was visiting the Herbal Man,' she said, as calmly as she could. 'Is there anything wrong with that?' She heard Eesa gasp and people whisper.

'And his dragon?' Trask queried accusingly.

The man's blunt question caused her to pause again and the crowd hushed to hear her answer. Tam wished that she could lie as easily as the Dragon Heart lied about her rescue, or as easily as her father lied about the summer dragon hunts. If she lied now, if she bluffed her way out of the confrontation, she could make Katris and Trask look foolish, protect her father and mother from heartache, and save Claryssa and the Herbal Man. But she knew lying was only a short-term solution. However she managed to spy on them, Katris clearly knew the truth because of what she described, and it would only be a matter of time before she, or Trask, or someone tried to find the cave in the mountain. Lies only bred the need for more lies. She fixed her gaze on Katris' face and said, 'Yes. We were with the dragon. I took Chasse to meet her.'

Protestations mixed with cries of horror, and the villagers shuffled restlessly, until Trask again shouted over the noise. 'You heard her admission!' he yelled triumphantly. 'There is a dragon on the mountain, a dragon over Harbin!'

'It will kill us!' a warrior cried. 'It will burn and destroy our homes!'

'Not if we strike first!' Trask roared. 'Not if the Dragon Fang bring it down!' He brandished his spear to exhort the crowd into action.

'To arms!' another warrior yelled.

'Stop this nonsense!' Kevan shouted. 'Hear me! People of Harbin! The Dragon Head commands you! Hear me!'

'No one listens to a liar!' Trask snarled. 'Your spawn are consorting with a dragon! Your son and daughter side with the enemy of Nakiades!'

'Hear me, Trask, or by Varst's mighty powers I will strike you down!' Kevan warned. He stepped in front of Trask and grabbed the shaft of Trask's spear. Katris screamed and rushed into the crowd. Warriors circled and encouraged the two men, and people crowded closer to watch the confrontation, while Eesa and others cried for the adversaries to stop.

Tam watched, pinned in the crowd and horrified, as Trask and her father wrestled for possession of the spear, muscles bulging in their arms and backs as they strained and twisted. Using his greater bulk to advantage, Kevan pinned Trask against a pillar, but he didn't anticipate Trask's left knee rising sharply into his groin. Kevan released his hold on the spear, and Trask hit out with his elbow, sending Kevan reeling back. Before Kevan could regain balance, Trask drove his spear into Kevan's exposed thigh. Eesa screamed as Kevan roared and staggered into the crowd.

Tam broke free of the press of people and leapt at Trask, but his reflexes were too quick. His right arm snaked out and caught her a stinging blow across the side of the face as she attempted to grapple his waist, and she was flung against the wall of onlookers. But her diversion gave her father time to recover. Ethen handed Kevan a sword and he straightened to face Trask, blood flowing from his thigh.

'Stop them!' Tam desperately appealed as the two men circled.

'Hush, girl,' Ethen remonstrated. 'It's time this was resolved.'

Trask prodded Kevan with the point of his spear, goading Kevan into an attack. Tam was no expert on fighting, but she saw the advantage that Trask held with a spear against Kevan's sword. He had a greater reach, and his opponent was wounded.

'Come on, old man,' Trask sneered confidently. 'Come and taste Varst's bitter cup. No one will follow a man whose own children are dragon-spawn!'

Kevan ignored the jibe and continued to circle silently, neatly dodging Trask's probing spear, and Tam suddenly realised the odds were in her father's favour, despite the weapon disparity and his wound. He was more disciplined than Trask, resolute and controlled. Her fear remained, but she sensed Kevan would win this encounter, and she saw that the watching crowd believed Kevan would triumph too. Trask's supporters were predominately younger dragonwarriors, but most villagers sided with Kevan. He was the Dragon Head.

Trask lunged, but Kevan's sword steered the spear away. Trask lunged again, and again Kevan turned the attack aside, but he also retaliated, and a cut appeared on Trask's cheek. Trask swore and jabbed ineffectively.

'Put up your spear, Trask,' Kevan ordered coolly. He seemed unperturbed by Trask's threat, but Tam saw her father was breathing heavily and his thigh wound was wider, the blood running down his leg and smearing the floor.

'Go to hell!' Trask spat, and he swung his spear in a wide arc.

Kevan effortlessly ducked, but he slipped on his own blood, and a collective gasp rose as the Dragon Head stumbled. Seizing his opportunity, Trask stabbed. Kevan twisted, but the spear pierced his shirt and dug into his side, and as he collapsed like a dropped sack of grain his weight tore the point loose. He rolled onto his back, his chest heaving, blood leaking onto the hardened earth floor. Trask swaggered towards his fallen opponent, grinning as he hefted his spear to deal the death blow.

Tam wrenched free from restraining hands and leapt across the intervening space to stand defiantly between Trask and her stricken father.

'Get out of the way, girl,' Trask growled hungrily. 'I am going to kill your father.'

As he raised his spear, another figure scampered out of the crowd to stand beside Tam, and a boy's voice shrieked, 'Touch my sister or my father and I will kill you!'

Tam stared in astonishment at Jaysin's unexpected show of courage, his lip quivering, his eyes brimming with tears, his tiny fists clenched.

Trask hesitated, and his grin widened as if Jaysin's defiance amused him, but then he frowned, saying, 'Pity your father never had your courage, boy,' and with a sweep of his arm he pushed Tam and Jaysin aside.

Tam screamed, 'Father!' as she scrambled to her feet, fearing she was too late to stop Trask's attack, so she was surprised to see Trask with his spear still raised. Then she saw the two dragonwarriors standing between Trask and her fallen father. One was Jon. The other was Raven. Neither held a weapon, but both were resolute in their stand.

'You have won, Trask,' Jon said sternly. 'The people witnessed your victory, and it is done. Do not dishonour the Dragon Fang or your newly won title with a foolish vengeful act. Enhance your honour by letting Kevan keep his.'

Trask held his spear aloft a moment longer, as if he was unimpressed by Jon's speech, but his expression melted into a grin, and he lowered the weapon. 'Fair words, Jon,' he acknowledged. 'Always the one with the fair words.' As he turned to address the crowd, Eesa rushed forward to her husband. 'You have borne witness, people of Harbin, people of my village. I stand before you as the new Dragon Head. Varst has filled me with renewed strength to rise to lead you, and through his will the weaker man has fallen. So do all dragon worshippers perish. The task of Nakiades is never done while dragons exist, while dragons live.' He drew a breath and continued. 'The gods have revealed to us through the girl, Katris, that a loathsome dragon roosts above our village.'

'She is harmless!' Tam called from behind.

Trask ignored her, saying, 'Dragons are our sworn and sacred enemy, and all dragons must die!'

Tam pushed beside Trask and pleaded, 'Claryssa is old! She has never hurt anyone!'

'Don't bring your lies here, girl!' Trask warned, and to the gathering he said, 'We must drive the dragon from the mountain! If we do not, it will steal down in the night to burn our homes, strip flesh from our bones, and eat our children, and Harbin will perish! We know this is true. It is why Nakiades hunted the foul beasts! It is the reason why the Dragon Fang journey every summer. All dragons must die!'

'There are no dragons!' Tam yelled in exasperation. 'You all know the truth better than I do! You tell lies and say you hunt them, but there are no dragons!'

'There is!' Katris retaliated. 'I saw it! You know I saw it!'

'Both of you be quiet!' Trask ordered. 'This is no longer a place for girls,' he announced, and added, 'or women. The Dragon Fang will meet in the Warriors' Hall to plan how to purge the mountain of this dragon and rid us for all time of the old fool who keeps it there. The rest of you go to your homes until the dragon is dead. The Dragon Head has spoken. Obey my words.'

People nodded knowingly, or shook their heads with concern, but they all began shuffling noisily from the Long Hall, discussing the sudden change of events, arguing the outcome, some happy, many worried. Tam glimpsed Chasse caught in the crowd at the doorway, but as she went to go to him her arm was grabbed by a strong hand and she turned to find another dragonwarrior, Adin, holding her. 'Keep her and her family in the Long Hall,' Trask ordered, 'and find Chasse.'

Tam pulled against the warrior's grip, but he held her fast and said, 'Don't be stupid, Tamesan. Trask is the Dragon Head now, and you are no longer the Dragon Head's daughter. You will obey Trask.'

Recognising the gravity of her predicament, Tam screamed above the general hubbub, 'Run Chasse! Warn the Herbal Man! Run!'

Chasse looked at her, saw two dragonwarriors moving towards him, pushed through the stragglers at the door, and ran.

'Get him!' Trask roared.

The dragonwarriors pursued Chasse.

Trask approached Tam and took her chin roughly in his hand. 'He won't get there,' he remarked sourly. 'The old man and his dragon are doomed.' Tam shook her chin loose and spat at him, which made Trask laugh, and say, 'You never did have womanly manners, did you, girl?' He chuckled grimly. 'A good man will teach you how to behave — if any man will have you now.' He turned away, laughing heartily, and joined a group of dragonwarriors waiting for him at the centre of the hall. As they reached the door, Trask turned to the four remaining warriors and said, 'Keep them here, and don't let any of the nosy ones inside, unless they have my permission.'

As night settled over Harbin, Tam dressed her father's wounds with Eesa's help, applying the lessons she learned from the Herbal Man, but lacking the necessary ointments and herbs to promote healing. Kevan was deathly pale from blood loss and he slipped in and out of consciousness.

Tam tried to enlist Jaysin's help, but her little brother lay in a foetal curl in the corner, refusing to acknowledge his sister or his mother. Tam was still in awe of Jaysin's stand against Trask because her little brother always avoided confrontations and fights with other children and hated weapons, showing none of the aggressive qualities expected of boys. Instead, Jaysin preferred being alone, and he was interested in odd things like the stars, learning reading and writing, and making up songs to sing. He did not fit Harbin expectations. Tam remembered the word Chasse used — unique. Jaysin was certainly unique.

Eesa convinced the warrior guards to let her fetch food, water and clean cloth to bandage Kevan. Before she left, she kindled a small fire in the Long Hall hearth, and when she returned she brought food for her family and the guards. The men expressed their gratitude, and the mood in the hall relaxed, but everyone was waiting to hear the Dragon Fang's decision as to the fate of the dragon on the mountain.

Tam ate a morsel of food, but her thoughts were with Chasse and the Herbal Man. She assumed Chasse escaped, or logically he would already be a prisoner in the hall. She knew there was a possibility he might have been injured or killed in the pursuit, but she refused to entertain either outcome. The other dragonwarriors wouldn't kill Chasse. He was one of them.

Tam rose and crossed to where Kevan lay, with Eesa stroking his greying hair, and asked quietly, 'Mother?'

'Yes?' Eesa responded, without taking her attention from her husband.

'Why didn't someone stop Father and Trask fighting? Theo would've stopped it.'

'Theo was good man,' Eesa murmured, 'and a very good friend, Varst rest his soul.'

'But why didn't anyone else stop them?' Tam asked.

'Must you ask so many questions?' Eesa complained, lifting her tired eyes to look at her daughter.

'I need to know,' Tam replied, as she sat beside Eesa.

Eesa sighed and gazed wistfully at Kevan, who was asleep. 'This has been a long time coming, child,' she said slowly. 'Your father knew this would happen – if not Trask, then someone else. If not this summer, then perhaps the next.'

'Knew what would happen?'

'Knew someone else would become Dragon Head, that someone would challenge and defeat him.'

'I don't understand,' Tam admitted. 'Do you mean Trask, or someone had to fight him? Why?'

'Oh, child,' Eesa murmured. 'You have so much to learn.' She sighed and stroked Kevan's hair as she explained. 'The Dragon Head must be the strongest warrior in Harbin, the one with strength to lead the Dragon Fang unrivalled and unchallenged. Every Dragon Head earns the title by defeating the man holding the title. Your father became Dragon Head by defeating Theo's father, Taen.'

'Father killed Theo's father? I thought Theo was Father's friend?'

Eesa chuckled, recalling a fond memory. 'Theo was our friend and Kevan didn't kill Theo's father. He hardly even hurt him. The challenge was all planned and agreed in advance. Taen chose your father as his successor. I wasn't Kevan's wife then, only a girl like you. Kevan was the most handsome and wonderfully strong warrior in Harbin. Everyone knew. Even the older men who travelled for years with Taen respected Kevan. He commanded respect. He was so perfect, so god-like.'

Tam listened, fascinated, as her mother described her father as a young man. Tam never imagined her parents as young people, like Chasse or herself. They were always old, distant and angry. Eesa sounded like a love-struck girl, a facet of her mother's personality that Tam had never witnessed.

'So,' Eesa continued, composing her emotions, 'Taen didn't want to face any more challenges to his position. Like your father now, he was getting old. He wanted less responsibility, and he believed Kevan was the right warrior to replace him.'

'What about Theo?' Tam asked.

'Theo never wanted to be Dragon Head,' Eesa replied. 'Like everyone else, he thought your father was the best candidate. It's why he never challenged Kevan all these years but stood by him.'

'So, what happened?'

'Taen arranged for Kevan to challenge him one afternoon, on the shore near the jetty. Everyone came down to watch, but they quickly realised the fight was staged, and people were laughing, almost to tears, at the antics those two men got up to. They exchanged mock blows for a short time, no one drew blood, and in the end Taen, Varst rest his soul, yielded, and declared Kevan the new Dragon Head. The celebration in the evening went on until the following morning, and few people worked the next day.'

'Why didn't Father name his successor like Taen?' Tam asked.

'He intended to, when the time came, but he wasn't satisfied with anyone yet. And there was always Trask. Trask's father, Marden, told him he would be Dragon Head one day, so Trask believed it. He's always been jealous of your father, for many reasons. But Kevan knew Trask would not make a good Dragon Head. Trask is too headstrong, too selfish. He's tried to take the title from Kevan before.'

'They fought before this?' Tam asked.

'Oh, yes,' Eesa affirmed. 'At least three times on the summer journeys, and twice in the Warriors' Hall. But your father always put Trask back in his place.'

'Why didn't Father kill him?'

Eesa shook her head, and answered, 'Because Kevan knows Trask is a good warrior and valuable to the Dragon Fang. He was angry that Trask wanted to supplant him, but your father always put the needs of Harbin ahead of his own, so he never let his anger override his decisions.'

'Does Trask know?' Tam asked.

'He does, Tamesan, but he wanted to be Dragon Head, and now he is. Perhaps he will mellow, now that he has what he wanted. Time will tell.' Eesa yawned, and said, 'I am tired.' She smiled at Tamesan, and added, 'But this time you can answer my question, Tamesan. What is the Herbal Man's dragon really like?'

Tam met her mother's gaze and was filled with warmth. It was time to tell the truth and share her secret world with her mother and it felt good. She tucked her knees under her chin and began with, 'Claryssa is the most beautiful thing I have ever seen.'

Twenty-Nine

Tam dreamed Chasse was whispering in her ear. 'You have to come up the mountain,' he urged. 'Hurry.' He pulled at her arm and urged her to get up. 'Tamesan,' he whispered. 'Come on.' Tam opened her eyes to find Chasse squatted beside her in the semi-darkness, tugging her arm. 'Sh,' he warned, as she went to speak.

She sat up on her rumpled bedding and glanced at the remnant coals glowing in the hearth. She quickly scanned the Long Hall. The sleeping forms of her father and mother lay side-by-side. Jaysin was still curled in the corner where he retreated. 'What about the guards?' she whispered.

Chasse shook his head and motioned for her to follow. They crept to the door, where Chasse held up a hand for Tam to wait while he peered outside. When he slipped through the opening, Tam followed.

Harbin was draped in fog so thick that Tam could not even see the Warriors' Hall across the space separating it from the Long Hall. She followed Chasse along the path until they reached the last hut, and then he led her across the goat pasture.

When they melted into the ghostly tree line, Tam grabbed Chasse's arm and broke the silence. 'What happened to the guards?' she asked.

'They're looking for me,' he said, grinning. 'I made an unexpected appearance and led them towards Meltsparkle. Then I doubled back for you. The darkness and fog made it easy to lose them.'

'Did you warn the Herbal Man?'

Chasse shook his head. 'I couldn't get up the path,' he confessed. 'The dragonwarriors cut me off, so I hid in the forest until they stopped searching. I decided to come back for you in case Trask did something stupid.'

'Then we better hurry,' Tam urged. 'The sooner we warn the Herbal Man, the sooner he can get Claryssa to safety.' She leapt ahead of Chasse and they climbed quickly.

As they clambered around a steep pile of tumbled boulders in the pre-dawn, a voice challenged, 'Where are you going?' Two dragonwarriors emerged from hiding, spears raised menacingly.

'I thought you said they'd given up looking for you?' Tam complained.

'Trask thought it wise to place a guard up here in case Chasse convinced the Herbal Man to come to the village,' one warrior explained, as he jumped down to confront Chasse and Tam. 'We didn't quite expect to see you coming up the mountain with your sister.'

'I didn't intend to be predictable, Alan,' Chasse replied.

'Stay here, Jak,' Alan told his companion. 'I'll take them down.' He turned to Chasse and rolled his spear fluidly in his hands, as he said, 'You won't give me any trouble, will you?'

'Me?' Chasse asked and laughed. 'Not with that thing in your hands.'

Alan laughed, and said, 'Let's go, then,' and he prodded Chasse with the spear. Chasse shrugged and began to descend, but Tam hesitated, until Alan waved the spear at her, and said, 'You too, in case you haven't worked it out yet.' Tam glared at Alan but fell into step with her brother.

'Now what?' Tam whispered to Chasse.

'No scheming,' Alan warned and sniggered. 'I think our new Dragon Head would commend me for skewering his enemy's offspring.'

'You wouldn't really do it for Trask?' Chasse queried.

'No, I wouldn't do it for him,' Alan answered. 'I'd do it for the fun of it.'

'Improvise,' Chasse whispered to Tam. 'Distract him.'

Tam abruptly stumbled, and cried in agony, 'Oh my ankle! My ankle!' She collapsed and rolled between a pair of tree trunks.

Chasse bent forward, asking, 'What have you done?'

'Hurt my ankle, idiot!' Tam exclaimed, and she wrinkled her face in pain as she clutched her leg. Chasse reached for her ankle, but she screamed, 'Touch it, stupid boy, and I'll thrash you!' Alan started laughing. 'What's so funny, goat breath?' Tam yelled.

Her outburst made Alan laugh harder, and he paused to say, 'I'm glad she's your sister, Chasse. Pity the man crazy enough to choose her at Procra's Dance.'

'It won't be a half-wit like you!' Tam jeered.

Alan stopped laughing, and said, 'Get her up. We have to get off this mountain before the sun rises.'

Chasse tried to lift Tam, but she yelped, and her position between the trees made manoeuvring difficult. 'Can you at least help me?' Chasse appealed to Alan.

Alan cursed and moved closer to assess the situation. 'Girls,' he lamented when he saw Chasse couldn't shift her alone. 'Who needs them?' He leaned his spear against a trunk and helped Chasse pull Tam to her feet. She protested as they shifted her into a manageable position, until she placed an arm over each set of shoulders, but as they eased her onto the path Tam crumpled left, putting all her weight on Alan. Caught off-balance, he fell with her, but Tam rolled away, and by the time Alan pushed up on his elbows Chasse stood over him, pressing the spear against his neck. Tam scrambled to her feet and stood beside her brother.

'Girls,' Chasse said, grinning triumphantly. 'They're useful too, aren't they, Alan?' Alan cursed and went to call for help, but Chasse put pressure on the spear and warned, 'I wouldn't, Alan. I have nothing to lose by killing you.'

Alan flinched, and gasped, 'We are dragonwarriors. We sail together.'

'Not according to Trask,' Chasse replied. 'And not according to your threat before.'

Alan shrugged, and asked, 'What do you want me to do?'

'Roll over, face down,' Tam ordered. Alan complied. Tam tore two strips from her hem and used one to bind Alan's wrists behind his back, the other to gag him. 'I've left your feet free,' she informed him. 'If you're silly enough, you can keep going down the mountain, but I advise you to stay here. I'm sure Trask and the others will be here soon.' Alan mumbled beneath the gag, but Tam and Chasse were already climbing the path.

Just before the point where Alan and Jak ambushed them, Tam and Chasse halted. 'Let me go a few paces up to check Jak,' Chasse requested. Tam nodded, and Chasse slipped into the forest.

Tam waited, her nerves on edge, concerned that her brother's movement through the undergrowth was too noisy. The dawn's light would break over the mountain soon. Small animals and birds shuffled and chirped in anticipation of the day.

A cry from lower on the mountain startled Tam. 'Jak! Watch out! They're coming back up!' She backed into the bushes, wondering where Chasse was and what Jak's reaction would be to Alan's warning cry. She knew Jak had to make a choice. Either he would stay in wait, or he would come to meet them.

As she decided to climb in search of Chasse, stones clattered on the path and Chasse appeared. 'Where are you, Tam?' he whispered.

'Here,' she said,' stepping from behind a thick bush and startling him into raising his spear defensively.

Chasse relaxed, and urged, 'Come on.'

'Where's Jak?' Tam asked.

'Never mind,' Chasse replied tersely. 'Come.'

They ran wherever they could, and scrambled up the steeper path sections, alert to further ambushes, until they emerged on the plateau. Morning sunlight sparkled on the snowy peak of Dragon Mountain.

Tam sprinted across the small clearing and hammered on the door of the Herbal Man's hut, but, as she expected, there was no answer. When she tried to turn the door handle and then pry open the window shutters, she was surprised to discover everything locked tight. 'He doesn't lock the windows,' she said, as Chasse joined her. 'We have to go in through the goat cave.'

She led Chasse out of the clearing into the lush green forest. Impressed with how easily Tam negotiated the undergrowth, Chasse assumed that she was following goat tracks, but he couldn't distinguish them in the tangled undergrowth. Tam led Chasse into a small clearing, facing a low cliff, where a small herd of the patchwork animals grazed on the dewy grass, and she headed for a tiny cavern, mostly obscured by plants. Chasse dropped to hands and knees to follow Tam in, and the cold interior was dark and stank of goat dung. He crawled for a distance and quickly could not see his way. Afraid he might miss a fork or direction change, he asked nervously, 'Are you sure this is the way?'

'Yes,' Tam replied. He crawled headlong into her legs. 'You can stand, Chasse,' she told him. 'We have to feel our way along the wall but be careful. The wall is rough.'

Chasse followed Tam blindly, hearing his feet scrape and his breath echo in the chamber, until he bumped into his sister a second time. 'Why have we stopped?' he asked.

'The door,' Tam replied. 'It should be here.'

'Have we gone in far enough?' Chasse asked.

'If anything, we've gone too far,' Tam said, and sighed. 'The door has – it's gone,' she said.

'What?' Chasse asked.

'It doesn't matter,' Tam replied. 'There's another way. Follow me. We're going back out.'

Chasse dutifully resumed his blind fumbling along the wall, until his head bumped the cavern ceiling and Tam tugged at his leg, telling him to kneel. He dropped to hands and knees again and crawled along the tiny tunnel, glad to see daylight appearing at the end.

Back in the clearing, Tam oriented herself and plunged into the forest, shadowing the cliff with Chasse in her wake, until she reached the foot of a narrow, steep path cut into the rock. 'This way,' she said, much to

Chasse's chagrin when he saw the difficulty of the path. Parts were barely wide enough for goats.

He clung to the mountain fearfully, as he trailed his sister, and he was grateful when she clambered onto a ledge, and he hauled himself onto it after her. As he settled beside Tam, Chasse saw the whole world of Harbin opened in a vast panorama in the morning light.

Tam cried, 'The Herbal Man's hut!' Directly below, black smoke rose on the plateau. 'Trask and the Dragon Fang must already be there.' She turned and disappeared into a cleft in the cliff.

As she led her brother into the cavern, Tam's mind whirled with confusing thoughts. Because Katris saw them in the crystal chamber, she must have found the trapdoor in the hut, which meant Trask and the Dragon Fang could get into the Herbal Man's underground sanctuary. The disappearance of the door in the goat cave was mysterious. There was the likelihood that the Herbal Man was searching for herbs on the mountain, as was his early morning custom, and if he was she couldn't warn him. She could get to Claryssa. It might be the best hope.

The cavern of the Dawn People was dark, but Tam led Chasse around the perimeter, feeling her way along the smooth walls. She hoped one day that she could show Chasse the ancient drawings daubed on the polished stone, but she urged him to keep pace. 'There's a tunnel and a stairway here,' she told him. 'We can get into the Herbal Man's chambers this way.'

Tam descended the zigzagging flights carefully in the dark, as quickly as she could go, leaving Chasse in her wake, until she heard him call above her, 'Where are you?'

'At the bottom,' she replied, her voice echoing in the stairwell. 'When you get here, wait for me. I'll come back for you. Don't go anywhere.'

Tam edged across the short landing, hands outstretched to touch the door leading into the Herbal Man's chambers, but her fingers met the solid stone of a cavern wall. She searched, walking her fingers around the walls to her right, until she faced the stairwell, but she could not locate the door she needed to find. She turned and searched the wall where the door ought to be again, but it was as if the door never existed. She heard Chasse arriving, breathing heavily. 'I can't find the door,' she confessed.

'You mean it's gone?'

'Yes,' Tam said, 'like the door in the goat cave. It's just not here.'

'There's air moving in here,' Chasse said.

'Where?' Tam asked. She stood still, concentrated, and felt faint movement to her left.

'There's another opening here,' Chasse said.

Tam followed the walls to her left and found a narrow archway, where Chasse stood in the inky dark. She tested with her foot. 'Steps down,' she said. 'This wasn't here before.'

'Now what?' Chasse asked.

'We go down.' Tam descended a dozen steps before the stairway ended at a level corridor. She sucked in her breath, and said, 'Chasse.'

'What?' he asked, as he joined her.

'Do you see it?'

Chasse stared into the dark and saw an amber glow. 'What is it?' he asked.

'Come on,' Tam whispered.

Tam and Chasse warily approached the light along a smooth and level corridor, and the glow steadily revealed the corridor was square, built with crafted precision. When they reached the end, they stood at the head of a wide flight of uniformly cut steps leading down into the heart of a huge chamber that was lit by a multifaceted amber crystal in the ceiling. Claryssa's reptilian form was curled in the middle of the chamber, and a figure in white flowing robes turned orange in the light was striding up the steps to meet them.

'You came,' the Herbal Man called, as he approached. 'I knew you would come if it was possible.'

'We came to warn you,' Tam blurted, 'but I couldn't find the doors.'

'I sealed them,' the Herbal Man explained, as he reached the landing. 'There are no more doors into this chamber, only the way you came in, and I can seal it if necessary.

'The Dragon Fang know about Claryssa,' Tam said. 'They're coming to kill her. And you.'

'I know,' the Herbal man said, matter-of-factly. 'The Seeing Waters told me.'

'They're burning your hut,' Chasse informed him.

'Yes,' the Herbal Man said, nodding. 'I thought they would. And the hideaway. Katris saw it all, didn't she?' He shook his head, disappointed, and mumbled, 'Very careless of me, that morning. I always knew I'd make a mistake eventually. It had to happen.'

'It was my fault,' Tam muttered. 'I led her to you when I brought Chasse. I should never have brought him here.'

'Nonsense, Tamesan,' the Herbal Man said tersely. 'She followed you. You had no way of knowing how her spite would vent itself. Besides,' he added, grinning wanly, 'it wasn't you who foolishly left things unlocked. I should have been more vigilant. An important lesson to remember.'

'But now your secret is lost,' Tam lamented. 'All your possessions, they're being destroyed.'

The Herbal Man chuckled conspiratorially, and replied, 'I told you I knew they were coming, so I retrieved everything of value and stored it safely out of harm's reach down here. The Dragon Fang will find a few old books and some jars of herbs that you or I can replace anytime.'

'But what about you and Claryssa?' Tam asked. 'Where will you go now? The whole village knows the truth.'

'It is time the truth is told,' the Herbal Man replied, and he frowned as he added, 'Too many lies make living impossible in the end, anyway. 'It's time for us to leave.'

'Where are you going?'

'Away,' the Herbal Man cryptically replied. He turned his head to gaze down on Claryssa. 'And I think it is almost time.'

'Time for what?' Tam asked.

'For the last wizard and his dragon to be seen in this world,' the Herbal Man announced with a deft flourish of his arms. 'Claryssa and I have reached a decision, so it is time to do what must be done.'

'Exactly what?' Tam asked, irritated by the Herbal Man's habitual ambiguity.

'You will see. But first there are things to put in order.'

The Herbal Man reached into his robes and withdrew three items. Into Tam's hands, he pressed a set of iron keys, a parchment, and an amber ring like the one he sent to Harmi. 'These are for you, my child,' he said. 'They are part of a gift from Claryssa and me. I would have liked you to complete a true and traditional apprenticeship, but it is no longer possible. You were a long time coming to us, Tamesan, and we stayed hidden too long to find you. But these gifts are yours. Your brother is witness that I gave these to you.' The Herbal Man clapped Chasse on the shoulder, and said, 'Be her champion, young man, her knight. The path she has chosen to walk is long, dangerous and lonely, but she is the right person to walk it, especially with you to walk beside her. Claryssa knows this to be true in her heart, and I have never doubted her wisdom, nor had cause to doubt it. There are also gifts for you in this chamber when today is done. Stand with your sister and give her strength and courage when she doubts herself. Trust her, as she trusts you, and never abandon her, no matter what strange or terrible challenges you may both face in times to come.'

Tam listened, amazed, as the Herbal Man spoke to Chasse, because his voice seemed stronger, deeper, more commanding, as if it had acquired new resonance. When he finished, she asked, 'But what are these things for?'

'The keys will become obvious,' the Herbal Man promised. 'The ring is an heirloom, a gift from my great-grandmother that was passed to my grandmother, to my father, to me and now to you.'

'I'm not your son,' Tam protested.

'You are my inheritor,' the Herbal Man said firmly. 'You have the right to wear the ring. Besides, I believe that my great-grandmother and grandmother would approve.'

'And the parchment?'

'Must not be opened until Claryssa and I are gone,' the Herbal Man warned. 'Only then can you read what is inscribed there. It reveals the last portion of our gift to you because it leads you to our treasure.'

'I don't want treasure,' Tam argued. 'I'd rather go with you and Claryssa. Why can't you take me with you?'

'You could not possibly go where we are about to go,' the Herbal Man replied. 'One day, perhaps, you might, but you are not yet ready. The path you are to travel is one much harder than the one we are about to travel. I wish I could make your path easier, but I don't have that power. Besides, what your path becomes is partly for you to decide. And what you decide will determine the paths of your brothers. They will share your journey.'

Movement in the chamber distracted Tam, who turned to watch the dragon uncurl her massive body and unfurl her delicate bat-like wings that rustled as they spread. Claryssa lifted her head and opened her eyes. The dragon's gold and russet colours were highlighted in the crystal's amber glow, and the light gave the dragon a menacing aspect that sent a shiver down Tam's spine.

'It is time to go,' the Herbal Man announced. 'Take this rod to find your way back to the cave of the Dawn People. To make it work you need only shake it like this.' The Herbal Man shook the rod, and it emanated a soft white glow, like a small lantern. 'If you go onto the ledge again, you will see what Claryssa and I have prepared for the Dragon Fang, but you must be patient. My old friend and I are slower than we used to be.' He handed the rod to Chasse, and Tam and Chasse waited after the Herbal Man turned to descend the steps, but he spun on his heels, as if he anticipated they would hesitate, and he entreated, 'Go now. Time is short. Go.'

Tam and Chasse backed into the long corridor, before turning and heading swiftly away from the amber chamber where the wizard and his dragon communed.

As she walked, Tam clutched the Herbal Man's gifts, wondering what fabulous treasure the old man and the dragon were leaving behind, and what dark roads lay ahead for everyone.

Thirty

'We searched everything,' Lance reported, emerging from the smoking ruins of the Herbal Man's hut. 'He's nowhere to be found. There's no dragon and no dragon cave.'

Trask spat on a charred hunk of wood, the remnant of the trapdoor to the Herbal Man's lower chambers, and said, 'It's a trick of some kind. The girl swore she saw the dragon in a chamber beyond the crystal one. Kevan's daughter admitted there was a dragon here.'

'We found the crystal cave, but there's only solid rock beyond it,' Lance explained. 'Maybe she imagined the dragon.'

'You don't imagine dragons,' Trask said, sneering contemptuously. 'Kevan's spawn must have warned the old man. When I get hold of them, I'll use them as examples to the rest of the village of what happens to those who lie to the Dragon Head.'

'It might be Varst's Fortune we didn't find a real dragon here,' said Neal, as he strolled from the forest in the company of several Dragon Fang warriors. 'How do you fight a dragon?'

Trask spun and strode towards Neal, eyes brimming with anger, and he struck the warrior a solid blow with the shaft of his spear, sending him sprawling at the feet of his startled companions. 'How do you think Nakiades fought his dragons?' Trask roared. 'A dragonwarrior knows how to fight dragons because it is in his blood! He fights!' He threw his spear across the clearing and impaled a tree trunk. 'Varst's Blood!' he swore. 'For years, we've searched for dragons to fight! For endless hell-blasted years! Now, when there's one on the mountain right above us, we can't find the cursed thing!' More warriors emerged from the ruins, faces blackened, and Trask asked, 'Any sign at all of the old man?'

'No,' Jon replied.

'I want him!' Trask bellowed. 'He crippled my son, and he must pay! He will pay! On Varst's Word I will make him pay!'

'Your personal vendetta isn't why we are here,' Jon reminded Trask. 'There is a dragon to kill.'

Trask glared at Jon and retorted, 'I am the Dragon Head now, and if I want the old man dead he will be dead! I am the law!' He held Jon's gaze to emphasise his authority, but when Jon did not relent Trask spat on the ground at Jon's feet and stalked away to retrieve his spear.

As Trask reached his spear, he heard Jon call, 'You wanted the dragon, Trask? Here it comes!'

Trask turned to find the dragonwarriors gaping stupefied, open-mouthed, at a creature sweeping across the face of Dragon Mountain on broad wings thirty times the span of a man's arm. The dragon scales shone like burnished gold, and its long snaky tail, shifting in the air currents, stabilised the dragon's flight as it glided in a controlled arc towards the plateau. The dragon descended, scythe-like talons glinting in the sunlight, to land among the terrified warriors who retreated to the forest fringe. Trask felt a sickening surge of fear, a mad urge to run and hide, as he stared at the terrible spawn of Blitzart, Shaddho and Arkamroth, a creature from Harbin's legends, but he steeled his will against his instinct and raised his spear defiantly.

Seated on the dragon's back was a white-haired wizard, beard flowing down the front of his dazzling white robes, wearing chains and pendants richly adorned with multicoloured jewels, and holding a gleaming obsidian staff in his right hand. The dragon lowered its huge reptilian head, so that its slit golden eyes stared at several anxious dragonwarriors who lowered their spears and backed deeper into the forest while it patiently waited for the wizard to dismount. When the wizard was safely on the ground, the dragon lifted its head and began preening its wings. The wizard faced

Trask, bowed his head politely, and said in a clear, commanding voice, 'I believe you wanted to see us.'

Tam watched in awe as Claryssa appeared above the north-western shoulder of Dragon Mountain, high over Meltsparkle gorge, and glided across the mountain's western face. The old dragon's scales shone majestically in the midday sun, and as she circled towards the plateau Tam found it hard to believe Claryssa wasn't as invincible as the great dragon Arkamroth described in Harbin's legends.

'We won't see anything from up here once they land on the plateau,' Chasse complained.

'Then we'll climb down,' Tam decided.

Chasse silently cursed for opening his mouth. He did not enjoy the climb up the treacherous goat path, and he did not like the prospect of descending the same way.

He started to follow Tam, but she turned, put a hand firmly on his chest, and said, 'I've changed my mind. I'm going down, but you're staying here.'

'I don't think so,' he disputed.

'Chasse, someone has to guard this entrance in case the Dragon Fang find it, and you will do it better than me because you're a warrior,' Tam argued.

'But-' Chasse started to say and was cut off.

'It's important, Chasse. For me. Don't come down, no matter what happens. Stay here,' Tam pleaded.

Against his feelings, Chasse relented, but as Tam disappeared over the lip of the ledge he wondered if he'd made a wise choice. 'Be careful,' he called after her.

By the time Tam reached the plateau, the Herbal Man was facing Trask.

Behind Trask, the Dragon Fang fanned in a broad arc, several holding their spears ready for battle, others less confidently standing in the fringe of trees watching the dragon. Claryssa had finished preening and was warily eyeing the warriors.

'I don't care for your history, old man!' Trask bellowed, as Tam nestled behind a thick bush to observe. 'The only dragon the people of Nakiades will ever praise is a dead dragon!'

The Herbal Man shook his head sadly, and replied, 'You speak the same tired and foolish words I've heard from the mouths of angry men for a thousand years. They are all forgotten dust in the winds of time. Learn from their bitter mistakes, my friend. Lead your people into the light of understanding.'

'Dust in the face of you and your abomination!' Trask cried. 'Nakiades taught us the truth about dragon kind, their treachery and cruelty. No man is a man until he slays the dragons preying upon our homes. And I will be a man!' He hurled his spear and struck the Herbal Man full in the chest.

Tam screamed, but before she could burst from her hiding place Claryssa's jaws opened and a stream of raging fire poured over Trask. Many of the Dragon Fang panicked and ran, but Trask's closest friends, and experienced warriors like Lance and Jon, courageously held their ground, spears raised to fend off the legendary monster. Claryssa rolled her head, raised her wings, reared on her hind legs, and spat another stream of fire five paces in front of the remaining warriors. The flood of intense heat drove the warriors into the forest and more dropped their spears and ran in terror. The few who remained rallied beside Jon, but they were bereft of desire to confront the dragon on open ground.

Tam sprinted to the Herbal Man who, amazingly, still stood, despite Trask's spear jutting from his chest. A bright red blood stain was spreading across his white robe and his staff lay on the ground. Tam caught his arm, but he looked at her with glazed eyes and said in a warning tone, 'Step away, child.'

'You need help,' Tam insisted.

'Step away,' he repeated. 'You cannot help now.' He turned from her and spread his arms wide. 'Get out of the clearing, Te-Amen-San!' he ordered. 'Go!'

Tam released the Herbal Man's arm and retreated. As she reached the trees, she heard him begin a litany in an ancient tongue, using words that flowed like the wild water over Watersdrop in spring, words of passion and power. A blue glow enveloped the wizard, intensifying around the impaling spear, and the old man's chant gained strength and volume. Like Tam, the remaining dragonwarriors were enthralled by the wizard's display of magical power as, little by little, Trask's spear disintegrated, until only the nub piercing the old man's chest remained, and it, too, dissolved. The blue aura flashed and vanished.

The wizard's chanting changed pitch, and his hands glowed as if they were aflame. He gestured at the trees where the dragonwarriors stood and a bush exploded near them. Another bush burst into flame beside Jon. The dragonwarriors bolted, but Jon stood his ground, until a third bush erupted, and he took to his heels. The glow faded from the Herbal Man's hands, and he crumpled to his knees. Claryssa sagged beside him.

The fires in the forest were dead and only thin coils of smoke twisted into the air to testify that the confrontation between the Dragon Fang and the dragon took place. Tam helped the Herbal Man to his feet and he limped towards Claryssa. The old dragon lowered her head. 'We are much too old for that sort of thing anymore,' the Herbal Man confessed, forcing a wry grin.

'But you were magnificent, so powerful,' Tam said, thrilled by what she witnessed.

'Illusion,' the Herbal Man wheezed. 'Part of the show.'

'Claryssa's fire was no illusion,' Tam argued. She glanced at the ashen patch where Trask perished and felt nauseous.

'It took almost every grain of poor old Claryssa's energy. We hoped that we wouldn't need to resort to it,' the Herbal Man admitted. 'So many men choose to be stupidly arrogant when they would be better served by admitting defeat and getting on with something else.' He coughed as he pulled himself onto Claryssa's neck. 'Pass my staff, please,' he requested, when the coughing fit passed.

Tam picked up the staff, feeling its mirror-smooth surface and noticing myriad glowing amber runes etched into its fibre. 'Is what you did magic?' she asked as he handed the Herbal Man his staff.

The Herbal Man shook his head, as he answered, 'It was a poor kind of magic. Being able to scare or destroy things isn't very impressive. There is much greater magic than I've shown here today.'

'Like what?' she asked.

The Herbal Man smiled and said softly, 'Like the magic you already possess. Finding answers to your questions, and earning your brother's trust, helping people see what is right and what is wrong, making people feel good. Honesty. Love. Make these things happen, Te-Amen-San, and you will wield the most powerful magic there is. Remember it.' He started coughing again.

'Can't you wait until morning before you leave?' Tam entreated. 'You both need rest.'

The Herbal Man studied the lengthening afternoon shadows, and said, 'No. We've tarried too long. I didn't expect to take so long recovering, but then I only wanted to talk reason into some heads. That way, the road you travel might be easier at home, but I fear we have only succeeded in making it harder for you.'

'Chasse and I will sort things out,' Tam replied.

'I'm sure you will,' the Herbal Man agreed. 'Claryssa believes you will.'

Tam glanced left and saw the dragon studying her. In daylight, the eye of golden liquid was condensed into a long yellow slit, making the dragon look sinister, but Tam remembered the great golden eye in the crystal room that was able to draw her into its depths.

'Time to go, old girl,' the Herbal Man murmured as he patted Claryssa's neck. The dragon lifted her head and unfurled her wings, but despite having rested the dragon was noticeably unsteady and exhausted. 'Te-Amen-San,' the Herbal Man called. 'Don't forget the parchment! Don't read it until we are gone but then make sure you read it carefully.' He looked around the clearing and asked, 'Where is Chasse?'

'I made him stay on the ledge. He's guarding the entrance to the Dawn People's cave,' Tam explained.

'He is in your care, Te-Amen-San,' the Herbal Man told her. 'And you in his. And both of you must look to Jaysin. His destiny lies in a place beyond Harbin.'

'How do you know?' Tam asked, startled by the prophetic message.

'It's written in his eyes. I've seen it. Look, and you will see it too. Protect him and let him become what he must become.'

Claryssa turned her body, rose on her hind legs and spread her wings wide. To Tam, she looked both huge and fragile at once as her wings tested the afternoon breeze.

'I'm going to miss you!' Tam called out. 'Where will you go?'

'To the west,' the Herbal Man replied.

'Will I see you again?'

The Herbal Man laughed, before he answered, 'Wherever you go, Te-Amen-San, Claryssa and I will be with you.'

'How?' Tam asked, confused.

'Trust my word,' the Herbal Man said. 'The answer is in your pocket.'

As Tam fingered the keys, the ring and the parchment in her pocket, Claryssa tensed and leapt into the air, and Tam hastily retreated from the downward push of air stirring the trees, generated by the dragon's powerful wingbeats. She watched the dragon and wizard rise rapidly, until Claryssa disappeared over the forest canopy.

Chasse charged out of the forest, yelling, 'The dragonship! It's setting sail!' Tam stared at him as if she didn't understand, so he took her arm and urged, 'Come on! I saw it from the ledge! The ship's already heading out of the bay. We've got to get down to the village!'

Tam followed Chasse through the plateau forest and on a mad scramble down the mountain, but for once she could not keep pace with her brother and by the time she reached the goat pasture Chasse was disappearing into the village. She ran through Harbin, past the Warriors' Hall and the Long Hall and the cottages and huts, to the jetty and joined Chasse who was standing at the end, staring at the horizon.

The sun was dipping low in the western sky and the last afternoon rays were playing across the ice-capped peaks. At the furthest reach of the bay, the dragonship's solitary red sail was fast fading from view. Tam looked back at the village. The first chill of evening was wreathing between the huts and she noticed the absence of hearth fire smoke from the chimneys. 'Where is everyone?' she asked.

Chasse turned from staring out to sea and studied the village. 'I don't know,' he replied.

'You won't find anyone here,' a deep voice said. Tam and Chasse turned to see Galt the goatherd emerging from the shadow of a fishing hut on the shore by the jetty.

'What do you mean?' Tam asked.

'They've all taken to the dragonship and sailed away,' Galt informed her as he climbed onto the jetty.

'Everyone?' Chasse asked.

Galt shook his head. 'Near enough. My sons and a handful stayed with your folk in the Long Hall. Your father wouldn't budge when they came for him. He thinks he's Nakiades now that there's a dragon to fight.'

'But why did everyone else leave so suddenly?' Tam asked.

'You ask such a foolish question?' Galt asked and snorted in disbelief. 'Your dragon friend scared them off. They think the dragon's coming down to fry them all.'

'Why didn't you go with them?' Chasse asked.

Galt scratched his head and spat to the side, before replying, 'Because I didn't. Maybe I'm too old to be frightened by much anymore. Maybe I'm an old fool.' He laughed. 'But the way I see it is, if you and your brother aren't frightened of the old man and the dragon, then why should I be frightened?' He jerked his thumb in the direction of the goat pasture. 'You know I lost Derin this past summer. He was my youngest boy. I have two sons still here. And I didn't want to lose that lot over there. They may be goats to you, but they're all I've got left to work with.'

Tam looked in the direction of the goats, but the animals were hidden behind the village buildings. Sunlight faded from the mountain peak, and the sky darkened into indigo and purple and amber traces as dusk spread. She heard a piping cry and searched first for a gull in the air, but when the sound repeated she looked down and saw Jaysin running towards her from the Long Hall.

'Tamesan!' she heard him cry as he ran onto the jetty.

She held out her arms and scooped him up, full of joy to embrace him. 'Where is everyone?' she asked, as she released him.

'In the Long Hall,' Jaysin said, panting. He turned to Chasse, who ruffled Jaysin's hair. 'You're not hurt.'

'Of course we're not hurt,' Tam said. 'The Herbal Man and Claryssa protected us.'

'I saw the dragon, Tam!' Jaysin exclaimed. 'I saw it fly away. It was magnificent! All golden, and so big!'

Seeing Jaysin's face full of light and energy sparked a memory of her dream when she saw her little brother sitting astride a dragon and laughing with delight as he clung to the creature's neck. She understood the dream. Jaysin had an affinity with dragon kind like the Herbal Man — he saw dragons as intelligent, awesome, beautiful creatures, capable of companionship of the highest order. And the Herbal Man's parting instruction came to her: *Look to the boy.* Like Chasse, she gave Jaysin's auburn hair a customary ruffle and said, 'Take us to the Long Hall.' Jaysin grinned and trotted ahead, Chasse following, but Tam turned to Galt and asked, 'Coming with us?'

Galt shook his head, replying, 'Not yet, young Tamesan, but perhaps, when I have the goats safely quartered, I will come to the Long Hall.' He looked in the direction of his dark hut, and added, 'There's not much point going home tonight.'

'I'll tell Father,' Tam said and smiled, and she followed her brothers.

More people than Tam expected were waiting in the Long Hall and she saw that not all the Dragon Fang had sailed. Jon and Raven, Galt's sons, Lynel and Kogan, and a half dozen more warriors and their wives, were present, along with Banni and Jara, Amarti, the fishermen and women, and a handful of artisan villagers.

'I've brought Tam and Chasse!' Jaysin announced as they entered, and he proudly led his siblings to the centre of the hall where Eesa stood with Kevan propped in a chair. Then, as if he remembered his shyness, Jaysin withdrew to the outer edge of the gathering.

Eesa greeted Chasse and Tam with hugs, and the women and men crowded around to welcome them. Banni hugged Tam as close as she could, Jara caught between them, and they laughed at their awkward embrace. Tam kissed Kevan and checked the state of his wound, despite his protests. And the questions started about events on the mountain.

'Did the Herbal Man provoke Trask?' Kevan asked.

'He was only trying to talk sense to Trask,' Tam insisted. 'Trask wouldn't listen.'

'It's true,' Jon chimed in. 'I was there.' He looked at his companions. 'We all were, and we saw what Tamesan saw. Trask attacked first. His spear-' and he hesitated, recalling the spear striking the Herbal Man, and the healing magic. 'His spear dissolved in the old man's chest.'

'Dissolved?' Eesa queried, while others gasped in disbelief.

'I saw it too,' Raven asserted. 'We were hiding in the trees, but we saw a blue glow. The spear disappeared.'

'Surely the old man died?' Kevan asked. He shifted his weight in the chair to be more comfortable and winced painfully from the wound. Eesa squeezed his hand.

'No,' Tam replied. 'He healed himself.'

'I saw it too,' Jon said. 'Even the bloodstains on his chest vanished.'

'But how can this be?' Eesa asked.

'Magic,' Tam stated calmly. 'The Herbal Man is a wizard. He knows how to use magic to protect himself.' Aware that the people were staring, she turned to Chasse.

'I saw it,' Chasse said in support.

'But what is magic?' Eesa asked, speaking for everyone else.

Tam shrugged, and replied, 'I can't easily explain magic. I don't really understand it myself, but it's a way of doing things, of making things happen that people can't normally make happen.' She knew her brief explanation wouldn't make sense to the others, but she was still grappling with the concept.

'Is it true the Herbal Man is gone?' Raven asked. Tam nodded.

'And his dragon?' Jon asked.

'They've gone,' Tam confirmed, and a knot of sorrow formed in her throat.

'Where have they gone?' Kevan asked.

'I don't know,' Tam replied. 'He said they were going into the west.'

'But there's nothing to the west,' Jon argued. 'The ocean is endless, and only Shaddho the death dragon flies there.'

'I saw the dragon flying west!' Jaysin interrupted, but when everyone turned to him he blushed and fell silent.

'They will come back,' old Amarti croaked and she nodded knowingly to her husband, Berikan.

'They won't be coming back,' Tam said, her eyes shining with tears. Eesa reached for her hand, and Tam welcomed her mother's comforting touch.

'How can you be so sure?' Raven asked.

'Because they're dying,' Tam said.

Her answer silenced everyone, as if the people in the hall turned to stone. Outside, Harbin was sinking into night and Tam felt tears streaming down her cheeks. She melted into Eesa's embrace, and cried for Harmi, and for Eric and Claryssa who only wanted peace in their old age but could not stay.

Thirty-One

Tam dangled her feet over the edge of the jetty, her legs pressing against the weathered wooden planks as she revelled in the brisk, biting pre-dawn air, feeling the waves lapping against the barnacle-encrusted pylons. She looked up at the creamy face of the moon peering down from the satin indigo sky and its tapestry of stars, and as she marvelled at the number and variety of constellations she thought of the maps the Herbal Man studied and his fascination with the heavens.

The few who remained in Harbin after the dragonship sailed shared the night in the Long Hall. Tam wept in Eesa's arms for a time before she succumbed to emotional and physical exhaustion and slept. And dreamed of Kevan and Trask struggling for possession of a spear, bright red blood spreading across the Herbal Man's chest, Trask's fiery death, and Eric and Claryssa flying into the amber glow of the setting sun.

When Tam woke, the hall was dark and the hearth fire cold, and she lay listening to the sounds of sleep in the hope that she would be drawn back into its realm, but she could not sleep. She held each gift from the Herbal Man in turn – the amber ring, the keys, and the parchment – and she remembered that there was one mystery to unravel before she could rest. She needed to solve it before the dragonship and its passengers returned – and she knew they would return when they believed the dragon was gone, so she slipped out of the Long Hall, without disturbing anyone, and walked through the twilight gloom. Her first thought was to cross Watersdrop and climb onto the roof of her cottage to wait for sunrise over Dragon Mountain, but the water attracted her, so she crept to the jetty.

Lighter hues appeared in the sky, night blue inexorably fading to grey, which gave way to a lighter blue seeping into the air from the mountain ridges and the ocean. She looked over her shoulder at the peak of Dragon Mountain and watched the snow slowly differentiate from the darker mountain bulk, whitening as a precursor to true morning. A soft golden glow bloomed on the peak, and she sighed – dawn's light. 'Te-Amen-San,' she whispered, and she felt magic course through the sound of her name, like it did when she was a child, promising a greater destiny to her. Tam smiled. *Perhaps*, she thought, *I do have a greater destiny*. The Herbal Man and Claryssa left her their legacy, so she would climb the mountain to discover what lay at the heart of their gift.

Shadows of old Berikan and Amarti emerged from the Long Hall, and the husband and wife headed down the worn path to their hut on the shoreline. Moments later, Galt stumbled out of the hall, clapping his hands to beat out the cold, his breath escaping in puffs of steam, and he headed for the goat pasture and the shelter where the goats sojourned for the night.

Tam did not want any of them to see her, but their appearances early in the morning reassured her that the simple and honest daily routine of Harbin life would continue. She waited until the village was quiet again before she left the jetty and headed for the mountain. She deviated around the Long Hall and halted at the edge of the buildings until Galt was busy driving the goats out of the shelter before she cut across the northern section of the pasture, shielded from Galt's view by a hillock.

Beyond the tree line, Tam extracted the small bundle from her pocket and slipped the amber ring onto her finger. As she turned it in the morning light, the amber sparkled with greens and yellows and hints of gleaming red, and its tessellated texture reminded her of Claryssa's scales. 'A dragon ring,' she said whimsically. She examined the keys. Four were familiar – keys to the Herbal Man's retreat that no longer existed except as a ruin. The additional three keys were unfamiliar, made of dark, dull metal. She guessed that they were for doors in the larger amber chamber where Chasse and she last saw the Herbal Man and Claryssa before their final confrontation with Trask. She slipped the keys into her pocket and held the rolled parchment. The promise was not to read it until after the Herbal Man and Claryssa were gone, and she had kept the promise. She was unknotting the grey thread encircling the parchment when a twig snapped to her left. Turning, she discovered Chasse approaching.

'Why didn't you wake me?' he asked, as he reached her.

'I couldn't sleep,' Tam explained. 'I didn't want to wake anyone.'

'You are quiet, Tam' Chasse said, grinning, 'but not that quiet. I heard you leave.'

'Why didn't you say anything?'

'Because I know what it's like to want time alone,' Chasse answered. 'You didn't want to disturb anyone. I didn't want to disturb you.'

'Thank you,' Tam said quietly, but she felt shame for underestimating her brother's sensitivity.

Chasse's gaze rested on the furled parchment. 'Have you read it yet?' he asked.

Tam shook her head. 'Not yet. I was about to, but I think I will wait until we reach the top.' She hesitated, before saying, 'Perhaps we should tell Mother and Father where we are going.'

'It's all right, Tam,' Chasse told her. 'I explained to them where we were going before I came after you.' Tam looked at him with questioning eyes. 'Truth,' he said, his expression serious. 'We made a promise, remember?'

Tam smiled, and replied, 'I remember.'

Sunlight sparkled on dew-laden rocks and leaves as Tam and Chasse climbed the familiar path through the morning, clambering over rocks and winding between trees, their spirits renewed by the world's pulsing beauty. The invigorating mountain air smelt fresher, the blue sky, dotted with puffy clumps of white cloud, expanded in every direction, and the western ocean was deep blue and serene to the horizon. Only when they reached the plateau, and stood before the dark smudge, the ruins of the Herbal Man's home, did Tam's high spirits dissolve. Memories flooded back – the mornings hunting for herbs, the days spent painstakingly learning the alphabet, the frustrating nights reading by candlelight, struggling to recognise the words. She felt sharper moments – the first vision of Claryssa's great golden eye staring at her, the Herbal Man's voice calling in the heart of the blizzard, the radiating light and enveloping warmth, the whispering of 'Te-Amen-San'.

'Tam.'

Chasse broke through her reverie, his hand on her arm. 'I'm alright,' Tam whispered hoarsely, choking back her surging sorrow.

'Tam,' Chasse repeated. 'Look at the forest.'

Tam refocussed and looked around. The leaves were yellow and brown, and the trees bare-limbed on the higher branches. Ferns, that were lush and taller than a dragonwarrior, were colourless and wilting. The birds and butterflies were absent. The plateau forest was dying. She stared silently, for a moment, before she turned to Chasse and said, 'Come on,' and she headed for the path to the Dawn People's cave.

'Why is everything dying?' Chasse asked.

'The magic is gone,' Tam replied, and, as they passed the goat cave, she fleetingly wondered how the Herbal Man's goats would survive with him gone.

When they reached the foot of the upward path, Chasse asked, 'Can I go first?'

'Why?' Tam asked.

'It's something I have to do,' Chasse replied. 'I was scared when you led me up here yesterday. I need to prove to myself that I am no longer scared.' Tam nodded and stepped aside.

By the time Tam clambered onto the shelf beside Chasse, the sun was sitting high over Dragon Mountain. 'This is a magnificent view!' Chasse declared as he gazed across the bay. 'Yesterday, I was so overwhelmed by the height and the rush that I didn't appreciate it, but this morning I understand why the Herbal Man lived up here.'

'Did you see them leave?' Tam asked, gazing at the western horizon.

'Yes!' Chasse replied. 'They circled the mountain three times, once so close to the ledge I could see the Herbal Man's face. He nodded to me. Then they headed straight out to sea.'

Tam wished she was on the ledge with her brother to watch the Herbal Man and Claryssa fly away, but, if she was there, she would not have been on the plateau to say goodbye. 'I want to read the parchment,' she murmured.

'Open it,' Chasse urged. 'Read it to me.'

Tam unrolled the document and studied the script, recognising the Herbal Man's handwriting because she was forced to copy it rigorously. She cleared her throat and read, haltingly.

"Te-Amen-San: Of all things that can be given from one to another, the greatest gifts are life, trust and knowledge. These three things Claryssa and I have shared, as all our kind have shared through time. But all things have an ending as they have a beginning. That is a universal law. So, before our days are fully counted, we entrust to you the fruit of our lives and knowledge, and we choose to share with you the one treasure we value higher than our own lives. Believe in what you are, Te-Amen-San, and the world will unfold before you."

The parchment carried no signature and no clue as to the nature or storage of the treasure. 'What does it mean?' Chasse asked.

'I don't know,' Tam replied. 'So many things the Herbal Man told me never made a lot of sense. At least, not straightaway. There might be an answer in the amber cave where we found him yesterday.' She furled the parchment and led Chasse through the cleft into the mountain.

'We can use this,' Chasse said as they entered the cavern. He pulled a familiar long rod from within his tunic, shook it, and the rod glowed.

The magical light made their progress easy. Tam showed Chasse the Dawn People's ochre art as they passed through the upper caves and descended the zigzag staircase. Tam noted with grim disappointment, when they reached the landing where there was an entrance to the Herbal Man's hideaway, that the wall was still solid, which made her wonder at the magic the Herbal Man used to permanently seal the opening. She was pleased, when they descended into the tunnel, to find that the amber glow still illuminated the far end, and she led Chasse to the head of the flight of steps leading into the chamber.

The amber crystal in the ceiling, the source of light, permeated the cavern and the air was comfortably warm, as if a giant hearth burned nearby. Where Claryssa had lain when they entered the previous day, Tam saw a raised circular space, and at its hub was a large, pink oval object.

Chasse and Tam descended warily, expecting Claryssa to suddenly appear, even though they knew she flew west, and when they reached the base of the steps they discovered the object at the centre of the gigantic cavern sat on a massive grass pile woven into a circular bed.

Tam cried 'Chasse!' and she ran to the nest, filled with exhilaration and fear.

'Wait!' Chasse warned, and he ran after his sister, puzzled by her excitement, but before he could stop her Tam climbed onto the grass mound. He clambered after her and found his sister sitting cross-legged, staring at the biggest egg he had ever seen. 'In Varst's Name!' he blurted. 'What is this?'

Tam, her face in rapture, her eyes riveted to the soft oval shape resting in the grass nest, whispered, 'A dragon's egg.'

'But how?' Chasse asked.

'It's Claryssa's. It's her egg,' Tam said. She stroked the scaly skin and found it was not at all like a bird's egg. She often collected bird's eggs, but this shell, despite the scales, was soft, flexible, leathery and warm to touch.

'But why would she leave her egg?' Chasse asked, bewildered.

'It's her gift,' Tam explained. 'This is what the parchment is about. Don't you see? This is Claryssa and the Herbal Man's treasure. The egg. It's life, and trust, and knowledge all wrapped up in one thing, and they passed it to me to protect and care for.'

'But I thought Claryssa was the last dragon?' Chasse said, as he settled in the nest beside his sister to stare at the glowing shell in the eerie amber light.

'No,' Tam replied, stroking the egg. 'Not anymore. The last dragon is here, Chasse. It's here, and we've been made its guardians. What greater gift could we have been given?'

The Legend

Tam sat beside Chasse and Jaysin before the burning hearth in the Long Hall, and she studied the faces of the listeners in the flickering firelight as Jon began the traditional tale of Nakiades, wondering if her father, her mother, or the people remaining in the village, would see the irony and the pathos in the story. Tradition bound the community, she understood that, just as she also now knew that tradition could be flawed and destructive to a community. She leaned against Chasse, drew Jaysin against her, and listened to Jon's narration, as she had listened to other men tell the story of Harbin's founding for more than fifteen summers.

'Na-Kia-Des' tiny ship raced out of Blitzart's jaws, the great white dragon's frozen breath thundering in its sails,' Jon recited passionately. 'Around the tiny vessel, the storm churned the wild sea white with fury, and lurking at the edge of the maelstrom, Shaddho, dragon of all darkness, waited to claim Na-Kia-Des and his people. Long raged Blitzart's storm. Dark was Shaddho's night. Na-Kia-Des' helpless craft rose and fell on the mountainous waves, and his people, terrified that Na-Kia Des had called the dragons' merciless wrath down upon them, huddled like water-rats in the flooded hull.

Only Na-Kia-Des defied the storm. When the winds tore away the sail, he lashed his body to the broken mast, turned his face into the full breath of Blitzart the storm dragon, and cried, 'Hear me, Lord of all dragons! Hear me, almighty Varst! Look down and see I am not afraid of your servants! I am Na-Kia-Des, first-born son of Esa-Ra-Tha! I am a warrior, brave of heart! I stand before you, and I will not kneel or cower in fear. I am not afraid! I am not afraid!'

Hearing Na-Kia-Des bellow into the face of Blitzart's breath, seeing him roped to the shattered mast like a madman, the people were filled with greater fear. Here was their mightiest warrior, Na-Kia-Des, screaming at the dragons and calling on the highest god of all, Varst, Lord and Creator of everything, as if he was challenging a man to combat. All night Na-Kia-Des yelled his anger and challenges into the wind and rain, until it seemed that his breath had mingled with the great white dragon, and all was one.

When morning broke, the people woke to find the storm gone and the ship rocking on a gentle swell. Grey though the skies remained, the worst was surely passed. When they peered up from the hold to look upon Na-Kia-Des, they saw his wild eyes were gazing straight ahead, fixed on a wondrous sight. Filled with astonishment, the people scrambled onto the deck and stared – and saw mountain peaks, forests, cliffs: a new world. 'Behold!' cried Na-Kia-Des as they stared in awe. 'Almighty Varst listened. He blesses us with a new home. He saw our courage and welcomes us into the world again.' Amazed and grateful, the people knelt before great Na-Kia-Des. They thanked him for his protection and for their deliverance, but he waved them aside, saying, 'Offer your prayers to Varst. He, not I, brings you here.'

So it was that Na-Kia-Des' people came to live at the foot of Dragon Mountain. Na-Kia-Des' battered ship drifted into the bay and there was great celebration when the people set foot on land. They found pasture and building stone, a fruitful forest and crystal water to drink. It was as if they had found the fabled paradise of Te-Akra-Sen. Those with craft set to building new homes, and the village of H-Ara-Bin – the place of peace – rose from the earth. Such was the happiness in those first days that Na-Kia-Des took a wife, the beautiful Se-Lese-Rin, daughter of Ka-Ra-Kas, and in no time the laughter of children echoed across the mountainside.

But Blitzart and Shaddho watched the people's happiness with envious eyes. Na-Kia-Des had mocked them by calling upon their lord and master to rebuke them. Angered and frustrated, they took their grievance to their older brother, great Arkamroth, the Earthfire dragon. 'Brother, come. Look at the children of men at play in our world,' they beseeched. 'See how they strut and frolic as if the world was their own.'

Wise Arkamroth, hearing his spiteful brethren, came to observe as they asked, and saw the people of Na-Kia-Des in their new home. 'Does this not anger you?' his brothers asked.

Arkamroth smiled and answered, 'No, my brothers, it does not anger me.'

Dismayed by his response, they tried to persuade him to act on their behalf. 'Help us, brother,' they pleaded. 'Use the earth to drive them back into the sea. Make the mountain rain fire down upon them.'

'No,' Arkamroth replied. 'I see no reason. Men have a brief moment before they are dust again, and there are so few of them here. What trouble are they to us?' So saying, he left his brothers and flew south, and then to the west to tend to his own matters.

Infuriated by their elder brother's indifference, they complained to the Master of all dragons, almighty Varst. 'O Great One,' said Blitzart, lowering his massive white head with respect, 'O Greatest of All, hear us.'

Varst turned from his tasks and, seeing his creatures bowed before him, he commanded, 'Speak.'

'It is not our place to question your wisdom, mighty Lord,' Blitzart began cautiously, 'but we feel you have done us a terrible wrong by letting the pitiful seed of Na-Kia-Des pollute our beautiful garden. He taunted us disrespectfully, and spited us when we were about our duties, and now he goes unpunished for his arrogance.'

Great Varst opened his golden eyes, and they glowed like the radiant sun. 'Are you saying I have done wrong?' he challenged.

Recognising his master's mood, Shaddho eased from Blitzart's side, but Blitzart, blinded by his intense desire for vengeance, did not heed the master's tone. 'I think it is wrong to let an arrogant man live without fear,' he insisted. 'I would not have let that be so.'

There followed a long and fearful silence as Varst stared at Blitzart, his golden eyes shining. Only then did Blitzart recognise the foolishness of his words and wish he had never spoken. His heart suddenly as cold as his breath, he slunk from his master's presence, and Shaddho silently followed.

'So, we are cursed to endure this braggart Na-Kia-Des,' Shaddho hissed when they were safely out of Varst's hearing. 'Still, as brother Arkamroth reminded us, a man's life is but a passing instant. Soon the name of Na-Kia-Des will diminish, and his people will wither and die. What is humankind to dragons? Dust in the winds.'

'It is not enough!' Blitzart spat angrily. 'Na-Kia-Des must be punished!'

'Then let him face a dragon's wrath,' Shaddho declared. 'If you insist he must die, brother, send one of our children to taste his flesh and burn his bones to ash.'

'Yes,' Blitzart agreed. 'I will send one of our children to teach these people of Na-Kia-Des that we must always be shown respect.'

Of course, Na-Kia-Des knew nothing of the dragons' plans for vengeance. He watched his new home grow and his children bloom like forest roses and felt he could at last put aside his warrior's sword and live his life in peace. Happy that all was well, Na-Kia-Des told beautiful Se-lese-Rin he would travel east into the mountains to see what lay beyond. He gathered a band of young men eager to travel with him, and provisions, and set out to discover what great mysteries Varst hid beyond Dragon Mountain.

In the days while Na-Kia-Des explored, the people of H-Ara-Bin continued to thrive and prosper. Then one night Shaddho threw a great darkness across the face of the moon and the people cowered in fear as they watched the Dragon of Darkness sweep across the sky and steal away the light. And down from the mountain came a breath so cold that it turned the earth white, and the water froze in the wells. The people knew then that cruel Blitzart stalked their land. 'What will become of us?' they cried. 'The dragons have come and where is Na-Kia-Des? We will all perish.'

Out of the darkness, across the waters, a shape loomed, a scaly beast with eyes of fire and jaws of flame. It burned the buildings and took whatever fresh meat it could find – animals and people. Again, and again it came, burning, killing, eating what it pleased. And each night that it came Shaddho hid the moon and Blitzart froze the air. The people cried and hid in terror, but still the monster came to feed and destroy.

In desperation, some of the braver men waited in hiding to ambush the ravaging creature. When it arrived, they leapt out, brandishing their stone-sharpened spears, only to find they faced a shining dragon of silver – one of Blitzart's earthly spawn. Undaunted, they heaved their weapons, but the war spears bounced off its scaly hide as if they were children's wooden play spears. Enraged by the futile attack, the dragon tore the hapless warriors limb from limb and left their heads on the shore as a warning to the people not to oppose a child of Blitzart. Then it slid back into the sea.

Fearing the child of Blitzart would soon return to plunder their homes, the people called a meeting. Several put forward bold schemes for driving the creature off, but they had all seen the terrible fate of the warriors who faced the silver dragon and knew they were in greater peril than ever before. 'There is no point fighting,' the men claimed. 'The dragon will come and take until there is nothing left to take.'

'Then we must stop it,' argued Se-Lese-Rin. 'Na-Kia-Des would.'

'But your husband is not here. And we are too weak ourselves to stop it,' the people replied. And they asked the fair Se-Lese-Rin, 'Where is your husband?'

'I do not know,' she whispered forlornly. 'I do not know.'

At that fateful moment, the roof of the meeting hall burst into flame and a silvered head appeared, eyes burning like the coals in a blacksmith's forge, sharp teeth glittering like diamond spear points. The people screamed and scattered, running for their lives to the safety of the forest and the mountain. Some even put out to sea in their tiny fishing boats to escape the wrath of the hideous child of Blitzart. For three days, the people hid, too frightened to return to the village lest the dragon was waiting.

When, at last, they crept back into the ruins of H-Ara-Bin, it was discovered Se-Lese-Rin was not among them. Na-Kia-Des' four sons returned with the old woman, Er-A-Bos, and told the people they had not seen their mother since the night of the dragon's attack. Then, in the ashes of the meeting hall, the old woman found the ivory bracelet Na-Kia-Des had given his wife, and all feared Se-Lese-Rin perished in the flames. A great sorrow descended on the people and their mourning songs rose to the heavens.

So loud and so deep was the sound of sorrow that it brought Na-Kia-Des and his band down from the mountains seeking the reason for the people's sadness. When they told him of the silver dragon and the fate of his beloved Se-Lese-Rin, he snatched a spear from the ashes and vowed he would slay the child of Blitzart to save his beautiful wife and return H-Ara-Bin to a place of peace. Those who were his companions in the mountains asked to go with him, but Na-Kia-Des refused their offer, saying it was his responsibility to face Blitzart's child since it was he who neglected his duty to protect his people.

Taking the spear, his sword and his armour, Na-Kia-Des left the village. He strode to the peak of Dragon Mountain and screamed a challenge to Blitzart to meet him face to face and be done with it.

For five long nights, he waited for Blitzart's answer, but the Storm Dragon ignored his challenge. On the sixth night, Na-Kia-Des came down from the mountain and went to the head of the bluff we now call Nakiades' Watch, and he waited for Blitzart's child to slink out of the sea.

When the dragon came, it was heralded by a day of freezing cold breath from Blitzart's jaws, and it rose from the waters with its silver scales glittering and eyes of coal-red fire shining with death. Mighty Na-Kia-Des stood on the bluff to meet the enemy in battle and stepped into the terrible dragon's path, brandishing his spear. 'Hear me, death-spawn of Blitzart!' he called. 'Where is my Se-Lese-Rin? Where is the beautiful wife of Na-Kia-Des?'

The dragon's eyes burned with hunger as it gazed on the solitary figure standing defiantly in its path. Its ugly maw opened, and a twisted hissing issued, the chorus of a thousand tortured souls caught in Arkamroth's fires. 'Man-thing!' it spat. 'You are nothing to me! When I have torn the flesh from your bones, ground your bones to dust, and eaten my fill of your people, only then shall I answer you!' So saying, the dragon sucked in and spat a stream of blue fire at Na-Kia-Des. But Na-Kia-Des leapt aside, the fiery heat rushing past his shoulder. He raised his spear and launched it at the child of Blitzart. True was his aim. Strong was the warrior's arm. Where spears of lesser men bounced harmlessly off the dragon's silver armour, Na-Kia-Des' spear struck home, piercing the smaller, softer underarm scales of the startled creature. A strangled scream rent the air and the dragon spouted green flames as it staggered backwards. Seizing his chance, Na-Kia Des rushed forward and plunged his sword deep into one of the dragon's red eyes. Though mortally wounded, Blitzart's child wrenched free of the warrior's death embrace, tossing Na-Kia-Des aside like a discarded dinner bone, and stretched its blood-spattered wings to take flight. It retreated towards the hill we call Varst's Bluff, pursued in its ever-weakening flight by Na-Kia-Des, until he stood over the dying dragon on the crest. He pulled his sword from its eye and let the dark green dragon blood ebb into the earth.

When Na-Kia-Des came back down to the village, holding his sword aloft with dragon blood steaming on its blade, the people rushed out to greet him joyfully. They praised his courage as they carried him to the centre of H-Ara-Bin, and they showered him with gifts, and bowed before him as if he was mightier than even great Varst, father of all dragons.

Na-Kia-Des, though, was deeply troubled. One among the people, the warrior Te-Era-Vis, kneeled before Na-Kia-Des and asked, 'Why are you not happy like us? You have brought peace to H-Ara-Bin and the people shout your name to the heavens. Mighty Varst himself cannot deny your greatness. Why are you so full of sorrow?'

Na-Kia-Des lifted his weary eyes to Te-Era-Vis and replied, 'I have lost what I most loved.'

Then everyone remembered Se-Lese-Rin had not returned. The most beautiful flower of all the village had not been found. The joy sank and the celebration ceased. The people of H-Ara-Bin left great Na-Kia-Des to his sorrow beside the dying embers of the fire and went quietly home to their own hearths.

The next morning, they found Na-Kia-Des at the water's edge, busy cutting, binding, and shaping wood. Ropes and raw sailcloth lay beside him. 'What is that you are doing?' they asked.

'I am building a boat, he answered, but he did not look up, and he did not slacken in his work.

'Why do you build a boat?' they asked.

'Because I am going to the land of dragons,' Na-Kia-Des told them.

His answer stunned them, and some stole away shaking their heads, believing Na-Kia-Des must have been maddened by his battle with the dragon, but good Te-Era-Vis knelt beside the great warrior and asked, 'What will you do in the land of dragons, mighty Na-Kia-Des?'

'Se-Lese-Rin is there. I will go to her and bring her home again.'

'How is it you know this?' Te-Era-Vis asked.

For the first time, Na-Kia-Des looked up and caught Te-Era-Vis' eye. 'Blitzart's dying child told me it is so. So, I will go to the south lands and take back what is mine. And I will punish Blitzart's children for what they have done.' Thus, having spoken, the mighty warrior returned to his task. Te-Era-Vis then took up a crafting tool and began working beside Na-Kia-Des.

When word spread that the great warriors were building a boat, a dragonship, more people came to the water's edge. First, they came to watch out of curiosity, but then some bent to work with Na-Kia-Des and Te-Era-Vis, and soon the whole village was working as one. And Na-Kia-Des' dragonship grew from the lumber and hemp and tar. The great sail was sewn by the wives and daughters of H-Ara-Bin while the men laboured over the boat. Na-Kia-Des released Te-Era-Vis from construction and directed his companion to teach all the young man the skills of a warrior, the skills of Na-Kia-Des the Dragonslayer, for they would be sailing with Na-Kia-Des into the land of dragons. There, they would face the children of Blitzart and Shaddho, and even great Arkamroth's offspring, and they would need to know how to fight and kill the fire-breathing creatures.

When the first dragonship was ready, Na-Kia-Des ordered the great sail be dyed red with the juice of the Bloodflower, which grows high on the slopes of Dragon Mountain. This would be a sign to the children of the dragons that Na-Kia-Des was coming to avenge the murder of his people by Blitzart's child. Then he gathered about him the warriors whom Te-Ara-Vis taught, and in the first weeks of summer they set sail.

Though he searched and searched, Na-Kia-Des did not find his beloved Se-Lese-Rin, but each year thereafter, before Blitzart's breath swept down from the mountains, Na-Kia-Des returned to H-Ara-Bin with riches and spoils gathered from the dragons slain by his warriors, and each summer, when Arkamroth's warm winds drove Blitzart's icy touch from the waters, the warriors took to the ocean in search of Se-Lese-Rin.

On his death-night, Na-Kia-Des made his warriors swear an oath, before almighty Varst, that they would never cease their search for Se-Lese-Rin, nor end their war with the children of Blitzart and Shaddho until Se-Lese-Rin and he were re-united.

And so it is, still, that every year the warriors of H-Ara-Bin, the Dragon Fang, take to the dragonship in summer and journey south to the land of dragons. And so it is that the law of mighty Na-Kia-Des is with us and makes our days strong and prosperous.'

Jon paused to look at Kevan, who nodded approvingly.

In a quieter tone, Jon said, 'We are the dragonwarriors. We are the Dragon Fang. We are the children of Na-Kia-Des and the people of H-Ara-Bin.'

ABOUT THE AUTHOR

Tony Shillitoe is a multi-genre author of fantasy, young adult, historical romance, science fiction and contemporary novels and short stories. Fantasy novels *The Last Wizard* (1995) and *Blood* (2003) were short-listed for the Best Fantasy Novel category in the Aurealis Awards and the teenage fiction *Caught in the Headlights* (2003) was listed as Notable Book for Older Readers in the Children's Book Council of Australia Awards.

A former high school educator, part-time TAFE and university lecturer and tutor, writing workshop convenor and writing mentor, International Baccalaureate teacher trainer, sports coach and player, amateur actor and radio show guest and very poor guitar player and singer, Tony is committed to fulltime writing to complete an array of projects while enjoying coffee and good times with family and friends.